STORM DREAMER

The Crossing Trilogy Book 3

JUNE V. BOURGO

OTHER BOOKS BY JUNE V. BOURGO

Snap Shots (Life Bites—Vignettes)

The Crossing Trilogy

Chameleon Games, Book 2

Magnolia Tree, Book 1

The Georgia Series

Missing Thread, Book 3

Chasing Georgia, Book 2

Winter's Captive, Book 1

*To Dennis—for always being there when
I abandon you to live in the world of my characters.*

ACKNOWLEDGMENTS

This book is the last of *The Crossing Trilogy* and it's time to say goodbye to all the characters I've spent time getting to know and grown to love over the years. Unlike my first series with the same main character throughout, this trilogy focused on a new protagonist with each book, the previous characters becoming secondary ones in the next book. A different style of writing and a new challenge, I'm pleased with how well all the characters grew as the trilogy progressed.

Storm Dreamer took a lot longer to write than the other two stories in this trilogy. The same way COVID-19 took the world by storm and changed all of our lives, some more than others, it took away my muse and my focus on writing just wasn't there. However, through the past winter months, my motivation returned, and I was able to complete this story. I've enjoyed the creation of all three books, but I have to say, this one is my favourite. There are a few people along the way who must be mentioned for their support and help in making *Storm Dreamer* an entertaining and believable story.

First, and foremost, my husband, Dennis—my best friend, my biggest fan; your constant support and input have never failed me.

To the group effort of Sandra J. Jackson, Megan Herlaar, and Ronald Bagliere, my writing partners (accomplished writers themselves), whose insights and edits are always enlightening and helpful to my developing story; thank you so much for your time and effort. Love our Zoom meetings.

And there's Heidi Frank, my editor-in-chief, who plays devil's advocate and calls me out if necessary. Your no-nonsense, straight-to-the-point input, never fails to push my creative juices forward, and you are so appreciated.

Of course, *Storm Dreamer* could never have reached a believable ending without the input of Sergeant Jason Bayda, Area Commander of the Royal Canadian Mounted Police, Osoyoos Detachment, Penticton South Okanagan Similka-meen Regional Detachment, Government of Canada. Your firsthand knowledge of policies, procedures, as well as forensic investigation methods as they pertain to my story has been an invaluable tool. Any errors in the use of your wealth of infor-mation in the telling of this story are solely those of the author, either for lack of interpretation or for creative license. Thank you for the time and patience afforded to all of my enquiries, even when I continuously came back for "just one more question".

A big thank you to Patti Roberts of Paradox Book Covers Design and the team at Next Chapter for the beautiful cover.

To my Publisher, Miika Hannila and the team at Next Chapter Publishing, thank you for all you do to make *Storm Dreamer* the best it can be, and the hard work you put into the marketing phase after publication.

❧ I ❧

A little while, a moment of rest upon the wind,
And another woman shall bear me

Khalil Gibran

PROLOGUE

The howling wind knocked tree branches against the bedroom window while golf ball-sized hailstones pounded the roof. Thunder and lightning sounded in the distance. Valerie Hayes stirred and rolled over in her sleep. The raging storm itself wasn't enough to awaken her and she slept on undisturbed until the chilling screams from the baby monitor echoed around the room. In a matter of seconds, the internal bond between mother and child kicked in. Her eyes shot open and she sat upright in bed in sudden panic. "Madie?"

Her shrill cries were indicative of something more than being hungry or a wet diaper. In a shot, Val was racing barefoot to her bedroom. Her daughter was standing in her crib, her little hands gripping the bars tightly. The muted blue light from the purple ladybug night lamp on the dresser illuminating the baby's frightened expression made the whole scene more distressing to her. Val picked up the nine-month-old baby, coddling the shaking child whose green eyes were huge with terror.

The child's moist red curls stuck flat to her head. "Oh, Madie, look at you," she said soothingly, feeling the cold wetness of the infant's sweat-soaked sleeper against her bare arms. Val felt the rapid beating of her daughter's heart pounding against her chest as she rocked her back and forth. "Shhh, baby girl, shhh, Mama's here."

As Val rubbed her daughter's back, the screams turned to sobs, then gasps and body shudders. Madie's breathing normalized and she began to hiccup. Val tilted the baby's face up to hers. She stared deep into her daughter's eyes. "What's got you so scared?"

Bad dreams were one thing, but the sheer terror on Madie's face unnerved Val.

"How about a warm bath?" She stripped the baby, but as soon as she ran the water, her daughter started to scream again. "Okay, no bath." Shutting off the water, the young mother hurried back to the bedroom, carrying her daughter, along with a warm wet cloth and towel. There she wiped down Madie and dried her, applying cream to her bottom and inner thighs, with a fresh diaper and sleeper completing her efforts.

"How about some warm milk? Hmm?" Val asked and carried the baby into the kitchen to warm up a bottle.

A few minutes later, she settled on the couch to feed her night terror-stricken daughter. For a while, Madie relaxed but the storm had moved closer, and with each boom, she tensed and tightly grasped Val's fingers. "It's okay, baby girl. Just a noisy rainstorm. It won't hurt you."

Exhausted, her daughter finally fell asleep halfway through her bottle.

Val took her daughter back to bed, placing her daughter on her tummy. She covered her with the blanket, making sure to place her favourite stuffed toy beside her. Val smiled at the long-eared white bunny. *Hopper* was almost as big as Madie and when she was up, she carried it everywhere. Picking up a snow globe from a shelf, she wound its key, setting the timer for twenty minutes. The soft notes of Brahms' *Lullaby* began to play.

Val returned to her own room and cuddled under the covers. But sleep evaded her. It broke her heart to see Madie so terrified. *I'm at my wits' end. Maybe it's time to talk to the doctor about it. Perhaps there are things we can do to help her.* By we, Val meant she and her husband, Brad who was in Vancouver at a medical conference. He was due home in a couple of days. They both worked at the local hospital; she as a lab technician and Brad as a radiologist.

Madie had been having the nightmares for a couple of months, whenever there was a storm. Normally, once down for the night, her daughter never woke up until seven in the morning. Outside, the rain pattered on the window, the worst of the storm over. Val heard a noise come through the monitor and listened to the sound of Madie sucking her thumb in her sleep.

A quick plumping of her pillow and Val settled down again. She loved being a mother and being home with her daughter. Soon, she'd have to return to her job at the hospital. Luckily, her mother offered to babysit Madie when she and Brad worked the same shifts. The idea of leaving her daughter to return to work bothered her, though, especially on nights like this. It made her feel like she was abandoning Madie.

And yet, here I am, unable to help her anyway when these episodes happen. Sometimes, I feel so inadequate as a mom. Yes, it's time to take her to the doctor and get an opinion on what might be happening with her. I mean babies can't talk; they have no awareness about the world beyond their family home. Feed them, change them, wash them, cuddle them, play with them, and love them; give them that and they're happy. And Madie's a happy child.

Val frowned. *Isn't she? Maybe babies can have bad dreams about the family dog chewing their favourite stuffed toy or maybe getting shampoo in their eyes. But what kind of nightmares could cause such terror?*

TWENTY-TWO YEARS LATER

*S*lipping *on the wet patio tiles, she tried to balance to keep from falling. The wind blew her long wet hair across her face, blinding her further in her quest to slip into the darkness of the grasslands. Even the cracks of lightning bolts, followed by thunderous booms, couldn't cover his yells and curses as he chased her through the night. She pushed her hair back and pulled hair from her mouth. Each time a lightning bolt exploded, the night sky lit up, allowing her to adjust her direction—it also allowed her pursuer to see her and continue his pursuit.*

"Stop. Dammit. We shouldn't be out here. It's too dangerous," he yelled through the rumbling.

But she wouldn't stop. She'd reached a flat plateau. Her lungs hurt and her chest heaved. She sucked in the cold air and found the strength to keep running. Fear was her adrenalin. The torrential rain had soaked her to the skin and her body shivered. The lightning strikes were getting closer.

In a matter of seconds, her hair stood on end and a tingling sensation spread across her skin. She crouched low to the ground with her feet together and balanced on the balls of her feet. The bolt hit the ground a few feet away and a reciprocating bolt left the ground and surged into the sky. That was way too close.

Frozen in her crouching position, she took a moment to catch her breath—too long a moment. As she stood, a hand from behind grasped her by the hair and pulled her backwards. Her feet flew out from under her and she hit the ground hard on her back, knocking out what little wind she had left. A series of lightning bolts exploded around them and she stared up at his jean-clad legs and saw his new black and white Nike Air Max runners as he straddled her.

THE NOISE GREW louder and more intense. The buzzing sound filled her head and her eyes flew open. "Uh …" Madie Hayes gasped. She groaned and reached out, fumbling around the nightstand until she found the button on the alarm clock and turned it off. She closed her eyes and relived the horrific dream she'd just experienced.

There she was again. Different scenarios but always the same woman and always the fear.

Madie sat up and rubbed her eyes. Her body shuddered. Her mother told her she'd had night terrors as a baby, lasting until she started school. She didn't remember any of them and had forgotten about them years ago. Now they were back. The dreams had been haunting her for a few months. But this one was particularly violent. *Why are they back? Why now? And who was this woman?*

The pinging of rain on the tin roof reminded her of the thunderstorm that had occurred in full force throughout the night. All she knew was the nightmares only occurred on stormy nights. *Why? Another unanswered question.*

Madie stood and headed to the shower. The hot steam settled her frayed nerves and her body relaxed.

Thirty minutes later she rinsed her coffee cup, grabbed her car keys and the lunch she'd made the night before, and headed to her car. It was a short drive to work at the Stoney Creek Wildlife Rehabilitation Centre. She worked closely as an Administrative Assistant with Chelsea Grey, one of the owners. Chelsea had survived a twenty-year abduction by a neighbouring farmer; freed by her daughter that she never got to raise and a mother who'd considered the farmer, and his deceased wife, a friend. Madie was impressed with the strength and compassion her boss brought to the Centre and looked upon her as a mentor.

The Centre had only been in operation for ten months and they were coming into the late spring and it was already busy. She'd started working for them a couple of months before they opened their doors, readying education and internship programs and working with Chelsea to set up Administration. They'd had a successful first year and Madie looked forward to the summer season. Her twenty-third birthday was coming up and she felt content that at such a young age she'd found her dream job.

She parked her car in the employee parking area, taking note of the extra cars not normally there. As she entered the administration building, her eyebrows shot up. The reception was full of people, sitting and standing.

A male voice beside her said, "Uh-oh, here comes another one."

She turned to see a young man in his mid-twenties staring at her. She could have lost herself in his deep blue eyes and boyish grin but, instead, she stared him down. "Are you refer-ring to me?" she asked.

"Welcome to the jungle," he said with a laugh.

"And you are?"

"Cody ... Cody Diaz." He put out his hand.

Madie shook it. "Madie Hayes."

"I should wish you good luck but hopefully it's all mine."

She stared into his eyes, sparkling with humour. She had no idea what he was talking about but decided to go along with it. "Well, Cody Diaz, my being here in the jungle has nothing to do with luck. So, it's all yours." She pushed her way through the crowd of people and entered her office at the far end of the reception.

Instantly there was a knock on the door and Chelsea entered, carrying a pile of folders. "Good morning, Madie. Quite the zoo out there."

"Hi. Have a seat and tell me what's going on."

"It seems we've lost Peter. He called Wenner on Saturday and told him he'd decided to take a year off to travel the world with a couple of friends."

Madie's eyebrows shot up. "Just like that? No notice?"

"Nope. Another friend had dropped out and they needed someone to take his place this week. Wenner posted it online right away and told people to apply in person Monday morning as the position was available immediately." Chelsea nodded over her shoulder. "We never expected this kind of response."

"Impressive. Where's Wenner?"

"Stitching up a deer caught in a wire fence. Came in thirty minutes ago. So-oo … he's left this up to you and me. I thought we could go through the resumes together and short-list the top five and send the others on their way."

"Sure. We can do that."

"It's not the usual way to do this, but since they're all here, we might as well weed them out now. I'm going to move them into the conference room and tell them I'll be back shortly with a short list."

Chelsea handed half the folders to Madie. "Here … you know what's required for Peter's job. Choose the top five and I'll do the same with my pile when I return. We'll cut them down further together."

It didn't take them long to go through the resumes. Peter's basic job consisted of helping Wenner with surgeries, training and managing the volunteers, cleaning the cages, feeding the animals, general maintenance around the animal compound, and everything else in-between that happened to pop up.

Madie pushed the files aside. "I only found three I think are eligible."

"Me too. We'll interview all six." Chelsea stood. "I'll go thank them for coming and let the deleted ones go. Are you up to sitting in on the interviews with me?"

"Absolutely."

Chelsea smiled. "Not exactly how we expected our morning to go is it?"

Madie laughed. "Nothing here at the Centre follows routine for long."

Chelsea wrote the names of the six interviewees on a piece of paper. "You've got that right. Here take the six files and I'll meet you in my office."

Madie crossed the hall and waited for Chelsea to join her. One by one her boss brought the candidates in for an interview. There were two women and four men. They got to the last one and Madie was surprised to see Cody Diaz enter with Chelsea. She'd forgotten about him, realizing that Chelsea must have shortlisted him. As soon as he saw her, his face turned red.

Before Chelsea could introduce them, Madie stood and shook his hand for a second time. "Cody, we meet again. I see that luck is working for you so far. Have a seat."

He looked sheepish and gave her a crooked grin as he sat.

"You two know each other?" Chelsea asked her.

"Not really. We met in reception earlier."

Chelsea nodded. "Well then, let's get started. I'm impressed with your resume, Cody. Tell us about your work in Africa."

"After I graduated from university, I worked my way around Europe and ended up at a wildlife reserve in Africa. It was a working holiday in Botswana. We repaired fences, built new compounds, and fed the wildlife. It was there that I knew when I returned home, my work had to include working with animals. I became a Conservation Officer, but it wasn't as satisfying as I thought it would be. Instead of conserving animal life, we spent most of our time putting animals down that interfaced with people. After three years, I had to leave. I've been working part-time at the Kelowna Wildlife Centre for the past six months but I'm looking for full-time work. I've been following your Centre since you opened your doors and when I saw Peter's position was open, I jumped at the opportunity."

While Cody and Chelsea chatted, Madie read his resume. *Impressive.* She studied his face. His look was unique with his black hair, deep blue eyes, and straight nose. *Not too hard to look at, that's for sure.*

"I assume you're willing to relocate to the area then," Chelsea said.

"Absolutely."

They spent some time talking about the position, wages, and benefits.

"Peter's job has evolved in the year since we opened our doors here. We have a lot of plans for the future and I expect as we grow, the position will take on more responsibility. We're looking for someone who intends to stay and grow with the job."

Cody nodded. "Just what I'm looking for. I did my carefree hitchhiking around the world after I graduated. I'm looking for stability and work in a field I love."

"Okay. If we did offer you the job, when could you start full-time?"

"I'd like to say right away but I do owe Kelowna some notice. I could start part-time tomorrow while I finish my part-time shifts there for the next two weeks."

Chelsea stood. "We could probably work around that and I respect your work ethic towards your employer. The others we interviewed were told we'd contact them later today with our decision. But why don't you wait in the reception area for a few minutes while Madie and I chat? I need to get this decision behind me."

"Of course."

Chelsea walked to the door and as Cody stood, Madie stared into his eyes. "Your lucks still holding, Cody."

He grinned and held up his hands with crossed fingers.

After Chelsea closed the door, she sat down and swung her chair towards Madie. "I like him. What do you think?"

"He's certainly qualified but a bit … cocky."

Chelsea's brow furrowed. "Oh? I saw confidence and enthusiasm. He's the most qualified. But … we're a small outfit and I want you to be comfortable with whoever we bring in."

Madie paused at that. "Well, maybe I was misreading him. I came to work in a mood this morning, certainly not expecting to see all these people. He didn't know I worked here, and I wasn't up to his teasing humour."

Chelsea studied her face. "Are you alright?"

"Yes. Fine. As for Cody, I think Wenner will like him."

"Mmm … me too. Why don't you take him on a tour and introduce him to Wenner? Take his resume."

"Okay. It'll give me another chance to reassess my initial reaction."

"Good girl. If Wenner likes him, I'm sold. Bring him back and process him, then turn him over to Wenner. And if you would, please call the other candidates with the bad news."

"Sure thing." Madie smiled as she headed to the door. Chelsea's mind was already made up.

She found Cody sitting in reception. One leg was wiggling nervously and when he looked up at her, for the first time, she saw insecurity in his eyes. "Come on, lion tamer. We're going on a tour of the place and to meet Wenner."

As Madie showed him around the Centre, Cody never said a word. Then, he blurted out, "Sorry about earlier in reception. I didn't know you worked here. I tried to use humour to cover my nervousness. I want this."

Okay, so maybe I overacted. "Hey, working here, a sense of humour is a definite must. You've already got Chelsea in your corner. If you win over Wenner, the job's yours." She felt Cody staring at her.

"And what about you? Are you in my corner?"

"Maybe, but I'm not the one hiring you."

"But you appear to be an important person around here, so your opinion counts."

Madie smiled. He wasn't only cocky, but a flatterer as well.

"Phew … finally, I made you smile. And it's a beautiful one too."

Madie laughed. "Save your flattery for Wenner."

Twenty minutes later, she and Wenner stood back and watched Cody bottle-feed a fox cub. He knew what he was doing and made it look easy. Madie caught Wenner's eye. "Whatcha think?" she whispered.

Wenner nodded yes and gave thumbs up.

Wenner Gibb was Chelsea's partner. He ran a small animal rehab Centre in Emerald Lake, where Chelsea had gone to heal and find herself. He'd offered her a job and the two worked well together, forming a close friendship. Wenner was a widower who'd thought he'd lost his husband in a car accident. But together, he and Chelsea discovered that his husband had stumbled upon a money-laundering scheme through his accounting firm, and it had cost him his life. The bond between Chelsea and Wenner became one of mutual healing and they'd moved to the Grey family acreage, split between Chelsea and her daughter Sydney. The Stoney Creek Rehab Centre was formed with Chelsea and Wenner as equal partners. To Madie, it was business first, yes, but the compassion and empathy the owners brought into the Centre, not only to the animals in their care but to their employees, bonded them all as a family.

Cody finished the feed and took the baby fox back to its cage.

Wenner watched him wash his hands. "I like him. He knows what he's doing, and I've heard good things about him through rehab circles."

When the young man rejoined them, Wenner put out his hand. "As far as I'm concerned, you're hired. Welcome aboard, Cody!"

❧ 2 ☙

Distant rumbling and the patter of raindrops on the tin roof filled Madie with dread. The pending storm was later than the weather forecast had predicted, dashing her hopes they would be spared another night of thunderstorms and along with it, a much-needed peaceful sleep. The darkening sky looked menacing as the black clouds rolled overhead. She snapped shut the curtains, prepped for bed and set the alarm for the morning. *Like I'll need it.*

Settled under the covers, Madie pulled the bedside lamp closer and picked up a book: a thriller suspense yarn that soon drew her into the engrossing plot of a missing woman. It wasn't long before her eyes drooped, and the book fell across her stomach as sheer exhaustion claimed her and Madie fell into a deep sleep.

The image in the mirror stared back at her. The soft glow of the night-light made her swollen cheek look grotesque. The imprint of his diamond and onyx ring could be seen on her cheek, even through the swelling and broken skin. She touched it and winced. Running the cold water, she

placed a wet cloth over the wound. It helped ease the pain. Her eyes reflected her despair and she knew the time had come for her to leave. His attacks were becoming more frequent and more aggressive. If I don't go, one day he might kill me. And she had more than herself to think of.

The bathroom light came on, blinding her for a moment. She blinked and once her eyes adjusted, her body tensed. His face appeared in the mirror, behind her left shoulder. As she held the compress to her face, he knocked it away with the back of his hand.

She winced and reacted to the instant pain. "Ow." Immediately, she bit her lip, knowing she'd made a mistake. Rather reacting to injury, he'd call it whining.

He grabbed her by the hair and pulled her backwards through the bathroom door and flung her against the wall in the hallway. She slumped to the floor.

"Take your pity party somewhere else. I need the bathroom." He slammed shut the door.

She held her hands over her mouth so he wouldn't hear her sobs. Dragging herself up from the floor, she crept down the hall and into the family room. She stood by the sliding doors and stared out at the torrential downpour. Lightning strikes lit up the desert beyond.

The sound of the bathroom door opening made her flinch. The hall light came on.

"Where are you?" he yelled. He found her in the family room. "Planning your escape?"

She spun around to face him and by the look in his eyes, she saw this wasn't over.

"Time for bed," he demanded.

Overcome with fear of more reprisals and disgust at the thought of having to lay silent beside him, she reacted the only way she could. She turned to the glass door, slid it open and ran onto the tiled patio. Her bare feet slipped on the wet smooth squares and she almost fell.

Seconds later, she'd disappeared into the stormy desert night.

MADIE'S EYES POPPED OPEN. An uneasy feeling filled her deep to the core. She lay still for a moment and turned her head to the clock. 4:00 a.m. She heard the crash of thunder in the distance and knew the storm was passing over. *Not this nightmare though. Might as well get up. No sleeping now.*

Heading straight into the shower, she let the hot water beat down on her shoulders and back. Her muscles released their tension. She blew dry her long red hair, pulling it into a ponytail. As she put on her make-up, she stared at her face in the mirror. What freaked her out most about this latest dream were the faces in the mirror. Over time, there'd been flashes of the woman's face reflected in a window or the mirror of a car. This was the first time Madie had got a good look at the woman of her nightmares: a much younger face than she'd first thought, full of innocence and vulnerability. And then there was the man.

A shudder shook her body. *Seeing him was a definite first. Who was he to this woman?* She'd never forget his cold, blank stare, and the hatred in his lifeless dark eyes. *Who are they? Why am I seeing them? What do they want from me?*

An hour later, she headed to work early. She had a ton of paperwork to process on the volunteers and part-time workers they'd hired for the summer season. She'd rather be working than deal with this. As she drove into the parking lot, she saw Cody's truck parked by the gate. *Wow, he's an early bird.*

Madie wandered across the yard. Cody was nowhere to be seen in the outer animal compounds. She reached the surgery unit that housed injured animals either waiting for, or recuperating from, surgery. When she entered the building, she saw Cody sitting in a chair halfway down the outer room. He was bottle-feeding a baby racoon.

He glanced up and grinned at her. "Good morning. You're in early."

"I am but you beat me."

"Nuh-uh. Been here all night. I relieved Wenner at

midnight, and the volunteers will take over in a couple of hours. Too many young ones have lost their mothers. It's ridiculous."

"You've had a long stretch then."

"I got some shut-eye before I came in."

Madie watched Cody return the baby racoon and retrieve another one. She sat on the floor with her back against the wall.

He sighed. "I'll be glad when we get past this phase. We're on overload right now. Wenner may be transferring some of our guests to Kelowna."

"That would be a great help. You seem to be settling in okay. Have you found a permanent residence?"

"I have. I've got a private cottage rental over on the river in Stoney Creek. Moving in this weekend. Aren't you over that way?"

"Yup. I'm in a cabin at the resort. It's small but suits me for now."

The small animal Cody held appeared to be having trouble latching onto the bottle. Cody manoeuvred the kit into a different position. "There you go, little guy."

"You're so good with them."

He glanced over at her. "Thanks. So-oo ... what's up? I'm sure you didn't come in this early to watch me work."

Madie shrugged. "I couldn't sleep."

"That was quite a storm last night." Cody gave her a crooked grin. "Don't tell me you're afraid of thunder and lightning?"

Madie felt guarded. She didn't feel comfortable enough with Cody to explain her dreams. Much to her surprise, she exploded. "Who are we? Kids in the schoolyard? If I was afraid of storms why would you make fun of that?"

"Whoa ... I was only teasing."

Instantly, she felt bad. "Sorry, not enough sleep."

Before Cody could respond, the door opened and Wenner

entered. He nodded at them. "Good morning."

Madie started to rise from the floor but he waved his hand at her. "Stay. No need to get up."

"Shouldn't you be sleeping still?" Cody asked.

"I'm good. I thought I'd relieve you until the volunteers arrive. I've got surgery at nine on the coyote that came in yesterday. Chelsea will help me and she's pulling double shifts today. Why don't you head home and get some sleep yourself?"

"You sure?"

"Yup. I just spoke to Kelowna. They're taking six of our charges. They'll be ready for them tomorrow afternoon and I'll need you to transport them."

"That'll ease things up around here." Cody returned the kit to his cage, washed his hands, and rejoined them. "I'll give you a rundown on things here before I go."

This time, Madie did stand. *Time to get to work.*

Wenner turned to her. "Ya think you could go with him tomorrow? Chelsea and I called in a supply order yesterday. If you two can pick them up after you've dropped off the animals, we won't have to wait until the end of the week for delivery."

Madie nodded. "Sure. I can do that. I'll call them and let them know we'll be stopping by."

"Thank you," Wenner said.

She headed towards the door. "I'd best get to my paper-work and put a dent in it." She threw a glance at Cody. "See you tomorrow."

"Sure thing." He gave her a wink and added, "Sleep tight tonight."

As she passed him by, Madie threw her head back and stuck out her tongue. She walked through the compound to the administration building with a frown. *Why do I let that man get to me? Just when I feel relaxed around him, he infuriates me, and I lash out.* "Aargh."

☙ 3 ❧

"Y ou can get dressed now. I'll be back in a few minutes." The doctor left the examination room, shutting the door behind her.

Chelsea sat up and slipped off the side of the examination table. She dressed and pulled a brush from her shoulder bag and ran it through her chin-length blond hair. Perched on the edge of a chair in the corner of the room, she rubbed her hands together, partly because it was chilly in the room but mostly out of concern about the results of her examination. Convinced the symptoms she'd been experiencing were signs of menopause, she had mixed feelings.

Aren't I too young for menopause? The idea she was ageing slapped her in the face. *Not that I ever expect to have more children.* But knowing that part of her life could be over reminded her of all the years she'd been lost in captivity with Arne. She was grateful he was sterile from a childhood case of the mumps. Childbirth under those conditions would have had added complications. She caught her breath and let out a sigh. *But still.* She extended her fingers, studied her painted nails to pass the time and distract her thoughts from the depression weaving through her.

21

The door opened and Dr Anna Carson slipped in. She shut the door, pulled her stool over, and sat facing Chelsea. A slight smile creased the corners of her mouth. "Well, I can tell you what we're dealing with here and it's not menopause."

"Okay. What's wrong with me?"

"I'd say you're about four months pregnant."

Chelsea gasped. Her hand flew to her chest. All she could say was, "No way."

"I'm surprised it took you this long to come in."

Her brain couldn't function. *Pregnant?* "My God, how is this possible?"

"It's unusual at your age for sure. Less than ten per cent of women after forty ever get pregnant with their eggs. But there it is. How do you feel?"

How do I answer that? Like I know. "I … I'm … it's a shock, to say the least." Tears filled her eyes and the doctor handed her a box of Kleenex. She blew her nose. "I don't know why I'm crying."

"Raging hormones for one thing, along with an unplanned pregnancy. There are a few things we need to discuss if you choose to have this baby—or if you don't. There are some potential problems associated with pregnancy and birth with women in their forties."

"Such as?"

"You can develop diabetes and high blood pressure, experience a difficult birth, and usually a pre-term pregnancy. Eighty per cent of post-forty aged women have caesarean sections at around thirty-seven weeks. There can also be extensive bleeding post-delivery, which means you may need transfusions. And a fifty per cent chance you can miscarry. Although, I'd say you're close to the safe zone for a miscarriage."

"That's a lot to take in. I thought you were going to tell me I was in early menopause."

Dr Carson nodded. "It's certainly a game-changer."

Chelsea expelled a deep breath. "And what are the risks for the baby?"

"A preemie baby would have to remain in the hospital until a certain development level. There's the risk of jaundice. Then there's the uncertainty of genetic defects. As a woman ages, her eggs begin to break down. There's no guarantee the baby will be born healthy without chromosomal abnormalities."

"You mean like Down syndrome?"

"That's one consideration. Now, there is a test we can do that will tell us if there are any chromosomal issues."

Chelsea's stomach knotted. "I read once those tests are pretty invasive and can cause miscarriages and infection."

"True. But luckily for you, there's a new non-invasive procedure. It's a simple blood draw. Researchers discovered that a baby's cells are discharged through the placenta into the mother's bloodstream. They float freely within the mother's blood. Usually, it's done at ten weeks and then again around sixteen weeks. You're past the first period so we can do one right away."

Chelsea hesitated. "I guess."

Dr Carson leaned into her and squeezed her arm. "I know this isn't what you expected to hear today and, since I don't know what your moral or religious beliefs are, let me present your choices. If the test result is positive, you still have the option of terminating the pregnancy—or not. I'm also ordering an ultrasound. They'll get you in within a few days. If the results of the blood work are negative, then you'll need to decide if you want to have a baby at this stage of your life. You don't have to decide right now but I want you to think about it."

"Okay. I guess until we know more, I have some time to think about all of this."

"Is the father part of this decision?"

That gave Chelsea a start. *Chaz! What's he going to think about all of this?* "Umm, he's part of my life, so I guess Chaz should be part of all of this."

"I suggest you discuss it with him. But, ultimately, the decision is yours to make. I know I'm hitting you with a lot all at once, but because you're so far along, we have a short window to work with."

I can't imagine how I'll bring the subject up to Chaz. "What a strange conversation that's going to be," she mused aloud.

What is it about me and surprise pregnancies? First Sydney and now this.

Dr Carson turned to her computer and printed out two requisitions. "Let's get the results of the blood test and ultrasound so you can make an informed decision. Take this to the lab at the hospital. We might as well do all your blood work. Take this one to imaging. Once I have all the results, we'll get you back right away."

"I'll go as soon as I leave here."

"Okay. Meanwhile, get some rest and try not to stress about this."

As if.

CHAZ RAN his hands through his hair. He was sitting across the kitchen island from her, sipping coffee when she told him. She'd been to see the doctor that afternoon and this wasn't the news he'd expected when he arrived this evening. He was aware she was studying his face as he digested the information. Surprise, shock, and then confusion engulfed his mind. *God, I might as well be sitting in a minefield.* He studied her face in return. *One wrong word and this whole thing could go sideways. Trouble is I'm not sure what the right or wrong words are.*

"Are you sure? Yesterday, you thought you were going through menopause. How can you get pregnant?"

"I guess I'm one of the ten per cent who can … do … and did."

"Wow."

Their eyes locked and they stared at each other in silence. He dove in with the first coherent thought that came into his head. "What do you want to do?"

Her eyes stared past him. "I don't know."

"Oh." It was all he could think of to say.

"I'm sorry, Chaz."

This snapped him out of his apparent state of disbelief. "Sorry? Don't apologize. We created this baby together. It's not a matter of blame." He reached across and took hold of her hand. "How do you feel about it?"

Chelsea snorted. "I have no idea. Like you, I'm flabbergasted. I wasn't going to tell you until I had all the facts. But you asked me how my doctor visit went today, and I couldn't lie about something like this. For the record, I was saying sorry for just blurting out, 'Surprise! I'm pregnant'."

"What do you mean about having all the facts?"

"I had a blood test at the hospital to see if the baby has any abnormalities. It does happen with women who conceive in their forties."

"Okay. You mean like Down syndrome. And if there are? How does it help to know that at this point?"

Chelsea looked down. "I could abort."

That startled him. "How far along are you?"

"Sixteen weeks."

"Don't you want to have this baby?"

She lifted her head, her eyes full of anger.

Uh-oh. Wrong question. Brace yourself.

"Yes … maybe. I don't know." She pulled her hand from his. "I did some research online on Down syndrome before you came tonight. They can live long lives but are more prone to infections that can affect their lungs, and they can develop early-onset Alzheimer's. Even if I lived to my nineties, I'd be leaving a middle-aged child alone with possible health issues. Is that fair? And understand Down syndrome is what everyone thinks of first, but other things can go wrong, too. It's so confusing."

"Did the doctor talk about the dangers to you if you go through with this pregnancy?"

"She did." Chelsea filled him in on the possible complications for a woman her age. "There is another point to consider here too. If I remain healthy and the baby survives, it will change our lives. God knows I've struggled the past two and a half years. You've been so patient and given me time to heal and learn to trust in people again. Having a baby scares the hell out of me. How will a baby affect us? And you?"

Chaz felt puzzled. "Are you worried I wouldn't want this child?"

"No. It may be a shock, but I know you well enough to know you'd step up to the plate on this. It … it's more complicated than that. It's hard to find the words."

He was aware that she'd pulled back from him. What he saw in her eyes was fear. She appeared to him like a caged animal, waiting for a chance to bolt. *Be careful what you say next, old man.*

Chaz stood and walked around the island. Sitting beside her, he turned her stool to face him. She stared into his face as he took her hands into his. "My first concern is your health. I wouldn't want you to go through this pregnancy if it becomes a health risk for you or the baby. On the other hand, if the test is positive and you decide to terminate, it's your decision and I'll respect it."

Chelsea slipped off the stool and into his arms. "Thank you."

They hugged in silence until Chaz pushed her back gently. Her eyes were misty. "But understand one thing: if you decide to go through with the pregnancy, even with abnormalities, we'll raise this child and deal with whatever comes our way *together*. You don't have to do this alone."

He saw her body tense. She started to say something, and he put his fingers to her lips. "Shhh. We'll figure it out."

Chelsea stared deep into his eyes. "I'm willy-nilly and all over the place with my emotions. But I do know one thing and you need to know it too: if I decide not to have this child, it won't be because the baby has abnormalities. It would be about immediate life-threatening issues for the baby or me."

Chaz pushed her hair back from her eyes. "Then one step at a time. Okay?"

❧ 4 ☙

The water on Tuc-el-nuit Lake rippled as a light evening wind blew across the spring-fed oasis, dropping the desert heat a few degrees. Madie sat back in her chair and breathed in the heady, intoxicating scent of magnolia blooms —a touch of cherry, lemons, with a hint of vanilla—and listened to the birds singing their evening song.

After work, she'd driven straight to her mother's place in Oliver for a home-cooked meal. Her mom poured them lemonade from a glass pitcher on the patio table. Madie studied her mother's profile as she handed her the glass. Her mom looked relaxed and through the course of their meal, she'd observed her smiling naturally, nothing like the forced ones she'd witnessed the past year. Her mom had lost weight over that time, which had concerned Madie. Her lean frame couldn't afford it. But today, there was a lightness to her step and a sparkle in her blue eyes. Her blond hair had been cut into a chin-length bob, which added fullness to her face and accentuated her blue eyes. *And she's wearing make-up. A good sign she's paying attention to herself.*

"What?" Valerie Hayes asked.

"Huh?" Madie answered.

"You're answering a question with a question. You're staring at me."

"Oh, sorry. You look good, Mom. More like your old self."

Val smiled. "Thanks. I feel good and I guess it shows. It's been a tough year with your dad's passing. But the time feels right to start living again."

"That's good to hear you say. Grief is so devastating. But Dad would want you to be happy and make the most of your life."

Val sighed. "On the day he passed, he made me promise to do just that. I think he knew it was his last day, even if I didn't." She paused and stared at the garden. "Look at my rhododendrons and the magnolia trees. Aren't the flowers gorgeous?"

Madie glanced at the garden. "Yes, everything's beautiful. Love the fragrant smells." She went quiet, sensing her mother had more to say.

"You know what he said to me? He said, 'Val, we've had a wonderful life together but I'm the one who's dying, not you. It's not your time. You have a beautiful, loving soul and I need to know you'll be here not only for yourself but for the other people in my life. And once you feel whole again—and I know you will—please be happy. Promise me you won't give up on the gift of life that's still yours'."

Madie's eyes teared. "That's Dad. God, I miss him."

"He made me write it down and put it away in my jewellery box. I'd forgotten about it over the past year; probably deliberately. But I was thinking about the anniversary of his death coming up soon and it came back to me full force. We did have a wonderful life together, and he's right, I should try to enjoy it. And I promised."

"I've been concerned you'd closed yourself off from everything. I hope this means you'll get out of the house more."

Val laughed. "Huh! That may not be so easy with what I

have in mind." She paused a moment. "I wanted to ask your opinion on something."

Madie was intrigued. *Mom's asking me for advice? Surprise, surprise! What's this about?* "Shoot."

"I really don't need all this space. Working full-time and maintaining the yard and a two-story home is too much. It was fine while I was re-adjusting to life on my own. It kept me busy. But now I'm finding it all a chore."

"So, you're thinking of selling and moving into something smaller?"

Her mother looked startled. "Heavens, no! I couldn't leave my beautiful gardens or the lake. I was thinking of turning the lower level into a rental suite. I could live upstairs quite comfortably and still maintain a guestroom on the upper level for family and friends."

"But isn't that adding to your workload with your job and all?"

"The mortgage is paid, and with the extra income and the life insurance policy your dad left, I could afford to work part-time and be home the rest of the week to work in the gardens. I'd need to do some Renos to separate the two levels and secure my place upstairs. It wouldn't be that hard to do. What do you think?"

"Being on the lake with a beach at the end of the property makes it a prime rental. You'd do well financially."

"I was thinking the large rec room could accommodate a small kitchen at one end, with a breakfast bar and stools to separate it from what would be a living room. And the bathroom is large enough to put a stacked washer/dryer in."

"Mmm ... it's doable," Madie said, noting her mother's exuberance and the excited sparkle in her eye. "Have you thought about moving into the lower level yourself? You'd get more money renting the upstairs and less work housework for you downstairs."

"No. First off, more money for the larger part of the house

would attract a family or a couple. I don't think I'd like people over my head. Besides, giving up the upstairs means I'd lose my deck and the view of the lake."

"Makes sense." On the one hand, she was happy for her mother's enthusiasm but, on the other, a little apprehensive about her opening her home to strangers. "You seem to have given this a lot of thought. You've always been a people person. If you think you could adjust to having strangers sleeping in the house, I guess it could work."

Her mother reached out and patted her hand. "I sense your concern with me being here on my own, but I'll take precautions. They'd be separate homes with the downstairs having no access to upstairs. The suite would only be suitable for a single person, preferably a woman. Whoever rents it would be carefully vetted. I might even be able to ask around and find a tenant through my friends, who can vouch for them. I've also been thinking of getting a dog as a companion. And there's this as well: having a rental suite would add to my security. I wouldn't be alone on the property."

Madie relaxed. "I guess you're right. It sounds like a great idea and if it gives you purpose, I'm all for it. And if you like, I could ask Jax Rhyder to have a look at the work involved. He'll draw up a plan and see if you like it. He does great work and won't stiff you either."

"That would be great. Give him my phone number and we'll set up an appointment. Now, let's talk about you."

Madie's eyebrows shot up. "Me?"

"Yes, you. I appreciate your compliments that I look good and all, but I'm afraid I can't reciprocate. During dinner, I sensed dis-ease. You look terrible … actually, tired."

"Thanks, Mom." Madie rolled her eyes. "Just what I need to hear."

Val smiled. "A mother always knows, right? What is it, dear? Work?"

"No. I love my job at the Centre. It's all good."

"It must be personal then. Man trouble?"

"No, Mom. I'm not seeing anyone."

"But you must be dating?"

"Nope."

Her mother looked aghast. "You're a beautiful young girl; there must be some available young men in Stoney Creek. It's not that small."

"I've been too busy with the opening year of the Centre. Dating just hasn't been on my mind."

"So, there's been no one since you broke up with that nice young man, Tom, a couple of years ago? Shame, that. He was such a handsome fella, stable too."

"Too nice. And a relationship needs more than stability."

"Gotcha, 'too nice' says it all." Val stared at her daughter. "Humph, at least I know you aren't jumping in and out of bed for the fun of it, inside of five minutes of meeting someone."

Madie gave a bemused smile. "Where is that coming from?"

"It's true! I see it on television all the time. Not on cable of course but those other channels. The other night this guy walked into a bar and ordered a drink, the bartender served him and, five minutes later, they were in the wine cellar doing it up against the wall. Don't you think—"

"Mom, are you done having this conversation with your-self? I assure you I don't have sex with men I've just met."

Val looked contrite. "Well, I'm not saying you have to wait until marriage. I'm not that prudish. Your father and I had sex before we married."

"*Mom* ... move on."

"Okay. But don't make me drag it out of you; tell me what's going on."

Madie wasn't sure where to start. *Try at the beginning?* "Remember when I was a baby and I had night terrors?"

Val wrinkled her brow. "I do. I haven't thought about them in years. Thank God they disappeared. I felt so helpless because I couldn't do anything to make them stop. You were *so* terrified."

"I don't remember them at all."

"Good thing, too. Your dad and I were so concerned, we took you to the doctor. What a total waste of time that was."

Madie poured herself more lemonade. "Want some?"

"No, thanks."

"What did they do?"

"At first, the usual rhetoric. Make sure there're no reflections on the walls from light that might appear menacing, make sure you got plenty of sleep, stayed hydrated, stayed on a regular sleep schedule, on and on. Nothing changed, and the nightmares continued. Then they sent us to Vancouver Children's Hospital, where they did physical exams, blood work—nothing was found. Next were the child psychologists, who examined our family's medical history and your father's, and our relationship. We felt like mice in a laboratory."

Madie pondered this information. "So, then what?"

"The final test was keeping you in for an overnight study in a sleep lab. They did brain scans, placed sensors on you to record brain waves, oxygen levels, heart rate, breathing, and body movements."

"Weird, I don't remember any of that."

"I can understand why you'd want to forget it. In the end, the final diagnosis: you were a sensitive child, prone to being neurotic, and eventually you'd outgrow the night terrors."

Madie reached across the table and squeezed her mother's hand. "I'm sorry I put you and Dad through that, Mom."

"Honey, you got the worst of it. I could never understand how an innocent child could have such terrifying dreams. We were so relieved when you started pre-school. Once you were in school, the dreams stopped and never returned."

Madie sipped her lemonade, deep in thought. "Did I ever give you any details about them?"

"Oh yes, I asked you about them because I thought I

could relate them to your bedtime stories—or maybe something else in our lives." Val paused. With a heavily creased brow, she asked: "Why are you asking about this now?"

Madie ignored the question. "Tell me about them."

"They were basically about a woman—always the same woman, who was afraid of something, and sometimes a man was chasing her. You described her as a young woman with long brown hair. You didn't know who she was. But sometimes she had 'owies' on her face and blood on her mouth or nose. Horrible dreams for a toddler."

Madie's skin tingled as she stared at her mother in silence, letting this tidbit of information sink in, then took a deep breath. "Well, I hate telling you this, but they're back."

Val looked confused. "They? Who's back?"

"The nightmares. I've been having them for the past couple of months."

Her mother leaned forward, wringing her hands. "Oh, no. I don't understand. Why after all these years would they come back?"

Madie hated that she'd upset her. "I don't know, and I'm sorry to dump this on you. But I just don't have anyone else to talk to about this."

"Don't be sorry, hon. I'm glad you told me. Are you sure they're the same dreams?"

"Well, it's the same scenario: a young woman with long brown hair, being chased in the desert, and always the fear. Has to be the same. The real question is what you already asked. Why after all these years are they back?"

"What are you going to do?"

Madie shrugged. "I don't know. Is there anything else you can remember about the nightmares?"

Val sighed, turning her glass around and around on the table. "One other thing. They only occurred during thunderstorms. Never during the day if you were down napping. Just after dark."

Madie's heart skipped. "Thunderstorms?" she asked in a whisper.

Val leaned towards her. "You've turned as white as a sheet. What is it?"

"Mom … my current nightmares? They only happen during thunderstorms, only this time—night *or* day."

5

Cody glanced over at Madie and smiled. There was no doubt she was sleeping. He'd never known her not to have something to say. She was the mistress of trivia with the ability to remember all the little details. He admired that.

They'd chatted nonstop on the way into Kelowna. After delivering their patients to the Kelowna Wildlife Centre, they'd picked up the supplies, and were sixty minutes into their hour and a half drive home. He turned the dial on the radio from raucous country music to a Seattle jazz station and turned the volume down.

A quiet snore escaped every once in a while from the back of Madie's throat. He glanced at her full, parted lips and something inside him stirred. Her long, dark red hair flowed around her face and shoulders in clusters of curls. She usually wore it up in a ponytail for safety reasons around the animals but had taken it down after they'd left the animal Centre. Cody thought of her eyes, which were an unusual sea green with a black outline around the edges. *Stunning.*

A feeling of warmth towards her caught him by surprise. *Stop it,* he thought. *We have to work together.* There were no rules at the Centre that said they couldn't date but he'd found in the past it was never good practice to get involved with a co-worker. Not only was it distracting, but if it turned sour, work could become a painful place to be.

His finding this job at the Centre was a dream come true. Wenner and Chelsea were wonderful and working with the animals and birds made it all the better. *And then there's Madie.* He snuck a glance at her. *What a gem she is. Hmm ... am I thinking professionally or personally? Okay, not going there.*

A sudden cloudburst brought rain from the darkened sky. Cody switched his attention to the road and traffic. Before long, his wipers were jacked to the highest setting as the downpour blasted across the windshield. The continuous sound of thunder in the distance told him it was moving closer as the whap-whapping of the blades lulled his senses. It took the sudden thumping of the rumble strip in the centre of the road to make him sit up straight. *Whoa, wake up man before you become a part of someone's truck grill.* He was about ten minutes from home. Cody glanced at Madie. *She really must be fried to sleep through this.* He turned his attention back to the road.

Then, it happened!

WHAM! An elbow whacked him in the right rib. Madie thrashed in her seat; her hands grappled something invisible at her throat.

"No," she shouted. "Mmm ... mmm," she groaned, gasping for air.

"Whoa," he yelled, shifting his body away from her to keep control of the car. "Madie—wake up," Cody shouted.

Her eyes flew open and her head came forward. "Uh ... uh ..." She panted, catching her breath. "Can't—breathe!"

Cody glanced at her.

She stared at him with horror in her eyes, her face pale.

He turned back to the road. "You're okay. Just a bad dream," he said softly.

She sunk back in her seat, releasing a long breath. "Fuck … fuck," flowed forth. "Sorry …"

"Hey, it happens. Must've been quite the dream. You alright?"

"It was much more than a dream. I'm fine, thanks."

"Just coming into town."

As they entered Stoney Creek, lightning hit the power pole ahead. The loud explosion shook the car as they drove past, sparks flying through the air. Madie jumped in her seat.

"Shit! That was close," Cody cried. They drove on through the centre of town. "We'll be at the Centre soon."

Madie responded in a shaky voice, "It'll be good to get off the roads."

After another glance at her, he sensed something more was going on than a bad dream.

She stared silently out the side window.

"Looks like the power is out in town. Must have been a transformer that blew back there. I wonder how the Centre is doing," he said worriedly.

She didn't appear to hear him.

Five minutes later, they pulled into the parking lot of the Wildlife Centre. Cody helped Madie carry the Administration supplies into the building.

She hit the light switch. "Power's still on here."

He gave her a look. *So, she did hear me.*

"Thanks for helping me with the supplies. Looks like Chelsea's home for the day. I'll put these away and head out too."

"Sure thing. I'll check in with Wenner and get this shit put away. Night." He left her reluctantly, not knowing what else to say or do, and not wanting to intrude.

Twenty minutes later, Madie sat in the parking lot, trying to get her car to start. *You're kidding me.*

Cody drove out of the Centre and stopped to lock the gate. Then, he drove over to her car and rolled down his window. "Everything all right?"

She lowered hers. "I think I have a dead battery."

"Try it again," Cody suggested, getting out and pulling his hoody over his head.

Madie turned the key. Nothing.

"I don't think it's dead. Sounds like your starter's gone." He peered down the road and then turned back. "The garage in town is closed now. No power anyhow. Lock it up and I'll drive you home. Tomorrow, you can have it towed in."

"Okay."

When they drove up to her cabin, the owner came out of her residence and ran over to the car. Madie opened her window.

"Hi hon," she said. "Isn't this awful? I'm afraid we've lost power. The winds are coming up too. We have no idea how long it'll be out. Bob placed a cooler on your porch full of ice for your perishables. We put some food in it for you since you won't be able to cook. And a thermos of hot coffee beside the cooler."

"Oh Connie, you guys are so good to me. Thank you so much."

"Bob placed some extra firewood on the porch as well, in case it chills down."

"Aww," Madie said with a grateful smile.

"No problem, love." She turned and ran back to her house.

"It must be comforting to know they've got your back. They seem like good people," Cody said.

"They've certainly made me feel at home here." She opened her door. "Thanks for the ride."

Cody opened his door and climbed out. "I'll help you bring in the cooler and some firewood."

They ran to the porch as another thunderclap boomed around them. A few minutes later, they'd brought everything inside. She turned on a couple of battery-operated lanterns. Madie opened the cooler and gasped. "Oh, man. She packed more than a dinner here. Look at all of this food—BBQ chicken, homemade potato salad, Caesar salad. Are you hungry? You might as well stay for dinner."

"Sure. I could eat. I'll get the woodstove fired up."

Madie placed the food on the table. Once she'd transferred her perishables from the fridge to the cooler, she finished setting the table. "Want some coffee?"

"Please. Black works."

"Same for me." She filled the cups and put the thermos down. "We're all set. Let's eat."

As they feasted on their dinner, the fierce storm continued. Every time a thunderclap sounded, Madie tensed.

"You don't like storms much do you?" Cody asked.

She hesitated. "I've always hated them."

"I've always loved them. Not driving in them so much. But lying in bed, listening to the rain hit the roof, especially a metal one—it's comforting."

"Good for you, I'll pass."

She caught him studying her. Finally, he said, "At least your colour is back. You were pale coming out of that bad dream … or, I'm guessing, it was a nightmare. You started to speak about it when the transformer exploded."

Madie put her chicken wing down and wiped her fingers. "Have you … have you ever had a recurring dream?"

Cody nodded. "All the time when I was little. I lost my mom when I was five. She died of cancer."

Madie didn't expect that. "I'm so sorry."

"Thank you, but it was a long time ago. Anyway, this grade-one teacher I had was really cool, you know? She was there for me when I had bad days. I started having this same dream over and over that my teacher died. I'd wake up crying, thinking it happened. I couldn't wait to get to school to check in with her. And there she'd be, with that warm smile, greeting me at the classroom door."

Madie felt sympathetic. "That's horrible."

"One day, I begged her to be careful. She asked me why. When I told her about my dreams of her death, she sat me down and explained that it was transference or something like that. Because I lost my mother, I'd grown close to her and my fears of losing my teacher were projected through my dreams in the form of her death too. She promised me she wasn't going to die. After that, the dreams never came back."

"Wow. I wish mine were that simple."

"Do you want to tell me about them?"

Madie fell silent. "You're the first person I've talked to about my dreams, except my mom. It's a little daunting."

"No fair. Never told anyone 'bout mine either. Not even my dad. You can trust me; tell me about your dreams."

Madie hesitated and, instead, asked, "So, where is home?"

"The island, Victoria. My dad still lives with my stepmother." Cody gave her a reassuring grin. "Come on, talk to me."

Madie relaxed. "Nightmares, not dreams. They're not exactly the same, as the situation always changes. But always the same woman—and now there's a man. The thing about them is they seem so real and the nightmares are getting more violent."

"That's scary shit. Do you recognize any of these people?"

"No. Haven't a clue. The woman's always been alone and frightened. But she doesn't feel like a stranger … it's like … she's me." Madie hesitated. "Now, you're going to think I'm crazy."

"Not at all. There has to be a reason it's always the same person."

"Probably, and now there's this man. He's hurting her. I know he's the one she's frightened of."

She watched him chew on her answer. Finally, he said, "How long have you had them?"

Madie sighed. "They started when I was a baby."

His eyebrows shot up. "Whoa."

"I don't remember them as a baby. My mother told me about them. I'd wake up with night terrors and it'd take her a while to calm me down. They stopped when I started school. Now, they're back."

"So, when did they return?"

"This spring, here in Stoney Creek. Ever since the rainy season started."

"The storms? You think that has something to do with them?"

"Yes. As a baby, I only had nightmares when it stormed. And, now, the same thing. Another thing: I only had them at night. But today, it was daylight, and the most violent dream of them all."

"That explains your going bat-shit crazy in the car coming back from Kelowna. You were sleeping peacefully until the thunder came—then bam!"

Madie leaned back in her chair. "I just don't know what to do. I'm afraid to go to sleep 'cause when I do, I don't know what's gonna happen. It's why I'm tired and cranky half the time at work. All those years passed without them. Why now?

Cody appeared to ponder that for a moment. "Perhaps it's the farm."

"The farm?"

"The Wildlife Centre. It's part of the original farm Chelsea grew up on. I don't know if you know its history but it's definitely a spiritual spot. See, when Chelsea was held hostage at the neighbour's farm, Arne, the farmer, killed his wife and Chelsea's father because they found out he'd kidnapped Chelsea. Her old man's spirit stayed to look over

Chelsea. And he played a part in her being found by communicating with Sydney and her mother."

"What a story! How'd you learn all this?" Madie asked, awed.

"Wenner told me some of it, and Syd's husband, Jax. Perhaps this woman is trying to tell you something."

Madie stared back in disbelief. "You think she's real?"

"Well, unless she's a figment of your imagination, why the same woman over and over again?"

"I … you … wow. I didn't expect that from you. I mean, do you believe in psychic phenomenon?"

Cody laughed. "Actually, I do. My grandmother is a channeler. She sees spirits that have passed over. I grew up on her stories and research."

The wind blew a broken tree branch against the window, causing them both to jump. "Looks like we have a helluva night ahead of us," Cody said.

Madie stared at the window, looking troubled. "Yeah! I can't go on like this. Especially with each episode getting more violent."

"Maybe we should talk to my grandmother. She might be able to help you."

She stared at him. "Ya think?"

"You have nothing to lose. We're both off work tomorrow. Maybe we can go and see her."

"Where does she live?"

"Rock Creek."

Madie let out a sigh. She got up and stared out the window, into the raging storm. When she turned back to him, she'd reached a resolve. "Okay. How long is the drive?"

She started to clear the table.

"Forty minutes. I'll call Grams and make sure she'll be home." He pulled his cell phone out of his pocket.

She finished cleaning up the kitchen while he was on the call.

"All good. She's excited to see us. And she'll do a reading on you. Hopefully, she'll see something that may help."

"Thank you for this," Madie said with a smile. "I do appreciate your support." Another thunderclap made her cringe.

"Listen, I've got an idea." He put his hands up and tilted his head. "It's just a suggestion. But hear me out. This storm isn't stopping any time soon. What if I stay? I can sleep on the couch over there and you won't be alone. I'd have to come back for you in the morning anyway."

"That's kind of you. But I can't expect someone to stay with me every time there's a storm. It's … it's not practical."

"Let's deal with tonight. The storms are expected to blow over tomorrow and maybe you'll have some peace for a while."

Madie studied him for a moment.

"Trust me, I'm only trying to help."

She let out a sigh. "Then follow me. Let's get you some bedding for that couch."

6

It wasn't a long wait in reception before Chelsea was called into Dr Carson's office. Chaz gave her arm a squeeze when she stood to follow the nurse. She gave him a nervous smile.

"I'll be here when you're done," he said.

Dr Carson was sitting at her desk when she was led in. "Have a seat."

She sat down, her body rigid, bracing herself for whatever the doctor told her.

"The blood tests came back normal for you and the baby. No genetic abnormalities. The ultrasound also shows a normal growth for the gestation period. The placenta is sitting at the back of the fetus at the moment but should move to the top further along when the baby is preparing for birth. Lastly, you're in top physical form for your age. There's no reason at this point why you shouldn't have a normal, healthy pregnancy."

Chelsea nodded, sat back in her chair, and relaxed.

"Have you thought about your options since we last talked?"

"I've thought of nothing else for the past five days.

Knowing there's no abnormality is a relief, but I have some questions."

"Sure. Go ahead."

"I did a lot of research into things you mentioned the last visit, like hypertension and diabetes. If I develop these conditions, how do you treat them?"

"You'll be monitored regularly and, if necessary, be given medication to control them. I suggest you purchase a blood-sugar level kit and a blood-pressure monitoring kit from the drug store and self-monitor at home."

Chelsea looked puzzled. "And the meds won't harm the baby?"

Dr Carson shook her head and smiled. "No. There are medications we can use that won't harm the baby."

"Good to know. I also read ageing mothers-to-be could have stillborn babies. How common is it?"

"Stillborns are associated with chromosomal issues. We've already determined that's not the case here. Anything else?"

"What else can I expect?"

"We'll do regular blood tests and ultrasounds, more than we would for a younger mother-to-be and I'll give you a prescription for special vitamins. You may have to consider quitting work sooner than most. You'll need rest and receive no additional stress factors."

Chelsea thought about that. "I'd hate to leave my business partner alone to handle things. But I live at the Centre; I suppose I could do computer work from home."

"Make a plan, then, but as I said, be mindful of your body." The doctor paused. "Can I ask if you've discussed this with the baby's father?"

"Yes, he's all in to support me in whatever I do. He brought me here today. He's waiting in reception."

"Then the only decision for you is: do you *want* this baby? I must remind you that time is of the essence here, considering how far along you are."

She stared past the doctor at the framed medical diploma hanging on the white wall next to family photos and one of a dog. The sea of smiling faces in the family pictures tugged at her heart. "When I was a teenager and pregnant with Sydney, my mother wanted me to either end the pregnancy or give the baby up for adoption. Despite how scared I felt about the future, abortion wasn't on the table at all and I was committed to keeping her. My abductor took away the right I'd fought for to raise her ..."

Chelsea paused as her decision became clear. Her heart pounded, knowing the words she was about to say would change her life. "As unplanned and shocking as *this* pregnancy is, a second chance has been offered. Nothing short of a medical emergency will stop me from having this baby."

"Then take this." Dr Carson handed her a brochure. "We've discussed you'll have this baby via Caesarean, but perhaps you and Chaz would like to attend pre-natal classes together. There's a lot more to the sessions than just prepping for birth."

Chelsea took the papers in a daze. She'd no idea what her decision would be about carrying this baby to term until she'd heard herself say the words moments ago.

"One more thing. Would you like to know the sex of the baby?"

Chelsea's jaw dropped. "You know the sex?"

"I do. The position of the fetus on the ultrasound made it very clear."

Know or not know? "That information wasn't available to me when I was pregnant with Sydney." She hesitated. "You know what? Yes, I'd love to know."

Dr Carson laughed. "You're having a girl."

Chelsea chuckled for the first time in days. "Of course it's a girl; we're a family of girls."

CHAZ SAT in the reception area, trying to focus on emails on his phone. The nurse called another patient and he looked up to see Chelsea re-enter the room. She stopped to talk to the receptionist, then turned to him and nodded at the exit door. She didn't appear as tense as when they'd arrived. He followed her out to the parking lot

When he looked at her hard, she said, "Let's talk in the car."

They walked side-by-side in silence. He was bursting inside but didn't want to push her. After they settled into their seats, Chelsea turned to face him.

He couldn't wait any longer. "So? What'd she say?"

"Everything's normal."

Chaz let out a sigh. "That's great." He studied Madie's face. Her expression was unreadable. "Isn't it?"

"It's a girl," she blurted out.

His eyes widened. "A girl!"

She nodded. Chaz raked his hands through his hair. *She avoided my question. But surely she wouldn't tell me the sex if she didn't want to keep the pregnancy.*

He steeled himself. "Does this mean you've decided to go ahead with the pregnancy?"

She smiled. "Yes, it does."

"And no health concerns for you or the baby?"

"Nothing so far and with careful monitoring, it should be fine."

Chaz couldn't speak. His heart was thrilled about becoming a father again, but his mind ran in a different direction. *A daughter? What does this mean about our relationship? How is this going to work?* Tightness welled in his chest and he realized he was holding his breath. He pushed out the air and gasped, then stammered, "This just got real." He grabbed her hands. "What happens now?"

A weak smile crossed her face and she shrugged. "I don't know."

Chaz raised her hands to his mouth and kissed them. Without giving it a thought, he exclaimed, "I love you."

The smile disappeared as Chelsea's face blanched; her expression went blank.

His brow furrowed. "What? What's wrong?"

She turned away and stared out the window. "Nothing. I have to get back to work. We can talk more later."

Chaz knew better than to push. He'd learned over the years when they needed to talk, it only happened when Chelsea wanted it to. He turned away and started the car. *What did I say?*

Driving to the Centre, he tried chit-chat, keeping it generic and non-personal, but she didn't respond. *Shut up, man. You're sounding like an idiot.* By the time they reached the Centre, he was angry. *She's fucking shut down like she always does when she feels pushed into a corner. I didn't do that—did I?*

Chelsea opened the door, stepped out, and leaned in. "Thanks for taking me to my appointment. See you later?"

Her tone was ice. *Goddamn it, he didn't do anything.* He almost gave in, as he always did when she frustrated him. *Not this time.* "You know what, Chelsea? This should be one of the happiest days of our lives. For two and a half years, I've been here for you. You know me, and you know you can trust me. But here you are shutting me out, *again.* Why? And you know what else? I'm so sick and tired of walking on thin ice around you. It's time you realize I have feelings too and it's not always about you. So, no … you won't see me later. Now, shut the fucking door and let me get out of here."

She never said a word. The shocked look on her face said it all. She closed the door and stood watching as he peeled out of the lot and sped down the road.

Shit! A part of him felt bad for his explosion but not for what he'd said. It was a long time coming. *Okay, peeling out of the driveway was a bit childish.* What bothered him more was his timing. He knew he could have picked a better moment to let it all hang out, and certainly in a less confrontational manner. "Fuck." He slammed his fist on the dashboard.

Well, it's done. I can't undo it. Better to air it now, before the baby comes. Guess I've been fooling myself thinking we'd be together one day. It's time I face the facts ... she can't commit. His throat tightened at the thought of having a daughter but not the woman he loved. He wanted them both.

He drove straight home, called his office to tell them he'd be gone for the day and shut off his cell phone. Changing into shorts and a tee, he poured himself a stiff drink, headed out the back door ... but returned to grab the bottle of Scotch.

A path at the end of the garden led him to the river. The fast-moving water, heading south, rushed past him, still high from spring runoff. Sitting on the bank, he leaned back against a tree; the roaring noise of the water drowned out his awareness of his complicated life and the whiskey dulled his senses.

❧ 7 ❧

C ody pulled off the Crowsnest Highway at the crest of the hill and into the lookout parking lot. They'd only been on the road to Rock Creek for fifteen minutes, but the view was worth the stop. They got out of the car and walked to the edge to look down on the town of Osoyoos and Osoyoos Lake. In the distance, the fruit orchards in wine country stretched for miles, their uniform rows filling the landscape.

"This view never gets tired," he said.

Madie smiled. "You've got that right."

He gave her a sideways glance. "You look rested this morning."

"Sitting up with you so I wouldn't have another nightmare was genius on your part. And just like The Weather Network said, the storm ended in the wee hours. Thank you for letting me sleep in and catch up."

"You're welcome. You must have slept heavily because I made a lot of noise searching through your unfamiliar cupboards to make coffee and breakfast."

She snorted. "Never heard a thing. You know, there's a

depth to you I never saw before. The whole holistic thing and, now, a great cook. You've surprised me."

"I'll take that as a compliment. You can thank my grams for that. She wasn't just a loving grandmother to me after my mother passed, but a guiding light as well. She taught me so much about life."

"Tell me something she taught you that you've always remembered. Something profound."

"Hmm … no pressure there. Let's see, probably the time when I was sixteen and I asked her why some people could be so blind to something obvious. She said, 'Because looking at the world through the front of your eyes, your vision sees only what's directly in front of you. If you look at the world from behind your eyes, your vision becomes infinite.' She's the most near-perfect being I've ever met."

"Wow. Only near perfect? She sounds wonderful." Madie opened a bottle of water and took a sip.

Cody laughed. "She's also the one who told me I'd love tofu hot dogs … she lied. She never told me they tasted like crayons. Even my dog, Murphy, turned up his nose at them."

Madie laughed as she swallowed more water and began choking.

Cody patted her back. "You okay?"

"Fine. I do love your humour. You're so much more than a lion tamer."

Cody chuckled. "Thanks, I think."

They got back on the road and climbed higher, following the highway east along the Canada/US border. They passed the north turnoff to Beaverdell and continued along the Kettle River to Rock Creek. The terrain had changed from arid desert to green meadows and areas of forested trees. Cody turned down a dirt road that led them to a cedar cottage by the river.

"Wow. What a lovely spot," Madie exclaimed. She followed Cody along a gravel pathway to a set of steps that led to a covered verandah facing the river. They paused to look at the white water running downstream.

Raising his voice above the noise of the rushing river, Cody said, "Water's still high from spring runoff. There's great fishing when the water calms down. Grampa and I caught many trout when I was a kid in the early morning hours. Great breakfast fry-up with potatoes and eggs."

The door behind them flew open and a small, wiry woman in her seventies charged out and into Cody's arms.

"About time you visited your old grams. Mmm ... so good to see you." She released him and turned to Madie. "Now, aren't you the prettiest little thing? Look at that red hair."

"Grams, this is Madie Hayes. Madie ... my grandmother, Kat Diaz."

"Nice to meet you. You have a beautiful spot here by the river."

"I do love it here. Come in, let's get comfortable."

Kat led them into a living room that reminded Madie of an era past. One wall was a floor-to-ceiling bookcase, broken into three sections of dark-stained oak. Some shelves were books, some ornaments, and others carried framed family pictures. The original wood-grained floor had an oval rug in front of a plush couch. Two other armchairs matching the couch sat in opposite corners of the room.

"I'll be back in a moment," Kat said, leaving them alone.

"This room is like going back in time. It's so warm and cosy. I like it," Madie said.

Cody nodded. "I don't think it's changed since I was a kid."

"The only new thing is the pellet stove."

"Yes, after Grampa died, cutting firewood was beyond Grams. She had the old wood stove replaced."

Kat returned with a tray of lemonade and homemade chocolate-chip cookies. She placed the tray on an old vintage steamship trunk serving as a coffee table. After pouring them each a glass and offering up the cookies, she lit some candles. The smell of vanilla wafted through the room.

"Grams, you still spoil me—my favourite cookies."

"Who else do I have to bake for?"

She asked about their work at the Centre and Kat and Cody discussed the events in the lives of their family members. After a time, she cleared away the tray and asked Cody to leave her alone with Madie for a while.

Madie sat up straight. "Please, can he stay?"

"I usually do sessions alone with people I don't know to protect one's privacy. You never know what might be exposed during a session. But if you're comfortable with Cody staying, it's your decision."

Madie looked at Cody. "I am, if you're willing."

"Of course."

"Cody's been part of my family sessions over the years. He knows what's expected of him." She turned to him. "Can you move over to the corner chair and let her have the couch?"

Once Cody planted himself, Kat concentrated on Madie. "So, tell me, have you ever experienced channelling before?"

"No, never."

"Then let me explain what to expect. First, I'll get you to relax through meditation. I will close my eyes and prepare myself to receive my spirit friend, Nikesh. He's the one who will connect me with any spirits that may wish to connect with you. Sometimes, it can take a few minutes and, sometimes, it takes longer. Relax and be patient. I'll let you know when he's here."

"What a beautiful name—Nikesh," Madie said.

"Isn't it? It means 'saviour'. If we're joined with any spirits that wish to talk to you, I'll pass along their messages. You can ask questions or remain silent. Nikesh will tell me when they're gone. Shall we begin?"

"Yes."

"Sit back and make yourself comfortable. Close your eyes,

place your hands in your lap, and join your forefingers and thumbs on each hand together to form two circles. This will protect your aura and keep you safe from unwanted spirits."

Madie relaxed into the soft cushions of the couch and followed Kat's instructions. She took her through a series of deep, slow breathing to relax her. When asked to visualize a white light of protection that surrounded her, Kat told her to clear her mind and wait for her to receive Nikesh. A few minutes passed until Kat spoke again.

"He's here with us now and telling me there's an elderly woman with him. She's got grey hair and is quite tall. I can't make out her name but I'm seeing the letter 'C' and he's showing me a small house. It's either a dollhouse or a playhouse—yes, a pink playhouse with rose bushes around it."

"Uh." Madie gasped. She should have been shocked, but instead, she felt surrounded by warmth and love.

"Do you know who this spirit is, Madie?"

"Yes, my maternal grandmother, Camila. She had a pink playhouse in her rose garden for her grandkids to play in."

"Nikesh says she's laughing and clapping her hands. She wants you to know your grandfather is here as well. Tom ... or is it Tim? Definitely a T name ... no, I think it's Ted."

"Yes, his name was Theodore. They called him Teddy."

"Teddy wants you to know he's very proud of you. But he wants you to listen to your grandmother. He says he must leave now and says goodbye." Kat was silent for a moment. "He's gone. Only Camila remains. Nikesh says she's looking very sad. She knows you're experiencing something extraordinary that has you fearful. She says you must stay strong and see it through. What's happening is not common to many but is very unique to you. As you follow this to the end, you'll find danger. You must protect yourself and stay safe. Does this make any sense to you?"

"Some of it."

"Nikesh is telling me she's gone now and there are no

other spirits. He's telling me my role today has been to lead you towards your journey and to let you know it's real. I must pass you on to someone else who will reveal what that journey is. My part will then be over." Again, Kat was silent for a moment. "Nikesh is gone. Relax, and take a few deep breathes to centre yourself. When you're ready, open your eyes."

Madie did so but stayed silent.

"Are you all right?" Kat asked.

"I think so. I feel a little bit like I'm outside my body, looking in."

"Very normal, but it will pass. Let's chat. That was one of the shortest sessions I've done but I trust Nikesh gave us all we need to deal with your present situation. What I need from you is for you to tell me about this experience you're going through so I can steer you to whoever it is you need to seek out next."

"Okay." Madie related her nightmares from her birth until starting school, then their recent recurrence.

"She's never appeared in spirit form while you're awake?"

"Never."

"So, you've only seen this woman when sleeping?"

"Yes."

"Hmm … and she didn't appear through Nikesh as a spirit from the other side either. This would have been the perfect forum for her to do so, if she's reaching out to you from the other side."

"So, where does that leave us?"

"It could mean she's not a spirit at all. Maybe she's still alive, but in danger."

Cody had been silent and unmoving through the whole session. But now he shifted in the chair and spoke. "I wondered that too."

Kat looked at him. "Except … if, for some reason, Madie's tuning into this woman's psyche, I have no idea who to send her to next, which Nikesh said is my mission in all of this."

She turned back to Madie. "And you have no idea who she is?"

"None," Madie replied softly.

Kat studied her. "At least you know something real is happening here. You aren't imagining it."

Madie smiled. "And I'm not crazy either."

"No, you aren't, my dear." Kat paused a second. "You said something to me earlier about feeling what was happening to this woman, was happening to you. Right?"

"Umm ... I can't find the proper words to describe it. The emotions are so real ... it's like they're mine, but it's her I'm seeing, not me." Madie shrugged. "That's it ... sort of."

Kat got excited. "Hang on ... she can't be a real person in current danger if she's the same person you dreamed of as a baby. We're talking twenty years or so, right?" She gazed into the distance. "There *is* another possibility. Why didn't I think of it? Why didn't Nikesh make it clearer?" She started to giggle.

"Grams?" Cody asked, perplexed.

Madie stared at her in anticipation.

Kat pointed at Madie. "You *are* her."

Madie looked from Cody to Kat. "I'm her?"

"Of course. She, whoever she is, died. But her spirit isn't on the other side because she reincarnated back into this world. Your soul is the incarnated spirit of this woman from a past life. She's you and that's why you're experiencing her past as if it happened to you."

"Grams, that's brilliant. It makes sense."

Madie felt speechless. "A *past* life?"

"Yes. And now I know exactly who to send you to. I have a friend who lives in Kelowna. She's a Past Life Regressionist Practitioner. She'll take you back in time under hypnosis. Her name is Sasha Taylor."

Feeling confused, Madie asked, "If this woman's from a past life and lived in some sort of danger, why did my grandmother pass on the message I needed to protect myself and stay safe? How can a past life experience hurt me in this life?"

"That I don't know. My role is done here. But perhaps a session with Sasha will tell you more. I'll set up an appointment for you. What I do know is that messages of warning passed from the other side are to be heeded and taken seriously."

"In that case, I'm glad I brought her here, Grams," Cody said.

Kat sat up straight. "After all my years of practice, I can say this with certainty: Cody, it wasn't a mistake, you bringing Madie to me today. We're all meant to be part of a great mystery that needs unravelling."

8

Chelsea dragged herself into the Centre. She hadn't slept much the night before. It had been two days since Chaz had cancelled his visit the night he'd driven her back to work from the Medical Clinic. In their busy lives, two days without contact meant nothing under normal circumstances. But this was different. His explosive rant was out of character which, in itself, emphasized the seriousness of the rift between them.

His emotional outburst had left her speechless. She'd wanted to reach out to him but felt at a loss as to how to approach him. Two days of soul searching hadn't provided her with any answers. *He accused me of ignoring his feelings—and I did.* Three words—I love you—had knocked her off her feet. It was the first time Chaz had said them. Instead of being elated, the words had added more tension to the already stressful situation they'd found themselves facing.

She went straight to the lounge to get a cup of coffee. Wenner was an early bird and always put a pot of coffee on for her and Madie before he visited his furry or feathered patients. She smiled to herself at the thought of him. *What a sweetie, a great business partner, and an even better friend.* As she entered the room, Madie was pouring herself a cup.

"Good morning," Chelsea said, coming up behind her to refrigerate her bagged lunch.

Madie spun around. "Hi. Want a coffee?"

"You bet. I'm half asleep this morning."

Madie poured them both a cup and handed her one. "By the way, a courier brought an envelope for you. I placed it on your desk."

"Thanks." She lifted her cup. "I'm going to my office and force myself awake on caffeine."

She checked her calls and noted none were of immediate concern. Her eyes settled on the envelope on her desk. She cut the end open with scissors and found a white envelope inside with her first name written on it. Curious, she tore it open and what she saw made her head jerk back. She stared at the signature on the paper in her hand. *A letter from Chaz? Why didn't he just come and talk to me—or at least call?*

Something told her she wasn't going to like its contents. Chelsea got up and shut her office door and settled back in her chair. With shaking hands, she steeled herself before focusing on the handwritten words.

Chelsea,

I apologize for writing this letter as opposed to seeing you in person. Call me a coward if you will, but I can only see my way to clearly stating my thoughts and emotions by writing these words. Face to face, I'm afraid I'd be unable to say what I need to. Please accept my apology for losing my temper the other day; nothing can be resolved through rudeness.

I've spent the past few days trying to figure out what I said wrong in the car that once again caused you to withdraw from me. It finally hit me. When you walked back into my life two and half years ago, after being gone for twenty years, I believed I fell in love with you all over again. I now realize I'd never stopped loving you. Two days ago, caught up in the excitement of the moment, three words slipped out of my mouth for the first time, 'I love you'. For me, they were freeing. The fact that they caused such a negative reaction from you hurt me to the core.

You were right to question what effect this child would have on our relationship. There is no doubt this baby means a lot to you and you can be sure, to me as well. Our baby is and will be welcomed and loved. But this new stage in our lives has forced me to be honest with myself—about us. I've been respectful and patient as you've gone through the healing process these past few years and I was content with the standing of our relationship. The past four months, as we moved to an intimate relationship, were the happiest I've been in years. But the realization that we're to be parents has changed my expectations. Simply put, I need and want more. I want us to be a family. My heart tells me you love me, but my brain fears this is not a step you'll be able to take with me. Not because you don't care, but because your well-being depends on your independence. Arne damaged you in ways I can't fix, but I do respect your struggle and your right to be you.

Where does that leave us? I guess nowhere. We can't continue in a relationship where we have different expectations. It would only lead to hurting us both more than we already have. Sometimes love just isn't enough. I'm asking for some space to come to terms with my feelings and my sense of loss. But know I will be there for you and our child. I intend to be an attentive, participating father and when the time comes, we'll have to reach a co-parenting agreement. I don't want to be a part-time dad who spends weekends and the odd holiday with our daughter. I want 50/50 custodial rights and wish to be an active participant in the decision-making. I hope you agree.

I wish you happiness and good health.

Sincerely,

Chaz

Chelsea dropped the letter on her desk. She swivelled her

chair to stare out the window. The view was wasted on her as her glazed eyes saw nothing. She sat for a while like this, feeling numb. Finally, she stood and walked out of the office. As she passed Madie in the hallway, the other woman asked, "Are you heading Wenner's way? I have some files he wants."

Chelsea never heard her. She left the building and headed over the hill to Sydney's property. She wandered through the magnolia grove to her favourite tree. Climbing onto a branch, she sat there with her head leaning against the trunk. It was a warm, still day and the lake water reflected like glass. *Maybe it was a little too quiet.*

Her heart was heavy. *He's gone. I've lost him.* There was no doubt in her mind it was her fault, but she wouldn't allow herself to examine it. *Not yet. It hurt too much.* She tried to stay in control but here, alone in the grove; it got the better of her.

Tears filled her eyes and poured down her cheeks as she gave in and owned her despair. After a time, she wiped her face with her shirt. A sudden wind came from nowhere, shaking the limbs. She climbed down, walked around the base of the tree, searching for an engraving out of her past. When she found it, her fingers traced the outline of the heart, moving to the letters inside: 'C & C'. *Chelsea and Chaz. Twenty-three years ago, young and in love, we carved our initials in the bark. Oh, Chaz, we hurt each other then and twenty-three years later, we've repeated it.*

"Uh." Her hands flew to her abdomen. A decisive feeling of fluttering butterflies interrupted her thoughts. *Your first movements.* Engaged in the sensation of her baby stirring for the first time was perfect timing. She headed back to her office a little less lonely.

9

The box teetered on the edge of the chair where Madie had placed it. Losing its battle with gravity, it fell sideways onto the floor. The loud bang startled Madie and she dropped the trash can, spilling its contents. "Dammit, anyway!"

She spun around to see the newly printed brochures outlining their upcoming summer apprenticeship program strewn across the floor. She was lost in thought on her hands and knees, picking up the pamphlets, when the outside door opened. A fierce wind blew into the room and the remaining brochures flew into the air, scattering them further away. The door behind her slammed shut.

"Fuck!" She sat on the floor with her hand over her chest. "Two heart attacks in a row here."

Cody grinned. "Sorry, that wind is pretty wild."

Madie stared up at him. "Never smile when apologizing. The sincerity factor is lost."

He chuckled and extended a hand to her, pulling her onto her feet. With a glance around the room, he said, "Quite the mess you've created here."

"I've created?"

"Hey, I assume you dumped the garbage and tipped the box. All I did was spread them around a little. Tell you what; let me help you clean up. Then, we're even."

"Deal," she agreed.

Madie studied his long lean legs and buttocks in his form-fitting jeans as he bent over to pick up the paper. *Definitely delectable. What's the current slang? Hottie? Sexy dude? Easy on the eyes? All of the above!*

Cody threw a glance back at her and caught her lost in her daydream. A crooked grin crossed his face. "Not fair, me doing all the work while you check me out. That's pretty sexist, lady."

Madie felt her face burn and straightened her shoulders. "You wish." She turned her back to him and picked up the trash, throwing it into the garbage bag. "Why are you here anyway? Don't you have an animal to care for?"

"Wenner sent me to pick up some files he needs. He thought you were bringing them, but I guess you were too busy trashing reception."

Ooh, he's so annoying. "They're in my office." She marched past him. "Come with me."

Cody dutifully followed and dropped into a chair opposite her desk. Madie sat down and pulled the files from a desk drawer. "I'm here alone so I couldn't leave. I've been waiting for Chelsea to return."

"Yeah, I saw her wandering the compound a while ago. Where'd she go?"

"Haven't a clue. I tried to give her the files as she was heading Wenner's way, but she just walked out the door without answering."

"Humph … maybe something is going around in the Admin Building."

Madie frowned. "Like what?"

Cody grinned at her with that wide smile of his. "I don't know, but you're both a bit dozy today."

She tilted her head. "Sometimes, your humour is down-right corny."

His hands went to his chest. "Uh … I'm injured. You've broken my heart."

Madie laughed. "More like your ego, lion tamer."

He chuckled. "So, how are you? Sleeping better now that the thunderstorms have subsided?"

"All good. The nightmares have stopped. Thanks for asking."

"Do you have an appointment yet with the regressionist?"

She nodded. "She called yesterday. Next Saturday."

Cody studied her. "How do you feel about it? Are you nervous?"

She shrugged. "More apprehensive than nervous. Hoping for something concrete to come out of this session might be wishful thinking. On the other hand, what have I got to lose? What do you think?"

"I get you don't want to have high expectations." Cody paused. "But no stone unturned—that's my motto."

"Yeah, you're right."

"So, listen up, I've moved into the cottage, and have a list a mile long of things I need. How 'bout we drive to Kelowna together? I'll drop you off, go shopping, and swing back for you later."

A slow smile spread across her face. "See? Now that's why, just when you've pushed me beyond the point of being pissed off, you redeem yourself as a human being."

An innocent expression crossed his face. "I piss you off?"

Madie ignored him. *Nuh-uh, you're not going to turn this into a joke.* "Your suggestion of travelling to Kelowna together because you need some things—it's an offer of support without saying so. I appreciate it."

Cody squirmed in his seat. "Oh that. Well—I really do have a rather long shopping list …"

Madie rolled her eyes. "Stuff it, lion tamer, and take the compliment."

He stretched his long legs out in front of him. "You sure have a funny way of dishing out compliments."

"Meaning what?"

"It's come to my notice, your compliments usually start with an insult, or admonishment of some kind. Almost like you think you should compliment me but do so begrudgingly."

Madie stared at him. *Omigod, he's right! But I'm not admitting to it; move on.* "So, Saturday."

"Does that mean I'm picking you up Saturday morning?"

"Sure. Say, nine am? When the session's done, it'll be good to have someone to talk it over with."

"And, since we're there, why don't we stay and enjoy Kelowna? Maybe go out for dinner? I know this restaurant on the lake with great food, but casual dress. They usually have a jazz quartet playing live music."

Madie wasn't sure how to take the invitation. "Is this a, well we're here anyway, might as well have dinner, type of thing—or, is this a dinner *date?*"

Cody suddenly looked uncomfortable. "Umm, it was more like a spontaneous, I love to eat out and know this great little place on the lake kind of thing." He gave her a crooked grin. "But we could make it a date. Whatcha think?"

Madie studied his face for a moment. I should have left it alone and not asked. Do I want a date with this man? Of course! But that would be breaking my rule of never dating people I work with. "I don't usually date people I work with."

"Me either, but it's just dinner between two friends. We *are* friends, aren't we?"

"We are, but having dinner with a friend isn't a *date* date."

Cody looked frustrated. "I think we're overthinking this. We'll be out of town, we'll both be hungry, so we'll eat dinner before we come home—or not."

Madie decided to end the discussion. *Oh, what the hey!* "You're right. I'd love to check out that restaurant on the lake. Dinner it is. Now, get out of here. I've got work to do."

"You bet." Cody stood, stretched, and grabbed the files. "Besides, Wenner will be sending a search party to find out where everyone has disappeared to today. See ya."

Madie watched him leave and listened to the front door open and close. For the life of her, she couldn't figure out how quickly she'd found herself opening up and confiding in him. *I hardly know him. Although, when he's not trying to be funny to avoid showing his emotions, he listens with the sympathy of a good friend. But the keyword is "friend", girl.* She knew she was attracted to him. But she didn't want to be distracted at work. *One minute, I'm relaxed and enjoying his company; the next, I'm on edge and frustrated by him. And for what? His silly teasing? I've got to get it together. Besides, a good-looking guy like Cody could have any girl he wants—and probably does.*

The outside door opened and Madie left her office to see who it was. She found Chelsea standing in reception. "It's chilly out there with that wind. How are things?"

"Fine, quiet here today." Madie noted her red, puffy eyes. *She's been crying.* "You all right?"

"Sure. Why?"

"Just that I spoke to you when you left. I guess you didn't hear me."

"Sorry, I didn't. I went home to get something I forgot. Was it important?"

"Nope. Taken care of."

Chelsea passed her, heading to her office. "Okay, I'll be here for the rest of the morning if you need me."

Madie returned to her desk. *We all have our secrets we don't want to share—or are afraid to share. Why is life so complicated?*

❦ 10 ❦

A soft tap at the door brought Chelsea's head up from the mail she was reading on her desk. "Come in."

The door to her office opened and her daughter, Sydney, poked her head in. "Hi, Mom. Am I disturbing you?"

Chelsea smiled. "Not at all. What's up?"

"Have you had lunch?"

"Not yet."

"Do you have some time to join me? We just finished the summer shoot for *Snuggle Butts*. The crew are gone and there are tons of leftovers."

"Oh? Another commercial? I thought you were done for the year with the latest one, *Toddlers on the Move*"

"Nope. They have a new swimmer's diaper on the market, designed not to leak or absorb water. This is the one I told you about a while back that also features Jax and me because the girls can't go in the water alone."

"Of course, I forgot. I'd have loved to watch them film that one. Let me call Madie."

She hit the intercom to let Madie know where she'd be and followed Sydney outside through the rear door.

"How'd it go?" Chelsea asked her daughter.

"Awesome. A shorter shoot than last time and loads of fun. They even shot the girls in the barn with the new lambs. We have two more commercials to go. One in the fall for toilet training pull-ups and a final shoot next spring for the overnight diaper."

Chelsea inhaled the fresh air. It was a warm day with no wind; not even the birds were singing. Listening to her daughter prattle as they walked, Sydney said, "I'll be glad when it's over. Our three-year contract is up next year. Don't get me wrong, we're grateful for the endless supply of free diapers. And the girls have enough money in their trust funds to cover college. It's just that it's hard on them, breaks routine, and it takes a while to get them back on track."

"Yes, routine is important—especially when you have triplets."

They entered the room through the French doors from the back deck. The dining table was covered with various salads, cheeses, fruits, and deli meats, and delicious pastries. "Ooh, look at that food. Beats my bagged lunch sitting in the fridge."

Chelsea spun around to squeals of laughter and the running of little feet behind her. As the triplets surrounded her, she kneeled and put her arms out. "Hugs and kisses." She wrapped them in her arms, and they planted wet kisses all over her face. "Didn't you have a fun morning? Swimming and seeing the baby lambs?"

The most outgoing of the three, Jenna squealed with delight. Kylie clapped her hands, while Willow stared with wonder at Chelsea and said, "Babas."

Bea, who worked as a housekeeper/cook for Sydney, entered the room. "The girls are bathed, fed and ready for a nap."

"I'll take them," Chelsea offered.

"And I'm headed to town to do some shopping," Bea said.

Sydney smiled at Bea. "Thanks for all your help with the girls this morning. Couldn't have done it without you."

"You know it's my pleasure. I love the little ones."

Once the girls were down in their beds, Chelsea joined Sydney. They filled their plates and moved to the living room.

"I think they fell asleep as soon as their heads hit the pillow."

"Not surprising. They were up early, and it was a very busy morning," Sydney said.

Chelsea knew it was time for her to share the news with Sydney about her pregnancy. *But let's eat first.*

"Ahh ... listen," Sydney said.

Chelsea's ears perked up. "I don't hear anything."

"Exactly ... the girls are asleep."

"I guess you take your moments whenever you can get them."

"You've got that right."

Finishing their plates, they returned to the table for dessert and coffee. Chelsea took a deep breath. *It's time. How will Sydney react to the news?* With conflicting emotions of excitement and apprehension, she decided to jump right in. Her stomach rolled over. *Easier said than done. Here goes.* "I've something to tell you."

"Oooh ... intriguing. What's up?"

Chelsea hesitated. "Well ... you're going to be surprised. I know I was."

Sydney rolled her eyes. "Mom, out with it. Tell me."

Her lunch sat like a lump in her stomach. With a deep breath, she blurted out, "Okay. I'm pregnant."

Sydney's blue eyes popped, and she choked on her coffee. "What?"

"I think you heard me."

"But you thought you were ..."

Chelsea threw her hands up. "Stop. *If one more person*

mentions menopause again—yes, I'm menopausal. And yes, women can still get pregnant."

"But ... how?"

Chelsea snickered. "The usual way."

"I know that, silly. I guess I meant who?"

"Chaz. We've been intimate for the last eighteen weeks, and that's about when we conceived."

"Omigod ... does he know?"

Her stomach lurched again as she was reminded of the last time she and Chaz spoke. The words of his letter filled her mind. *Arne damaged you in ways I can't fix.* "Yes, he knows."

"But isn't it dangerous to have a baby in your forties?"

"It can be. But I've been through all the tests. I'm healthy, the baby is healthy, no abnormalities, and we're past the normal miscarriage stage."

"But what about giving birth?"

"Caesarean, sometime in November. My odds of having something go wrong are the same as with any pregnant woman, regardless of age."

Sydney sat with that a moment, sipping her coffee. She spoke in a quiet voice. "Mom, please tell me you're not planning on having this baby."

What? I expected shock, but this? She threw her head back; a feeling of unease overtook her. "I know you're concerned for my health, but the decision to continue my pregnancy was reached with a lot of advice and heavy thinking."

Sydney put down her coffee cup and leaned forward. "There's more to consider than the pregnancy. You have a great business with the Wildlife Centre. What about Wenner? You and Chaz have an awesome relationship. The two of you are moving into a stage of your life where you can enjoy each other and do things—like travel. Why in heavens name would you want to have a baby now?"

Chelsea hesitated. *Don't make me second-guess myself. I've made my decision.* It was bad enough that Sydney's reaction was a very negative one, but she knew she had to tell her daughter the rest of it. "Chaz and I are both looking forward to being parents and plan to co-parent—but we aren't a couple."

Confusion crossed Sydney's face. She ran her hands through her short blond hair. "I don't get it. You've been close for two and half years, recently moved into intimacy, got pregnant, which you both accept, but you're not going to stay together? So, why even have this baby? It makes no sense."

It does to me—at least it did until your negative attitude showed up. "I take the blame for that. I'm not sure I can commit to us being a 'family' together. Not in the normal sense."

Sydney's face went blank. "So, you've chosen between Chaz and a baby?"

Chelsea felt her face burn. "No. It wasn't a decision on my part. Chaz walked away."

"He walked away? Now I'm more than confused. You just said he was happy about the baby, so why would he do that? It's not his way."

Chelsea was finding it hard to find the words to express her thoughts. "It's complicated."

Sydney stood and paced back and forth. "Anyone can see that Chaz adores you. He's been wearing his heart on his sleeve while you healed from Arne. We all expected you two to get together one day." She stopped in front of her mother and, with a hardened face, she said accusingly, "And now you're going to have his baby and cut him out?"

"You're being unfair."

Sydney raised her voice. "You're being unfair—to Chaz. I think having this baby is ridiculous. You're already a mother … and a grandmother of triplets. That's the way it should be. Isn't that enough for you?"

Her daughter's reaction was way over the top of what she expected. Chelsea felt attacked. "It's not a matter of being enough. It is what it is—I'm pregnant."

Sydney's outburst continued, tuning out Chelsea's words.

Her voice had risen to a shout. "This is always the way it is with you, isn't it? Selfish. You don't care who it hurts. Why do you feel the need to keep on competing with me? It's my turn, not yours. Why can't you be content just being my mother and the girls' grandmother?"

The words stung and Chelsea stood and faced her daughter. "Are we talking about me and Chaz—or me and you here?"

Sydney's rant stopped and she sat down in silence.

It was Chelsea's turn to run with the conversation. "And what are you asking of me? That I have an abortion? This isn't about you, Sydney. It *is* about me, my body, and what I want—and I want this baby, goddamit. I'll be damned if I'll use abortion as birth control because you seem to think it's abnormal for me to want this baby."

Chelsea knew it was time to leave. The situation was out of control and if she stayed, more things might be said that could never be taken back. Sick to her stomach, she held herself tight to control her emotions. "I'd hoped you'd be happy for me. I'm sorry you find it so … ridiculous."

Chelsea bolted from the room and down the hall, afraid she'd burst into tears. *Damn hormones.* She left the house, slamming the door behind her.

SYDNEY STOOD and stared after her mother, jumping at the loud sound of the door banging shut.

"That went well."

She spun around to find Jax leaning against the dining room wall with his arms folded across his chest. She knew that expression; he wasn't pleased.

"How much did you hear?"

"All of it. I came out of my office to get a cup of coffee."

Sydney frowned. "Did your dad talk to you about this? Did you know?"

"Not until I heard you yelling at your mom about it."

Her eyes narrowed. "You're judging me. Stop."

"I think you should be judging yourself."

"How do you feel about your dad starting over again as a father?"

"It's not my business." His face contorted a little, which showed Sydney he wasn't as sure about it as he was acting.

"Do you think my mother should be having a baby at her age?"

"I don't know. But if she and my dad decided to have the baby, maybe we should be supporting them."

"But you heard her. Your dad walked away. They were so good together and now this baby is driving them apart."

Jax took in a deep breath and let it out slowly. "I'm sure it's been a shock to them both. Let them work it out. Bottom line: we can't live their lives for them."

"Oh? So, you're okay having a baby brother or sister who'll be younger than your daughters? That's weird."

He tilted his head and nodded. "Kinda, but it's life, Sydney. Your mom said it. It is what it is—she's pregnant."

Sydney thought about that. "I don't get it. After all she's been through, why would she want to have another baby?"

"If you'd given her a chance to answer the question, she might have told you."

Sydney frowned. "You mean not attacking her. I'm only concerned."

"Don't do that, Sydney."

She screwed up her face. "Do what?"

"Deny you went off on her. You accused her of competing with you. Really? Come on, that's childish and you know it. She came here to share something important to her and you lashed out. You owe her an apology."

A feeling of guilt engulfed her momentarily. She knew

she'd reacted badly but wasn't ready to give in. She crossed her arms over her chest like Jax and stared back at him defiantly. *After all, he is taking her side against mine!*

"You know, when Arne abducted your mom, she lost the right to raise you. She's been given another chance with this baby. Maybe she's excited about it."

She didn't know what to say to that. *Maybe he's right.* But she stood her ground, dropped her head, and stared at the floor in silence.

He threw his hands up and stepped back. "I'm not going to fight with you. But I *am* going to tell you what I'm sensing."

"What?"

"You're jealous."

Her jaw dropped. "What?"

"You lost your mother, Sydney. Then you found her. It was a rocky relationship until your mother found her way and the triplets were born. I think you're afraid you'll lose her again to this baby. Pure and simple jealousy. It's beneath you, Syd." He turned his back on her and disappeared into the kitchen.

❧ 11 ❧

C helsea finished the entry in the financial report on her computer and sent it to the printer. As she waited for the machine to do its thing, Wenner appeared at her open office door.

"Are you ready to meet?" he asked.

"You bet. Come in and close the door behind you, please." Chelsea ignored the sound of the printer and watched her partner sit down in front of her desk. For his fifty-four years, he was still youthful looking. His wavy, dark hair fell across his forehead, with a tinge of grey at the sides.

"What's up?"

"I have some major news to tell you which affects you and my work here."

A frown crossed his brow. "Oh dear, you're not sick, are you?"

She shook her head. "Not in the way you're thinking. But I am suffering from morning sickness." Chelsea waited and watched him digest that news.

His eyes widened, his mouth dropped, and then a smile broke across his face. "Omigod … you're pregnant? How wonderful."

She breathed a sigh of relief. It was nice to face someone who shared her excitement after her confrontation with Sydney.

"When are you due?"

"November, but I'll probably be booked earlier for a Caesarean." It dawned on her that the triplets were born in October. This might cause more resentment on Sydney's part. She stared off lost in thought.

Wenner snapped his fingers. "Hey … come back to earth. I've lost you."

"Oh, sorry."

Wenner titled his head, his eyes questioning. "You *are* happy about this, right?"

A wide grin spread across her face. "Yes. It's a surprise but I'm healthy and so is the baby. Chaz and I are both excited about it."

"Then I am too. Tell me your plans."

"Well, I think I may have to leave my position at the end of summer." A stricken look crossed Wenner's face. "Temporarily. After the baby is born, I really would like some time at home before I return to work. But for the first few years, I want to work part-time. How do you feel about that?"

"I was asking about your personal plans, but we can get back to that in a minute. The Centre is doing well. You and Madie have done wonders running administration and finance. I'll be sorry to lose you but if you promise you aren't leaving entirely, we can work it out. You know me, I'm all about the animals and not much on the numbers, so whatever you suggest, I'm all ears."

Chelsea reached for the report on the printer. "I ran some figures. It's all in this report. I think Madie is ready to take on more responsibility. I'd like to see her take on my position but strictly on the administration side. With her running the volunteer and adoption programs, it'll be enough."

"Okay. And what about the financials?

"In my opinion, the Centre can afford to hire a part-time finance clerk to handle payroll, accounts receivable and payables, as well as help Madie on the admin side. I think I could handle running the monthly reports for the accountant from my computer at home. I'd still be on top of everything that's happening here."

He reached for the report. "Sounds like you have it all covered. I'll read it tonight, but I trust your judgement on this."

"Thanks, Wenner."

He relaxed back into his seat. "Wow ... so we're adding a permanent little critter to the Centre."

Chelsea sputtered through her laughter. "Are you calling my baby a 'critter'?"

He had a glint in his eye. "When you drop the calf, we'll have to plan a show-and-tell day at the Centre for the public, as we do for fundraisers."

Her chin dropped. "Did you really say that?" Chelsea couldn't help but laugh.

Wenner threw his arms up, "I did. I guess I've been hanging with the wildlife too long."

"My friend, you need a social life."

Wenner chuckled. "The critters and birds *are* my social life. Unconditional love ... and the odd bite, it's all I need. Relationships are too complicated. Speaking of which, back to your personal plans, what are they? I mean with you and Chaz? I had no idea you two had progressed to afternoon delights."

Chelsea rolled her eyes. "I love your little sayings. Chaz is ready to step into the role of daddy." She paused, her face clouding over. "He'll be there for the baby but we're taking a step back."

"Umm ... isn't that a step in the wrong direction?"

She tensed and clamped shut her mouth.

He gave her a knowing look. "I see. You don't want to talk

about it. How about the rest of the fam? Sydney must be thrilled."

Chelsea's chest tightened. "Afraid not."

"Oops, seems I've put my foot in my mouth yet again."

"Actually, it appears I'm the one who did that by getting pregnant. She's definitely not happy about me having a baby. Ridiculous and weird—her words not mine."

Wenner's eyes shot up. "Really? Maybe she's worried about your age."

"I assured her everything was fine. It's more she's accused me of competing with her."

"Competing? In what way?"

"Umm ... like I should be a mom to her and grandma to her girls? Not having babies? I have no idea what's going on in her head right now. I can't even discuss it with Chaz."

"And why not?"

Chelsea hesitated. "With him being Jax's father, I don't want to start a family war."

"Right, family dynamics. I forgot about Chaz being his father and you being Sydney's mother. As for Sydney, I kinda see where she's coming from."

Shocked, Chelsea leaned forward in her chair, raising her voice. "What? I didn't plan this pregnancy and she said some pretty hurtful things to me."

He threw his hands up. "Whoa. Don't go all hormonal on me. I'm not condoning her behaviour. But she may resent that this baby will take up all your time."

Chelsea snorted. "Like hers isn't taken up with the triplets?"

"You're missing my point."

Her eyes flashed. "Which is?"

"This baby will get to experience growing up with you as its mother. Sydney didn't have that opportunity when Arne nabbed you. I bet the main crux of her behaviour is tied to jealousy."

Chelsea's hand flew to her mouth. "You think that's it? Oh boy. I've been so caught up with this whole baby thing. Is it healthy? Am I? What if it's deformed or mentally challenged? And then the dynamic of my relationship with Chaz, the Centre, you." Her eyes glistened. She felt deflated. *What kind of mother am I? I never gave a thought about how Sydney might feel in that regard.* She slouched back in her chair. "She's right about one thing. I've been so self-absorbed and blind to everyone else's needs."

A movement by her side caught her attention. She eyed Sage, the golden retriever she'd adopted a couple of years ago. The dog, sleeping by her feet, roused herself, sat up, and placed a paw on Chelsea's knee.

"I think she's tuning in to your distress."

Chelsea rubbed the dog's ears absentmindedly. "It's okay, girl. I'm okay." Her eyes lifted to Wenner. "Funny, ever since I became pregnant, she won't leave my side. She whines if I leave her at home. It's like she knows what's going on."

"Sage is intelligent, and definitely bonded to you. I have no doubt, she's in protection mode where you're concerned."

"She's a great comfort to me, that's for sure."

The dog moved over to the corner of the office and curled into a ball, keeping a watchful eye on her mistress.

"Listen, don't beat yourself up. These past few years you had to put your needs first. You've come a long way, my dear, and we're all very proud of you. As for Sydney, give her some time to work it out; she'll come around."

"I hope so." She sighed.

"And Chaz? I think he's proven he loves you. He's a good guy. I'd love to see the two of you work it out, but that's up to you."

Chelsea pursed her lips. "Sydney said that too."

"Then just let me add that I don't think it's a matter of trusting him, but a matter of trusting *yourself.* You have good instincts that have served you well in your work with all of us at the Centre. You've also applied them to your struggle to heal. Trust what your heart and instincts are telling you and you'll be fine."

Chelsea smiled. "You're a wise man and a good friend. Thank you."

"You're welcome. Now—let's talk about me. I was thinking of going home to Saskatchewan for a week to spend some time with my folks. With a busy summer ahead of us, I figured September. With you probably out of here by then, perhaps I should go now. Things are back to normal with Kelowna taking some of our patients. Cody's capable of handling the compound and you both can take care of minor surgeries. Anything major would have to go to Kelowna. What do you think? You okay with it? Me leaving now?"

"Go, by all means. You haven't seen them since last summer when they visited. It'll give you a break before the summer chaos starts."

"Good. I'll bring Cody up to speed and fly out the day after tomorrow."

Wenner stood and headed to the door. He opened it and stepped out but before closing it behind him, poked his head back in. "Congrats, Mama. It's all good. I'm gonna love being called Uncle Wenner."

❧ 12 ❧

Madie was on the phone when Wenner left Chelsea. He gave her a smile and a wave as he passed her office. When her call was done, she left her desk and went to see her boss. She tapped gently on the door.

Chelsea glanced up and waved her in. "Come, sit. You're just the person I want to talk to."

Madie joined her. She knew why she'd sought out Chelsea but wondered about her boss' intentions. *Uh-oh! Was she and Wenner discussing my obvious distraction to my work? My timing to fill her in on my personal issue seems about right.*

Chelsea sat back and folded her hands on the desk. "You look so serious. What's up?"

"Some things are going on in my personal life and I feel I owe you an explanation. I want to apologize because I know they've affected my daily work of late."

Madie couldn't read her expression but did notice her body tense.

"I've noticed you've been distracted. Why don't you tell me about it?" Chelsea requested.

Madie filled her in on her night terrors. "They're affecting my sleep and my sense of wellbeing." She told Chelsea about falling asleep on the trip back from Kelowna with Cody and the nightmare that ensued once the thunderstorm started.

"How terrifying for you. And it's always the same woman?"

"Yes. Because of it, I'm tired and distracted and I wanted you to know why. Cody took me to Rock Creek on Saturday to see his grandmother. He also convinced me to talk to you. He said the farm is a spiritual hot spot and maybe that's why the nightmares have come back. He felt you'd understand what I'm going through."

"I'm beginning to." Chelsea appeared to relax. "And I'm relieved."

Madie's face registered surprise. "Relieved? Why?"

"Oh, I'm not trivializing your situation. I did notice the changes in you, and you were so serious when you sat down— I was afraid you might be planning to leave." Chelsea furrowed her brow. "You're not, are you?"

Madie was surprised by the question. *At least she's not planning to let me go.* "Uh … no. I love my job here at the Centre."

"Good. We'll get back to that in a minute but, first, let's talk about your nightmares. Why did Cody take you to his grandmother?"

"She's a channeler of spirits from the other side. He thought she might be able to help me."

"Did she?"

"To a point. We discussed some theories and …" Madie squirmed in her seat; not sure of how Chelsea would react to her session with Cody's grandmother, she felt a little uneasy opening up to her.

"Please, relax. I truly want to hear this."

"Well, first maybe this woman died and her spirit's reaching out to me. We ruled that out because no spirit came forward during our session and she should have once the portal was opened."

"Fascinating, continue."

"Maybe the woman's alive and in trouble. Perhaps she's seeking my help. But that doesn't fly because I had the same dreams twenty years ago. It's not feasible. The third theory, ruling out psychosis on my part, is that I'm connecting to a past life of mine."

Chelsea nodded. "Hmm, a past life. So, where do you go from here?"

"Kat's contacting a friend, a Past Life Regression Practitioner in Kelowna. Hopefully, I'll learn more."

"Kat?"

"Sorry, Kat is Cody's grandmother."

"I see. He's right about the farm being a spiritual place. With all the right elements crashing together, I can see a past life overlapping into this one." Chelsea glanced at the clock on her computer. "Did you bring your lunch?"

"Yes, it's in the fridge."

Chelsea stood. "Mine too. Let's take our lunch and go for a walk. I know just the place for us to picnic." She looked over at Sage, who was sitting on point. "Come on, you. Time for a walk."

The two women were soon walking along a trail from the Centre that took them over a hill into a magnolia grove. The trees were in full pink bloom. Sage bounded ahead, stopping every few feet to sniff the ground and dig into the dirt and debris, and once satisfied there were no treasures to be found, she moved on.

"This part of the old farm is on Sydney's property. Isn't it beautiful?" Chelsea asked.

Madie stopped and sucked in the sweet odour of the flowers' cherry-vanilla scent. "Mmm, love that smell." She followed her boss through the trees and Chelsea led her to a lone magnolia tree.

They spread out a blanket and sat down to eat. "This tree has quite a history. I used to play in the grove as a child." Chelsea pointed up. "I sat on that limb for hours, daydreaming. Chaz gave me my first kiss up there." She paused.

Madie noticed a momentary sadness in her eyes that quickly passed.

Chelsea looked at her and asked, "Have you heard of soul travel?"

"I have, but I don't know a lot about it."

"Well, it's also called Astral Projection and is defined as the soul leaving the body and travelling to some sort of new plane of consciousness. When Arne held me captive, I use to soul travel and sit in this tree. Sydney sat on that same limb until they left the farm when she was five. As a child, I'd soul travel to her room and we'd have tea parties together. She didn't know who I was at the time as she was a year old when Arne took me. Her grandmother thought I was an imaginary friend. I couldn't talk to them, of course, but I found peace here on the farm, watching over them."

"Wow. I didn't know about that."

"That's only part of it. My father's spirit visited here too and with me at Arne's. He wouldn't leave me alone as long as I was incarcerated. When my mother and Sydney returned to the farm, he visited them as well and helped Sydney put it all together about my disappearance. He's crossed over now."

"No wonder Cody thought you'd understand my situation."

"He's right. Perhaps your coming to work here was fate. This place, the storms, the nightmares, the right mix of people. They're all coming together—the right elements I was referring to earlier. You're going to figure this out and when you do, there'll be peace. And we're all here to support you."

Despite her weariness, Madie felt a sense of relief for the first time in weeks. "Thank you. It's nice to be able to open up about this to people other than my mother. She worries about me so."

Chelsea looked pensive. "Remember when we interviewed

Cody? You weren't keen on him, but he was meant to be here too. He's one of those elements."

Sydney grinned. "A total misread on my part. He's so much more than I gave him credit for. He's been a supportive friend."

"Good to hear. Let's talk about work and your place at the Centre."

"Okay."

The dog inched her way onto the blanket, eyes focused on their lunch bags, with her nose sniffing the air.

"Sage—no! No scraps for you." The retriever put her head down and looked up at her from under hooded lids. "Oh, don't you give me those puppy-dog eyes. You know better." Turning back to Madie, she said. "We're very pleased with your contribution. You've proven to be invaluable and I'm going to be relying on you more and more in the future because I have some news of my own."

"Okay," Madie said, curious. *News of her own? How does that affect me and what does relying on me mean?*

"So, my news: I'm pregnant."

"Oh Chelsea, that's wonderful. More surprises."

"You've got that right. As unexpected as it is, I'm excited about it."

"Congratulations."

"Thank you. Now, here's what it means to you, my dear. I'm going to be taking maternity leave at the end of summer, meaning that along with your existing job, I'd like you to take over the administration of the Centre temporarily—except the financials. This means a raise for you, of course. We'll hire a part-time finance clerk for payroll, payables and receivables and help you might need while I run reports from home. Eventually, I'll be back part-time. I have every confidence you can do the job if you want it."

Madie's heart raced. "If you think I'm capable, yes."

"I do, and so does Wenner. Don't forget, I'm living right on the property. You can call me or pop over anytime."

"You can count on it."

"When we get back to the office, I want you to go home for the rest of the day. Tomorrow's Friday. Take the day off. I don't want to see you at the Centre until Monday morning. The storms are diminishing and we're in for good weather, so you can get caught up on your sleep."

"Are you sure?"

"Of course. You haven't taken any holidays since we opened the Centre. Go home. Next week, we'll begin training. Oh, Wenner's flying home Saturday to see his family for a week before the summer peak begins. We'll all be busy with additional duties, so it's a good time for you to take a couple of days off."

They finished their lunch and packed up to leave.

Chelsea chuckled. "I'd say it's been a good day, considering when you walked into my office, you thought I was going to let you go, and I was concerned you were planning to leave."

As they passed out of the grove, Madie saw Sydney standing on her deck. She gave her a wave, which wasn't returned, then stole a glance at Chelsea, who had stopped. Mother and daughter stared across the meadow at each other and Madie saw Chelsea tense. Without a shout or gesture of acknowledgement between the two, Madie sensed some sort of family discord and chose to mind her own business and continued walking. Her boss caught up to her and they walked back to the Centre in silence with Sage leading the way.

❦ 13 ❦

Madie sat in the office of the Past Life Regression Practitioner and waited for the woman to join her. The room was done in warm shades of green and beige, while soft piano music played in the background, all of which relaxed her.

The door opened and a petite woman in her fifties entered. Her silver hair was pulled back in a ponytail. Long bangs fell past her eyebrows but not enough to cover her sparkling, pale grey eyes. "Hi Madie, I'm Sasha Taylor. Welcome and please call me Sasha."

Madie stood and shook hands. "Hi." She sat down again, a little unsure of the situation and not sure how to explain to this stranger why she was here.

"I've gone over your chart and I see this is your first experience with a PLR Practitioner."

"Yes, it is," said Madie. She tried not to show her nervousness.

"Let me explain some things to you about PLRs and if you have any questions, we'll address them. Our focus is on resolving events in our lives that are believed to be interfering with our present mental and emotional wellness. These events aren't restricted to our present life but can apply to a past life that has carried traumatic and symptomatic effects into this one," Sasha said with a soft tone that was very calming.

She leafed through Madie's chart and continued. "A PLR session isn't dangerous to clients unless you have serious health conditions in this life that could be triggered by stress. Viewing past lives can be stressful but it can also be beneficial by releasing pent-up emotions. This is why we're so thorough with our chart questions. I see nothing here to cause concern. Any questions?"

"How long is the session?"

"Usually about thirty minutes, but I don't adhere to a clock. It's as long as it needs to be to help you—or if I think you should come back into consciousness at a certain point, I'll bring you back. Anything else?"

Madie shifted in her seat, still feeling uneasy. "Can you explain how the session works? I'm a little uncomfortable not knowing what to expect."

Sasha smiled. "A perfectly normal reaction. Once you're settled on the recliner table, I'll take you through some exercises to relax your physical body and your mind. When you're ready, we'll begin a transgression from your current life backwards to before you were born. I'll coach you on how to deal with anything you see and feel that's stressful and I'll bring you back into consciousness when the session is complete. All you have to do is listen to my voice and follow my suggestions. Are we good?"

Madie nodded. "Okay."

"Why don't you tell me about these dreams you've been having—when they began, how often, and the content."

"According to my mother, they started when I was about nine months old and continued until I attended pre-school. I have no memory of them, but she said I'd awaken terrified and she'd find me standing in my crib, soaked in perspiration, and screaming. As a toddler, I'd run from my room hysterical and crawl into bed with my parents."

"I see you've recently celebrated a birthday; you're twenty-three. When did the dreams begin again?"

"About four months ago."

"What's the theme of the dreams and are they new dreams or the same repetitive images?"

"Always the same young woman: fearful, crying, running ... but always different scenarios."

"Is there ever anyone else in the dream?"

Madie squirmed in her seat and let out a deep breath. "Not until my last dream. There was always a feeling someone else was there with her, but not in view ... but with the last one, I saw a man. The girl in my dream was in a bathroom looking in the mirror. Her cheek was swollen. There was dried blood under her nose and her left eye was turning black. As she examined her face, a man walked into the bathroom. I could see his reflection in the mirror over her shoulder. Her body stiffened and she froze. There was fear in her eyes."

"And do you recognize either one of them?"

"No."

"Past life memories often are revealed through dreams. This kind of dream is different from our typical dreams, where there's a beginning, middle, and an end. Life dreams begin in the middle. Knowing this, how would you categorize your dreams?"

"Definitely the middle. The dreams always start in the middle of something that's happening. They aren't like regular dreams at all."

"When you wake up from them, what do they feel like? I don't mean how do you feel emotionally but how does the dream feel?"

Madie frowned. "I'm not sure I understand the question."

"I'm sorry. I don't want to put words in your mouth. Umm ... do you feel like you've been dreaming?"

Madie's eyebrows shot up. "No. That's the frightening part. It feels so real like I've experienced it. Only, I haven't because it's her experience and I don't know who she is or anything about her. Does that make any sense?"

"Yes, it does," Sasha said.

"It does? Then I'm not crazy?"

Sasha gave her another warm smile. "No, you aren't crazy."

"It's good to have it reinforced. Kat said the same thing."

"Do you feel ready to have a session?"

As Madie soaked up Sasha's words, the weight dropped off her shoulders. *Maybe Sasha can help, and I'll finally get some answers.* Feeling a sense of resolve, she nodded. "I'm ready."

The practitioner led her into a small room. The furniture was sparse with one chair and a recliner bed. A small table with incense and candles sat against one wall. The room was in the same warm colours as the adjoining office. Potted trees and plants filled the empty spaces. The same soft music filled the air. Madie lay on a padded table and Sasha raised the back of it into a partial sitting position. Sasha lit the candles and the smell of vanilla filled the small space.

"The plants are beautiful," Madie said, staring at the fauna display in front of her.

"I leave the walls bare so there are no picture suggestions that could invade your subconscious. The plants help to make the room cosier." Sasha reached to a shelf under the table. "I'm going to cover you with a light blanket to keep you warm. A subconscious state can leave your body chilled and we don't want any physical distractions. Are you comfortable?"

"Yes."

Sasha settled into the armchair. "Listen to my voice and follow my words as I take you into a relaxed state. Now, close your eyes and take a deep breath, hold, and exhale."

Madie listened to Sasha's soft voice and before long her calming words had her in a state of relaxation.

"I want you to envision a white light at the bottom of your feet and as it's absorbed through your skin up to your ankles and into your legs, feel the warmth of that light. The light is moving into your upper thighs and it's slowly and gently pushing all your stress ahead of it. Follow the light as it moves into your torso and fills you with a sense of peace. It's moving upwards into your chest and back area. From the neck down, your body is warm and weightless. Feel the light pushing all the stress through your shoulders and down your arms, until the warmth of the light leaves your hands, tingling as all the stress slips through your fingers and disappears from the tips of your fingernails. This soft, white light meanders its way back up your arms, through the shoulders, into your neck and pushes its way up the back of your head, circulating to the front of your face. And as it finds its way to the top of your head, envision the remainder of your stress dissipating into the atmosphere. Feel the release as your facial muscles relax and your lips part. Lightness embraces your body."

A feeling of weightlessness spread through her, followed by calmness and a sense of peace that left her at ease.

"This warming light has encased your body; you are protected from any negatives you may encounter as we travel on. Madie, are you ready to move forward with our journey?"

"Yes," she said in barely a whisper.

Sasha's voice was quiet and soothing. "Go back to your childhood, to a day where you were very excited and happy. Describe to me where you are."

Madie smiled. "I'm playing in the backyard, waiting for my daddy."

"How old are you?"

"Six."

"Look at your feet and tell me what you have on."

Madie looked down. "Pink runners with glitter and purple laces."

"And what are you wearing?"

"Pink tights and a flowered multi-coloured t-shirt."

"And why are you excited?"

"Because Daddy's taking me to a wildlife sanctuary. I can't wait to see the animals there."

"I want you to go to the end of the day now, after you visited the sanctuary. Where are you?"

Madie paused. "I'm in bed. Mommy and Daddy are kissing me goodnight."

"How are you feeling?"

She smiled and felt a sense of contentment. "Tired but happy. It was a fun day."

"Does that mean visiting the sanctuary was everything you expected it to be?"

Madie laughed. "Oh yes. I'm going to work with animals when I'm big."

"Good. We're going to move on now. I want you to go back to before you were born. Are you ready to move on?"

Madie pursed her lips. Her heart fluttered. "Yes."

"Find yourself at the top of a flight of stairs. Let me know when you're there."

"I'm on the landing at the top."

"What do you see?"

"Numerous flights of stairs, with wooden bannisters; it's a long way to the bottom."

"As you begin to descend the stairs, you may see fleeting images. When you reach the bottom landing, know that whatever you experience and feel can't hurt you in your current life. Remember, I'll be here to help you. Do you understand?"

Madie gulped and took a deep breath. "Yes."

"Are you ready?"

In barely a whisper, Madie said, "Yes.

❧ 14 ❧

C helsea pulled back her head from inside the cupboard under the bathroom sink, cocked it towards the bathroom door, and listened. A distinct knock could be heard on the front screened door.

"Shit!" She pulled off the rubber gloves she'd worn to wash down the cabinet and headed towards the hallway to investigate its source.

As she approached the door, her irritation at being interrupted disappeared and she let out a cry of delight. "Mom?" She opened the door and pulled her mother inside. The two embraced in a tight hug. "You're home early. When did you get in?"

Elizabeth Grey pushed her daughter back, a Cheshire-cat smile lighting up her face. "Last night. I came straight here this morning to see you."

Chelsea led her mother into the living room and they sat at opposite ends of the couch, facing each another. Elizabeth's short silver hair framed her face, her sparkling blue eyes, and a Grey family trait stood out against her tanned face. "You look wonderful."

"Thanks."

"So, how was the rest of your trip?"

"All good. Scotland was beautiful and Gord's relatives—oh, let's just say they're a wacky, fun-loving bunch. A great time."

"In that case, why'd you cut it short? You're home ten days early."

"Because ..." Her mother hesitated a moment, then continued. "We were ready to come home. We did a lot of travelling in three months and it was time. Gord and I are looking forward to relaxing on the lake for the summer."

"Fair enough. I've loved following your photos online. I appreciate seeing you so soon, but you must be exhausted after such a long flight."

"We stayed in Vancouver for a day to rest up before flying to Kelowna yesterday. I'm good." Elizabeth studied her daughter's face. "How are you doing?"

Chelsea felt startled by the question. Not expecting to see her mom so soon, she wasn't prepared to jump in just yet with the news of her pregnancy. She responded with the first word that came to mind. "Oh, I'm—healthy." *Dumbass answer; bring attention to your physical state of being right off the bat.*

Elizabeth's brow wrinkled. "Good to hear and see. But I meant more, how's life? How's work?"

"The Centre's great. Entering our busy season. Did I tell you we hired a new man to work with Wenner? Cody Diaz. He's fitting in great, doing a super job."

Elizabeth plumped up one of the olive-green pillows under her arm. "That's wonderful, dear. Have you seen Sydney lately?" she asked, staring at the pillow and picking off pieces of lint and placing them on the coffee table.

Chelsea's bullshit detector went off. Her mother was acting too casual. *She knows.* "I saw her last week just after the *Snuggle Butts* shoot," she said and continued cautiously. "Have you talked to her since you got back?"

"Not yet. I spoke with her last week." Her mother raised

her head and stared back at Chelsea with probing eyes. "So, tell me—what's going on with you two?"

Here it comes. "What did Sydney say?"

Her mom frowned. "It's not what she said, it's what she wouldn't say. I know there's something wrong. As soon as I mentioned your name, she told me to talk to you, as it wasn't her place to say anything. Now I'm asking you and you're doing the same thing."

Another thought crossed Chelsea's mind. Aghast, she asked, "Mom—please tell me you didn't cut your vacation short because of this? You could have called me on the phone."

"And got the same runaround? Rest assured, Gord and I had already talked about coming home sooner. But after my call with Sydney, I knew something was wrong and as your mother, I felt the need to be here to help you through what-ever it is that has you and Sydney at odds." Elizabeth sat up straighter. "Now, no more nonsense. You talk, I listen."

Suddenly, Chelsea felt the need to reach out to her mother. She had no idea how her mother would react to her news, but she wanted to hear her perspective. "In two words: I'm pregnant."

Elizabeth stared back, dumbfounded.

Chelsea prattled on, waiting for it to register. "Well, I guess technically that's three words, not ..."

Her mom reached for her hand. "Ssssh," she said, squeezing it. "Chaz?"

Chelsea nodded.

Elizabeth drew a long breath. "I assume this is unplanned? Have you seen a doctor?"

"Yes and yes, had all the tests. I'm healthy, so's the baby, and it's a girl."

"A girl?" A chuckle escaped Elizabeth's lips. "What else would it be? We Greys only have girls. What are your plans?"

"Other than having a Caesarean birth, that's a bit up in the air right now."

"Well," Elizabeth patted her hand. "Not what I expected to hear. How's Chaz taking it?"

Chelsea sighed. "I'm afraid I've royally fucked up things. We'd only just started moving forward when I got pregnant. He's very supportive and we agreed to take it day by day, but …"

"What?"

"After I knew there were no problems with the baby, I decided to continue the pregnancy. He was excited—but I … I panicked."

Her mother gave her a questioning look. "Meaning?"

"He said our lives were going to change. In a nutshell, he saw the three of us as a happy family, raising our daughter. I envisioned myself losing my independence … in lockdown like with Arne."

"But you can't feel that way with Chaz, can you?"

"I know he's not Arne. And I thought we'd have some time to talk it all out, one day at a time, but before I knew it, I felt like he was pushing me."

Elizabeth nodded. "You felt like you lost control?"

"Exactly!"

"But you *do* want this baby?"

"Absolutely. It's not quite like I saw my forties. But no question about it, I want her."

"Perhaps, you and Chaz need to give it time. Things have a way of working out."

Chelsea shook her head. "No. I hurt him, Mom; I pushed him away. He wrote me a letter saying he'll be here to support the baby and we can co-parent together. But he broke it off with me. He thinks I'll never heal from what Arne did to me and he wants more than I'm capable of giving."

"Oh, honey. Do you believe that?"

She shrugged. "Maybe he's right."

Her mother stared hard at her. "What I think is, you're both overwhelmed with the idea of being parents at this stage of your lives. It's an adjustment for anyone. I can't tell either of you what to do with something like this, but I have a suggestion. Talk with Dr Sauvé. It's been a long time since your past sessions."

Chelsea mused over the suggestion. "Maybe." She turned to her mom, studying her. "What?"

"Do you believe Chaz loves you?"

Loves me? Yes, but I'm the problem, not him. "No question."

"Taking yourself out the equation for a moment, if any other woman found herself pregnant by Chaz, and asked you about him as a father, a man, and should she commit to him, what would you say?"

Chelsea gave her mother a wry smile. "I know where you're going with this. I'd probably tell her she couldn't find a more supportive and caring man. But she wouldn't have travelled in my shoes, would she?"

"Then, tell me this: do you love Chaz?"

Chelsea cringed, sucking in her lips. "Yes—but Chaz says sometimes love isn't enough."

"Because of Arne?"

Chelsea nodded. "Yup."

Her mother shifted closer. "Do you remember when you spoke at the Women's Victim Survivors Conference at the University in Kelowna?"

"Of course, why?"

"After you shared the horrors of your twenty-year captivity with Arne, you told the audience you refused to be defined by that experience—you were a survivor, not a victim. I was so proud of you that day."

Chelsea's face clouded over. "It was a lot easier to believe when I only had me to consider."

"No, it wasn't. Please listen to me. You worked so hard that first year. You made bad choices and suffered slip-ups, trying to find yourself. It was a tough year, but you survived. The feeling of losing control because you think Chaz and the baby will take over? Wrong, so wrong. Building a life with someone is never going to be easy, but the ups and downs make you closer and stronger together—especially with a man like Chaz."

Chelsea weighed her mother's words. Deep down, she knew her mother was right. *So, what's holding me back?*

"Do you know who *really* took your control away?"

"Who?"

"Arne. He was a psychopath who made you a victim. But, honey, he's dead. You're not, your baby isn't, and Chaz isn't. Don't let Arne reach out from the grave and take your power. If you could survive your time with him, you're strong enough to handle anything that life throws at you and Chaz. You deserve this."

Elizabeth stood and held her arms out. "Come here."

Chelsea stood with glistening eyes, melted into her mother's arms, and clung to her as she had as a child. The two of them held each other in silence for a long time. Finally, Chelsea pulled back and said, "Why would I need Dr Sauvé when I have you?"

"Just being a mom. Now, tell me, how does Sydney fit into all this?"

Chelsea rolled her eyes. "Oh, God! Once I'd decided to have the baby, I wanted to share my excitement with her. I totally misread her reaction. At first, I thought she was concerned with her menopausal mother having a baby and all the health issues that could arise. I assured her about that, but she flipped out, accusing me of choosing between Chaz and a baby and pushing him away. Then, she accused me of competing with her and the triplets and I should be happy being a grandmother. I should have seen it right then; she was afraid of losing me again and being replaced by this baby."

"Oh dear. She was overwhelmed too."

Chelsea nodded. "It took Wenner to point it out to me. No baby could ever replace her and the triplets. I should have assured her of that."

"Jealousy." Her mother's expression turned stern. "Why in heavens name didn't you call me?"

"Because I didn't want to ruin your holiday. And after Sydney's outburst, and the mess I made with Chaz, I wasn't sure what to expect from you."

Her mother snorted. "I *will* offer an opinion, if I may."

"Please, do," Chelsea said.

They resumed their positions on the couch and this time Elizabeth took both Chelsea's hands in hers. "You've decided you want this baby. I think she's the next step in your new life, a chance to make up for some of what you lost. All the rest, Chaz, Sydney, whatever—it's just domestic family 'fluff'. That's not diminishing it. Just saying it'll take care of itself. As for me? I'm excited as hell—another grandchild."

❧ 15 ❧

Sasha studied Madie's facial expressions as her client followed her instructions to descend the stairs. Madie's eyes moved constantly under her closed lids; her breathing quickened.

"Are you seeing images as you move down?"

"Yes. Flashes of arid grasslands and a backyard."

"You're almost there. Take a deep breath and relax. Are you at the bottom?"

"Yes."

"Look down and tell me what you're standing on," Sasha said.

"The desert floor."

"What's around you?"

"Nothing. It's dark and when the lightning lights up the sky, I can see out in the desert."

Sasha wrote some notes and asked, "Are you male or female?"

"Female."

Madie was talking so softly, Sasha moved closer to hear her. "Are you an adult or a child?"

"Adult."

The practitioner noted it was nighttime and stormy. "Tell me what you're wearing."

"Black jeans and a white t-shirt."

"Why are you in the desert at night in a thunderstorm?"

"I'm running away."

"I see. Are you alone?"

Madie's face contorted and her eyes began twitching again. "No. There's a man," she said, her voice denoting fear.

Sasha focused on the changes in Madie's tone. "Do you know who this man is?"

"Yes. My husband."

"And why are you running away together into the desert?"

"Not together. *I'm running away from him.*"

"Tell me what you're feeling," Sasha requested.

Her body shuddered. "Scared. Cold. Wet."

Sasha observed Madie's physical reactions. Not wanting her to lose control, she said, "Breathe deep through your emotions."

She watched as Madie took deep breaths. Her body relaxed and she calmed. "And how old are you?"

"I'm twenty."

Sasha was surprised. *So young.* "How long have you been married?"

"A year; we married as soon as I finished high school."

"Why is your husband chasing you?"

Madie squirmed. "He's angry at me."

"Why?"

"Because I'm leaving him. Going home to my parents."

"Can you tell me why?"

"He hurts me. He's bad."

"Do you have any children?"

Madie hesitated. "No. But I'm three months pregnant."

Sasha was pleased with the details Madie was experiencing. She wrote furiously as they progressed. "I see. Is that why you're leaving? So, he can't hurt your child, too?"

"Yes."

"Tell me about the desert. Do you know where you're running to?"

"Rock cropping. To hide."

"Do you make it to the rocks?"

"No. The lightning strike is close. The ground is shaking, and my body is tingling. I'm crouching down for protection."

"Tell me what happens next."

"The lightning just hit the ground right in front of me. I catch my breath and stand." Madie licked her lips and her eye movements began again. Shallow, rapid breaths overtook her body.

Sasha picked up on the warning signs and led Madie through her trauma. "Deep breaths, in, hold, and release. Again … and again." When Madie relaxed, Sasha asked her to continue.

"He's caught me from behind and is pulling me by the hair onto my back. He's straddling me and kneeling over my body." Madie's body stiffened and shook.

"Control your emotions with your breathing."

Madie wasn't listening. Her body thrashed on the raised table and she gasped for air. With arms flying in all directions, Madie's face contorted and her head tipped back.

Sasha tried again. "Deep breathes, in, hold, and release."

Madie continued to struggle. Fearing she'd fall off the table, Sasha brought her out of the regression. "Madie we're moving on. See yourself in a beautiful place where you feel safe. Go there now."

Madie stopped moving and settled into a quiet state.

"Breathe slowly, knowing nothing can harm you here. Enjoy the tranquillity of this peaceful retreat you're in. Relax. That's it. Now, open your eyes and find yourself back with me as Madie."

Madie opened her eyes and focused on Sasha's face, her cheeks damp with tears.

"Stay still, until you regain your balance. I pulled you out because you were in a lot of distress and not hearing my commands."

"It seemed so real."

"Do you remember what was happening just before you came back?"

"He was straddling me—her. Shaking her and yelling."

"Do you remember what he was yelling?"

Madie shuddered. "He wouldn't let her leave. Called her ungrateful, selfish." Madie stopped and looked at Sasha, wide-eyed. She sat up on the edge of the bed. "He called her Tara —her name is Tara."

"Good. Anything else?"

Madie concentrated, closing her eyes as if reliving her experience. "Nothing."

After a moment in thought, Sasha said, "I think you were experiencing her death. I'd like to continue and take you back through it, but I'm not sure you're ready. How about we book another session?"

Madie looked at Sasha, weighing the option. A determined look crossed her face, pushing her shoulders back and nodding with renewed strength. "No, let's do it now. If I was experiencing Tara's death, and her husband killed her, I need to know now."

Sasha looked at her notes. She studied Madie for a moment, coming to a decision. "Alright, lay down and we'll begin again. But if your trauma returns to the point that I think you can't follow my commands, I'll pull you out again. Okay?"

Madie nodded. She leaned back on the raised padded table and closed her eyes. Once again, Sasha took her down the stairs to the bottom. Madie descended easily into her past life and Sasha took her back to the moment they'd ended in the first session. She noted that Madie appeared relaxed and her breathing was normal.

"You're on your back and your husband is straddling you. He's yelling at you for running away. Tell me what's happening."

"I'm trying to push him off me. It's hard to see with the pounding rain on my face. I feel his hands around my neck, squeezing. I'm fighting back, trying to scratch his face, pounding his chest with my fists. It hurts so bad."

Sasha gauged her degree of distress. In a matter of moments, Madie gasped for air. "My fingers are caught in the pendant around his neck. It breaks and comes away in my hand. Can't breathe … can't breathe."

Sasha spoke to her in a soothing tone. "It will pass soon. You won't feel any pain. Tell me what you're feeling now?"

In a quiet, raspy voice, her client answered, "Hopelessness. Fear. Death."

"You're taking your last breaths, now—feel at peace."

She watched as Madie's facial expression relaxed and her breathing returned to normal. Instinctively, Sasha knew she'd passed through death. No matter how many times she'd taken clients through this moment, she never got used to it. Something she'd never share with them of course, but her sense of peace returned, and she let go of her inner tension.

"Where are you now?"

"I'm floating above my body."

"Have you passed through death?"

"Yes."

"And how do you feel?"

Madie's mouth curled into a smile. "Free and at peace."

"What's your husband doing?"

"Sitting beside my body with his head in his hands."

"Are you sad you're leaving this life?"

"Yes. I worry about my parents." Madie's voice caught. "And my baby—my baby will die inside me."

"What's your husband doing now?"

"I follow him home as he carries my body back. He wraps

JUNE V. BOURGO

me in a tarp and ties it around me with rope, then places me in his ATV, along with a shovel. He sits until the storm passes and rides out to the hills," Madie explained, letting out a deep sigh.

"Is it still dark?"

"Yes."

"And where are you now?"

"I'm sitting on top of a rocky hill, watching him bury me within a circle of rocks below my perch."

"And how are you feeling now?"

"Sad. Angry."

"Your husband has finished burying you. What does he do next?"

"He's transplanting some sage in front of the opening to the enclosure of rocks to hide the entrance."

"He's finished planting; tell me what he's doing now?"

"He's on his ATV, heading home."

Sasha decided it was time to end the session with one more question.

"Do you know what the date is?"

"Early Sunday morning, June 14, 1998."

"Excellent. Now, it's time for you to relax. I want you to go back to your beautiful safe place. Tell me when you're there."

"I'm here."

Sasha could see the tension leave Madie's body, a slight smile at the corner of her mouth. "Enjoy the moment and its serenity. From here you'll return to your present life." Sasha paused. "I want you to regain your consciousness as Madie. Know you can live your life in peace without fear of thunderstorms or nightmares. Now, feel your body and wiggle your feet, and experience the weight of your body. You're returning to full awareness, here with me. Open your eyes."

Sasha watched her client stretch. Madie opened her eyes and stared at the ceiling for a few moments.

"Are you okay?"

"Yes."

"Do you remember what you experienced?"

Madie nodded and sat up, swinging her legs over the edge of the table. "Oh yes. Do you think I was Tara in a past life?"

"I do," Sasha replied firmly.

"And the repressed memories from that life only surface during rainstorms in this one because she was murdered during a storm?"

"That's right."

"Wow." Feeling overwhelmed, Madie waved her fingers, fanning her face. "She was so young. Only twenty."

Sasha stayed quiet, allowing Madie to ground herself.

Madie's hand slipped to her throat. "It felt so—so real. I can still feel his hands pressing on my neck."

The practitioner handed her a Kleenex.

Sitting on the edge of the table, she dabbed at her eyes and blew her nose. "What do I do now?

"It's safe to say you were Tara in a past life, and that's been haunting you in this one. With this knowledge, you should find peace."

"Which is great for me, but what about Tara? She deserved more than what she got."

"Yes, she did," agreed Sasha.

Madie stared at her. "There may still be a family some-where who don't know what happened to her."

"Probably. They've had no closure."

Madie was quiet a moment, her gaze tunnelling in. Finally, she said, "Do you think she wants me to be her closure: hence, the nightmares and visions? I have to find out who she is and find her husband. He can't get away with it."

Sasha handed her a bottle of apple juice. "Here, drink and rehydrate. There's not much information. How will you start?"

Madie shrugged. "I have a first name and a date. June 14, 1998 is my birthday. He murdered her the night before I was

JUNE V. BOURGO

born. She reincarnated right away." She drank the juice, deep in thought. "You know, when I was born, I almost didn't make it? They did a last-minute Caesarean." Madie ran tense fingers through her hair and sighed. "You know, if this happened in '98, she'd be, what? Forty-three today?"

"I guess. But if you go looking, there's danger in what you're proposing. Remember her husband is a murderer."

"During my session with Kat, my grandmother's spirit warned me to be careful. Now, I know why. Believe me, I won't do anything stupid."

"Good. If you find out anything concrete, promise me you'll take it to the authorities."

"I promise. And I'm making a promise to Tara. There's a reason I've been reliving memories of her. I won't give up until I find out where he buried her. He'll pay for what he did to her and her family."

Sasha studied her client. "If you pursue this, you may continue to have nightmares."

Madie weighed that. "At least, I know why."

"I only say that because my clients usually are ready to put the past in the past and move forward in their present life. What I'm sensing, Madie, is you aren't ready to do that yet. I want you to be prepared and ready for the next step of your journey. And take heed of your grandmother's warning."

༄ II ༄

The two most important
Days in your life
Are the day you are born
And the day
You find out why

Mark Twain

C ody held the tranquillized fox in position on the surgical table while Chelsea removed the bandage from the animal's hindquarters. She examined the remaining stitches and dabbed a bead of antibacterial cream on the wound.

"It's healing nicely," she said, walking to the sink to wash her hands. "I think we can leave the bandages off now, but we'll keep the recovery cone on his neck for a couple more days until all the stitches have dissolved; otherwise, he'll be gnawing them or licking the wound. He should be ready for release soon."

"I think you're right," Cody said. As he lifted the animal and carried him to one of the recovery cages in an alcove off the back wall, the main door opened to the surgery.

Wenner stuck his head in and glanced around. "All clear to enter?"

Chelsea spun around, drying her hands with a paper towel. "Hey you, come on in. I heard you drive in late last night. How was your trip home?"

He entered the room, followed by a taller man with a slim build and greying black hair.

"Wonderful. It was great to see the folks." He turned to

the younger man beside him. "Let me introduce you to Chelsea Grey, my partner, and our compound manager and assistant, Cody Diaz. This is Jordy Lewis, a freelance writer. He wants to do a story on our Centre for a wildlife magazine."

Chelsea approached them. "Welcome." She shook hands with the visitor and stood back.

Cody returned to the sink to wash his hands. "Hi there, Jordy, good to meet ya."

Wenner turned to Chelsea. "Jordy was finishing up another assignment in Woodview. We met quite by chance and when he learned about the Centre, he decided it should be his next story." He eyed her expectantly. "I think it's a great idea; what do you think?"

"Well, the story could be a great help to our fundraising efforts." She considered Jordy. "How long will you be with us?"

"A couple of weeks to follow you all around, shoot photos. I promise you won't even know I'm here. There'll also be individual interviews, some scouting around town to learn its history and soak up the flavour."

"Jordy will be staying with me, in the guest room," Wenner piped in.

The two men gave each other a smile that wasn't lost on Chelsea. With their eyes locked and the heightened colour on Wenner's cheeks, the attraction between them was obvious.

Chelsea smiled inwardly, noting Jordy, with his greying dark hair, dimpled cheeks, and boyish smile was a good-looking man. She glanced at Wenner, who was staring back at her with a look that told her he knew what she was thinking and fell over his next words. "He ... umm ... he needs to experience the routine here—he can't do that unless he's a part of our family."

She gave him a nod and a crooked smile. *Good for you! About time.* "Hmm, makes sense," she said as Madie entered the room.

"Hi, Wenner, welcome back." Madie smiled. "Sorry to interrupt you all, but I just got an emergency call from Conservation. They need someone to meet them at Sandhill Pointe. They have a coyote in distress with a kill snare around his neck. He broke the trap free, but he's in serious trouble."

Wenner's jaw went rigid and his face coloured. "Goddammit! Trappers are trained and licensed to set those bloody things so this doesn't happen. As much as I hate snare traps, no animal should be able to break one free." He turned to Cody. "Can you get the truck ready while I grab the first-aid gear?"

"Sure thing." Cody pushed past them and left the room.

"Someone will be waiting for you at the junction of Carey Road and Desert Rat Trail," Madie said.

Jordy stepped back, seemingly to observe the rush to action. "Is it okay if I tag along and do my thing with the camera?"

"You bet." Wenner grabbed drugs and syringes from the cupboard.

"I'll run to the house for my equipment," Jordy said.

Wenner yelled after him as he rushed from the room. "We'll pick you up by the gate." He turned to Chelsea. "I need Cody, too. Are you able to finish his chores? We should be back by noon."

"Not a problem. Get going! And welcome home!"

Left alone with Madie, Chelsea asked, "Think you could finish the government reports I've been working on? They have to be filed by end of the day."

"Sure thing. I'll head back to the office."

Chelsea leaned against the counter, staring after Madie. She nodded to the empty room. *No worries with that one. She'll take over things just fine.* Lost in her thoughts, a noise from the alcove caught her attention. *Earth to Chelsea!* A check on the fox confirmed he was waking up from the medication. He moved into the corner of the cage when he saw her but remained calm.

"Don't worry, little guy. You'll be going home soon."

Thirty minutes later, the surgery room was scrubbed, and the instruments were placed in the sterilizer. Chelsea glanced around the room, nodding in approval while she breathed in the fresh, clean smell of the antibacterial cleaner. She grabbed the patient clipboard and headed to the kitchen to prepare formula for their younger patients.

THE WILDLIFE TRUCK from the Centre followed the conservation jeep along the dusty trail towards Sandhill Pointe. Ten minutes later, Wenner reached their destination and pulled over. The coyote was lying in a bramble of sagebrush and juniper shrubs at the base of the rocks. He grabbed the first-aid kit and turned to Cody. "We need the net."

A moment later, Wenner, Cody and Jordy approached the frightened animal, struggling to push himself up onto his legs. He had no strength and collapsed on his side. As Wenner moved in on the distressed coyote, gasping for breath, their eyes locked.

"For fuck's sake—he's been dragging the whole harness, including the goddamn pole," Wenner said, his temper boiling over.

Cody looked beside him. "He's skinny. I think he's been caught in that thing for days. He's lucky to still be alive."

One of the two conservation officer's standing nearby, asked, "You gonna tranquillize him?"

Wenner shook his head. "No, he's too weak. I don't think we'll need the net either. If you and your partner circle him and hold his back end down, Cody can hold him at the shoulders while I cut him loose. You're both up-to-date on your rabies booster shots, right?" When they nodded, he added,

"But wear your gloves; he could still have some fight left in him and land a nasty bite."

As the coyote's frightened eyes darted back and forth between them, they moved into position around him. "Okay, let's do this on the count of three," Wenner said, and they lurched forward and pinned the animal that offered a feeble attempt of a struggle until, at last, it gave up and lay still. "Easy fella, we're here to help you." To Cody, he said, "Poor guy's exhausted."

As he worked, Jordy circled them, snapping pictures.

But Wenner paid him no mind as he squatted down for a closer look. He wrinkled his nose at the musky smell of the animal and the strong odour of urine filled his nostrils. "Poor thing just peed himself. Let's take a peek at that damn wire." He parted the fur around it. "Jesus, it's cutting into his neck all the way around. Okay little guy, let's cut that trap off and clean you up so I see what's going on."

With a quick snip of his nippers, he cut the trap away from the wire and tossed it aside. The usually long, soft fur around the wound was matted and coarse to the touch with dried blood and dirt. Wenner cut it away with scissors. When the embedded wire was exposed, he sat back on his haunches. "Wow, the wire's uptight to his trach." He pressed his lips together, rubbing his chin. Whether the coyote had suffered internal injuries, he didn't know, so he moved slowly with his mini snips and cut the animal free. He looked up at Cody and the two conservation officers. "Hard to tell if he'll need surgery til we get him back to the Centre."

"One thing's for sure, there's an infection going on," Cody put in.

Wenner treated the wound with antibacterial gel and wrapped it in gauze. "All done," he said, then stood and stretched. "Jordy, could you help me carry the cage to this little guy while the others keep him down? We should be able to lift him in. It'll be less traumatic."

"Sure thing."

Inside of fifteen minutes, they were back on the road, heading to Stoney Creek. Jordy remained silent while Wenner and Cody discussed their plan for the injured animal. Once they were silent, Jordy asked, "What did you call those traps?"

Wenner spat the words, "Kill Snares."

"Are they even legal? And is it legal to kill coyotes?"

"Yes and yes. From September 1 to June 30. I wish it wasn't so but it's not my call," Wenner said grimly.

Jordy frowned. "But it's July."

"He's been dragging that trap around for about a week I'd guess, which is why he was so lethargic. Made it easy for us, but bad timing for him, poor fella. It was probably towards the end of June when he got trapped."

"Making it legal, then," Jordy said.

"Yep."

"There's a lot more depth to this piece than I anticipated. I think my research for this story is going to take me in directions I hadn't considered." Jordy was quiet a moment and Wenner could see him looking over his shoulder at the cage in the back. "What are his chances of survival?"

"Not sure yet. I need to do a thorough examination. Depends on if the trach's been cut, and how much debris's in the wound. Then, there's the infection, and if there's any tissue necrosis there. The important thing now is to stabilize him and get him ventilated. The rest is up to the coyote and his will to live."

❧ 17 ❧

The glare of the computer screen caused her eyes to water and Madie blinked to clear her vision. She took a break and padded to the kitchen to get some water. Since her session with the regressionist, she'd spent every spare moment searching Google sites for a missing woman in the late 1990s called Tara—to no avail. A couple of drops of Murine cleared her eyes. She put it down to eye strain. *Between my day job and long evenings online too, not good.*

Back at the computer, she found a reference to *The Highway of Tears* and got lost in the story.

A little-known highway in Northern BC—The Highway of Tears is a 724km (approx 450 miles) length of highway, known as Highway 16, that stretches from Prince Rupert, BC, on the west coast, to Prince George, BC, in the interior. It's hard to explain to people that haven't been here how remote and isolated the communities are that dot that highway. Twenty-three First Nations communities border the Highway of Tears, named thus due to a large number of missing and murdered women linked to the highway. These small communities are, unfortunately, mostly poor and lack things like public transit, doctors and, in many cases, places to get groceries and even gas for your car. These conditions force people in these communities to resort to hitchhiking to get to larger communities for those things we take for granted.

Madie read on to read that dozens of these women and girls had gone missing from 1969 to 2006, with two serial killers working independently of each other found to be responsible for about fourteen of the murders. The police expected that there could be more than two serial killers and most of the murders may never be solved. Having driven that stretch of highway in the past, it made her skin crawl at the secrets hidden along its isolated and lonely path.

A pounding on the door made her jump. "Holy shit!"

She glanced at the clock and saw it was just after 9:00 p.m. Madie went to the window and peered through the curtain, let out a long sigh of relief, and opened the door. She leaned against the door frame. "To what do I owe the pleasure of a visit from the one and only lion tamer?"

Cody pulled his hand out of his pocket and held up a gold bracelet. "Are you missing this? I found it on the floor between the front passenger door and the seat."

"Omigod! Thank you, thank you, thank you!" She took it from him, and then glanced down at her clothes. "I'm in my PJs but what the hell. Come in."

Cody followed her and she explained, "My dad gave me this bracelet the year before he died; it was my grandmother's. I've been so bummed out thinking it was lost and I couldn't remember when I last wore it."

"I'm thinking it was on the day we took the animals to the Kelowna Wildlife Centre. The clasp is broken, and it may have happened on the drive home, when you were thrashing about in your sleep during the storm."

"It's possible. I'm so grateful you found it." She gestured the couch. "Sit. You want a beer?"

Cody sat and stretched out his legs. "Sure. I found it tonight at the car wash and could have given it to you at work, but I was driving by and saw your light on."

"Glad you stopped in. I could use a break." She popped the tops off two bottles of Corona and joined him on the couch, tucking her feet under her.

"Thanks. A break from what?"

"Oh, researching missing women for Tara. So far nothing. I've been searching in British Columbia but it's time to go further afield. Maybe I'm wrong, thinking she lived by the desert; maybe they were vacationing near one and lived elsewhere. Anyway, I'll extend my search."

"Don't give up; you'll find her."

"I hope so. Since the rains stopped, no more nightmares, and that means no more clues. Crazy, isn't it? Before I knew what they meant, I'd have given anything for them to disappear; now, I wish I knew more."

"The storms will be back and with them the nightmares. Wherever he buried her, she isn't going anywhere, so enjoy the peace."

"Uhh." Madie leaned over and smacked him on the shoulder. "Not nice."

He gave her a crooked grin. "Sorry. If you find her, what will you do then?"

Madie sighed. "I have no idea." She paused, looking thoughtful. "Probably track the husband next and see where he's at. After that?" She shrugged. "One thing at a time."

A frown crossed his brow. "Remember, he comes with danger, so please include me on that search. Promise me you won't be a lone crusader."

Madie took a swig of beer. "Okay. How's Wiley doing?"

A puzzled look crossed his face. "Wiley?"

"Wile E. Coyote, your patient?"

"Oh, right. Clever. Better this week. The wound's healing nicely and his fur is starting to grow back. Another couple of weeks and he can go home. His mate came back again today. She sits by the compound fence and calls to him."

Madie's eyes glistened. "The fact she knew where to find

him is such a wonder. Shows how tight a bond they have once they mate."

"She doesn't stay long, probably has pups back in their den, and with him out of the picture, she has to do the hunting for food. Today, he was very alert to her presence. When she called, he raised his head and tried to answer. It was the first time, he attempted it. I think she's giving him the strength to fight back and heal."

"So cool. We have the best jobs in the world, don't we?"

They locked eyes and Cody reached out and squeezed her hand. He put his beer down, took hers and placed it on the coffee table, pulled her to her feet and cupped her face with his hands. He leaned in and kissed her gently at first on the lips.

Madie froze as the sensation of his kiss sent tingling throughout her body. Building to a fervent need for something more, her arms reached out, embracing him, and she pressed her lips harder against his.

His tongue darted back and forth, and she opened her mouth, exploring his tongue with hers. Her sudden need took control and one kiss led to many more. Madie led him to the bed where she pulled his sweatshirt off and he unbuttoned her pyjama top. They both kicked their lower clothing off and fell onto the bed in feral abandonment.

As they explored each other's bodies, Madie lost herself to his adept lovemaking. Her experience was limited to a boyfriend in Kelowna, both of them virgins when they got together. Being older than her, Madie expected Cody to be more experienced sexually than her—he was. She feared she might disappoint him. As his fingers worked their magic, and their passion grew, Madie became more confident.

Her hand slid down his thigh, searching between his legs and shock coursed through her. *Wow, he's huge, compared to ...*

She pushed thoughts of her one and only experience out of her mind, concentrating on stroking his thick offering.

Cody rolled on top of her and Madie stretched her arm over to the night table. Her fingers found the knob to the drawer and she pulled it open. Between her gasps, as his mouth found her nipples, she fumbled in the drawer and pulled out a condom and slipped it into his hand.

Cody paused to open it. He stared into her eyes while he rolled it in place and Madie heard herself whisper words she had no intention of saying, "Should we be doing this?"

Cody hesitated, pushing her hair away from her face. "Do you want to stop?"

Forsaking her brief moment of sensibility, she throatily answered, "No way." Madie pulled him down and Cody accepted her invitation, groaning in unison as he entered her.

At first, he was gentle, taking his time, teasing her with his strokes. Worried she might not be able to take in his size disappeared as Madie relaxed in the knowledge they fit together well. Cody's strokes became faster and harder, a wanton need growing between them as their bodies moved as one in a feverish climb ... until they peaked together at the top and tumbled down, side by side, into each other's arms, gasping for air.

Cody pulled the comforter over them as they rolled over to face each other. "What just happened?"

Madie grinned. "You're asking me?"

He ran a finger down her nose and stopped at her lips. "Do you always answer a question with a question?"

She kissed his finger. "When I don't have the answer, I do. Are you sorry?"

He smiled. "To quote this girl I know, 'no way'."

Madie knew they'd just crossed a line as coworkers but now was not the moment to examine it. "Well, that girl you know would probably say: figure it out tomorrow. So, let's relax and enjoy the moment, lion tamer."

"You're amazing. You're such a petit little thing; I wasn't sure you could take me, but you proved me wrong."

Madie sighed contentedly. "I had my concerns at first too."

Cody's infamous crooked grin surfaced, "Sorry if I scared you."

"Actually, my first thoughts were, 'my God, that thick one certainly wouldn't float in the bathtub'."

Cody laughed and Madie giggled, red-faced she'd actually said that. He rolled onto his back and pulled her in close, and she placed her head on his shoulder. They cuddled in silence while he ran his hand along her hip bone and she stroked his abdomen.

With a raspy voice, Cody whispered in her ear, "Next time, we'll take it a lot slower."

❧ 18 ❧

With their meeting over, Wenner and Jack Pruitt, the Centre's accountant, stood and shook hands. Jack then leaned across Chelsea's desk and shook hers. "Congrats and all the best to you and the baby."

"Thanks, Jack."

"I'll walk you out," Wenner said.

They'd just ironed out the details for their new part-time hire and Jack had assured them, they were good to go.

Wenner returned and stretched out in his seat with hands crossed over his chest. "All settled. I'll leave the posting details and interviews to you and Madie. This is gonna work out fine."

"It's good to hear Jack's support." Chelsea studied her friend. Changing the subject, she said, "I see Jordy is still with us."

Wenner gave her a wide smile. "Yes, he is. The magazine has decided to run it in three parts. It's taken on a political side he hadn't anticipated, so more research is required with trips to Vancouver and Victoria. And he's combining this story with a little vacation time. I've invited him to stay for the summer."

Chelsea raised her eyebrows and gave him a knowing look. "Are you two a thing?"

Wenner chuckled. "We're—*something*!"

"Hey, give it over. I told you about me and Chaz."

"Oh, right. Like you could keep it a secret as your belly grows bigger. Not the same thing at all."

"Huh! Like looking at the two of you together doesn't say it all."

Wenner looked surprised. "Oh, really? And what is looking at us together saying?"

"That you're happy, relaxed, and wearing a smiley face—a new Wenner. Now, stop playing coy and talk to me. I don't need all the details, just the definition of 'we're *something*'."

Wenner sighed. "Okay, we're taking it slow, with both of us coming from a place of pain: me dealing with Brian's murder and Jordy losing a relationship because his work took him away from home too much. We're both into our work and enjoying our friendship. It's all either of us needs for now."

"Good for you. I love seeing you happy."

"How ironic that I ran away from Westwood, vowing never to return and years later I find a new relationship there."

"Life is about the strangest thing I ever did see," Chelsea said, feigning a southern drawl.

Wenner gave her a puzzled look.

She laughed. "The movie, *Missouri Breaks*? Actor Randy Quaid said that line."

"Ah, gotcha. So, how's life treating you these days?" He gave her an expectant look.

"My mother's home from Europe. It's nice to have someone else on my side about the baby."

"I take it nothing's changed with Sydney and Chaz then?"

Chelsea didn't answer him. A strange feeling she could only describe as a "whoosh" in her lower abdomen caught her by surprise. She looked down into her lap to see a reddish stain seeping through the front of her tan slacks. "Uhh," was all she could say, followed by a feeling of panic.

"Chelsea?" Wenner leaned forward. "Chelsea, hon, what's wrong?"

She lifted her head and stared wide-eyed. "I'm ... I'm bleeding."

Wenner flew out of his chair and rounded her desk. "Okay, hon. Stay right there, don't move." He picked up her phone and called 911. "Yes, this is the Stoney Creek Wildlife Rehabilitation Centre. We have a five-month pregnant woman here who is haemorrhaging, and we need an ambulance right away."

Chelsea began to panic as she listened to Wenner talk. *Stay calm.*

The operator asked a question. "She's sitting and no, we won't move her." He turned to Chelsea. "Are you feeling any pain?"

She shook her head.

"No pain. Okay, thank-you, so much." He hung up the phone. "They're on the way." He pulled a chair close to her, sat down, and held her hand. "You're going to be fine, hon."

Her fear rose and a feeling of despair overwhelmed her. "What if I'm losing the baby?" she cried.

"We don't know that. A little bleeding happens sometimes during pregnancy; let's wait and see what the doctor says, okay?" He squeezed her hand reassuringly and stood.

"Where are you going?" Chelsea grasped his hand tightly. "Don't leave me."

"I'm just going to get Madie to sit with you while I check in with Cody. I'll be back in a minute, don't worry. I'm going with you to the hospital. All right?"

"Okay."

The room spun before her. Not sure if it was because of what was happening to her body physically or because she felt on the verge of a panic attack, she took deep breaths through her nose and released them via her mouth. The wetness she felt grew and she closed her eyes tight. *Please don't let me lose my baby.*

Madie rushed into the room and sat beside her, placing an arm around her shoulders. "They'll be here soon. Can I get you anything?"

"My mouth is so dry. Could you get me some water?"

"Sure thing, I'll be right back."

In the distance, Chelsea heard the sirens growing louder as they approached; when they stopped, she knew help had reached the Centre, and she breathed a sigh of relief. The front door opened and slammed shut. The sound of running feet echoed down the hallway. Chelsea focused on the open doorway to her office, expecting paramedics.

Instead, her daughter, Sydney, wide-eyed, with a face full of fear ran into her office, stopped to catch her breath and gasped, "Mom?"

CHELSEA SAT in the hospital bed hooked up to monitors and an IV. Sydney sat on one side and Wenner on the other. Several tests had been completed. The bleeding had stopped, and she was waiting for the doctor to come and talk to her.

"Are you comfortable? Do you want an extra pillow or another warm blanket?" Sydney asked softly.

Chelsea gave her a weak smile. "I'm fine, thanks." She was so grateful to have Sydney with her. Their argument still hung between them, but in the end, Sydney had risen to the occasion and shown up to support her when it counted. The paramedics had come into the office right after Sydney, so they'd had no time to talk. She could see her daughter was very concerned. Her manner was contrite, and Sydney was going out of her way to be there for her. "All I need is you by my side."

Sydney squeezed her hand. "I'm not going anywhere."

Dr Carson arrived and stood by the end of the bed. She directed her words to Chelsea. "You've had quite the day." She glanced at the other two.

"I'm her daughter, Sydney, and that's Wenner, Mom's business partner and a close family friend."

Wenner stood. "I'm going for coffee while you chat." He turned to Sydney, "Be back shortly."

"Would you like me to leave as well, Mom?"

"No, please stay."

Wenner headed to the door, "I'll bring you back a cup, Syd."

"Thanks."

Dr Carson took Wenner's empty seat and smiled at Chelsea. "First, you and the baby are both fine. No worries there."

Chelsea breathed a sigh of relief. "That's good news."

"Last time I saw you, I told you the placenta was in the back of the fetus, which in itself isn't that unusual. And that it pushes the fetus forward, which is why you felt the baby's movements sooner than most mothers. I also said at some point it moves up above the fetus as the baby prepares for birth and drops into place at the entrance to the cervix."

Chelsea nodded. "Yes, I remember."

"In your case, the placenta hasn't risen but dropped below the fetus, blocking the entrance to the cervix. The condition is called a placenta previa. This would be upsetting for a young mother who wouldn't be able to have a normal delivery. However, in your case, we've already determined you're having a Caesarean birth."

"Okay. I know there's a 'but' coming here. What is it?"

"The placenta is pressing on the cervix and it can only get worse as the baby grows and the inner space of the uterus grows smaller. That's what's causing the haemorrhaging. We've stopped it for now. Your haemoglobin level is a bit low as well, so we'd like to give you a pint of blood and keep you in overnight. If nothing changes, you can go home tomorrow. How's that sound?"

"I'll do whatever you think is best."

"Good to hear because here's where the 'but' you mentioned comes in. You're going to have to change your life-style. For starters, you need to rest laying down most of the day."

Chelsea sputtered, "*Most* of the day? You're kidding, right?"

"No, I'm not. You can sit for a couple of hours or take a short walk, but no hills. No exercising. No heavy lifting. Quick showers and bathroom breaks. Nothing more. Then, lay in bed for several hours. Rotate the routine. Only lay on the left side; it helps the blood flow. No sleeping on your back."

Chelsea felt deflated. She looked at Sydney in horror. *Maybe Sydney was right. I shouldn't be having this baby.*

"Mom, you can do this. I had to with the triplets—remember? You have a lot of people around you who can help. If I could do it, so can you; you're stronger than me."

"It could be worse," the doctor interjected. "You might be in bed full-time if you keep haemorrhaging. You can expect some spotting off and on. That's normal—but anything like today, you come in right away."

Chelsea asked, "Okay. Since I live at the Centre, is it okay to go to work for a couple of hours?"

"If it's a flat walk, and you're sitting at a desk, once a day for a couple of hours is fine, but the stress level must be mini-mal." The doctor stood to leave. "I'll be back tonight before I leave to check on you. The nurse will be in soon to set up the transfusion. Now rest."

Chelsea locked eyes with her daughter, who was still holding her hand. "You asked me why I'd want to have a baby at this stage of my life. I'm beginning to wonder that myself right about now."

Sydney's face clouded. With glistening eyes, she said, "Mom, what I said to you that day—it was uncalled for and mean. Yes, I was concerned about your health, but I also resented the baby. It took Jax to make me see it. I'm so sorry."

"It took Wenner and your grandmother to help me understand your reaction. I'm sorry I didn't consider it before talking to you."

"You were excited, and I reacted selfishly. I saw this baby as a threat to me; I wanted you all to myself. It was immature and silly. Forgive me?"

For a moment, Chelsea held back, envisioning herself as a teenager, asking her mother's forgiveness when she told her she was pregnant. Sydney reminded her so much of herself when she was young and impetuous. She smiled at her daughter. "We'll forgive each other. You know, your baby sister may well become jealous of you."

"What? Why?"

"Because her big sister is my best friend. After all we've been through, we have a very special bond. But this baby doesn't need a best friend; she'll need a mother who'll give her rules and discipline, at least until she's an adult."

Sidney laughed and leaned over, hugging her fiercely. When she drew back there were tears on her cheeks. "I love you, Mom."

"I love you, too." Chelsea reached up and brushed the tears from her daughter's face, then smiled. "No more tears, okay?"

Her daughter sat back in her chair. "Back to your question about having this baby … you've been given a chance to be the mom Arne took away from you when he kidnapped you. You're entitled to that. I see it now."

"I thought I'd lost the baby. Now that I know she's okay, I'm committed all the more to this pregnancy, but I'm scared. More scared now than I was when I had you. Yes, I'm strong, but having you here to support me means the world."

"And I do support you, Mom. Now that we're talking again, it's kinda cool having a baby sister—weird, but cool."

Chelsea chuckled. "Our family *is* weird. At one time, you thought Chaz might be your father and worried you may have slept with your brother. Thank God that wasn't the case. Now, I'm sleeping with your father-in-law." She paused and her gut tightened. "Or I was. My baby will be your baby sister, your husband's baby sister, and your kids' auntie."

Sydney shook her head. "Definitely weird. Oh, Jax and Chaz are in Vancouver. They left yesterday. They're helping Jax's grandma move into an independent living complex. I left a message for Jax to call me."

"Please tell them not to come rushing home on my account. I'm fine." She took a long breath. "I could never understand why, after her husband died, his grandmother stayed on the coast. Why wouldn't she want to be closer to the only family she has left?"

Sydney shrugged. "Chaz tried to talk her into moving closer, but her life is there, I guess. She never liked small-town living and referred to Stoney Creek as that 'place' her husband dragged her to when they married. And she never got over Chaz giving up what the city had to offer him when he returned to the sticks—not to mention, bringing her only grandchild with him."

"You're right. She hated it here and Chaz gave up a long time ago seeking her approval."

"They should be home Friday. So-oo, back to the baby. Since you know it's a girl, have you given any thought to names?"

"I'd like to name her after Chaz's grandmother, Margaret …"

Sydney's mouth dropped. "Margaret? My mother, who dyed her hair pink like Cindy Lauper and named her first-born, Sydney—a man's name, by the way—wants to call her daughter Margaret? It's so—so old-fashioned. She's gonna hate you, Mom."

"I hadn't finished. I was thinking of using the Gaelic form of the name: Maisie."

"Maisie?" Her daughter chewed on the name, then finally grinned and nodded approvingly. "Maisie Grey Rhyder. It could work." Then, she frowned. "Isn't there a singer called Maisie Grey?"

Chelsea laughed. "Macey, not Maisie. And Gray with an 'a', not an 'e' like ours. But please don't tell anyone until I talk to Chaz—that is, if he ever talks to me again." *Oh, Chaz, I miss you so much.*

"Mom—of course, he will. You both need time, just like you and I did." Sydney squeezed her mother's hand comfortingly. "And he'll love this little angel."

❧ 19 ❧

Two days after her overnight trip to the hospital, Chelsea sat in her office with Madie. "Thank you for holding it together on such short notice, Madie. I'm glad we got a couple of weeks of training done before the doctor clipped my wings."

"You're welcome. I'm glad you're okay."

Chelsea sat back in her chair. "It's all good. I think we're caught up for the moment and the only thing left is to get a job posting together for the new finance clerk. Now I'm on short hours, we need to move on it right away."

Madie pulled out a folder from under her pile of papers and handed it to Chelsea. "I got a hold of a copy of the Kelowna Wildlife Centre's job description for its finance clerk. With a little modification, I think this may cover what we're looking for."

Chelsea read the document and chuckled. "Right on. You're going to push me out of a job, young lady. If you get it up on the website right away, we can schedule interviews for next week. You're a godsend to me, you know, especially right now. I'm impressed."

Madie's face lit up. "Thanks. Just trying to help where I can."

The outside door to reception opened and closed. "Ladies? Where are you?"

"Back in my office, Wenner," Chelsea shouted.

He poked in his head, nodded at Madie with a "Hi, new boss lady," and pointed to Chelsea, "Hey, you! It's been two hours already; home to bed with you."

"Yes, Daddy!"

"But before you go, come join me and Cody in the compound for a few minutes. We decided this morning it was time to turn Wiley loose. He's been sunbathing in the hot sun in the outer cage and, a few minutes ago, he stood and stared out across the desert flats. Now, he's pacing back and forth along the fence line. I think his mate is coming. We haven't seen her for a few days."

A lone howl filled the room. "Uhh ... she's here," Wenner said. "Let's go."

An answering call from Wiley could be heard. Sage stood from her favourite sleeping spot in the corner of the office, ready to follow Chelsea. "No, Sage. Stay! I'll be back for you."

The female coyote sat outside the compound, watching Wiley run the fencing around his cage. Jordy snapped pictures from every angle while Wenner approached the cage. "Cody, why don't you open the side gate into the compound."

They watched the female bare her teeth and give Cody a growl as he unlocked the outer door and swung it open. She backed away and sat down, watching them warily.

Wenner opened Wiley's cage. "Time to go home, little fella." He joined the others at the bottom of the administration stairs.

In a shot, Wiley was out the door, running across the compound and out the open gate to the desert flats. His mate rushed forward, teasing him by pulling on his leg, sniffing his neck where the closed wound had healed nicely. The two animals ran around each other, ducking and evading, swinging to the left and then to the right. The group watched, mesmerized by their reunion antics until, finally, the pair ran off side by side and disappeared into the grasslands.

Wenner spoke first. "And this is why we do this work—for days like this one. Whatcha think of our little home, Jordy?"

"Awe-inspiring." He held up his camera. "I can't wait to sort through all these pics. But I'm going to love ya and leave ya, off to town to the Stoney Creek Museum to do a little research. See ya later."

"Later, then. Back to work everyone," Wenner said. He looked at Chelsea. "Not you ..."

"Yeah, yeah! I'm going home. But I have to clear my desk and get Sage first."

Wenner laughed. "Good girl, I'll pop by tonight and we'll have some tea."

Heading back to her office, Chelsea spoke over her shoulder, "*You* can have tea. Had to give it up; it gives me heartburn."

"Really? Sure, glad guys can't get pregnant; I'd die without my tea."

They all laughed and headed to their destinations. Chelsea heard the phone ringing in her office as she and Madie entered the building.

"I'll get it," Madie said and ran down the hallway. Seconds later, she met her at the office door. "On hold for you."

Chelsea sat behind her desk and picked up the call. "Chelsea here."

"Hi, it's Chaz."

Her throat constricted and her chest felt like someone had thrown a hard punch to her gut. It took a moment to comprehend that he was on the other end of the phone.

"Are you there?" he asked.

"Uh, yes. You still on the coast?"

"I am."

Chelsea felt her heart race and she fumbled for words, not sure what to say next. Feeling like a shy teenager, she managed to ask, "How's the move going?"

"It's going. Umm—I called the hospital a couple of times but all they'd say was you're doing fine and resting. If it wasn't for Sydney, we'd be in the dark. I'm guessing since you're out of the hospital things are okay with you and the pregnancy, but I wanted to make sure."

"Apart from some restrictions, we're good," Chelsea replied. She paused, and then added, "I appreciate your call." *Appreciate? Dumb thing to say. Too formal, really talk to him.* Her head was spinning. Chelsea decided to follow his lead, since he'd called her.

"That's great. Umm, we're supposed to be home Friday, but it looks like we need an extra day." Chaz fell silent, then added, "Maybe Sunday, I could pop over—for a few minutes?"

Pop over? That's something. But for a few minutes? Maybe he's finally got the courage to see me and confirm face-to-face it's over with. She wanted to talk to him, but her mind was a jumbled mess of words that wouldn't come together. Chelsea knew this whole mess was her fault and she was scared it was too late to fix things between them. "Umm … sure. Sunday's good."

"Right, take care of yourself."

Panic welled inside her chest. Chelsea didn't want the call to end. *Say something.* "Chaz? I'm so sorry for …"

Chaz interrupted her, "Chelsea, I can't talk now. Just wanted to check on your health."

Chelsea hesitated, feeling deflated. *He's pushing me away this time.*

"Bye," Chaz said. It was a short, curt end to the call.

Before she could reply, the dial tone echoed in her ear. She stared at the receiver, a wave of depression washed over her, mixed with anger. She slammed down the phone. *He did his duty and checked on us both; that lets his conscience off the hook.* Sage came to her and placed her head on her knee. Lost in thought, Chelsea absentmindedly stroked her head.

"You're so in tune with me, girl. I know *you* love me."

Unconditional love. It only exists with pets and souls. What does that mean—unconditional? No matter what someone does, even the bad stuff, you just accept it? Of course not. I know Chaz loves me, but not unconditionally. And that's how it should be, or we'd never grow or change. I think I can change. The question is—can I convince Chaz of that?

"Enough reflection. Come on, Sage, let's go home and have a nap."

Chelsea mused while walking home, realizing how much she'd missed the sound of Chaz's voice. Despite the awkwardness of their conversation, hearing his voice was comforting, even if what he had to say wasn't. She sighed. *That makes no sense.*

She opened the sliding door and let Sage run into the house first. "I need to make some changes in my life, girl, even if it's too late for me and Chaz."

❧ 20 ❧

The wind brought in the black clouds from the southwest, blocking the morning sun. The sky opened up and what started as a few drops of rain quickly became a downpour. Madie grabbed her cup from the table on the deck and went inside for a refill. Standing by the picture window, she stared out into the storm.

Distant thunderclaps were followed by lightning strikes that lit up the darkened sky. *I wonder if it had rained last night if I'd have experienced any nightmares. It hasn't rained in weeks since my past life regression session. Even expanding my search, I haven't found out anything more about Tara. I'm at a standstill.*

Madie focused on the farm fields across the road. *The farmers will be happy with the much-needed water.* At that moment, a strange thing happened. The fields began to fade; her body began vibrating, leaving her in a state of weightlessness. She sat down in the nearest chair, putting her cup down before she dropped it, her eyes riveted on the disappearing world outside the window.

JUNE 13, 1998, LATE SATURDAY AFTERNOON

The hot sun beat down on twenty-year-old Tara's head as she hurried out of the park to her car. *Why'd I forget my hat? Everything's gone wrong today. Now I'm late getting home to make dinner.*

She got into her car and headed out of town, passing the huge billboard advertising her husband's real estate firm. His name, Douglas Crawford in bold, black lettering sat underneath the smiling face that stared down at her. Her body twitched with nervousness. Her long, dark hair clung to her head and sweat dripped down her forehead.

Douglas expected dinner to be ready when he returned from work and, since to his mind, she did nothing all day, he felt it wasn't much to ask dinner be ready to serve the moment he walked in the door. *Why did I go to the park today? I knew I was running short of time.*

It was the music. The sound of classical music playing at the bandstand, serenading her as she'd placed her groceries in the car. She loved classical music. Douglas hated it. It had been so long since she'd heard music that soothed her soul, she'd found herself floating into the park, lost in its tempo. After the news she'd received today, she needed to chill and think things through.

She glanced at the car clock and sighed, running the list of fresh foods she'd bought through her mind. Okay, Caesar salad, pork chops, and leftover mashed potatoes in the fridge with mushroom sauce that could go into the microwave, pickles, and buns warmed in the oven. She nodded as she turned into the driveway. *You can do this.* As she turned past the grove of trees, her newfound sense of confidence left her. Douglas' car sat in the driveway. *Oh no. He's home early.*

She parked the car and hurriedly gathered up her bags. Racing into the house, she found him pouring himself a glass of water from the fridge.

"Hi, hon," she said, with a nervous smile. "You're home early. Dinner will be ready in twenty minutes."

"I don't smell anything cooking. Where have you been?"

"There was a fender-bender on the road. Held me up until the police arrived and cleared the vehicles." She could feel his eyes on her as she unpacked groceries and put them away. She prattled on, asking about his day while she tried to act normal.

Finally, he left the kitchen. "I'm going to shower."

Tara took a deep breath and rushed around the kitchen, prepping dinner. *Got away with that one. He's so unpredictable.* She'd married Douglas straight out of high school. He was six years older than her. A shy and sheltered girl, who'd fallen in love with love, her parents weren't happy about it, but couldn't stop her since she was of legal age. He was well off and provided for her but there was something about him they didn't like. In the year they'd been married, she learned he wasn't who she thought he was.

In the beginning, he'd been so charming and loving but it all changed once he'd put a ring on her finger. She'd learned to weigh his moods and avoid confrontation—most of the time. Sometimes, what she thought would set him off, made him laugh. And what she thought would make him laugh, had backfired into a verbal and, sometimes, physical confrontation where she was always the loser. Her parents lived an hour's drive away and over time he'd managed to cut her off from them and her old friends.

At first, she was quite happy to spend her time with him and leave her friends behind. She was a married woman now and had responsibilities, while her friends were going to clubs and still acting like high school kids. Madie decided they were immature. She missed her parents but didn't miss the disapproving looks they gave her husband. It was easier to follow Douglas' lead and make excuses when they wanted to make plans. Madie felt her place was to be at her husband's side and until her parents came to accept Douglas, she'd keep her distance. But she'd begun to question that decision lately.

Everything was ready, except the mashed potatoes. She opened the microwave to retrieve the potatoes just as he entered the kitchen.

"Leftovers? You know I hate leftovers."

"It's just the mashed potatoes, hon. What am I supposed to do with them? Throw them away? That's so wasteful."

She approached the table with the bowl and, noting the sneer on his face, dropped her eyes and placed the potatoes on the table. In an instant, he raised his hand and knocked the bowl flying off the table onto the floor. It smashed into pieces, scattering potatoes and shards of glass across the tiled floor.

"You want wasteful? That's wasteful."

Tara felt the old fear well up in her chest. Her body became taut and wary and she stood perfectly still, staring at the floor.

"If you knew how to cook for the two of us, there would *never* be any leftovers, unless it's roast beef or chicken that could be put into a casserole. Do I have to teach you everything?"

She bit her lip and said nothing, in the hopes his tantrum was over. Sometimes that worked—not today.

Douglas grabbed her arm. "I'm talking to you. Don't ignore me," he shouted in her face.

She recoiled. "You're hurting my arm." She tried to pull away but he tightened his grip, making her wince.

"You think that hurts? How about this?"

Before she knew what was happening, he backhanded her across the chin, which caused her to bite the inside of her lower lip. Her head snapped back when the blow landed, and she could taste blood in her mouth. This was the worst he'd ever hit her, and it shocked her. She moaned from the pain and managed to pull away from his grip and back away.

His face reddened and his eyes bulged with anger. He

reached out grabbed her by the hair. "You can't get away from me. It's over when *I* decide it's over."

She thought he was going to hit her again and braced herself. But he turned on his heel and walked out. "I'm going out for dinner, and when I return, this kitchen better be spotless."

Tara held a wet cloth to her swollen lip. She parted the drapes and watched his taillights disappear down the driveway. A storm was brewing outside, and she studied the sky. She wrapped her arms across her chest, running her hands up and down her chilled arms. *Isn't it ironic how the storm outside reflects the storm raging within these walls?*

Would he come home still upset or would it all be forgotten? She had no way of knowing. Tara knew she was afraid of her husband. He'd threatened to hurt anyone who helped her if she ever thought of leaving him—especially her parents. She couldn't go on like this, especially now that she was pregnant. That's why she'd gone to the park after seeing the doctor earlier in the day, to try and sort out her emotions. Under normal conditions, as a young couple, they should be celebrating the news tonight. Tara wanted this baby, but saw it as a trap, tying her to Douglas even more.

I hate this. I hate being complacent. I hate Douglas. And I hate myself for living in fear. Why did I stay so long?

She watched what had started as a sprinkling turn into a light rain, and progress into a pounding rainstorm that turned puddles to rivers running down the driveway. Drops of rain on the window pooled into rivulets, distorting her vision of the world beyond. *Isn't that what happened to my life?*

Her marriage had been romantic in the beginning—until his true nature surfaced. His loss of control led him to search out objects he threw around the room, such as couch pillows and magazines. Tara had thought it so childish at the time, until

his abhorrent behaviour progressed to deliberately

smashing things, especially possessions that were special to her, like a glass vase given to her by her Auntie Tess.

Oh, it wasn't worth much monetarily, but since her aunt had passed recently, it had special meaning to Tara—and Douglas knew that.

That look she'd come to recognize in his eyes before he'd lose himself to a violent tantrum had changed in recent months. She'd always backed away until he'd finished his rampage, but now that look was directed at her. Objects were no longer enough. But no more. The only one who could stop this was her.

It's time. She turned and ran up the stairs to the bedroom and pulled a suitcase from the bedroom closet. Tossing it on the bed, she emptied her dresser drawers into it. Turning back to the closet, she took a few of her favourite things. Most of her clothes had been picked out by Douglas and she hated them.

Pulling an overnight case from under the bed, she filled it with toiletries, jewellery, and personal pictures, then rushed about throwing a few more things into the two bags, anxious to get out of the house before he returned. Nothing else mattered. He could keep it all.

"Peace of mind and freedom—that's all I need." Excited to finally escape, she carried the bags downstairs to the hallway, grabbed a jacket from the closet and headed to the kitchen to get her car keys. The thought of calling her parents to tell them she was coming home was short-lived. There would be too much explaining to do, and she didn't want to waste any more time.

She took in the mess on the floor of potatoes and broken crockery, the cold bowls of food sitting on the table and dirty pots in the sink. She felt disgusted and defiantly shouted out, "Guess who gets to clean up this time, asshole!"

Self-absorbed as she was, she never heard the car pull in the driveway, never heard the key turn in the front door. She hurried to the hallway to grab her suitcases and stopped short. Her hands flew to her chest. With her heart pounding, she gasped for air.

He was standing in the open doorway, staring down at her bags. The next few moments passed as if in slow motion. Finally, he lifted his head and stared at her.

Tara watched his shocked expression fade, replaced with anger. She saw his neck turn red and the colour rising to his face until he spat, "Going somewhere?" His hand reached behind him and he slammed shut the door.

The loud bang of the door made her jump. "I—I can explain. My m-mom ... she's, y-yes," Tara stammered, as fear took hold.

"Your mom's *what?*"

"Sick ... she's sick. I need to go see her. I ... I was going to call you on the road." She gestured feebly at him. "But here you are." Tara tried to distract him. "Why'd you come back?"

"Because I forgot my wallet. Good thing I did." He was studying her face intently.

"Oh. So ... umm, I need to go."

Douglas frowned at her. "You're lying to me."

Tara tried to sound strong, licked her swollen lip and swallowed her fear along with the blood still trickling from the split in her mouth. Staying was no longer an option and, somehow, she had to get past him and out the door. "No, I'm not. And I'm leaving."

Douglas walked towards her. "You're not going anywhere."

Tara backed away.

Douglas lunged and caught her by the arm. "You were leaving me. I know it. Well, that's not going to happen—ever." He twisted her arm and backed her into the kitchen.

Slipping into her old habits to protect herself, Tara knew better than to challenge him. She fell silent and let him lead her across the floor. She knew she couldn't get away from him

—not tonight. She was scared of what might happen next, but she tried to pull herself together. Stay calm. She'd have to be strong and wait for another opportunity. But she knew, one way or another, she was leaving.

Douglas pushed her down onto a chair and towered over her. "We talked last month about you visiting your family. I said it wasn't the time. So, you were going to sneak out and go anyway?" His eyes took in the messy kitchen. "And you left me to clean up this mess you created? And what about tomorrow night's dinner with the Bakers? Huh?" He slapped her hard across the face, drawing blood from her nose. "You're so selfish. Thinking only of yourself."

Tears welled in her eyes. Tara stared down at the floor, her hand wiping the blood from her face.

"Look at me when I'm talking to you," he shouted.

She looked up at him, trying not to show the hatred she felt.

"Bitch!" Douglas back-handed her on the left cheek so hard, she flew off the chair, landing on the floor.

Tara curled into a fetal ball, wrapping her arms around her head as she sobbed. He sat down at the table and stared down at her with a look of contempt. For several minutes, they both remained silent.

Maybe it's over for now, she thought. She pulled herself up slowly, gauging her body aches, and leaned against the cupboard. "I'm sorry, I was just lonely for my family. I wanted to see my mom," she said in a whisper.

He pulled his car keys out of his pocket and played with them. He'd calmed down and spoke in a quiet voice. "You've ruined my night. What's wrong with you? Why do you always push me to the point of losing my temper?"

Anger welled inside her, but she dared not show it. *Of course, it's always my fault. Tara felt her face.* She could feel the swelling, open skin where his signet ring had cut through, and blood dripping off her chin. It hurt like hell and she winced, certain he'd broken her cheekbone.

Douglas sighed. "Tomorrow night is out too. We can't go to the Bakers' with you looking like that. Why do you always try me?"

"I need to pee. Can I go to the bathroom?"

He stared hard at her. "Where are your car keys?"

"In my jacket pocket."

"Give them to me and take your jacket off, along with your shoes."

Tara stood and did as he asked. He placed her keys into his pocket with his own set. "Go."

THE POUNDING of her heart filled her ears. Madie sat still, waiting for her senses to return. Her eyes cleared and the farmers' fields, in all their glory, were back in her line of sight. *What just happened? This wasn't a nightmare, nor is it nighttime.* It took a few minutes for her to feel grounded. Overwhelmed with fear and excitement, she searched for her cell phone, punched Cody's number and when he picked up, without so much as a hello, she sputtered, "Holy Shit, Cody. You're not going to believe this. I just experienced Tara's life in a vision, and I saw a huge billboard with his face on it. He's a realtor and his name is Douglas Crawford."

🌿 21 🌿

Madie ran to the door, flung it open, and pulled Cody by the arm into the cabin. "I think I found something." She bounced up and down on the balls of her feet, bubbling with excitement.

"Already? That was quick."

"I couldn't wait for you to get here so I Google-searched her name. Nothing. Then I typed in Douglas Crawford, Lawyer. I was about to check out the site when you arrived. Come and see."

She pulled another chair beside hers and pointed to the laptop screen. "Look. Douglas Crawford: Owner, Carson & Crawford Realty Inc., Osoyoos, BC."

Cody clicked the mouse on the *About Us* page. The first name that came up was Eric Carson with a photo and bio; scrolling down, up shot Douglas Crawford.

Madie groaned and her hands flew to her face. "Omigod … that's him," she croaked. She was staring into the face of a man about fifty, with greying dark hair. His dark eyes drew her in and made her shudder. Her body began to shake. "Twenty-something years older, but it's him; I know it. I *feel* it."

Cody slipped an arm around her shoulders. "You okay?"

146

She nodded. "Yeah! It hit me how close he is to us. Just down the road in the next town."

"It says the company has been in business since 1990," Cody said.

A residential name search in the Osoyoos area by Cody proved fruitless.

"All it means is he's either got an unlisted phone number or only uses his cell phone. What's next?" Madie asked.

"Hmm ... you couldn't find Tara Crawford. Let's try this." He typed, "Wife of Douglas Crawford, Osoyoos Realtor missing."

They watched in silence while Google brought up possible answers. The first item to pop on the screen stunned them both. They stared at each other, speechless for several seconds.

Cody pushed the mouse to her. "You should have the honours."

Madie clicked on the heading and held her breath while it loaded. The first thing that caught her attention was the picture of a dark-haired young woman: her woman, Tara.

Madie's throat constricted and she shivered. "It's her. We've found her," she whispered.

Cody read the Missing Person Bulletin aloud. "Osoyoos RCMP are seeking the public's help in locating the missing wife of Douglas Crawford, an Osoyoos resident. Scarlett Rose Crawford was reported missing on June 17th, 1998. She was last seen at home on the morning of June 14th, 1998 by her husband. Miss Crawford supposedly left that day to visit her parents in Cherryville but never arrived.

"Crawford is described as: Caucasian female, 20 years old, 5 ft 4 in (162 cm), 115 lbs (54.43 kg), brown hair, brown eyes. She is believed to have been wearing tan slacks and a white t-shirt, and a black jean jacket. She was driving a silver 1996 Jeep Cherokee; licence plate number: 768 TDT. If you have information related to Crawford's disappearance or have any information that could assist the investigation, you are asked to contact the Osoyoos RCMP at 613-555-0134."

Madie sat back in her chair in a daze. "Scarlett? So where did Tara come from? She's a real person, Cody. And I was her."

"It has to be a strange feeling, knowing you didn't imagine her."

The nausea settled down but Madie certainly didn't feel normal. "It's like I'm on the outside of my body looking in—only looking inside Tara."

Cody typed the name Scarlett Rose Crawford. There were newspaper reports of her being missing, quoting the RCMP bulletin. He sifted through and found a news clipping.

Osoyoos RCMP has called off the search for missing person, Scarlett Rose Crawford, a resident of Osoyoos who went missing last June. Her car was found in Rock Creek. Her black jean jacket and suitcases were found in the car. The RCMP believes foul play is involved and the case is ongoing.

If you have information related to Crawford's disappearance or have any information that could assist the investigation, you are asked to contact the Penticton RCMP at 613-555-0090.

CODY SEARCHED the web for Douglas Crawford in Osoyoos, to no avail. There was an article about him donating funds to upgrade the Osoyoos Fire Hall last year. "Look at this. They called him an outstanding citizen and named him Citizen of the Year. What a joke."

"He's a murderer. At least we know he's still a resident. We have to go and find out where his house is," Madie declared.

"And then what? We can't prove anything and if he connects us to Tara, we'll be in danger."

Madie sighed. "I don't know, but at least we'll know where to find him." She jumped up. "You up for it? Let's go." She ran for her shoes and cell phone.

"A little Saturday afternoon adventure, chasing a killer? Can't think of a better thing to do today."

Inside of thirty minutes, they found themselves standing on the street in front of the real estate offices of Douglas Crawford. They peeked in the windows and saw a couple of real estate agents, but neither was Crawford.

Madie turned to Cody. "So, short of walking the streets and searching out stores in the chance we see him, what do we do now?"

Cody turned full circle, taking in the surrounding buildings. "This whole block is comprised of commercial businesses. Look over there." He pointed to a courtyard across the street. "There's a coffee shop. How much you want to bet, they all frequent it during their workday and know each other? You ready for lunch?"

"Good thinking, lion tamer."

The cafe was busy with lunch patrons. They found an empty booth by the window where they could see Crawford's business. The decor was a mix of old wood walls, floor and ceiling, a wooden bar for take-out service, plenty of plants, but modern display coolers, and barista coffee machines on the bar top. An opening in the wall behind the bar exposed a modern stainless-steel kitchen, with busy staff hustling up orders.

Their server was really friendly and talkative, which made it easy for Cody to chat with her. During the meal, he noted that not knowing the area, they were lucky to have found a place with such great food. This, in turn, led the waitress to ask what brought them to their town.

"Actually, I'm trying to hook up with a distant relative. I'm from back east and haven't connected with him in years. His home address isn't listed on the web, probably for privacy reasons. He's a realtor."

The waitress' blue eyes opened wide and she tossed her blond ponytail back over her shoulder. "What's his name?"

"Douglas—Douglas Crawford."

"Well, didn't you come to the right place?" she chortled. "His real estate business is right across the street." She pointed out the window. "Right over there? Did you know that?"

Madie took in a wink from Cody, along with a raise of his eyebrows as he followed her finger in mock surprise. "What? You're kidding, right? What are the odds of that?"

"Well, we're still a small town after all, but, luckily, you chose this place to eat at. Too bad it's Saturday; he works from home on the weekends. On weekdays, he comes in at three pm every day for coffee and a treat. But I can tell you where he lives: north of town on the Crowsnest Highway. A couple of kilometres down on the left, there's a dirt road that leads into a canyon. I can't remember the name of it but it dead-ends at a grassland's protection area. There are only about half a dozen acreages out that way; I'm sure one of them will know which one's his."

"Thanks so much. I'm grateful."

After the waitress left, Madie leaned towards Cody, speaking in a soft tone, and smiled. "Hmm … I'm not sure if I should trust you anymore. You make such a good liar."

"I'd prefer to say I'm a great actor—Oscar material. Hand me my award and let's finish up and get out of here."

They knew the Crowsnest Highway, having driven it many times. Madie watched for the dirt road and when it came up, pointed it out. "There it is."

Cody made the turn and followed the road. It was a well-groomed road that led them past acreages.

"Let's do a run through the canyon and scope out the properties," Madie suggested. Good bumps rose on her arms and she rubbed her hands over them. A familiar feeling passed over her. "I know this road—not as Madie, as Tara."

Ten minutes later, they had passed most of the properties; the ones on the passenger side had homes visible to the road. A couple on the driver's side weren't visible but Madie could see a long ravine behind them on the flats. "She lived on my side of the road—I know it."

They approached the last driveway on the right.

Madie shouted, "Stop!"

Cody pulled over to the side of the road and she pointed to the one on the right. "This one. This is it."

He looked at her quizzically. "How do you know?"

"I have no idea—I just do. The house is back there—hidden." She glanced past Cody at the other side of the road. "That side, the property drops off back there. See the ravine? Same for all the houses on the left. Now, look on my side. The grasslands stretch for a few miles to those hills."

Madie shivered and reached out to grab Cody's arm: her fingernails digging into his skin.

He winced and closed his hand over hers. "What is it? What's wrong?"

Her eyes never left the flats and when she spoke, Cody had to lean close to hear the faint whisper of her words.

"That's where she is." She pointed with shaking fingers. "Tara's somewhere in those hills."

22

Lark sparrows sang their complicated song,: a melodious jumble of clear notes and trills interspersed with harsh buzzes and churrs. Earlier that day, a summer storm passed through and now there was no sign of it.

Chelsea leaned back in the lounger, closed her eyes, and lifted her face to the hot, late-afternoon August sun. Soft snores made her smile and she opened one eye to observe her dog. Sage was sleeping on her back between Chelsea's legs.

Eyes shut again, she sighed and settled back in the chair. It was Saturday and day five since her race to the hospital. At just over six months pregnant, she knew she was in for the long haul over the next couple of months until her scheduled delivery date. Chaz and Jax were due home today and tomorrow; she'd see Chaz for the first time in a month.

A part of her was excited to see him and finish the conversation she'd started on Wednesday on the phone. *But he cut me off in the middle of an apology. Is that because I hurt him so badly, he won't talk to me? He knew what he wanted, and I cut him off at the knees.* Chelsea took a deep breath. With no idea, what they would say to each other, she knew it was a hurdle they had to cross—for the sake of their baby. *How do I explain my feelings when I'm just beginning to understand them myself?*

Sage shifted position, her soft fur tickling her bare legs, and Chelsea felt her tail whop back and forth across her shins. She opened her eyes to see Jordy crossing the yard.

"Hi, Chelsea, how're you feeling?" he asked. When he reached the deck, he sat down on the edge of it and leaned back against a post.

"Hi, Jordy, all good. Whatcha up to?"

"Wenner's in the shower. When he's ready, we're going out to dinner in town to celebrate six weeks together."

Chelsea smiled. "Six weeks, eh? Congrats."

Jordy chuckled. "I know it's not very long, but Wenner's a romantic—and I think I'm becoming one too."

"He's reached a new level of happy and I guess we can thank you for that."

"It works both ways, believe me."

Chelsea studied him for a long moment. "You know, it took him a long time to get over Brian's death. And when we discovered it wasn't an accident and Brian was murdered, his depression returned. Reuniting with family and building the rehab centre brought him back. I know he's a big boy and understands your commitment to your work, but one day, it'll take you away from him. Please, always be honest with him—don't hurt him—if you do, you're going to have to deal with me."

Jordy nodded and gave her a tiny smile. "Point taken. Believe me, I have the utmost respect for him. I've never met anyone quite like Wenner and the last thing I want to do is hurt him."

"Sorry, he's not just a business partner, but a best friend." She shrugged. "I'm a little hormonal these days—probably the last person who should be giving a warning."

Jordy bent forward. "For the record, I've given some thought to retiring as a freelance journalist. Different time zones, different weather seasons. I'm not enjoying living out of a backpack like I used to."

"Really? What would you do if you settled down in one place?"

"Well, I'm mulling over an offer from an old college friend. He's a publisher." Jordy stretched his legs out on the deck, crossing them at the ankles.

"Interesting."

"Over the years, I've amassed a large collection of photos and written diaries of important world events that never made it into my assignments. My friend Paul believes a series of books based on what he calls my 'journalistic treasures' would sell."

"Sounds promising."

Jordy shrugged and grinned. "All I'd need is a desk and a computer."

Chelsea studied him for a moment. "Do you think you could make the transition from travelling the world to sitting at a desk?"

"It's a big decision, for sure. If you'd asked me that question two years ago—never. But now it has a certain appeal. My article at the Centre here is my last contracted commitment. There've been other calls, but I put their offers on hold for now."

Chelsea nodded. "I get that."

"I'll decide in the fall when I'm done with this story."

"So, Jordy, where was home before you landed here?"

"Toronto, born and raised. When I go home, it's to a condo I bought many moons ago. My folks live in the 1000 Islands area near Lake Ontario. They retired to their summer cottage, where we spent holidays when I was a kid." A wide grin spread across his face. "Lots of great memories of summers spent on the river."

The honk of a car horn caught their attention. Wenner drove into her driveway and rolled down the window. "Hey you, mind if I steal that handsome devil? We have an important dinner to attend to."

Chelsea waved. "He's all yours, my friend. Enjoy and stay out late for once."

Jordy stood and put his palms together, nodded to her and said, "It's been a pleasure." He gave her a wink and bounded over to the car.

After they left, Chelsea watched Sage snoop around the yard. He chased a squirrel up a tree and began digging a hole in last year's vegetable garden. *Oh, well, no home-grown vegies for me this year.* The summer heat was becoming unbearable and Chelsea stood to go back in the house. *Time for a lay down anyway.*

Sage stopped digging to watch her. In an instant, she felt that familiar flow of wetness; this time followed by sharp pains in her abdomen. She cried out, "No, no," and attempted to walk to the doorway. But a uterine contraction doubled her over in pain.

She dropped to her knees and sat on the deck, grasping the chaise lounge as Sage came bounding beside her, licking her face and whimpering. "Oh, Sage, I'm in trouble."

Why now? My cell's in the house on the charger and I'm afraid to move.

Another pain took hold and she laid her face on the lounger cushion. There was no one at the Centre and she heard a mower running at Sydney's. *No sense yelling, no one would hear me anyway. Maybe I could crawl into the house to the phone.*

Chelsea tried to push herself away from the chair but didn't have the strength. She saw blood seeping through her beige shorts. "Sage, you must go for help." She raised her arm and pointed to Sydney's house. "Go get Sydney, girl. Go." The dog stared at her, looked towards her daughter's farm and took off barking all the way and running full speed. Even after she disappeared over the hill towards the magnolia grove, Chelsea could hear her continuous bellowing.

She clung to the chair as another wave coursed through her. The sound of the mower stopped and there was silence. Suddenly, Sage appeared at the top of the hill, turned towards Sydney's farm, and barked again. A moment later, a figure appeared beside the dog and the two of them ran side by side down the hill towards her. Once they reached the deck, Chelsea managed to focus long enough to recognize him.

"Jax? You're home," she whispered, before losing consciousness.

❧ 23 ❧

Lost in their thoughts, Madie and Cody stared at the distant hills in silence for several moments.

"So, now what?" he asked.

Madie turned to him. "Let's drive down the driveway. I want to see the house."

Cody's eyebrows shot up. "What if he's home? He'll want to know what we want."

Her brow furrowed as she thought about it. "We'll lie. Make up a story we're looking for someone and must have the wrong address."

He looked dubious, but she was insistent. "I have to see the house, Cody." She squeezed his arm and threw him a sly smile. "Show me your acting chops again. Please, just drive."

He took a deep breath. "Okay, but we stick to that story and get the hell out of there." He turned right onto the long, dirt driveway and slowly drove on.

Madie took in the scotch pines and white spruce groves ahead. "All the houses have tree breaks for protection from the strong winds that blow across the flats, but the houses are still visible. This one is thick with windbreaks, maybe deliberately to hide the house from view?"

"Definitely hidden," Cody agreed.

A strange awareness passed through her mind. Her heart raced and she could feel her blood pounding in her ears. "A little déjà vu is happening here. We should be rounding a curve to the right just past those scotch pines up ahead, back to the left again, opening up in front of the house—a white house with white columns on the deck."

Cody glanced at her red face. "You okay?" He reached the first turn and manoeuvred the vehicle along the narrow path.

"Yes, it's all a little surreal …"

Her voice trailed off as they followed the last bend and the driveway opened to a white rancher sprawling before them. Cody stopped behind a black pick-up parked in the circular driveway. Madie stared ahead at the familiar structure as every nerve in her body tingled. "It's the house in my vision. Tara lived here," she whispered. In a trancelike state, she opened the car door, stepped out, and walked towards the dwelling

Cody jumped out of the vehicle and stood by the door. "Madie, wait."

At that moment, a blood-red Jeep pulled in behind them and a man with a much younger woman got out. A tall man about fifty years of age, with greying dark hair, and piercing blue eyes walked up to Cody while the woman held back. "Can I help you?"

Madie turned and stared at the man. "Uhh." Her hands flew to her face and she froze in place.

Time had moved forward, Madie knew, but the older man she saw before her morphed back to the Douglas she'd been married to in a past life. The scene before her faded, replaced by one she'd experienced all those years ago as Tara …

Tara lay on her back in the desert, rain pelting her face. She gasped for air, having hit the ground hard when he pulled her backwards. A series of lightning bolts exploded around them and she stared up at his blue-jeaned legs and saw his new black and white Nike Air Max runners as he straddled her. He bent over and his hands closed around her neck, squeezing hard as he spewed words of hate at her. Tara fought back and struggled to breathe. As hard as she tried to push him off, his weight held her to the ground, her heartbeat pounded in her ears, and her lungs ached for air. Tara knew she wasn't just losing the battle; she was losing her life. The last thing she saw was the wild rage in his bulging eyes; his face contorted like a grotesque Halloween mask.

CODY STOLE A GLANCE AT MADIE, who seemed rooted to the spot, her hands at her throat. He smiled at the man, trying to think up a good story. "We're from out of town. I thought this was the Sanders' home."

"Don't know them. You've got the wrong place." Douglas looked at Madie and frowned. "What's wrong with her?"

Cody focused on Madie's blanched face, which was in large contrast to the bright pink he'd seen moments before. Her hands pulled at her neck and she began to cough and gasp. *Oh, shit!* He rushed over, put his arm around her waist, and walked her back to the car while his mind raced to think up a response.

"Umm ... too many hours on the road. She suffers from car sickness." He turned to Madie. "You're not going to throw up, are you?"

She shook her head.

"Let me help you into the car."

She didn't move. Cody followed her stare to the younger woman as if Madie were seeing her for the first time. She looked over at Douglas and back to the woman, and spat out, "Omigod!"

Cody leaned in close and whispered, "Madie, get in the car, *now.*"

For once, she listened to him and he slammed shut the

door, hurrying around to his side, where he flashed a smile at Douglas, "Sorry, man. We'll get out of your hair."

Douglas stared at him blankly. "Hope you find your people."

Cody drove around the circular driveway and glanced in the rear-view mirror as they passed Crawford's parked car to see him and the young woman staring after them; he shook his head in disdain while she looked wide-eyed and confused.

"What happened to you back there?" he asked.

Madie ignored his question. "Did you see her, Cody? She's pregnant."

He hit the road, turned left, and drove towards the highway. "I saw. You okay?"

"Yeah. I knew it was him right away. Then, a vision took me back to that night he chased her through the desert." Madie gulped. "Where he strangled her. All the nightmares, and the vision I had earlier today, came together in those few minutes. He murdered her because she was leaving him, going back to her family." She stared past him, over the flats to the hills beyond. "And she lies somewhere up there."

Cody pulled over before they turned onto the highway and faced Madie. He took her hand in his. "At least your colour is back. You were as white as a ghost."

"I feel better now. Sorry I left you on your own back there."

"Understandable. He suddenly became real to you and, throwing a vision into the mix, no wonder." Cody thought about the whole situation with trepidation. "Look, Madie. We've reached dangerous ground now. At this point, this Crawford guy doesn't know what we know, and we can't let him find out either. Maybe we should go to the police and tell them the whole story; let them handle it from now on."

"We could. But if they didn't arrest him twenty-three years ago, they have nothing to prove his guilt. They'll think, along comes this young girl who wasn't even born the night Tara died, with a cockamamie story of reincarnation and visions. It's not enough for them to go digging around the desert for a body."

"You're right. It won't be enough."

"At the very least, it's not enough for them to re-open her case. I can't stop here; we have to find her body."

Cody turned and his eyes searched the hills. "No small feat there. Do you know how big an expanse those hills cover?"

"Near impossible, like a needle in a haystack."

He had an uneasy feeling about this newest development. He swivelled back to Madie, reaching out to stroke her hair. "Promise me one thing? You won't do anything more about this without me by your side? Remember what your grandmother told Grams. There's a danger with this knowledge."

Madie studied him for a moment. "Okay, I promise."

"Good." Cody looked past her at a brightening sky as the sun appeared from behind the fast-disappearing clouds. "Let's head home and do something ordinary."

"Good idea. I need to put some miles between us and this place and do something to take my mind off of all of this Tara business."

Cody gave her a sample of his crooked smile, along with a mischievous glint in his eyes. He pulled her close and brushed his lips against hers. "I can think of something we could do that would definitely take you away from all of this."

Teasing, Madie feigned surprise. "You mention doing something ordinary and bring up sex? Is that what you think of our intimacy: ordinary?"

"No connection whatsoever," he whispered throatily.

Madie licked her full lips and pulled them into a pout. She moved closer and kissed him with a light touch, running her tongue over his lips.

Cody felt a stirring between his legs and leaned into the kiss, but Madie pulled back.

"Nuh-uh! Drive on home, lion tamer. We have the rest of the day and night to turn ordinary into something magical."

❧ 24 ❧

Chelsea stared through the open-screened window of her bedroom, watching the Western Kingbirds with their lemon-yellow bellies, grey heads and backs, and black tails, hawking for insects. The flycatchers were prolific this season, returning from their winter migration in Mexico to their summer home here in Canada's arid desert. *Won't be long before they head south again.*

Propped up in bed, a loud sigh escaped through her lips as she thought about her present plight. It was Sunday noon, the day after Jax had found her on the deck. An ambulance had once again taken her to the hospital, where Dr Carson assured her the baby was fine. *That* was the good news. The final diagnosis: if Chelsea wanted to keep this baby until her scheduled delivery date, she'd have to stay in bed permanently.

So, here I am, home again and confined to my bedroom.

She appreciated the silence—a sharp contrast to the hospital emergency room. This was the first moment of peace she'd had since yesterday's ordeal and she needed to focus on how being "bedridden" would affect the functioning of the world around her for the next few months. She glanced around the room of greens, creams, and beiges, a fig tree in the corner by the window, a rust La-Z-Boy in the corner. Flowers from well-wishers lined the dresser and the small table beside the armchair, adding a sweet fragrance to the room. *At least it's a comfortable, soothing room, if it's to be my life for a while.*

She absentmindedly rubbed Sage's ears, who was curled up on the bed beside her. Soft whimpers drew her attention to the sleeping dog and Chelsea watched as Sage's body twitched. *Dreaming, girl? Hope they're happy ones.*

Sage had her own bed to sleep in, but the dog had more than earned this spot on the bed after her heroics of the evening before. In the days to come, the golden retriever would be her companion and, during the day, Chelsea decided joining her on the bed would be okay. She picked up a long beige dog hair from the olive-green comforter with its beige-and-rust pattern and smiled. At least your hair blends in with the colour scheme. Chelsea dropped the hair into a wastebasket beside the bed and returned her gaze to the window and the flycatchers still feeding.

Deep in her soul, a feeling of defeat overwhelmed her. She felt a weight in the pit of her stomach, thinking about the Centre. She was leaving them in the lurch, in the middle of hiring and training a new employee. She had no idea how to make it all work from the confines of her bed. Remembering the looks of concern from Sydney, Jax and her mother at the hospital, she felt a wave of guilt engulf her. She realized the burden they were once again carrying over her safety.

Sydney was in the kitchen making lunch. Voices could be heard from somewhere in the house, telling her she had company. The mixed chatter grew closer to her room, drawing her attention from the window to the doorway.

Sydney appeared. "Can we come in?"

"Of course," she answered, her eyebrows shooting up as a delegation of family members and friends poured into her room.

Sydney, Jax, her mom and her husband, Gord, Wenner,

Madie and Cody formed a ring around her bed, all smiling, and addressing her in unison. "Hi, Chelsea."

She glanced around the semi-circle. "Wow, what's this? An intervention?"

Sydney giggled. "Of sorts. We held a family meeting this morning because we know how hard the next few months are going to be for you and we want to make it as easy as possible. We know you can't be living here alone, being confined to bed, so we were trying to decide if you could move in with me or Nan—"

"Or me," Wenner interjected.

Chelsea leaned forward and talked over them both. "No way. Leaving my home isn't an option."

Sydney threw up her hands. "Mom, please let me finish. We already concluded that your independent streak would win out on that one. So, we need to put a plan in place. None of us wants you to ever be alone. Thank God for Sage. God knows what would have happened if you'd been left here, collapsed on the deck for any length of time."

Chelsea settled back against the headboard. "Okay, shoot."

"First off, Bea will be sleeping here overnight, Monday to Thursday, in the guest bedroom. She'll make your breakfast in the morning before she comes over to our house. Lunches and dinners for you will be made with ours. One of us will bring it over to you. Nan will be here in the mornings to keep you company and do laundry, etc. Social services are sending a nurse every afternoon to monitor you and the baby, and help you shower. Nan will go home when she arrives. Between me and my girls, Wenner, and all the rest, someone will be here until Bea comes back for the night after dinner. That takes us to Friday afternoon. Bea will go home after lunch for the weekend and come back Monday morning to make your breakfast and start all over again. You with us so far?"

"There's more?" she asked, surprised.

"Jax and his work crew will maintain your yard work and all of us, at some point, will go into town to shop ... so, keep a list on the night table and we'll check if you need something. That leaves weekends. We haven't worked it all out as yet, but we've got all week to figure it out."

"Don't forget me and Cody," Madie piped in.

"And me," Jordy stepped into the room and stood behind Wenner.

Chelsea looked around the room at each of them, feeling overwhelmed by their support. A lump formed in her throat. "I hate that I've become such a burden, but I know there's no way I could handle this alone."

Elizabeth stepped closer. "That's what family and friends are for—to step up and help a loved one when they need it most. That's not a burden; it's called love."

Chelsea felt her eyes moisten but she kept her emotions in place. "Thank you, everyone. You've made me feel a lot better about all this."

"All you have to do is lay back and enjoy a life of leisure. We'll do the rest," Wenner said.

Another voice projected into the room, "I'm available weekends."

The group turned to the door and parted away from the bottom of the bed to reveal Chaz, leaning against the jamb. "If I'm needed, I'll be here."

Suddenly, everyone else in the room faded away and all she saw was Chaz, with his handsome face full of concern, a question in his probing gaze as to whether he had a right to be here.

Her heart melted. She wiggled over closer to the middle of the bed and Sage and patted the spot beside her. "Come, sit."

Chaz strode over to the bed and sat where she'd indicated.

Chelsea glanced up at the group, who was staring at them in stationery silence, like they were afraid to move in case the spell would break. She caught Sydney's eyes, who snapped to attention. "Okay everyone, lunch is ready. Why don't we all head to the kitchen? Chaz, you can get a plate for you and Mom when you're ready."

They filed out of the room, leaving them alone.

"Thanks for coming, Chaz."

"I'm glad you're both okay. You've had a scary week, but I think everything's going to be okay now."

Chelsea placed her hands on her abdomen and smiled down. "She's a tough one. I'll do whatever I have to, to keep her safe."

"I know you will. But you won't be doing it alone. We'll all be here for you."

"I'm grateful for everyone. But I don't want to overtax Wenner, Cody, or Madie. They're going to have their hands full running the Centre during our busy season."

"I get that. I want to help, that's why I'm here. I can get the baby stuff you want, or you can order online. On weekends, I can turn the spare room into a nursery …"

Chelsea cut him short. "Wait."

His face fell. "Or not."

"Before we get to that, we need to talk about the day you took me to the doctor."

"Look, the important thing is seeing you through this pregnancy and bringing our daughter into the world. The rest doesn't matter right now."

"Yes, it does. We can't ignore it, especially if you're planning to be here on weekends. I hurt you, Chaz—deeply. Everything happened so fast and I panicked—I'm so sorry."

Chaz took her hand in his, rubbing her fingers. "I know you are. I also know you have to be you. We're going to be co-parents and if we want our baby to feel wanted and secure, we're going to have to be friends too. So, I suggest that I stay on weekends—in the guestroom, work on the nursery, and help you enjoy this pregnancy as best you can. And it won't hurt that I'm a good cook. No pressure, no complications …

just friends. Now, why don't I go get us some lunch?" He stood and headed to the door.

Chelsea sighed. "You're a good man. I don't deserve you."

Before he disappeared down the hall, Chaz stopped, turned around, and leaned back through the doorway. With strong conviction in his voice, he said, "If you hang on to garbage, you'll end up living in a dump. You deserve better, Chelsea. That's all I want for you: something better."

MADIE WATCHED Wenner sort through the resumes of the people they'd interviewed the past couple of days for the Finance Position. He picked up one and shook it.

"This one—I thnk she's perfect. She has experience, only looking for part-time, and she's available to start immediately. Whatcha think?"

She took the resume from his hand. *Patricia Wallace—I knew he'd pick her.* Madie couldn't argue with his logic about her credentials. *But still...*

"Everything about her seems right..." Madie hesitated, "...on paper."

"On paper?" Wenner looked at his watch and frowned. "Don't you think we could use her expertise? And she can start tomorrow. Losing Chelsea so quickly, Patricia would make the transition a lot easier for us—mostly for you in your new position." He glanced at his watch again.

Madie knew he was due for surgery and Cody was waiting for him, not to mention the poor critter who'd been brought to the Centre a short time ago in pain and needing help. She couldn't put her finger on it. Call it a feeling, but Madie had reservations about the woman's demeanor and her ability to work with her. But Wenner was waiting to leave and wanted a decision from her right now. It was understandable, it was a busy time for them.

"I can't deny her qualifications and how it would quickly solve our problem…" Madie began.

Wenner stood, "Good, glad that's resolved. What a relief. I'll let you handle the rest. I'm off to surgery. " With that said, he turned and hurried out of her office, leaving Madie staring after him.

She was stupefied he hadn't at least let her voice her concerns—and angry he'd made the decision for her. *Aren't I in charge of admin?* Madie understood his desire to get the problem behind them, but how could she accuse him of over-stepping her position when he was an owner and technically her boss? *If I wait until later and call another meeting about this, he'll probably be angry with me and it'll look like I'm questioning his judge-ment. Do I really want to have an argument with my boss during the first week of my new position?*

Madie picked up the resume and reread it. There was no arguing the woman's capabilitiy or experience. *Still.* She let out a sigh.

"Okay, Patricia Wallace, I guess you're it—our new Finance Clerk.

❧ 25 ❧

THREE WEEKS LATER ...

M adie stretched out in the chair on the deck of Cody's cottage, watching the easy flow of the river before her. She slipped her hand to the back of her neck and massaged the taut muscles down to the top of her spine.

Cody joined her with a couple of Okanagan Lights. He handed her one of the bottles. "Here."

"Thanks." Madie took a couple of swigs. She bent her head from side to side, cracking the bones to release the pressure.

Cody put his beer down and stood behind her. "Sit up, I'll rub your shoulders." After following his instructions, he kneaded her tight muscles. "Whoa, knots. What's got you so tense?"

"Mmm," she murmured, eyes closed. "Ask again when you're done."

He continued manipulating her shoulders and neck until she felt relaxed and put a hand up over one of his. "Thank you, that feels so much better."

Cody sat on the railing and took a long drag of his beer. "So, what's up?"

She gave him a long stare and shrugged. "I don't know."

"Sure you do. Talk to me. Is it Tara Crawford?"

Madie wrinkled her nose. "Well, certainly I'm frustrated on that front. I was talking to my Mom this morning about having found out who she is. She thinks I should leave well enough alone—I think I freaked her out a little by putting a name and face to my nightmares.

As for Tara, I just don't know where to go next with her. I mean, when she disappeared, the cops would have checked out her husband as a possible suspect. They never found any evidence to charge him—and never found her. Without a body or new evidence, they probably wouldn't re-open the case."

"Probably not. The past few weeks, we've studied topographical maps, and the area is too vast for us to search. It could take years to find a gravesite in those hills—if ever."

Madie watched the nighthawks' aerial acrobatics as they fed on the insects flying above the river. "I don't think he'd have taken her into the hills. She's probably somewhere on the fringes. But I agree with you about searching. And after all these years, the terrain could be totally different."

Cody nodded. "Perhaps we should take a break."

"I was thinking I could go back to Sasha and have another session. We might learn something helpful. But, in all honesty, with everything that's happening at work, I agree we should step back and revisit Tara later."

He sat in the chair beside her and placed his feet on the railing. "Is there a problem at work? Why haven't you talked to me about it?"

"Because I need to work this out on my own." She paused and scanned the river. "And ... because we work together, we need some distance."

Cody looked pensive and took another swig of beer.

Finally, he turned to her. "You know you can trust me. The fact we work together and sleep together needn't be compli-cated. Anything we talk about concerning the Centre stays between us."

Madie smiled, reached for his hand, and squeezed it. "Of course. When I used the word distance, I meant our personal life should be free of shoptalk and we should cherish our time away from the Centre."

He relaxed. "Gotcha. But it's different if you're upset about something. Are you finding the extra workload too much?"

"Not at all. I thrive on being busy and working at a fast pace."

"Then shoot, out with it."

Madie picked at the label on her bottle of beer and spat out a name. "Patricia."

"The new finance woman?"

"Yup. I wasn't sold on her when Wenner and I interviewed the applicants. I tried to voice my concerns but Wenner was happy with her because she was well-qualified. He hates the finance side of the business and figured she'd do a good job, making things easier for me. Being new to my position, I didn't want to push my concerns on Wenner and decided to give her a chance."

Cody smirked with that tell-tale glint in his eye. "Like you did me, when I was interviewed?"

Madie laughed and smacked him on the arm. "Yeah, like that."

"What were your concerns?"

"To Wenner's point, she only wanted part-time and knew her stuff. But she retired from a large corporation as their Financial Officer and I thought she was *over*-qualified. She's also old enough to be my grandmother and I couldn't see her being happy with me as her boss."

Cody nodded. "And she's proving you right."

"That's putting it mildly. She dresses so formally just like a corporate employee, and frowns on how I dress for work ... she doesn't get that we *all* dress casually because sometimes we have to multi-task and help with the animals. I like how casual the Centre is; it doesn't mean we aren't doing our jobs."

"Have you tried explaining it to her?"

"Oh ya! But Patricia said because I'm the head of Admin, I should dress accordingly you see, and keep work clothes in my office. If I'm needed for the animals, I can change."

Cody snorted and choked on his beer, splattering liquid down his shirt. "When Wenner calls Admin for help, it's usually an emergency. He *can't* wait for you to change clothes."

"I told her that. All I got was a condescening look as she marched back to her office, which was *my* office I told her she could use until Chelsea comes back. She packed everything I'd hung on the walls along with my accessories, put them in the storage room and brought in her things. I understand making it familiar and cosy for herself, but a complete overhaul when she's only here a few days a week?"

"How long has she been here now?"

Madie rolled her eyes. "Three *long* weeks." She was on a roll, finally releasing pent-up frustration. "And another thing, if a volunteer comes into reception and we have a little chat and a giggle about something, Patricia gets up and slams the door shut to her office, like we're children playing too loud. She doesn't fit in, Cody."

"I can see that. Why don't you talk to Wenner about it? You're the boss and it should be your call."

She took a deep breath and let it out slowly. "I will, but I want to give her another week to make it a full month. That should be sufficient time for Wenner to understand I gave her a fair shot."

"You're handling it right. Now, relax. How about another beer—or maybe a relaxing hot shower with the guy with the magic hands? He's great at massaging other body parts besides shoulders."

A coquettish smile was her answer. Cody grinned, pulled her to her feet, and led her through the cottage to the master bedroom. They shed their clothes and stepped into the shower in the en suite.

"Now, close your eyes and clear your mind."

Madie relaxed to the heat of pounding water on her back and the touch of Cody's hands lathering her with fragrant soap. He massaged trigger spots that released her muscle tension, but also aroused her sensuality. Turning her around to face him, he claimed her mouth with his, instantly setting her skin on fire.

"My turn," she purred. Madie stepped back. She turned him around, soaping his shoulders in a slow, circular massage, working her way down to his buttocks. When she finished, she gave him a slap on the cheek and turned him back to face her. Her eyes never left his as she soaped his chest, working her way down over his stomach, and finished her teasing body wash by paying close attention to his lower dangling bits— until he begged her to stop.

They both rinsed off and Cody used his tongue to tease the places he knew would build them both into a frenzy. He lifted her with her back to the wall, her legs wrapping around him.

"Please," she begged. "I need to feel you inside me."

Cody pushed inside of her; she groaned, tightening her legs as he began a slow rhythm in and out, until she cried out, "Harder."

He plunged deep inside her and Madie matched his fast pace, their eyes locked until they both climaxed. They clung to each other in trembling silence, letting the hot water pound soothingly on their sensitive still tingling skin.

❧ 26 ☙

The key slid into the lock to the file room; Madie turned it and opened the door. She slipped inside and headed to the designated cabinet that housed financials. Pulling open the first drawer, her brows shot up. *Empty?*

She moved down to the middle drawer and the third. "What the hell?" They were all bare. She checked the other cabinets to find them untouched. She marched out of the room and down the hallway to Patricia's office. The door was shut and locked.

"Fuck me!" The Finance Clerk wasn't due in for a couple of hours while Madie had come in early to prep for a breakfast meeting she was due to have with Chelsea.

Finding the spare key to her old office on her key chain, she entered the room and found a new cabinet in the office, which was locked. "Hmm, maybe she has a key in the desk." A tug on the desk drawer told her it too was locked. *No reports for me.* Fuming, she went back to her office to call Chelsea.

"Hey, unfortunately, I'm not going to make it for our meeting until later in the morning. Are you good with that?"

Chelsea chortled on the other end of the phone. "Sure. I'll be doing the same thing then as I am now. Except you're going to miss breakfast. Why don't you come for lunch instead? I'll let Bea know."

"Can do. See you then."

Madie went to the fridge to retrieve her lunch bag, grabbed a fresh cup of newly brewed coffee, and retreated to her office. *Leftover pizza for breakfast it is!*

Two hours later, she was absorbed in the work schedule for the volunteers when the outer door opened, and she heard someone enter the reception. A moment later, Patricia appeared at her door.

"Someone's been in my office. The door is unlocked and open."

"That would be me. Please, come in and sit."

The older woman sat opposite her, looking peeved.

Madie linked her sweaty fingers together and placed her hands on the desk in front of her to steady her nerves. *Here we go.*

"Can I ask why you see the need to lock your office and your desk? We don't do that here at the Centre."

Patricia raised one eyebrow. "For security. Maybe it's something you should think about doing, as an acting Administrator."

Madie chose to ignore the slight. "First off, the building has an alarm system which is engaged when we lock up at night. With three separate residences sharing this property, we're quite secure. We also have a file room that is locked to secure all of our files."

Patricia opened her mouth to speak, but Madie held her hand up. "Hold on, I'm not finished. You took all the financial files and placed them in a locked cabinet in your office. Why?"

"Because I'm Finance and it's inconvenient for me to have to leave my office every time I need a report. It makes sense to have them with me."

"Perhaps, if you were a full-time employee. I would have appreciated it if you'd discussed it with me first."

"And if I did, I doubt you'd have agreed. It's obvious to me, you want total control."

It was Madie's turn to raise an eyebrow. "Let me remind you when you first started, I explained to you all our files were kept in one place because the file room is fireproof, and the door is secure. We have no objection to files being kept in an office when in use, but even the owners of the Centre return their files to central filing.

"The second reason for that is that we are a small outfit with all of us wearing many hats. If someone is called away to Kelowna, on animal rescue, or assisting with a surgery, the rest of us don't have to go searching for a needed file. The owners live here and pop over at odd hours to check on surgical patients long after you and I are tucked in our beds at night, often doing paperwork while they are here. We don't lock our desks or our office doors from each other. We work together as a team."

Patricia stiffened. "It certainly doesn't seem efficient or a secure way to run things."

"Who are you worried about that would want to rifle through our files?"

"Well, during the day, all kinds of people have access to this building."

It struck Madie her employee had an answer for everything. Her heart rate increased but she kept her facial expression stoic. "Patricia, we aren't the Department of National Defence, only a small rehab Centre. Guests and volunteer employees are more interested in the wildlife here at the Centre than our filing system. This morning I had a breakfast meeting with Chelsea and needed some financial reports to prep for it. Needless to say, since they were locked in a cabinet in your locked office, the keys probably locked in your desk; I had to cancel the meeting …"

Patricia fired back, "Why would *you* be having a meeting about financials with Chelsea? You're Admin, I'm Finance—*I* should be having that meeting!"

The woman's angry outburst and damning words left Madie's mouth dry and her stomach tied in knots. But Madie stayedcalm, secure with what she was about to do. "I think you've misunderstood the parameters of your position. You aren't the Financial Officer of a large corporation, you're a part-time Finance Clerk. Most of the files you locked up in your office have nothing to do with your duties."

"So, this little meeting is so you can put me in my place … as a lowly File Clerk. You're far too young to be an Administrator. You don't know what you're doing."

The woman's gall amazed her. "No one at the Centre would trivialize any of our jobs, Patricia. They're equally important and they all serve a purpose."

Patricia looked contrite.

Madie took a deep breath. "I think the problem here is you're very experienced and used to running your own department. The truth is you're over-qualified for this position and I don't think you'll ever be happy here. This is the third time in your first month of employment I've had to talk to you about overstepping your job. I'm sorry, but I feel I must terminate your employment, effective immediately."

Patricia's jaw dropped. "*You … you* are firing me? I want to talk to Wenner or Chelsea about this."

"As acting Administrator, it's one of my duties to hire and let staff go. They'll support my decision. I'd like all your keys, please." Madie leaned forward and put her hand out. "I'll have the paperwork and your final payout with severance ready for pick-up tomorrow."

"The file cabinet in my office is mine."

"Leave me the keys. I'll remove the files and you can pick it up tomorrow with your papers. If you bring some boxes, you can clean out your things as well."

"What about payroll?"

"I'll finish it."

Patricia stood, took the keys off her key chain, and threw them on Madie's desk. "If you can do payroll, why ever did you hire me?"

Madie ignored the question. "On behalf of the Centre, I thank you for your work this past month, and I hope you find a place more suited to your qualifications."

The angry woman marched out of the office and down the hall. Madie held her breath until she heard the outside door open and slam shut.

Breathing a sigh of relief, she relaxed back into her chair. *That certainly wasn't pleasant, but necessary—and I handled it.* She dropped her shoulders, realizing how taut her muscles were; taking in a few deep breaths to relax her whole body. She could have let her finish the week and complete payroll, but Madie knew with Patricia's attitude it would be an intolerable situation for them both and anyone else who'd have to deal with the woman.

But I still have to answer to Chelsea and Wenner. A classic, comedic television show, *I Love Lucy* came to mind. As a kid, she'd watch reruns with her mother and grandmother. Madie thought of Desi Arnaz' infamous line, repeated in episodes over and over again: *Lucy, you got some splainin' to do!*

Madie laughed out loud. *Nothing compared to handling Patricia.*

THE MID-DAY HEAT would've been intolerable if it wasn't for the breeze blowing from the southwest. Madie strolled from the Centre to Chelsea's house. One of the volunteers was in reception to answer the phone and greet any visitors while she was gone. The tension she'd been carrying for far too long was gone—almost. Her thoughts turned to her bosses and how to explain her decision.

As she approached the back deck, she heard Chelsea call out to her. "Come in and join me in the bedroom."

The master bedroom sat at the back of the house; she entered to find Chelsea in a wheelchair, sitting at a table set under the bedroom window.

"Oh, this is new. Nice table," Madie said, taking a chair opposite her. "I didn't know you were allowed up,"

"According to the doctor, we're doing so well, I can sit up for an hour a few times a day. Still no walking though. Chaz decided I should have a table by the window to eat my meals."

"Aww, that's awesome."

Chelsea beamed. "Sitting here, I can see my beloved magnolia grove on the low side of the hill. It's lifted my spirits."

Bea appeared at the door. "Anyone ready for lunch?" She entered the room carrying a tray.

"Hi Bea, I'm sorry I missed breakfast this morning. I hope I didn't inconvenience you."

Chelsea chortled while Bea said, "No worries, dear. Nothing went to waste." She gave Chelsea a pointed stare.

Chelsea grinned. "Guilty. My morning sickness is gone and my appetite is back. I was ravenous."

Bea shook a thumb in Chelsea's direction. "Two breakfasts for that one; she ate it all."

They shared a laugh. After Bea left, Madie decided to wait until they'd eaten lunch and had their meeting before bringing up Patricia's departure.

A while later, with full stomachs and their meeting completed, Chelsea sat back in the wheelchair with her hands on her bulging abdomen. "I'm going to have to watch what I'm eating before I turn into more of a blimp than I already am. Bea's cooking is so damn good." She held up one finger. "But—not until after dessert and coffee."

Voices could be heard in the hallway and, seconds later, Wenner and Bea entered the room.

He pulled out a chair. "Can anyone join this tea party?"

"Of course, the more the merrier," Chelsea said.

Bea cleared the table. "I'll be back with carrot cake and coffee."

"Do you want some help with that?" Wenner asked.

"Nope, you sit down and relax."

Madie's mouth went dry and she felt her nerves tingle. She hadn't counted on talking to them both at the same time, but here it was. Intuitively, somewhere deep inside, she had a niggling feeling that it was no coincidence he'd joined them.

"How's it going, Madie?" Wenner asked.

How do I answer that? I'm good? All good? Shit! Just do it! The confidence she'd felt earlier dissipated and she couldn't have felt more inadequate than at this moment. Madie locked her hands together to keep from wringing her fingers. "Umm, I need to discuss something with you both."

"Shoot," he said, leanng back in his chair.

Bea came back in with a tray of coffee and cake, giving Madie a moment to bolster her courage and decide how to open the topic.

"Yum, that cake looks and smells delicious, thanks," Chelsea grinned.

"Right about now, anything edible would be delicious to you. I bet I could serve you dog food and you'd eat it up and ask for more," Bea added.

They laughed as Bea left the room.

"That woman is a godsend." Chelsea looked across at Madie. "So, what's up, hon."

This is it. Sell it to them, kid. "I did something this morning I believed needed to be done—on reflection, I probably should have discussed it with you both first...but..." Madie gulped, fumbling for words, "It needed—I believe—to be handled at the moment. I, umm ..."

Chelsea looked confused but said nothing.

Wenner smiled at Madie. "Relax, you did the right thing.

And it's part of your job as an Administrator. I'm sure it wasn't easy."

Madie let out a sigh of relief but stared at Wenner, surprised. "Oh! You know?" She nodded and gave him a semblance of a smile. "I did do right, didn't I? It *was* the hardest thing I've ever had to do."

Meanwhile, Chelsea looked from one to the other. "It's obvious you're both in agreement with whatever Madie did, so maybe one of you can fill me in?"

Wenner said, "Oh—that. She fired Patricia."

Chelsea looked surprised. "Okay."

"It was the right move on Madie's part," he added with a nod.

"How'd you know?" Madie asked.

"Because I was confronted in the compound by a very angry, arrogant—and rude I might add—woman, who told me to keep my eye on you. Everything she said about you, which I won't go into detail about, I knew not to be true. Then, she turned on me and said we were running the Centre into the ground. None of us knows what we're doing, you see."

"Well, I guess we didn't when we hired her," Chelsea added solemnly.

"That's on me. Being hopeless with numbers myself, and a little shook up about losing you so quickly, I chose her because I thought her experience could make things easier for all of us, especially you, Madie. I pushed her on you and for that, I apologize."

Chelsea looked pensive. "What about the labour board? Are we covered if she puts in a complaint?"

Madie addressed that. "We're good. She was on a three month probationary period so under the act we could fire her. But I don't remember explaining that to her in so many words when she was hired, so I gave her two weeks severance pay as a precaution. She just wouldn't accept me as her boss and fought me on everything." Madie explained the ongoing issues, right up to the locks and missing files.

"Why didn't you talk to us about it? We would have backed you up," Chelsea declared.

"Because I felt I needed to prove that I could handle it, along with the responsibilities of my job."

"No worries there, my dear," Wenner said. "May I suggest, with emphasis on the word *suggest*, you pull the names of the ones we interviewed? You choose who you think is suitable and see if they're still available."

Madie nodded. "If not, I'll rerun the ad."

Chelsea leaned towards her. "You do whatever you need to. We have every confidence in you." She sighed and pointed to her empty dessert plate. "Now, who wants another piece of this delicious cake?"

❧ 27 ❧

Chaz pushed his plate away, stood, and gathered their plates. "I'll clean this up and then I want to show you something."

"Thanks for dinner. Another amazing meal," Chelsea said with a smile.

When he returned, he pulled her wheelchair back from the table and headed to the door.

"Where are we going?"

"It's a surprise."

"Ooh ... I love surprises."

It was Labour Day weekend and Chaz had spent his Saturday in the baby's room, working non-stop. *Probably where we're headed.*

She was right about their destination but had no idea what he'd been doing this past month in that room, having given her strict instructions it was a no-go zone. Oh, they'd poured over online catalogues together and chosen furniture and accessories, but Madie never saw any of it. Painting the room and adding accessories were one thing, but she'd heard him sawing out in the shed and hammering in the room on occasion. He and Jax had been carrying things in and out for a couple of weeks. Her only request was something different, not your traditional pink girly stuff. *What's he been up to?*

"Close your eyes," Chaz instructed.

Chelsea giggled. "Done."

He opened the door to the nursery and pushed her in. "Okay, you can look now."

Speechless, all she could do was gape at the room with her chin dropped. Her eyes went everywhere in the room, settling on the one wallpapered wall in pale green with birch trees and baby animals sitting on the forest floor, on tree branches, or swings: racoons, possums, deer, birds, skunks, rabbits, squirrels, and bear cubs.

"Oh, they're so adorable. I love it."

The dark wood floor had been replaced with a soft grey wood grain, with an oval rug in shades of greens and greys, a huge sun in the middle and the words joy, dream, and hope scattered throughout. The walls were painted taupe. There was a white crib and a bassinet, and the customary dresser, but what caught her attention next was the large closet.

Chaz had removed the doors and converted the space into an open alcove. Floor-to-ceiling shelving sat at either end, recessed into the wall. Cloth baskets lined the shelves on one side for storing diapers, bibs, towels, and the like, for all of the baby's needs. The shelves at the opposite end held Rubbermaid baskets for toys and a bookshelf. In the middle of the closet sat the changing table, with soft recessed lighting lining the top of the wall at the ceiling.

"Oh, Chaz. It's beautiful," she gushed, her eyes glistening. But what took her over the top was the rocking chair in one corner of the room with a new dark green cushion. Her throat constricted as tears poured down her cheeks. "Uhh … your … your grandmother's chair from the cabin at Emerald Lake." Overwhelmed, all she could do was cry.

Chaz kneeled beside her wheelchair and wiped her cheeks

with his thumbs. "I take it this means you're happy with the nursery?"

"Damn hormones," she whispered, laughing through her tears. "I love it, Chaz. You've done such a beautiful job. Considering this baby is living at a wildlife Centre, the animal theme is brilliant. And the soft greens and browns—colours of nature. Thank you."

His eyes swept around the room at his handy work. "I couldn't have done it without Jax and Sydney. I wanted to buy everything you'd need and fill the room with stuffed animals and toys, but Sydney curbed my enthusiasm and told me I had to leave something for people to buy when the baby comes."

Chelsea giggled and studied his face. She could tell he was pleased with his handywork, as well as with her reaction. She hadn't felt this content for a long time. Their eyes locked, and the love she saw on his face sent chills up and down her spine. No words were spoken, nor were they needed. A bonding of mutual feeling and connection passed between them.

Chaz leaned over and brushed her lips lightly, a kiss filled with tenderness and love. "Let's get you back to bed," he advised. "You need to rest up for the Labour Day goodbye party for the summer volunteers."

"It'll be so nice to see everyone."

"Only for a short visit, then I'm wheeling you home," he said in a protective voice.

Back in her room, propped up with pillows, Chaz sat on the edge of the bed facing her. "When's your next appointment for an ultrasound?"

"Wednesday."

"What time?"

"Ten in the morning."

"Would you like me to pick you up and take you to the hospital?"

Chelsea smiled. "Thanks for the offer but not necessary. This is the millenium, hon. The care nurse is bringing a hand-held ultrasound that connects to her cell phone. She'll take the pictures and they'll transmit real-time to my doctor's office."

His mouth dropped. "You're kidding. Humph … technology today."

"Not everyone has them yet, but rural areas and nursing homes are being supplied first. Dr Carson can tell me instantly what's happening, and I don't even have to get out of bed. When we spoke last week, she said it may be the last one needed because the bleeding has stopped."

Chaz took her hand in his. He stroked her fingers with his free hand, "I couldn't imagine having to stay in bed most of the day, 24/7. Nor could I imagine a stubborn, independent person like you, following the rules, but you have and I'm proud of you."

She dug her nails gently into his skin. "Stubborn?"

"Ouch, come on—you know you are."

A crooked grin crossed her face. "I know it. I don't know how you've put up with me."

"The teenage girl I knew was a bit of a wild child, fiercely independent and ready to take on life. That's the girl I fell in love with and that's the woman I've waited to see re-emerge since the abduction." Chaz shifted, moving closer. "I've been reading a book by Simone Weil, a French philosopher, political activist and mystic. She died at the age of 34, in 1943, after escaping with her parents from France to England. Suffering from different ailments, she refused treatment and based her food intake on what she thought her fellow countrymen of German-occupied France were eating. She starved herself and died of cardiac arrest."

"How awful."

"For sure, but I'm digressing. In this book about philosophy and spirituality, she writes: *You must live by the light of your own mind.*"

Chelsea pondered the words. "Say it again," she requested.

Chaz squeezed her hand. "You must live by the light of your own mind—that's what I want for you."

Live by the light of your own mind. Everything came clear to her; all the talks he'd shared with her these past months, and the sweet, caring gestures revealed a genuinely selfless man who wanted to share her life—not control it. It was a profound moment, one Chelsea knew she'd never forget. Everything she'd feared, and even the unknowns that probably would never happen, disappeared.

"So, tell me, how would a stubborn, independent woman —forget the wild part, that's behind her—fit into your life?"

"I spent most of my adult life raising Jax and married to a business. A woman like you've described, has brought me out of myself, shown me what I've been missing personally, and taught me what's most important in our lives."

"Even if her need for space and independence drives you crazy?"

Chaz smiled and spoke with a quiet raspy voice. "I love crazy."

"And I love you, Chaz Rhyder."

They stared at each other in silence with their hands entwined. Chelsea believed Chaz, like her, knew they were sharing a quiet moment that said much more than spoken words could ever say.

After a time, she said, "Bea never says anything but she's carrying too much. I'd like to send her home on weeknights to sleep in her own home. Am I speaking out of place if I suggest —if you want—you stay weeknights too?"

A wide grin slowly spread across his face. "I want." He climbed onto the bed beside her and took her into his arms.

❧ 28 ❧

It was a beautiful Sunday afternoon at the Centre Labour Day weekend. Madie had arrived moments before and stood in the compound watching the activity around her. Wenner and Cody had set up tables on the grassed area that held picnic tables for visitors. Bea had been contracted to provide a feast, and she and her staff were busy putting finishing touches to the food table.

Their annual summer send-off was to say thank you and goodbye to their summer volunteer staff, and interns, including family and friends. A DJ had been hired to play music and Cody and Jax had raked one of the animal compounds (now empty). They squared it off with hay bales for people to sit on. Jordy had set up a pay bar and hired a bartender. Madie and Kelly, the new Finance Clerk (Patricia's replacement), had worked together coordinating the event and Madie was happy it all came together so easily.

Madie sat on a bench to take it all in before joining the others. She ran a mental checklist through her head, happy to note everything was ready and all they needed were the rest of the guests to arrive. She took in the heady smell of the hay bales, felt the bright sun warm on her face, and listening to the animated chatter of those around her, Madie knew it was going to be a great day.

She watched Kelly, a former volunteer, and Jordy standing at the makeshift bar. The girl conversed easily and it was the fit at the Centre Madie had been looking for. She mused about how smooth things ran since hiring her.

She flashed back three week previous to the day Kelly had knocked on her door. Ironically, Madie was going through the past applicants for the financial position and was about to make some calls, when Kelly, a summer volunteer, asked to talk with her.

MADIE LOOKED up from the paperwork on her desk when a volunteer knocked on her door. "Hi, Kelly, what's up?"

The girl spoke with a quiver, sounding a little nervous. "Do you have a few minutes?"

"Sure, come and sit."

"I was away on holiday with my family when Chelsea had to leave. By the time I came back, Patricia was already hired and working in the office with you. I was disappointed I didn't get a chance to apply. Now that Patricia's gone, I was wondering if I could apply for the position? I've been taking accounting courses online this past year and this fall I'll be starting business college in Penticton. I need to find a part-time job to carry me through, which is why I'm leaving at end of summer as a volunteer."

"I didn't know you were taking accounting. Do you have a resume?"

Kelly bent over and opened a backpack she'd been carrying. "Got one right here."

Madie sat back to study the pages. "I was just going over past applicants. Give me a minute to read through yours." The office fell quiet as she scanned down the resume.

"I wish you'd been here last month when I began interviewing." She turned her attention back to Kelly. "So, what are your long-term plans when you're finished schooling?"

"I'm not sure. I'd prefer to stay local because I love country living. But to land a good job and utilize my training, I'll probably have to go to a bigger city."

"I see. The plan here at the Centre is not set in stone, but Chelsea wishes to have a couple of years at home with the baby and handle part-time work from home. Even if she comes back to the office, it would be limited days per week. Wenner expects by then, the Centre will have grown and so will the finance position.

"So, the position as it is now is being offered part-time, with the potential for more hours down the road. We expect that my workload will increase as well, and if you didn't mind doing some admin work to help me, you could gain more hours."

"Not at all," Kelly said enthusiastically.

Madie pulled a sheet from a file and handed it to her. "Here, read this. It's a job description and wage breakdown."

As Kelly read the sheet, Madie couldn't believe her luck. When the girl finished reading, she looked up.

"Any questions?"

"What hours would I be working and what days?"

"Well, that's something we can work out together and change if necessary in accordance with your class schedule. The only deadlines are paydays, and I'm sure we can set it up for you to handle. Are you just starting your shift with Cody?"

"Yes."

Madie looked at the clock on her desk. "As far as I'm concerned, the job is yours if you want it."

"Really? Yes, I'd love to stay on and become an employee."

"Okay then, you'd best get going before I make you late. Cody will be mad at me as it is for stealing one of his volunteers. Come back after your shift; we'll talk about your schedule for the next month and you can sign some paperwork."

"Thank you so much. I'll see you later." Kelly gathered her things and headed to the door.

"And Kelly, welcome to the team."

. . .

"What are you looking so smug about?"

Madie looked up to see Cody walking towards her.

"I was just thinking how well things worked out this summer. It was certainly a challenge."

Cody sat down beside her. "That it was. It's good to see you looking so relaxed. Wenner is happy with your choice in Kelly by the way."

"She's great. I don't know how long we'll have her, but for now, it's all good."

People were arriving and the DJ had started playing upbeat country music. Cody jumped up, grabbed her hand, and pulled her to her feet. "Come on, let's dance."

"Already?" She eyed the dance floor. "No one else is."

"Then let's get this party started. You dance, don't you? Or are you one of those people who need to get pissed first?"

Madie feigned insult. "How dare you. Have I not shown you my dance trophies? Wait until you see my moves, lion tamer."

As he led them across the compound, Wenner called out. "Hey, Cody! Could I borrow you for a minute?"

"Sure, be right there." He turned to Madie, looked down at her with a glint in his eyes. "I'll be checking out your moves later." He leaned down and kissed the tip of her nose, winked, and left her to join Wenner.

Caught off guard by the public display of affection, she glanced around to see if anyone noticed. No one at the Centre knew about their personal relationship.

At that moment, Jax appeared beside her, interrupting her thoughts. "Hi Madie, great day!"

She threw him a smile. "Yup. How're you?"

"Couldn't be better. Look, I never got the chance to thank you for the referral of your Mom's renos. We finished the work last week; have you seen it?"

"Not yet. But she told me she's happy with what you and the guys did."

Jax grinned and shrugged. "That's great. She drew up a plan of what she wanted; she did a good job with the space she has. When I made up the blueprints, all I added was a couple of space-saving ideas. It's a nice suite for a single person—and right on the lake."

"It's a beautiful spot all right."

He looked past her and waved at someone. "Speaking of your mom, here she comes. I'm heading home to get Sydney and the girls. See ya soon and thanks again."

"You're welcome." Madie turned to see Val approaching with a huge smile on her face.

"Hi Mom, glad you made it."

They embraced and Val pushed her back, staring straight into her eyes, still wearing a Cheshire cat smile. "*You* have been holding out on me."

Madie's head flew back. "I have? About what?"

Her mom's eyes travelled to the right and she nodded at Cody and Wenner, carrying cases of beer over to the bar. "*Him!*"

Shit! Of all people to notice his affectionate move, it had to be my mother. "Cody and I are good friends."

Her mom gave her a knowing look. "Oh, give it up. I wasn't born yesterday. You have good taste; I'll give you that. He's a handsome devil."

Madie laughed. "I didn't say anything because we have to work together, and I wasn't sure if it was a good idea. No one at the Centre is aware we're dating."

"Silly girl, I watched the two of you from the parking lot. The two of you were positively glowing together, the chemistry is *that* obvious. Believe me, they know."

Dumbfounded, Madie stared at her blankly. "Really?"

"And the fact that he kissed you here shows he's not afraid to let people know about your relationship. So, relax—and at some point today—I expect you to introduce me to your new boyfriend."

"Of course, you do. And if I didn't introduce you, you'd seek him out and introduce yourself."

"You know me so well. Now, tell me what's happening with this Tara Crawford thing. You haven't mentioned her for a few weeks."

"Umm ... been too busy here at work. I needed to think about what my next step should be."

"Have you?"

"Nope, I need more time."

"Fair enough. How about we walk over to that bar and get a drink?" She linked her arm through her daughter's and pulled her towards the crowd standing in front of the drink table.

Madie snickered. "Oh, Mom, you're so obvious."

Val's eyebrows shot up as she responded with a voice dripping with sarcasm, "Whatever do you mean?"

"That it's not a drink you're after."

They reached the bar and Madie addressed Cody who was chatting with a group of volunteers. "Hey, lion tamer, come and meet my mom."

He strode over and put out his hand. "Hi, I'm Cody. I've heard a lot about you."

She shook his hand. "Hello, I'm afraid I'm at a disadvantage because I've heard nothing about you." She gave Madie a pointed look. "But you can start by telling me why my daughter calls you 'lion tamer'."

"It's a nickname because I worked at a rehab Centre in Botswana."

"How fascinating. Madie is due to come this week for dinner and see my new rental suite in Oliver. I expect her to bring you along, and you can tell us all about your African adventures. How's that sound?"

Madie's mouth dropped. *Jesus, she didn't waste any time.*

Cody appeared unaffected by her sudden invitation. "I'd

love to, thanks. Have you been to the Centre before, Mrs Hayes?"

"Call me Val, and yes, I came to last year's opening. It's expanded a lot since then, though."

"How about I take you on a tour and introduce you to our current in-patients."

Val looked pleased. "I'd love it." She unlinked her arm from Madie's and stood beside Cody.

"You two go ahead. I see Chaz and Chelsea have arrived and I'd like a word with them. I'll catch up to you in a bit," Madie said.

She watched them walk away together and bubbled over with laughter when Cody offered Val his arm.

She slipped her arm through his, glanced over her shoulder at her daughter with eyes widened and an open mouth, sending her a nod of approval, a wink, and a thumbs up with her free hand.

❦ 29 ❦

A week had passed since Labour Day and Madie had spent a quiet Saturday catching up on household chores. Cody was called out with Wenner to rescue a white-tailed deer with a broken leg found by hikers. She was on her own this Saturday evening and decided to curl up in bed with a good book and a bowl of popcorn. Much-needed rain pelted the roof; it had been a long, hot month with no storms.

A few hours later, she'd fallen asleep, sitting up with her book across her lap. Oblivious that the storm had morphed into a windy, torrential rainstorm, it was understandable that when the first thunderclaps hit like sonic wave shocks, followed by lightning bolts, Madie suddenly jerked awake, bolted out of bed and in a panic shouted, "Holy shit!"

She ran to the window and peered out into the night. Wrapping herself in a fleecy blanket, she curled up on the window seat and watched the violent storm play out.

She marvelled at the fact it was the first time the storm hadn't evoked nightmares or visions of Tara Crawford. *Because there's nothing more to know, except where she's buried, the most important detail that still eludes me. But why wouldn't she show me where he placed her? Humph … maybe she doesn't know. Perhaps her soul left after he killed her, and she didn't experience the actual burial.*

Madie stared into the forceful storm, as far as visibility allowed, and spoke aloud to Tara. "If that's true, then we'll never know where you are. Why would you take me this far and not give me the final piece to the puzzle?"

A lightning bolt lit up the open field across from her cabin, illuminating a small knoll in the distance, reminding her of the foothills Tara had been trying to reach that fateful night in the desert so many years ago.

She gasped, a slow wisp of an idea forming in her mind. *Wait, maybe—just maybe—if I follow in Tara's footsteps through the desert in a similar storm, she'll lead me to where she is.*

She stood, her heart beating faster. "Is that what you're waiting for, Tara? For me to simulate your path?"

Madie rushed to get dressed and pack a backpack. *Snacks, water, topographical map, first aid, hunting knife; all here.* If she were going to do this, it had to be now, before the storm abated.

She dressed warmly, with a hooded rain jacket and hiking boots. Pushing aside thoughts of danger, or the futility of such a search, she felt compelled to make the trek, no matter how ridiculous others might believe it to be. The idea grew into an obsession and, in no time, Madie headed out of the cabin and began the drive down the highway to Osoyoos. She found a truck pullover on the Crowsnest Highway, just before the turnoff to Tara's house. Madie pulled in and parked, deciding to hike the kilometre down the dirt road and avoid leaving her car where it might be seen by neighbours. She glanced at the dash clock, noting it was 4:30 a.m. She had a couple of hours of darkness before the grey of daylight would begin to appear.

Fifteen minutes later, she'd completed the trek in the pounding rain to the driveway and trudged on until she stood in front of Tara's former house. Wisps of hair had escaped her hood in the fierce wind and blew her wet tresses across her face. The lightning lit up the white stucco structure with its stone pillars, creating an ominous picture she'd seen in her nightmares so many times before.

I promised Cody I wouldn't put myself in danger. She knew she shouldn't have come alone but her impulse outweighed common sense. She pushed the hair back from her eyes and studied the landscape. *Why'd I come here? What am I hoping to gain?* She switched to thinking in the third person. *Go back, girl. You can sneak back down the curving driveway to the safety of your car and go home.*

Instead, Madie crept up the stone pathway that took her around the corner of the house to the back. Lightning forked across the sky and a thunderclap sounded shortly after. She stepped forward, mesmerized as the desert floor stretched out before her. It was déjà vu. This was the starting point of Tara Crawford's run into the desert that night so long ago that haunted Madie in her dreams. Not paying attention to her movements, her toe caught under the edge of an uneven stone. She flew forward and crashed into the patio table and a terra-cotta planter fell to the ground, breaking into pieces.

"Shit!" Madie dove into some shrubberies nearby and hid.

A light came on in the house and seconds later a porch light lit up the patio. She heard a door slide open and Douglas Crawford peered out. Madie sucked in a breath and froze behind the shrubs. She saw his eyes settle on the broken pottery. *Damn … I'm so stupid.*

His head moved slowly around as he studied the patio, scanning for some sign of what or who had knocked the planter on the ground. Before he turned in her direction, his head stopped, and his eyes fixated straight ahead into the desert. "Go on. Get out of here, you mangy critter."

Madie followed his gaze and saw a coyote running across the plateau.

"Come back again and you'll get a bullet between your eyes." The door slammed shut and Madie could hear the lock fall in place.

She released the breath she'd been holding, and her muscles relaxed. *Thanks, little buddy.* Soon, the lights went out and all was quiet. Madie remained in place for several minutes in case Crawford was staring out from the darkened house. Finally, assured he'd returned to bed, she made her way out onto the flats.

The lightning was far enough away that she wasn't worried about the bolts hitting too close. But they offered enough light for her to see she was following in real-time, the same path that Tara Crawford had taken. The rugged hills flashed in the light of the storm ahead of her, all so familiar. The thunder and lightning moved on, but the rain remained, and Madie needed a flashlight to continue. She adjusted the pack on her back and trudged on.

By the time she reached the rock base of the hills, the darkened sky had turned to a muted grey as daylight approached. Madie wandered around the base but nothing appeared familiar. She looked up and studied the looming rock face. *That's where I need to be. On top.* She took a few swigs of water and nibbled on an energy bar before tackling the climb up the rocks. *The rocks could be slippery from the rain. Be careful, girl.*

Her summit to the top coincided with the sun peeking from behind the distant hills to the east. The winds blew the clouds away and the rainstorm subsided. Madie sat and watched as the dark shadows across the desert floor rescinded, slowly at first, then gaining speed as the sun rose and the grey shadows sped away to the west. She soaked up the warmth of the morning sun as she rested, the heat taking away the chill of her damp clothing. Finally, she stood and traversed back and forth across the hill line, studying the rocks below. Then, she saw it.

Her body stiffened and she stared at a crevice in the rocks, about fifteen feet long by ten feet wide. *That's it.* A lump formed in her throat and her eyes glistened. Her knees weakened and Madie sat down abruptly, her gaze unbroken. *Oh, Tara. You're down there, aren't you?*

There was nothing to prove the fact, but she knew. Madie began to shake and she felt a growing terror envelop her. She couldn't stop staring at what she believed to be Tara's gravesite. A tightness welled around her neck and Madie found herself gasping for air. Her hands flew up to her neck and she furiously flailed to no avail, at the invisible pressure that grew tighter. A manic panic overwhelmed her at a new realization: *this isn't a bad dream or an awareness I'm experiencing, it's real.*

Nausea welled in her heaving chest as she ran out of air, her breathing growing increasingly shallow—until blackness claimed her.

❦ 30 ❧

JUNE 14, 1998, EARLY-DAWN SUNDAY MORNING

Tara sat on a boulder on the top of the hill staring at the rocks below. How strange! She knew she was dead … at least, in the physical sense. *How else can I be up here looking down at a blue tarp housing my former body?*

Her gaze shifted to a gap in the rocks where her earthbound husband was digging a hole in the sandy soil. *Bastard!* If she still had her body, her blood would boil. She took in the rocky cliffs around her and the deep crevices. *This was where I was running to in my effort to escape Douglas. If he hadn't caught me on the flats, I could have hidden out here until he gave up.*

Tara released a deep sigh. *I finally got up the courage to leave—damn him for forgetting his wallet and coming back for it moments before my departure. My packed suitcase in the hall was the giveaway and nothing I could do or say could appease his rage.*

The rain had stopped, and the clouds were moving away at a high speed. But one round, misty cloud moved towards her. How strange. The closer it came, the bigger it grew, until a long oval shape stopped beside her. The mist took on a human shape and morphed into that of a middle-aged woman.

She smiled at her and spoke in a soft, melodic tone. "Hi, Tara. I'm Arielle. I'm here to help your transition."

Tara frowned. "Transition?"

"That's right. I can help you return to your source and rejoin your soul tribe."

Tara looked down and watched Douglas pull the blue tarp into the makeshift grave. "But I don't want to return. I was too young to leave my current life. My journey was only beginning."

"I understand. But it certainly wasn't a happy life, and now you're free from human abuse."

Douglas appeared to take a break before he covered the body. He leaned on the shovel and glanced around. Suddenly, he pushed his head back and stared up to the top of the hill, as if he sensed being watched.

Tara knew he couldn't see them, and she took comfort in the fact that she no longer feared him. But at that moment she did hate him. She focused her energy on a pile of small rocks at the base of the boulder she sat on and used her mind to create a whirlwind which swirled the sand and rocks faster and faster, until the pile flew off of the edge and cascaded downward, landing a few feet away from Douglas.

He jumped back and stared back up the hill. She sensed his fear as he began shovelling quickly to bury her abandoned body.

Arielle laughed. "Nicely done. Shall we go?"

She turned to Arielle. "I don't want to. Can I stay?"

"You don't want to return to your soul source?"

She listened to the sound of a shovel throwing sand on her former body below. "He can't get away with this. There must be a way for me to get justice for my former self."

"Hmm-mm." Arielle studied her face for a moment. "Is it justice or revenge you seek?"

Tara watched Douglas dig up the sage brush and replant it at the narrow opening in the rock face, hiding the entrance to her gravesite. "Maybe both, Arielle." Her eyes followed Douglas as he walked back to the ATV. She followed the cloud of dust trailing behind as he headed towards what was once her home. She looked at the spot where he'd buried her and doubted that anyone would ever find her body. "If I stay, what are my options?"

"You have two choices. Should you stay in this worldly plane in spirit form, all you can do is haunt him and destroy his peace. This can give you revenge but no justice, and it's such a lonely path to seek. Many who have chosen this way are doomed for eternity. I don't recommend it."

"And the other?"

Arielle shrugged. "You can reincarnate into another vessel. But generally, a new worldly life forgets the old one. Again, there's no justice gained. But perhaps you can experience a happy existence and continue your soul mission."

"In my life here as Tara, I'd read that some people remember their previous lives."

"My dear, the reason that we leave our ethereal clans and reincarnate to this plane is to influence earthly beings to be the best humans they can and recognize what's best for all, not just for one. Is it not?"

"That's true."

"Then why would you want to reincarnate and have another being experience such terrible memories?"

Tara felt guilty. "I guess that would be selfish of me. Perhaps that person will be stronger than I was and if that being does remember, maybe whoever it is will handle it better than I did. In any case ... I want to go back and continue our mission."

"Even if your new being never remembers this one?"

Tara pondered that for a moment. "Yes. I have more lessons to learn before I return to my soul clan."

"Then it's time for me to leave and for you to find your new life. Remember, there's always karma. Douglas will face his sooner or later. Good luck."

With that Arielle faded into a mist and floated back up into the sky. Tara followed the white cloud until it disappeared from view.

She stayed to watch the morning sun pop over the ridge and warm the desert air and long enough to witness the drying of the arid floor. *You'd never know it rained. Time to find my new life.* Tara stared in all directions. Where to go? *Somewhere close to my past life ... just in case my new life collides with the old. Maybe, and it's just a maybe, my new being will be the karma Douglas faces.*

In an instant, Tara found herself in the busy corridors of the Penticton Regional Hospital. She stood to the back of the hallway reading the directory. She soon found herself in the maternity ward on the second floor. She wandered through the rooms and visited the nursery. Standing behind the nurse's station, she listened as they discussed the patients. There were two pregnant women admitted that day into the ward, both in labour. All the other women had already given birth.

One of the women was a visitor to the area on holidays from the coast and the other was from Oliver, north of Osoyoos, right here in the Okanagan. Tara found the room of the Oliver couple and observed the woman with her husband by her side. He was very supportive; rubbing his wife's back, counting for her when contractions came and went. In between contractions, he held her hand and his love for his wife was apparent. She left their room, giving them their privacy.

Tara had no idea why she'd suddenly landed at the hospital. Souls usually connected with the fetus around six months, when the brain began its development. The souls weren't permanently attached to the fetus and could come and go to prepare for the birth. During the latter months, they stayed with the fetus and connected permanently at birth. But something had brought her here and she decided to wait it out.

It didn't take long. Alarms went off and the intercom rang out, beckoning staff. They all came running for the room of the Oliver couple. The mother-to-be was rushed down the hall to an operating room. With all the people in the hallway, Tara almost missed the woman standing halfway down the corridor, who watched as the staff pushed past, until they disappeared through a set of double doors. The woman turned and their eyes locked. Tara recognized her as another soul.

The soul joined her. "Something's happened to the baby. I was to be her soul, but I've been called to another mission and my connection is broken. They're doing Caesarean and you're the one she needs. You haven't bonded as yet so, initially, she'll have a rough infancy."

They watched one of the nurses try to calm the frantic husband. "They're good, loving people. You'll have a good life with them."

Tara now knew why she was here.

The woman pointed down the hall. "Hurry, it's time. You must use the portal before the infant enters this world, or the child will be stillborn. Go—now."

❧ 31 ❧

The noise forced its way through her senses. Madie's eyes flew open. Her heart was pounding, and she gasped for air, causing her to cough up phlegm. Her head ached, while her pulse beat in her ears. If anything could convince her she was Tara Crawford incarnate, this happening was it. *But that noise. What is that?*

She sat up and looked out into the desert. The noise grew louder, and she could see a plume of dust heading her way. *A dirt bike.*

The rider stopped to her left and climbed off the bike. He removed his helmet and placed it on the seat.

A gasp escaped Madie's lips. *Douglas Crawford.* She threw herself onto the ground and peered over the edge. He looked all around and walked to the rock cropping below her, stopping at an overgrown sagebrush community. He pushed his way around the shrubbery, stepping through a small opening around a large boulder that led him into the enclosure that housed Tara's grave. *No wonder I didn't see it when I was down there.*

Douglas walked around the perimeter of the hidden area, appearing to study the surface of the ground. *Perhaps to see if it's been disturbed? It certainly doesn't look like it.* The surface of the inner sanctuary was flat and hardened from time and arid conditioning. Small rocks and tumbleweed debris had blown into the gravesite. He stopped and stared hard, appearing to be lost in thought. He kneeled and stared across the enclosure towards the back rock face; with a shake of his head, he returned to his bike and rode in the direction he'd travelled from.

Madie sat up and watched the cloud of dust he'd created get smaller and smaller, until it disappeared. *What brought him here today of all days? My God, what if he'd come earlier when I was standing down below or visible climbing up the rocks?* Her body shook at what might have happened. She pushed away the thought. *Don't go there. But didn't he just confirm our dear Tara is indeed resting right here?* She stared down one last time, burning the rock formations into her memory.

"Don't worry, sweet girl. Now I've found you, I'll get you home to your family. You won't be alone much longer—and I promise, he'll be punished for what he did to you."

She opened her backpack and pulled out the map she'd studied before coming. There was no way she could hike out of the desert the way she'd come. She walked to the other side of the hill and stared across the flats. *It'll add an extra hour to my hike but it's safer. Before I start down, though, I need some food.*

She found a flat rock to sit on and rummaged through her backpack. A meal of raisins, mixed nuts, some cheese, and the rest of her energy bar, polished off with water. A calmness replaced her frayed nerves and she began the descent down to the desert floor and her journey home.

A few hours later, Madie drove into her driveway. She was surprised to see Cody's jeep parked out front. Asleep in the armchair, he woke up when she opened and closed the door. She dropped her backpack on the floor and took off her jacket. "Hi, I didn't expect to see you this early. How long have you been here?" She sat down to tackle her wet hiking boots.

"Since five this morning—came straight from the Centre after surgery on the deer brought in last night." He eyed her damp clothes and backpack. "Where were you? Looks like you were out in the storm."

Madie ignored the question while pulling off her boots. "So, you haven't slept yet? You should have gone straight home to bed, silly."

"It was the first storm in weeks. I wanted to check on you in case you had more nightmares."

She threw him a smile. "That's sweet. No dreams, but I do have some news. How about you make some coffee while I jump in the shower?"

Cody frowned. "You're gonna make me wait until you shower to tell me?"

"I need to get warm and lose some of this grime."

He studied the dirt on her face and hands, the damp dirty jeans she was wiggling out of, and said, "Fine. Why do I get the feeling you're putting me off?"

Madie flew past him. *Because maybe you're right?* "I'll be quick. Coffee, please."

Fifteen minutes later, she sat on the couch in flannel PJs and a woolly robe with a hot cup of coffee. "How's the deer? Will it be okay?"

"Too soon to tell. It was a white-tailed buck; don't see them as much as mule deer. He's got a badly infected wound. Wenner did what he could; it's up to the deer now."

Madie stared into her cup. "You must be exhausted." She looked up to catch Cody watching her.

"Your turn. You're warm, clean, got your coffee —what's up?"

She studied his face for a moment, then blurted out, "I found her, Cody."

He looked puzzled. "Who?"

"Tara! I found her gravesite." Madie watched the confusion on his face, saw the wheels turning in his eyes, and anger replace it all before Cody leaned forward, raising his voice. "You went out in that storm in the dark, hiking through the flats? Do you know how dangerous that was? You promised me you wouldn't go alone."

"I know I did, and I'm sorry. But I was compelled to go, and you were working."

"What were you thinking? What if you'd been injured? No one knew where you were. What if Crawford saw you and went after you? Really, Madie? I thought you were smarter than that."

Madie squirmed through his tirade. *Should I tell him Crawford was closer than he knows—twice?* She was impatient, waiting for him to finish chastising her, wanting to talk about Tara instead. In an irritated tone, she said, "Well that didn't happen, did it—so move on."

His face turned to stone and he stood abruptly, "You don't get to do that, Madie."

She stood to face him, hands on her hips. "Do what?"

"Trivialize my concern." He headed to the door. "Move on? How dare you!"

"Where're you going?"

"*Home* … to get some sleep." Cody opened the door, rushed through, and slammed it hard behind him.

Dumbfounded, Madie stared at the closed door. *He never even asked me what I'd found.* "Men!"

She stomped to the door, locked the deadbolt, threw her robe on the floor, and crawled under the covers. Luxuriating in the warmth and comfort of her bed, a moan of pure pleasure soon turned to a groan when she heard a knock at the door. "Aargh."

Madie got up and padded to the door. She flung it open to see Cody leaning against the jamb.

"I thought you were going home?"

"I'm too tired to drive." He pushed past her. "How do you know where she's buried?"

"Got a few hours?" Madie closed the door and turned to see Cody flop on the couch and pat the cushion beside him. "More than a few. Sorry I lectured you. Thinking of you wandering out there in that wicked storm freaked me out."

Madie sat beside him and he pulled her into his arms. "And I apologize for upsetting you," she said. She relaxed, wrapping her arms around his waist, and they sat in silence for a few minutes, Cody stroking her hair. "I've never seen you that angry; I just wanted to talk about Tara."

He pushed her back and leaned in to give her a quick kiss. "I'm all ears. Start talking."

"I woke up last night about two and sat watching the storm. It occurred to me there might not be any more nightmares or visions because we knew all we needed to about Tara, except where she's buried. We were at a dead end and I either had to give up the search or do something drastic."

Cody gave her a crooked smile. "And you chose drastic. What'd you do?"

"Something pushed me to go to Tara's house and follow her path through the desert to the foothills. I mean it wasn't a whim—it felt like a force inside me. The feeling grew until it was like an obligation. I *had* to go."

Cody frowned. "So, you went right to the house?"

"Well, I parked on the highway at a pull-out and hiked down the road to her house." Madie explained creeping into the backyard, knocking over the pottery and Douglas Crawford searching the yard while she hid in shrubs.

Cody sucked in his breath. "Oh, Madie, it could have gone so wrong."

For the first time, she felt contrite. "I know." She took him through her hike to the hills and the climb to the rocks above.

He listened in silence to her description of physically experiencing Tara's death, her decision to reincarnate, and finding herself at the hospital in the early morning hours after her death and uniting with Madie in birth.

"I saw it all. The strange thing is, I recognized the burial spot as soon as I saw it. I knew she was down there. And suddenly, there was Crawford, checking it out."

Fear crossed his face. "What? He was *there?*"

"Yeah, it's so weird he came the morning I discovered her grave. He entered the compound where he buried her, checked it out, and left on his dirt bike."

"Thank God he didn't see you. Maybe because you and Tara were so bonded in this life, he sensed something. But, Madie, it was so dangerous."

"I see that now. But I knew I could only do it during a night storm. Once it was daylight, I had to hike down the back of the hills. I couldn't head back towards his house in case he saw me."

Cody took her hands in his and squeezed them. "I don't know if I should admire your determination and strength—or chide your recklessness. Anyway, it's over and you're home safe."

Madie took in his exhausted expression, which mirrored how she felt. "I think we both need some sleep. Let's go to bed."

He nodded in agreement. Cody stripped down to his boxers and they climbed into bed, facing each other. "Whatcha wanna do now?"

Madie gave him a puzzled look and grinned. "Umm … sleep?

Cody wrinkled his brow. "That's a given. I meant about Tara's gravesite."

"Ohh-hh, I thought you meant we could—you, me—like fool around?"

His eyes widened. "What? There's nothing sweeter than make-up sex, but we're both bushed. The thick one wouldn't measure up, I'm afraid. You're such a horny wench."

Madie giggled. "Just me, eh? Anyway, next step, the police, I guess."

Cody closed his eyes, muttering, "Mmm, okay."

She studied his face, knowing he'd already slipped into sleep. She kissed her finger and placed it on his lips. "Good morning and good night, lion tamer."

❦ III ❧

*"I believe...that the soul of man is immortal and will be treated
with justice in another life, respecting its conduct in this."*

Benjamin Franklin

❧ 32 ❧

I t was early afternoon; the sun disappeared behind the house, bringing the shadows closer to the deck. The air temperature instantly changed. Sitting in her wheelchair on the deck, Chelsea zipped her sweater, pulling the collar around her neck. She and Wenner were finishing off their lunch meeting with coffee. "Summer's over. The nights are getting downright chilly."

Wenner nodded. "I, for one, *love* the fall. The cooler temps mean better sleep; hot nights don't agree with me. It also means our busy season is over and we can slow down: do repairs, figure out what worked this past season and what didn't. Madie can concentrate on grant applications and education programs."

It had been ten days since their end of summer party. "Things have been quiet this past week. I've been worried about leaving you all in the lurch and how it would affect business; I'm happy to see you made it through okay."

"We'll know more when the accountant crunches the figures, but considering our first year finished in the red, I think we almost broke even this season. We had a good fundraiser last spring and I expect next year will be even

better. Stop worrying. Your main job right now is to take care
of that bulging tummy of yours and, when the baby pops, be
a mommy."

Chelsea laughed. "Your choice of words cracks me up."
Changing the subject, she said, "Madie's happy with the new
hire, Kelly. How about you? Is she working out?"

"Absolutely, the two of them work well together. Madie
made a good call there."

"Good to hear. What about expansions this year? Got any
plans?"

"Cody and I were talking about building one more pen,
with a closed-in lean-to for now, a larger one for the big
animals that have to stay longer. We got lucky this year, jock-
eying them around, but it could be a big problem in the
future. That's it for this year."

"Probably a good idea to move slowly, considering we have
an additional employee to pay for."

"Yup. By the way, Jordy finished his story and submitted it
with the magazine. The first part is slotted for publication a
month before our spring fundraiser; the other two will follow
consecutively for the next two months."

"Hey, great timing. We can use it in our advertising,
leading up to the event and follow-up."

"Sounds good. Now, that's enough business talk. Let's get
to the good stuff. It's been a few days since Chaz moved in.
How's it going with you and Daddy?"

Chelsea giggled. "Not much of a change for me, I'm still
laying around getting fatter. A big change for Chaz, though.
He's taken on a lot—laundry, cooking dinner and weekend
meals. I insisted that we hire a cleaning service to come once a
week. What with running his business and taking care of me,
it's enough. He's been a real trouper."

He sighed. "True love."

"You're such a romantic, Wenner. I'm glad everyone else

can get back to their own lives and routines. Mom and Bea, bless them, still drop off casseroles to help Chaz out."

"I'm happy for you, hon. You deserve this."

Chelsea grinned. "I do, don't I?" She stared over to the magnolia grove, thinking of her special tree where they'd carved a heart with their initials. "It's a strange way to finally start our life together, but it's certainly awakened me to recognize the goodness in Chaz. I don't need him to prove himself to me over and over, anymore." She pensively watched a squirrel gathering food and scurrying up a nearby tree to hide it in its winter den. "Can't do any better than him, can I?"

"No, my dear. He's a catch. What's he going to do with his house?"

"He bought it as an investment. And since Jax and Sydney got married, he's found it too big for one person to lumber around in. He hasn't decided if he'll rent it or sell it."

"So, you'll stay here on the property as a family, then?"

"Yup, the house is big enough for a family of three. I could never leave the Centre. Of course, my office is now a nursery, and we want to keep the one guest bedroom, so we've talked about adding on to the house to give us each an office and a workshop."

Wenner leaned back and stretched his legs, taking in the landscape. "There's plenty of room to expand the house."

Chelsea studied her partner and best friend. She hadn't seen his friend, Jordy for a few days but was afraid of overstepping by asking about him.

Having made it obvious, he asked, "What? You're staring."

"Oh—I was thinking I hadn't seen Jordy around. Is he on assignment?"

"No, he went home to visit his family. His mother had a fall."

"How awful. Is she okay?"

"She will be. A few bruises and a twisted ankle."

Now that she'd brought him up, she decided to dive in about Jordy as he had about Chaz. "Last time we talked, you and Jordy had become more than friends, and he was settling in for the summer." She paused, thinking out her next words. "And …"

"It was a *great* summer. Sorry, I cut you off—*and* what?"

"And summer's over. After his family visit, will he be coming back?"

Wenner stared at her with a blank expression. "Let's just say, he packed up his things and moved out of the guest bedroom …"

"Hi, Mom."

They turned to see Sydney coming down the hill from next door, cutting off Wenner's words. When she reached them, she leaned over to kiss her mom on the cheek. "Hi, Wenner," she said, her eyes taking in the paperwork on the table. "Am I interrupting a meeting?"

"Hi, Syd," he said. "All over with. Just chatting over coffee."

Chelsea smiled at her daughter, noting the casserole dish in her hands. "More food from Bea?"

Sydney looked wounded. "No, *I* made this one, Spanish rice with chicken. Jax told me Chaz is in Kelowna today and I figure he'll be tired when he gets home. Since Bea is leaving early today, I made one for my family and one for you guys."

"It smells delicious. Thanks."

"You're welcome. You feeling okay?"

"I'm fine."

"Well, I'm going to put this in the fridge and clear this table for you. Bea is watching the girls until I get back."

Wenner stood, "Let me help." He gathered up their dishes and followed Sydney into the house.

Chelsea sat back in her chair and took in the quiet peacefulness. A sudden breeze blew across the property, lifting the orange and red-tinged leaves from the ground, swirling them through the air. She glanced at the trees, noting they were almost bare of their cover. Her eyes followed the tree line to the compound and over to Wenner's house. Chelsea stared at the home and her thoughts went back to her conversation with him just before Sydney had joined them. She felt terrible for him. He'd seemed so happy with Jordy here.

Sydney and Wenner returned. "Mom, do you need me to help you to bed?"

Wenner sat down, "I can do it if you need to get back." He held up his cup. "As soon as I finish my coffee."

"Awesome. I'll be heading home, so Bea can leave for her appointment. Enjoy!" She jumped off the deck and started back towards the hill.

Chelsea shouted after her. "Thanks, sweetheart."

"No problem," she yelled over her shoulder.

"What's with people and Monday appointments? Madie and Cody are leaving an hour early today, too."

Chelsea smiled. "They make a cute couple, don't they?"

"They do." He drained his cup. "You ready for a nap, your highness?"

"In a minute," she replied with a deep sigh. "Wenner—I'm so sorry about how things worked out with Jordy."

He lowered his head, then gave her a sad look. "Yes, Jordy. What was I saying when Sydney interrupted us?"

Full of empathy for her close friend, she flinched. "You said he'd packed his things and moved out."

Wenner held up a finger and wagged it back and forth. With a glint in his eye he said, "*No-oo*, what I said was: Jordy packed up his things and moved out of the guest bedroom," he paused for emphasis. "And right into the master bedroom. We're not a 'something' anymore, we're a 'thing'."

Chelsea's eyes widened. "Uh. You're *so* bad! And here I was feeling sad for you. If you were sitting closer, I'd smack you. Don't ever do that to me again."

Wenner gut-laughed. "So glad you're happy for us."

"I'll be ecstatic, once I'm over being angry. Does this mean he's giving up his freelancing and becoming an author?"

He beamed. "Signed the publishing contract before he left. Like you, we have some renos to do. My third bedroom has been a storage room until now. Jordy's going to turn it into his office."

"Oh, Wenner. I'm so happy for you both. What a summer this has been, Chaz and me, Madie and Cody, and now you and Jordy."

"Love is in the air." They shared a laugh and Wenner added, "At least, if I don't get to see Jordy for a while, it won't be because he's travelling somewhere far away; it'll be because he's locked himself behind a door to write."

"Sounds like someone I know, who buries himself in his work here at the Centre. Sooner or later, you'll both surface for air."

"And food and wine, laughter—and a little love."

❧ 33 ❧

Cody pulled into the visitor parking stall in front of the Osoyoos RCMP Detachment. Madie stared through the windshield at the entrance doors, feeling apprehensive.

"You ready?" he asked.

"They're going to think I'm crazy."

"No, they won't. Police work with psychics more than people know."

She turned to look at him. "Incarnate, not a psychic. I'm going to walk in there and tell them I'm the reincarnation of a missing person who was murdered twenty-two years ago." Her eyes grew large and she grabbed his arm. "What if they charge me with public mischief? I could go to jail."

"Madie, you aren't going to jail. They'll take your statement and assess it. It's their job to consider all tips and decide if they're viable or not. They'll either corroborate it or reject it."

Her face clouded over. "And what if they reject it? He'll get away with murder. And all of this would've been for nothing."

Cody laid his hand on hers. "That can't happen. Be

strong, sincere, tell them your story; you can't give in before you've even started. Shall we go?"

Madie stared through the windshield at the entranceway, sucked in her breath, opened the car door, and stepped out.

Ten minutes later, after they were asked to sit in the waiting room, they were approached by an officer. "Hi, I'm Sergeant Davis, Area Commander."

Cody and Madie stood and shook hands with the Sergeant. He turned to Madie. "I understand you have some information about a missing person's case?"

"I do," she replied solemnly.

Sgt. Davis spoke to Cody. "Are you witness to this information, as well, sir?"

Cody, appearing taken back by the question, glanced at Madie and back to the Sergeant. "Umm—some of it, yes."

"I'd like to talk with Miss Hayes. Would you mind if Corporal Murray gets a statement from you?"

"No problem," Cody said.

Madie knew they wanted to separate them, and she tried not to let it bother her. She should have expected it, considering she'd come here to talk about a possible murder. *Well, I know it was murder, but at the very least, they suspect foul play.*

"Good, I'll send him out. Miss Hayes, if you'll follow me?"

Sergeant Davies led her to a room, and they sat down at a small table. "Can I get you anything? Coffee, water?"

"No thanks, I'm good." She glanced around the tiny room with the barest of furniture and stark white walls. It did nothing to calm her nerves.

He placed a recorder on the table. "Mind if I record our conversation?"

"That's fine."

Davis turned on the recorder, stated the date and time, and identified himself. He relaxed into his chair with a pad and pen in front of him. "Why don't we start by you giving me your full name, address, contact number, birth date, if you're working and where."

Madie gave him her personal information, then added, "I work at the Stoney Creek Rehabilitation Centre as an Administrative Assistant; at the moment, I'm Acting Administrator."

"That's the Centre run by Wenner and Chelsea?"

"That's right."

"I was there last year at your open house. You're providing a great service. Can I ask you about Cody Diaz? Is he a friend?"

"Cody works at the Centre as well, an assistant to Wenner, and he runs the Internship Program. He's a good friend." Madie hesitated. "Umm, a little more than a good friend. We're dating."

"You say you have information about a missing person; can you provide me with a name?"

"Tara Crawford—she went missing in 1998."

The Sergeant's face was friendly, his brown eyes warm, but his expression had been stoic—until she mentioned the year of Tara's disappearance. One eyebrow shot up. "The year you were born?"

Here we go. "Actually, just hours before I was born."

"So, you never knew Tara Crawford. Are you related to her?"

Madie took a deep breath. "Not genetically," she whispered.

"Why don't you explain what that means?"

Madie rubbed her hands together, feeling like a fish out of water. "This is much harder than I thought it would be."

The Sergeant smiled. "Relax, take your time. Any information you can provide us regarding this case is welcome."

"Tara Crawford was murdered the evening of June 13th, 1998."

The smile on his face disappeared and the stoic look returned. He was on point.

Shit, I didn't mean to start with the word "murder". Her hands were sweating, now. "She—Tara—reincarnated hours later in the early morning of June 14, as me, Madie Hayes."

There was no mistaking his reaction. His head shot back as his eyes widened in surprise. Still, he said nothing and Madie watched him scribbling on his yellow pad. It gave her a moment to compose herself. *There, the worst is over, I said it. Not quite how I planned but the rest should be easier.*

"Why don't you tell me how you've come to know this?"

"As a baby, I had terrible night terrors, right up until I went to pre-school. My parents had all kinds of testing done and nothing was found wrong. The nightmares were always the same, about a young fearful woman. Through my school years, I forgot about her.

"Last spring, during the terrible thunderstorms, the nightmares came back. Same woman, the same fear, and only when I was sleeping during thunderstorms. During one dream, I saw the man she feared for the first time; I went through regression therapy in Kelowna and learned the woman's name was Tara. I tried researching on the internet but couldn't find anything."

Realizing she'd run out of air from talking so fast, Madie paused to catch her breath and slow down her telling of the story. "Her name is Scarlett. I have no idea why I see her as Tara. Then, the visions started, and I saw the man who murdered her. There was a billboard with his face on it, advertising his real estate firm. It was her husband, Douglas Crawford."

Davis stopped writing to glance at her but didn't interrupt. He went back to scribbling on his notepad while she told her story, including finding Douglas Crawford's offices in Osoyoos and visiting the home where he had lived with Tara and still lives.

"I recognized him as soon as I saw him. We pretended we had a wrong address and right there and then, I had a vision

… just a quick flash. I saw him straddling her in the desert, he bent over her and strangled her." Madie began to shake. "I … umm … physically felt it. I could feel his hands on my neck and started coughing and gasping. Cody told him I was suffering from car sickness; we'd been driving for hours. He hustled me into the car, and we left." She paused. "Do you think I could have some water?"

"Of course." Sergeant Davis turned off the tape recorder and left the room. When he returned, she felt a little more composed, although her hands shook as she sipped water.

"Shall we continue?" Davis asked.

"Yes."

He hit the recorder button, "Whenever you're ready."

"Cody and I didn't think we had enough information to give you, to re-open her case. Things were busy at work, and we decided to put Tara aside for a while and re-think the whole thing. Then two nights ago, we had another storm."

Madie took him through what led her to Crawford's house, her journey through the grasslands to the foothills. "Something led me to climb to the top of the hill, and immediately I saw the enclosure within the rocks below. Intuitively, I knew Tara was buried there. This time, I physically experienced her death at his hands—to the point I passed out. She was leaving him because she'd found out she was pregnant."

Madie explained her vision, filling in the details that lead up to Douglas chasing Tara into the hills and ultimately killing her.

Sitting perfectly still with that stoic expression, scribbling notes as she talked, she noticed the change in his body language when she told him about waking up on top of the hill to Douglas Crawford arriving on a dirt bike. His body straightened and he put his pencil down, listening to her every word.

"It was the noise of his bike that brought me back. I peered over the hill and watched him walk straight to the enclosure. The reason I hadn't found the enclosure when I walked along the base of the foothills was because he'd planted sagebrush to cover the small entranceway. Over the years they'd thickened and grown tall …"

Sergeant Davis stopped her. "How do you know Crawford planted them?"

"I saw him, in the vision. Back to yesterday morning, he pushed his way through and stood in the enclosure, staring at the ground. He walked around, examining the surface, kneeled on one knee, and stared towards the back rock face. Then he left, straightened up the bushes to hide the entrance, got on his dirt bike and headed in the direction of his home. She's in there. My bones are aching as I say this—Tara Crawford is buried there." She fell silent and stared at the sergeant.

"What did you do then?" he asked.

"I checked the map, walked to the other side of the hill, 'cause I knew I couldn't go back the way I came, had a bite to eat, some water, hiked down the back of the hill, across the flats to Crowsnest, and walked the highway back to my car."

"You drove straight home?"

"Yes, I got there about ten a.m."

"You live alone?"

"Yes, but Cody was there. He'd worked in surgery with Wenner into the night and came over to my place to check on me because of the thunderstorm."

"Check on you?"

"He was with me one day when I had a bad nightmare about Tara, and he was with me when I had the vision at Douglas Crawford's house. Cody was worried I might have had another vision or more nightmares. I told you they only happen during storms."

"Yes, you did. I wanted to clarify his reason for checking on you for the record."

Madie nodded. Now that she'd finished her statement, her

mind moved to other thoughts. She leaned forward, staring into his eyes. "You do believe me, don't you? I'm not crazy."

Sergeant Davis studied her in silence for a moment. "Madie, I do believe you've experienced something strange, something that has affected your life for a long time. It's not my job to psychoanalyze you or to pass judgement. My job is to take the facts as you've presented them, determine the verity and, if so, decide whether they will effectively help us re-open this case."

"So, what do *you* think? Are they?"

Sergeant Davis gave her a half-smile. "It's too soon to determine that. We have some follow-up work to do first. And I have to pull the cold case file." He sat back in his chair. "I'd like you to do something for me. Sometimes, when remembering events of an emotional experience such as yours, important details can be forgotten. So, here's what I'd like you to do. Start at ten a.m. yesterday morning, and tell me what happened in reverse, all the way back to when you were sitting at home at 2:30 in the morning watching the storm. Can you do that?"

Madie shrugged. "Sure, if it's important."

"It is," he nodded.

Twenty minutes later, she'd retold the story backwards as requested, sat back, and drank more water. "Did it help?"

"Yes, it did. Thank you. I do have a few questions for you. The night you say you saw Tara running away on the flats, do you recall what was she wearing?"

Madie frowned. "Umm … black jeans, bare feet, her hair was in a ponytail. I think she was wearing a white tee; that's all I can remember."

"And what about her husband?"

A pained look crossed her face. "When he pulled Tara backwards by her ponytail in the desert, he straddled her; I saw blue jeans and new black-and-white Nike air runners."

"What about jewellery?"

Madie ran her fingers across her chin and stared at the table. She looked up at the officer. "She was in the bathroom that night after he hit her. She brought her left hand up to her left cheek, examining it in the mirror. She thought he broke a bone in her cheek and touched the swollen wound, wincing. She was wearing a white gold narrow wedding band and a white gold engagement ring with a round diamond, and a ring of smaller ones around it."

"What about Douglas Crawford?"

Madie tried to concentrate and watched the face of Sergeant Davis disappear. In his place, she saw the face of Douglas Crawford. Everything in the room faded to black, except Crawford. He was smiling, holding up two pendants, his and hers. The scene changed, and they were back in the desert the night he killed Tara, with him straddling her. She saw his face come closer as he leaned down and placed his hands around her neck. The pendant around his neck fell forward and she saw the detail as it moved closer. Again, the scene changed, with Tara in the bathroom, examining her bruised face in the mirror, a smaller matching pendant around her neck.

In the distance, she heard a voice calling her name. "Madie, *Madie*, what's wrong? Can you hear me?"

The room came back into focus and Madie saw the concerned face of Sergeant Davis. She licked her lips and her eyes took in the room and the table they were sitting at. Feeling disoriented, she waited until her senses returned.

"You're back. You appeared to disappear into a trance. Are you feeling okay?"

Madie took a deep breath and exhaled slowly and drank water. "I'm fine, thanks … vision … flashes."

The man gave her a puzzled look. "What did you see?"

"They were both wearing matching pendants that night. Madie's was a little shorter than his. Can I have your pen and a piece of paper?"

She drew a long twisted chain with a spearhead hanging from it. "They were silver chains with a silver spearhead and the engraved inserts across the spearhead were set with black onyx."

Sergeant. Davis took the paper and wrote some notes on it. "We're almost finished here. Just a few questions. Have you ever seen Douglas Crawford before you met him at his home three weeks ago?"

"No—only in my nightmares and visions."

"Have you ever heard his name before you saw him in your vision, or on the internet three weeks ago?"

"Never."

"Have you ever met or talked to Tara Crawford's family and friends?"

"No, I have no idea who they are or where they live."

Davis nodded. "Last question, to satisfy my curiosity. Finding out a past life is the cause of your nightmares must have given you a sense of peace. You could have carried on your life and forgotten about it. What motivated you to continue on the search and come here with your findings?"

"Because I knew she'd been murdered, and I wanted to know more about her life. Then, when I found out it was still an unsolved case, I couldn't let it go. Being the only one who knew who her killer was, and knowing her family still had no answers, no closure, I had to go on."

"Okay, I think we're done here, Madie. We'll have your statement drawn up and have you back in to sign it. If you think of anything you'd like to add," he passed her his card, "call me. Meanwhile, I'll pull the file on Tara Crawford. The next step will be to organize a trip to the area where you saw Douglas Crawford on his dirt bike; would you be willing to take us to the area and show us the rock enclosure?"

"Of course," Madie answered.

He stood and extended his hand. "Thank you for coming

in today and providing us with this information. I'll contact you soon."

Madie shook his hand and followed him to the door.

Before he opened it, he turned to her. "The work you've done on this was very thorough and it took a lot of courage for you to go to the Crawford house, never mind hiking to the hills during that storm. But if the information you've provided is verified, you've placed yourself in possible danger. I'd ask that you stay away from Douglas Crawford and let us do our work."

Madie nodded. "I think my part is done; the rest is up to you now."

❧ 34 ❧

Sergeant Davis sat at his desk reading the file of Tara Crawford's disappearance. The last time the department had reviewed the file was ten months ago; the standard practice was to check cold files at least once a year. He wasn't familiar with the case because he was new to the detachment and this was before his deployment to Osoyoos.

The file was also periodically reviewed by an officer filling the duties of Southeast District Missing Persons and Unidentified Human Remains. Checking the notes, nothing had been added to the initial file. Cold files were a part of their work that kept them awake at night. This was why all tips were followed up, no matter who provided them or why. Davis remembered his cold file training at Innisfail, Alberta. *Working a cold case is a marathon, not a sprint.*

Tara's parents were still alive and living in Cherryville outside of Vernon. The notes confirmed they'd had no contact from Tara since her disappearance. He read Douglas Crawford's statement, in which he said Tara had left the morning of June 14th, 1989, to visit her parents.

After three days of no phone calls from her, he'd called her parents who told him she'd never arrived. A week after she'd disappeared, her car was found on the Crowsnest Highway outside of Rock Creek; her suitcases were inside and rifled through. Since her husband was the last person to see her, police had him as their number one suspect.

A search of their home provided no evidence of foul play, neither did her car. Although Douglas Crawford was never cleared as a suspect, there was no evidence to incriminate him, no crime scene, and no body. Eventually, the case reached a dead end.

Sergeant Davis looked at the evidence bags. There was a hairbrush for DNA purposes, should remains ever be found, and a manila envelope containing dental records. Another brown envelope had photos printed on it. He opened it and dumped the photos on his desk. Picking up one, he stared into the face of a young girl about nineteen years old, a smiling face full of sweetness and innocence. He noted the long dark hair that Madie had described. His blood chilled as he put the photo of Tara down because she reminded him he had a teenage daughter of his own. He pushed away the thoughts conjured up should anything ever happen to her. *Don't go there.*

He sighed and picked up another picture showing Tara and Douglas together. *They look happy enough.* But Davis had learned over the years of his career to never rely on photos of a smiling couple. He turned it over. Someone had written: *Tara and Douglas, Juniper Park, August 1997.*

Flipping the picture back, the first thing his eyes focussed on was a necklace around Tara's neck. He opened his desk drawer and pulled out a magnifying glass and studied the enlarged image, moving the glass to the image of Douglas, and swore. "Fuck me!"

Davis fumbled through the papers on his desk and pulled up Madie's drawing of the pendant in her vision. Her depiction of a pendent was dead on to the matching pendants worn by Tara and Douglas in the photo, taken almost a year before Madie Hayes was born. Shivers ran up his spine. Regardless of what he thought about reincarnation or Madie's fantastical story, he couldn't deny something was happening here. Madie knew things no one else did and Davis knew what needed to be done next. He spent the next few hours making phone calls and assigning follow-ups to other staff members.

Later that day, the sergeant sat in the conference room with staff members. "So, we've all read the file and the statements of Madie Hayes and Cody Diaz. You've seen the photos and Hayes' drawing of the matching pendants. Her statement bore out when she recounted it backwards—no missing details or out of place remarks, no detection of mistruths.

"The Diaz account of events he witnessed backs hers. An initial check on Diaz and Hayes turned up nothing. They're both clean. Tomorrow morning, we'll fly over the area and, hopefully, Miss Hayes will be able to pinpoint the location she hiked to Sunday morning. To start, we'll be searching for evidence of dirt-bike tracks and footprints in the vicinity. After the recent heavy rains, the ground surface will have been soft enough to leave traces of such activity. We'll also search on the hilltops for footprints of Miss Hayes to confirm she was there. There'll be me, Miss Hayes, Constables Friesen and Timmons … and Corporal Jennings, our Forensic Identification Services (FIS) officer, who's been called out from Penticton to photograph the scene and collect any specimens. Casual dress for hiking and appropriate pack supplies."

"Is head office sending a chopper?" Constable Friesen asked.

"No, it's in use elsewhere. We're using the Osoyoos/Oliver Search and Rescue helicopter. Miss Hayes and Mr Diaz will be here in the morning to sign their statements. Chopper leaves at ten o'clock sharp everyone. Be ready."

THE HELICOPTER ROSE into the air, facing east, completed a circle, and headed west over the town of Osoyoos. Madie watched their ascent and flight across the flats with fascination until she felt a tap on her shoulder. She turned to see Sergeant Davis pointing at the headphones on the back of the seat in front of her and motioned for her to put them on.

Once they were in place, he asked, "Have you flown in a chopper before?"

"No, my first time." They were well over the grasslands, heading towards the hills. "After my long hike the other day, I can't believe how quick it is to get there by air."

"I hear ya, frees up a lot of our time. We're following the path you walked and when we get to the hills, I'll get the pilot to come down lower. Hopefully, you can point out where you climbed up the hill and show us the enclosure from the air."

A few minutes later, they had reached their destination. Madie studied the terrain below. "There." She pointed to a group of rocks to the right of the hill. "That's where I ascended."

The pilot flew over the area and once they reached the top, Madie looked to the left. Knowing what to look for, she saw it immediately. "Down there. See it? That's the enclosure."

The FIS Officer snapped pictures of the hill and the enclosure as they circled a few times.

Sergeant Davis gave instructions to the pilot to land on the flats an appropriate distance away to protect the potential crime scene. They disembarked and he handed a book to one of the constables. "You're the designated log officer, you know the drill; time record of arrival, names and badge info of all of us here, times of comings and goings for all personnel who arrive or leave, evidence retrieved, etc." He turned to Madie. "I'm going to take you a little closer and ask some questions. You can wait there with Constable Timmons, only myself and the FIS Officer will proceed further to determine a perimeter."

Madie followed the three men towards the rock face.

Davis held up a hand and she stopped in place. "Does the area look familiar, Madie?"

"To the right, around the corner of that large cropping, that's where I climbed to the top of the hill." Her eyes moved to the left, following the foothills. "There." She pointed to a flat facing. Looking above it, she saw the top of the hill where she'd stood and looked down into the enclosure. "Partway along that flat facing, there's a community of sagebrush. See? That's where the opening to the compound is hidden from view."

Madie stood with Timmons and watched the two men move in closer. They stopped about ten feet away from the sagebrush, examining the ground. The FIS Officer stopped to stoop and take pictures. He stepped gingerly towards the wild brush, choosing his steps carefully, examined it, snapped photos, and pushed some of the brush aside and peered behind it. Proceeding towards the right, ground examination and photos were repeated; at one point, the two officers stared across the desert to the east. They disappeared around the large cropping, returning a few minutes later to walk back to Madie and the Constable.

Sergeant Davis nodded to Timmons. "We'll convene at the chopper."

They stood in a circle, addressed by the sergeant. "Constable Friesen, I'd like you to set up stakes and police tape. Corporal Jennings will show you the perimeter." He turned to Madie. "Madie, grab your pack; once Jennings collects specimens, I want you to take the Corporal up the hill, following the same route you took on Sunday morning. He's looking for your footprints, anything to show you were up there. Constable Timmons, you're to follow the dirt-bike tracks we found, hopefully back to the source. If you reach a final destination, take photos, but don't engage unless necessary. When you're done, return. I'll be flying out to make some calls. We need Search & Rescue out here with a dog."

Madie followed the Corporal to the perimeter and waited while he pointed out to Friesen the area to enclose with tape. He led her to the rocks just outside the perimeter. "You might as well wait in the shade while I gather specimens."

A little confused, she asked, "What kind of specimens?"

"Botany—soil and plants." He walked over to the sage-brush community hiding the enclosure, put on surgical gloves, pulled out a small cutting tool, a plastic bag, and snipped samples off the plants. "See these broken branches?"

"Yup."

"Someone pushed through here to get through the opening and snapped them. This is evidence." He cut off the broken pieces and placed them in a separate bag and, using a felt pen, wrote on it.

"Douglas Crawford did that, I saw him," she stated.

Jennings nodded and turned back to the sagebrush. He cut them back to expose the entry and walked inside.

Madie studied the rocks in front of her. She climbed up and positioned herself to observe Corporal Jennings in the enclosure. He looked up at her and she gave him a wave.

He smiled and got back to work. He photographed foot-prints in the soil and gathered soil samples, marking each evidence bag as before with the plant samples. He stooped down to study one set of prints, snapped more photos, and then stared towards the back rock wall. "See these?" he said, indicating the prints, "He bent down here and balanced on the balls of his feet like he was studying something. This confirms your statement."

It felt good to be validated. It hit Madie that all this evidence wasn't just to establish a possible crime scene but to clear her of public mischief or of being crazy. She could tell

Jennings was enjoying having a novice audience where he could share his knowledge.

He stood, studying the rest of the ground towards the back wall from one side to the other. "There are no tracks back there, only across the front." He paced back and forth, staring to the back, almost like he didn't want to step back there. "If you study the ground about two feet from the rock face, you can see a slight indent in the soil." He snapped more pictures.

"Meaning?"

"That if—and at this point, it's a big if—someone dug into the ground and refilled the hole, the soil would eventually settle and leave an indent."

Chills ran down Madie's spine as she stared at the indent. The investigators had a lot more work to do before establishing this spot as a burial site, but not so for Madie. *You're down there, Tara. I know it. My bones are aching with the knowledge the remains of the person you once were, will soon be found.*

"Bear with me while I make casts of footprints and tire tracks. Then, I'll be done here for the time being."

Madie stayed put while he completed his work. When he returned for her, he said, "Shall we head up the hill?"

She climbed off the rocks and joined the man outside the enclosure. She peered through the opening. "You're going to find her. She's in there."

He gave her a long stare, then said, "We'll walk the perimeter line to the east to avoid contaminating the potential crime scene. When we turn north to get around the rock face to climb, I'll point out bike tracks for you to step over."

"Crawford's bike tracks?"

"Allegedly. If we're lucky, Timmons will be able to trace them back to his house."

Once they reached the side of the hill, Madie took lead and led Corporal Jennings through the rocks, and they began their ascent. On the hill, she walked the line across the top until she reached the spot where they could look down into the hidden gravesite.

Jennings took more photos. He studied the ground and found some footprints. "These must be yours." More photos. "You wearing the same boots as Sunday?"

"I am," Madie replied.

"See this right footprint? Place your right foot beside it and lean into it."

When she was done, he smiled. "Perfect match," he said, snapping more pics.

Madie took him to the other side of the hill and showed him where she climbed down and walked the flats to the highway. They finished at the place she'd sat and snacked before her descent.

Corporal Jennings kneeled, took some camera shots, and pulled another bag out of his pack. Using tweezers, he picked up an object. "What did you eat?"

"Cheese, crackers, and trail mix."

"A-ha ... behold, a raisin." He put it in the bag and stopped for something else. "Peanut," he said, picking up a few more morsels. "Okay, we're done here. Let's get back to base."

They reached the bottom just as the helicopter returned. Jennings left her by the rocks to talk with Sergeant Davis, who had exited the chopper with a dog handler and his German shepherd dog.

Madie sat on a rock and drank water from her pack, observing the activity in front of her. The FIS officer climbed onto the chopper, disembarking a few minutes later with a machine that looked similar to a big lawnmower, but with larger tires, and unloaded plastic tubs and a large canvas bag.

Sergeant Davis waved her over and she joined him by the chopper. "The pilot will take you back to the detachment now. You've been a real help to us, Madie."

"Will you let me know if you find ... anything ... her?"

The fact there may actually be a body became a reality at that moment, and she couldn't bring herself to use Tara's name.

"Of course, you'll be the first to know if we find something; but, know if we do, it'll be a while before we can confirm the identity."

"Thank you."

"You know, you were lucky it was still raining when you hiked in. It washed away your footprints. Otherwise, Crawford might have noticed them and not entered the enclosure—or he might have been spooked and searched for you. I'm happy that didn't happen. Thank you, Madie. We'll be in touch."

The chopper lifted and circled overhead. Madie could see the handler enter the enclosure with his dog in tow. Fascinated, she'd have loved to stay and watch the dog at work; of course, the sergeant would never have allowed that. *My role is finished. Besides, I know what the outcome is going to be.*

The idea that her connection to the subject of her lifelong nightmares would soon play out in real-time shook her to the core. Feeling chilled, she wrapped her arms across her chest. *A little too real, I don't think I could handle seeing the unearthing of Tara Crawford.* On the flight back, Madie considered the sergeant's words. She knew he hadn't meant to scare her. *Or had he?* Still, she took it as advice to stay away from Douglas Crawford and let them take the case where they will.

35

Madie drove into the parking lot at the Centre; right away, she knew something was wrong. The gates to the compound were closed and locked, the closed sign visible on the gate. *What?* A glance at the clock on the dash read 1:30 p.m. The parking lot was empty save for two vehicles: Kelly's and Pete's, a volunteer. *What's going on?*

She exited her car and heard someone calling her name. She looked up to see Bea coming towards her from Chelsea's yard. Madie waved and walked across the parking lot. "Hi, Bea. Do you know why the Centre's closed? Where is everybody?"

"Chelsea's been waiting on you. Come on in and she'll explain."

Madie followed her into the house to the bedroom, where they found Chelsea propped up in bed. "Hey, don't you look cosy?"

"Yup, fat and cosy," Chelsea said, patting the bed beside her. "Come, sit. I want to hear all about your day, hon; but first, let me fill you in on what's happening here."

"Yes, please do. But I'll drag a chair over. I'm sweaty and dirty from hiking." She settled beside the bed and gave

Chelsea her full attention while Bea cleared lunch dishes from the table and left the room.

"Thanks, Bea," Chelsea said, turning to Madie. "There's been a horrific accident on the highway between Stoney Creek and Oliver—a multi-vehicle crash, with multiple injuries. Wenner and Cody were called to help because a sheep carrier flipped over. The highway's closed."

"Oh no, how terrible. Do you think they need me?"

"Actually, Wenner would like you to prep the number two surgery in the big barn in case he needs it," Chelsea replied.

"I can do that. Where's Kelly and Pete?"

"They're next door, preparing Sydney's barn. The sheep were being transported to a new farm in Armstrong. Sydney and Jax are still up at the cottage at Emerald Lake, and they've permitted us to use the barn for the animals with minor injuries and the second pasture for the rest. The ones badly hurt or in need of surgery will come to the Centre. Kelly and Pete will open the water troughs and take feed up to the pasture."

"Sounds good. How are they going to get the sheep here?"

"Wenner borrowed Sydney's transporter."

She nodded and stood. "I'd best wash up and get the surgery ready."

"When you've done that, would it be an imposition to ask if you could come back and sit with me? Oh, this is *so-ooo* frustrating. Chaz is returning from Kelowna and can't get through the closed highway. He's heading up through Rock Creek and down the Crowsnest into Osoyoos, a much longer trip, and Bea has to leave soon for an appointment she can't miss. Since I'm not supposed to be alone …"

"Not a problem. Is a half-hour to forty-five minutes okay?"

"Perfect, thanks so much. And then you can tell me all about your day."

Inside of an hour, Madie was back with Chelsea. Bea had left them a thermos of tea and fresh-baked chocolate-chip cookies. As they nibbled their way through a plateful, Madie related the details of her trip to the desert.

"Oh, wow! A cadaver dog? At least you know they're taking you seriously," Chelsea said, awed.

"I can't believe it'll all be over soon. Tara can go home, and no more nightmares and visions. What a surreal day this has been."

"You've done a good thing and I'm proud of you."

"Thank you. But how could I not? Now, her family can have closure."

Chelsea chuckled. "We're talking about this like it's a given they're going to find her there."

Madie gave her a knowing smile. "That's because *you*, of all people, and I know they will. I saw Crawford bury her in that enclosure on Sunday in a vision. And then to have him show up at that exact location an hour later? No doubt at all."

"Mmm … I hear you."

"Perhaps I should call Cody and see how they're doing." Madie reached into her pocket but her cell phone wasn't there. She stood and searched all her pockets. "Strange— must've left my phone in the car. An expression on Chelsea's face caught her attention. "Chelsea?"

The woman stared at her with a look of shock; her chin dropped and her eyes grew big like saucers.

"Chelsea? What's wrong?"

Chelsea winced and doubled over in pain. "My water just broke," she croaked.

Madie froze. *My God, not now. The highway's closed. How'll we get there?* Her thoughts fired all over the place.

Chelsea grabbed her arm and squeezed. "I'm scared, Madie. I can't deliver this baby safely."

Madie heard the fear in her voice and it snapped her into action. "You're going to be okay, Chelsea … you and the baby," she said soothingly. "Stay calm. I'll be right back."

Madie left the room to make a call. She punched 911 and waited forever for them to answer.

"911, what is the state of your emergency?"

"I need an ambulance in Stoney Creek; my boss' water broke, and I can't get to the hospital in Oliver because the highway's closed. She's scheduled for Caesarean in a couple of weeks because she has a condition and can't give birth naturally."

"I'm sorry, but you won't get an ambulance for ages. They're all busy at the accident site."

"What about Medi-vac?"

"Medi-vac and Search & Rescue helicopters are working the accident site as well. It's quite a mess out there. A lot of casualties. It would be faster if you can get her to the hospital yourself, using another route."

Madie thought for a moment. "Is the accident on the Stoney Creek side of Black Sage Road or the Oliver side?"

"Hang on." There was silence for several seconds. "It's on the Oliver side. I think that's your best bet."

Madie hung up and raced back to the bedroom. Chelsea was sitting on the edge of the bed, taking deep breathes. She picked up Chelsea's cell and put it in her pocket. "Okay, I'm driving you. Stay put and I'll get you a clean nightgown."

"Second drawer on the left."

Madie got a clean nightie. "Let me help you stand. There you go. I'll slip this one over your head. Now slip your arms through this one— and it's on. Here's your housecoat and we're done."

Madie got her into the wheelchair, giving her a pillow to hold. "We're off."

She wheeled her through the house and onto the back deck where Chaz had built a ramp. A few minutes later, they reached Madie's car. Once Chelsea was settled in the front passenger seat, Madie put the seat half down and placed the pillow behind her head. She grabbed a light blanket from the back of the car and covered her. "There you go. Snug as a bug in a rug." *Where did that come from? Not something I've ever said.*

She grabbed her backpack from the backseat, searching for her cell phone. "What?" *The pocket she usually kept it in was unzipped. Oh no, I must have lost it on my hike up the hill. Damn!* Madie got in the car and turned the ignition. *No time to worry about that now.*

They pulled onto the road into Stoney Creek, Madie driving at high speed.

Chelsea was in pain and concentrating on her breathing.

"It's gonna be fine, Chelsea. We'll be there in no time."

A car pulled out of a driveway right in front of them and Madie swung into the oncoming lane, speeding right past it and back onto her side of the road. The car honked at them and the driver put his arm out the window, giving her the finger.

Chelsea huffed and puffed between breaths. "Please … slow down … or … we won't … get there … at all."

"Sorry." Madie slowed down and realized she should have her hazard lights on. She punched the button on the dash to set them flashing. Once she reached the town, she turned south.

"Shouldn't we go … north?" Chelsea asked.

"Highway's closed, remember? We'll take a secondary road, Black Sage Road.'

"Oh, good … wine country … love that drive. Maybe … we could stop … for samples." Chelsea groaned with pain shot through her. "Might help my pain."

Madie's laughter was a little loud and forced, but the moment needed it. "Look at you—still got your sense of humour."

She turned left, crossing over the highway, and they were heading north again in no time. She took Chelsea's phone out of her pocket and searched contacts for Chaz's number.

It rang and rang.

"Oh, come on, come on, pick up." It went to voicemail and she left him a message. "Don't know where you are at this moment, Chaz, but Madie here. Chelsea's water broke and I'm driving her on secondary roads to Oliver. She's fine. We'll see you at the hospital."

The same thing happened when she punched in Sydney's number and then Cody's. She left a similar message with both.

Chelsea's pain settled for a moment. She burst out in anger. "Where the hell is everybody? Cell phones are supposed to keep us in contact."

"I guess it's a helluva day for us all, Chels. It's you and me against the world, kid."

"Who you calling kid? I could be your mom."

They shared a nervous laugh, easing the tension. Madie glanced over at Chelsea and the smile on her face froze when she saw the telltale signs of blood seeping through the beige blanket. *Oh, shit!*

Her eyes focused back on the road. The traffic had increased, and before long she was in bumper to bumper traffic, slowing their speed down considerably. "Fuck!" *A fat lot of good it's doing, having my flashers on.*

Chelsea's breathing became shallow. "What's ... wrong?"

"Everybody and their donkey are on this road, but don't worry, we're almost in Oliver."

Once they reached the town, they inched along at a snail's pace, until the traffic stopped completely.

"Dammit, anyway," Madie said, pounding the steering wheel. She looked at Chelsea, who'd become quiet the past few minutes. "Chelsea? *Chelsea!*"

Chelsea opened her eyes and looked at her as if from a faraway place. "Tell Chaz ... I love him," she whispered. Her eyes closed.

"No—*no!* Don't you dare leave me. Chelsea! You hear me? Stay with me," Madie yelled.

She looked at the road ahead in a panic. She could see the

hospital on the left-hand side, about three long blocks ahead. It sat on the corner of Black Sage Road and McKinney Road, but it might as well have been on the moon. "I'll never get there."

There was no shoulder she could pull onto to finish the last few blocks, as illegal as that would be. "Like I give a fuck." Madie looked to her left and saw a narrow paved road that ran parallel to the hospital up ahead. It only ran for about three blocks and was devoid of traffic. There was a wide, fairly flat arid meadow between Black Sage Road and the hospital road. She looked at the traffic in the opposite lane, coming towards her. *Not nearly as busy leaving town, as our side of the road going in … as we're at a complete standstill.*

"Fuck it!" Madie turned her wheels and waited for a break in traffic that would allow her to cross through. Seeing the moment, she floored it across the double solid line, her tires squealing on the hot pavement. A glance at the oncoming traffic made her heart pound. "Oh shit!"

A pick-up was almost on her, travelling faster than she'd first anticipated. Her foot hit the gas pedal harder and the car flew across the lane, clearing the vehicle just in time. She hit the edge of the paved road and bounced her way down an incline, coming to a full stop right in front of a telephone pole.

"Oh my God!" she yelled.

Realizing she'd held her breath through the whole thing, she let it out and gasped for air to the sound of honking cars on the roadway behind her. She looked in her rear-view mirror and saw people giving her the finger and heard them shouting obscenities. She shouted back, "Fuck you!"

Madie drove around the pole, across the open field, taking out sagebrush and floored it up the incline onto the narrow road. Picking up speed, she raced down the road, into the hospital parking lot, and came to a halting stop at the entrance to the ER. She turned to Chelsea with no idea if she was even alive. She put a finger on her neck, felt a pulse, and breathed a sigh of relief. "Thank God."

Madie jumped out of the vehicle and ran through the doors, stopping cold in her tracks. Emergency was a complete zoo. The waiting room was full of patients, who she assumed were accident victims with temporary bandages for various wounds; some sported blood-soaked clothes. It was like a war zone.

Madie tried to work her way up to the registration desk but couldn't get through. People pushed her back, telling her to wait in line. Madie turned in circles, not sure of how to get help for Chelsea.

In a panic, she stepped away from the chaos and calmed herself. She pulled Chelsea's phone from her pocket and found her doctor's number. When the receptionist answered, Madie told her where she was and what was happening. The receptionist put her on hold.

. "Madie, Dr Carson here. I'm in the hospital, I'll be right down with some help. Where is Chelsea now?"

"She's in the car unconscious, in front of the ER doors—she's haemorrhaging, doctor!"

"Okay, go wait with her and we'll be right there."

❧ 36 ❧

Sergeant Davis stood at the enclosure entrance, watching the dog handler take his charge through its paces. The handler walked the dog from one side of the compound to the other, and back again, moving further into the compound with each pass. They'd reached the middle point and so far the dog hadn't shown any behavioural changes.

He turned to see Constable Timmons approaching him. "You're back. What did you find?"

"I traced the bike track to Crawford's backyard. A dirt bike was parked behind a shed. I took some pics."

"Good work. Did you see anyone?"

"Nope." Timmons glanced at a stockpile of machinery and gear sitting against the rock face. "Where's the chopper?"

"There's a fatal multi-vehicle accident on the highway north of Stoney Creek. They've called in Oliver and Penticton staff to work it. The chopper was needed to transport casualties to various area hospitals. He'll come back if we need him. Army personnel from Vernon are on standby, should their chopper be required."

Timmons pulled out his water bottle and took a swig. The two men turned their attention back to the dog, who was sniffing his way across the enclosure some four feet from the back rock face. When he reached the halfway point, he stopped. The handler stood still and lengthened his lead.

The shepherd sniffed back and forth and in a circle. Moving inside the area he'd circled, the canine took a passive behavioural position by sitting down and staring at the ground beneath him. Davis noted that the dog was sitting in the indentation in the soil, pointed out to him by the FIS Officer. His handler took a marker out of his pocket and placed it on the ground in front of the animal.

"Good dog, Turbo," he said, rubbing his canine partner's head. He took a treat out of his pocket and fed it to his charge before leading him out of the enclosure. "It's all yours; something's down there." He took Turbo outside the perimeter and gave him some water.

Corporal Jennings, the Forensic Identification Services (FIS) officer climbed down from his perch on the rocks, where he'd watched Turbo do his job, and joined Davis and Timmons. "I guess it's my turn. If there's something down there, it should be an easy read in sandy soil. Let's get to it."

Jennings pushed the GPR—ground penetrating radar—machine into the enclosure. He charged it up and adjusted the small screen on the handlebars. He guided the GPR over the entire enclosure, following the path of Turbo and his handler. When he reached the area identified by the dog, the FIS Officer repeated a rectangular pattern. Using markers of his own, he identified a grid area on the ground surface. When he finished, he took surface soil samples within the grid and some photos. He rejoined his colleagues. "Now, the real work begins."

"What'd you find?" Davis asked.

"Whatever's down there may be wrapped in a tarp. Tarps tend to bounce a clear reflection on the screen—mine lit up like a Christmas tree. The inner grid represents the approximate size of the object, which just happens to be about the size of a human body."

The hairs on the back of Sergeant Davis' neck stood on end. "Madie Hayes said Crawford rolled his wife in a blue tarp."

The men stared at each other in silence.

A tent was set up over the grid site, with digging tools and forensic supplies on the ready.

Some hours later, the FIS officer stood at the gravesite, calling Sergeant Davis to join him. After digging, and soil sample retrieval at various levels, they'd discovered the object detected on the GPR. Davis joined him and stared into the shallow grave. The reality of what he saw left him speechless. He glanced over to Jennings, who said in acknowledgement, "There it is, your blue tarp."

Sergeant Davis shook his head, taking in the size and shape of the exposed tarp. "It could house a body. This is the strangest case I've ever worked."

Corporal Jennings shot more photos of the open grave. "I'll need to make a small incision in the tarp to confirm the contents and, if it's what we think it is, we'll have to wait for the Coroner to arrive on scene before proceeding, as well as the District Major Crime Unit to take the lead in the investigation."

A short time later, Jennings confirmed there was indeed a human skeleton inside the tarp. Davis left the tent to make the calls to request a Coroner on site and an MCU Investigator.

DR MASON THORPE, the Coroner from Penticton, and a certified doctor, stood by the gravesite with Corporal Jennings and the MCU investigator. Constable Friesen, the log keeper in charge of exhibits, stood to one side with Sergeant Davis; Constable Timmons had returned to the Detachment. The

Coroner was now in charge of the crime scene and he'd been brought up-to-date on all specimens gathered thus far, as well as provided with photos taken.

"The tarp is two layers; I'll cut them back one layer at a time," Jennings announced.

The process was a slow one, designed not to disturb any evidential material that might be on the tarp or the skeleton. Once the tarp was open and the skeletal remains were exposed, the FIS Officer did his thing once again with the camera. "There's some jewellery here—a necklace around the neck, another one intertwined in the fingers of the right hand, and two rings on the left wedding finger."

Sergeant Davis' body stiffened with the memory of Madie's statement, putting him on alert. "Let me guess. Silver chains, silver arrowhead amulet with black onyx inserts, white gold wedding band, engagement ring with a single round diamond, encircled with small diamonds."

"Could well be; the silver necklaces and ring bands are pretty tarnished, but arrowheads and diamonds look about right." Jennings moved away to allow the Coroner to inspect the bones and skull.

Because the area had been undisturbed through the years and the grave was shallow, the skeleton appeared to be fairly intact. But Sergeant Davis knew from experience that if they tried to remove it, it could easily fall apart. *We got lucky this time; it can be transported in the tarp.*

When the Coroner finished his initial inspection, he stood. "It's female. There are no obvious wounds, no bullet holes, or apparent broken bones or fractures. There is some damage to the facial and neck bones, but I need to examine them more carefully in the morgue." He addressed the FIS Officer. "You can collect the jewellery as exhibits now."

Jennings removed the jewellery evidence from the skeleton, bagging and labelling each of the pieces. His eyes moved over to the pelvic area and rested on a spot between the two femur leg bones. "Now, this is a rare sight." He pointed to a pile of small bones. "She was pregnant at the time of her death—at a certain point of decomposition, body gases pushed the fetus out of the birth canal. That's what's known as a coffin birth."

You could hear a pin drop as all eyes stared in silence at the infant remains. Davis glanced at Constable Friesen, knowing it was his first time working this type of crime scene. The young man was visibly shaken. His face was ashen, and he was taking shallow breaths.

Afraid he might vomit, and contaminate the area, Davis said, "Short break, everyone." He leaned toward the young man. "Why don't we go outside for some fresh air?"

Once outside the tent, they removed their masks. "You okay?" Davis asked his fellow officer.

Friesen took some deep breathes. "Fine."

"It's been a long day for us all. You've done well for your first gravesite. I remember my first, it leaves a lasting impression. It never gets easier, but you learn coping mechanisms. This case is one for the books. And you—you've been very professional."

"I was okay until he mentioned—the coffin death."

"Hey, we're all still human. It's when it doesn't bother you anymore that you should be worried." He placed a hand on his broad shoulder and squeezed. "You ready to go back in?"

"Yeah!"

They returned to finish their work. A large piece of plastic had been spread beside the open grave. Jennings closed the tarp and it was lifted out of the ground with the remains still intact. It was wrapped in the clear plastic sheet and zippered inside a body bag. The FIS Officer snapped photos of the empty gravesite, took more soil samples, and sifted through the soil that lay under the body for twenty-two years, searching for more evidence.

"I think we're finished here," Jennings stated with a nod.

The Coroner took possession of the remains, which would return with him to Penticton for closer inspection at the Morgue. He addressed Sergeant. Davis and the MCU Investigator. "I'll call you in the morning when I've scheduled the examination. It'll probably be mid-afternoon, tomorrow."

Sergeant Davis nodded, turning to Corporal Friesen. "You'll attend the Coroner's inspection to continue logging and take possession of any more exhibits. Meanwhile, you'll take control of today's evidence; it'll return with us to the Detachment until we can arrange transport to the Forensic Lab on the coast with the body." To the Coroner, he said, "We have dental records at the station. I'll send them up with Corporal Friesen tomorrow.

❦ 37 ❦

The waiting room in the maternity ward was overwhelmingly quiet compared to the noise decibel level and chaos in Emergency. In fact, Madie was the only person there. She was waiting for Chaz to join her. He'd called her en route to say he would be there in twenty minutes. Sydney had checked in as well and was on her way from Emerald Lake. She'd spared them both explicit details, only saying Chelsea was in surgery.

Madie placed her head back against the wall, closed her eyes, and reflected on her day. Her body ached from the hike up the hill with Corporal Jennings; she felt sweaty and dirty. *I need a shower and a soft bed. Not much I can do about that right now though.*

"Madie." At the sound of her name, she opened her eyes to see Chaz and Sydney standing in front of her.

"We pulled into the parking lot at the same time," Chaz said.

"Thank God you're here," Madie said and sighed softly.

Sydney sat beside her. "Any more news?"

Madie shook her head. "No, she's still in surgery."

Chaz pulled over another chair and sat in front of the two

women. "Thank God you arrived back at the Centre when you did. I'm so grateful, Madie. Who knows what would have happened if you hadn't?"

Madie felt pained. "I wish I could have got her here sooner. The traffic was horrendous; maybe I should have taken Crowsnest and cut through White Lake."

Sydney reached over and squeezed her arm. "That's the longer route around and it was backed up too. You did good, Madie."

"Apparently, the highway will be closed until tomorrow. Have you talked to Cody?" Chaz asked.

"No, we keep missing each other and leaving messages. He and Wenner are back at the Centre dealing with injured sheep. A lot of them died at the accident scene."

Chaz studied Madie. "You've had a helluva day. You look exhausted."

"I'm okay. Is it alright if I stay with you until she's out of surgery?"

"Of course," he said with a grateful smile.

Twenty minutes later, Dr Carson joined them. Nodding to Sydney, she turned to Chaz and shook his hand. "You must be Chaz. I'm Dr Carson. Congratulations, you have a baby daughter. She's small but she's holding her own."

Sydney's hands flew to her face. "Omigod, a baby sister."

Chaz stared at her in disbelief. "Thank you. How's Chelsea? Is she awake?"

Doctor Carson grabbed a chair. "She's weak but stable. Let's sit." Once they were all settled, she said, "Chelsea lost a lot of blood and we're giving her a blood transfusion. Because her blood pressure dropped to a low reading, Dr Abrams and I decided to keep her in an induced coma for a few days, to allow her body to adjust to the shock and heal."

"A coma?" Chaz asked, looking perplexed.

"Yes, she needs complete rest; our main concern is to

avoid blood clots. As soon as her blood pressure normalizes and we see she's stronger, we'll wake her up."

Chaz ran anxious hands through his hair. "She *is* going to be alright, though. Right?"

"As I said, she's stable."

"Can I sit with her?" he asked quietly.

"Of course."

Madie listened to everything in a state of shock. She hadn't uttered a word, watching the others interact like she was off to one side and not part of the conversation.

Dr Carson continued. "Your daughter is in the MICU in an incubator. She'll remain in the hospital for three to four weeks before we can send her home. If you want to follow me, I'll take you there."

The three of them went with the doctor. They stood at the glass window, watching the tiny bundle of life hooked up with wires to monitors, an IV in her little arm.

Chaz stared at his daughter with glistening eyes. "Little Maisie," he whispered.

"She's beautiful. So tiny, but perfect," Sydney said in awe.

Madie's eyes blurred, her body shook, as a multitude of emotions pulled her in different directions. *I have to get out of here.* "She *is* beautiful. Congratulations to you both. If you don't mind, I think I'll head home now."

"Are you okay to drive?" Chaz asked, worried.

"I'm okay."

Sydney looked at her with concern. "If you want to wait until I see my mom, I could drive you home."

"No, you should be here with Chaz. Really, I'll be fine."

Chaz moved forward and hugged her. "I can't thank you enough. Get some sleep. We'll call if anything changes."

"I lost my phone somewhere in the hills, so call the Centre. Hopefully, one of the officers out there will find it," Madie said.

She pulled Chelsea's phone out of her pocket and pressed

it into Sydney's hand. "It's Chelsea's. Cody's number is in there too."

Sydney took her in her arms. "Thanks, so much. See you soon."

She left, sensing they were both staring after her. She needed to escape it all and be alone. When she climbed into the car, her hand went to her chest. "Uhh!" Her eyes locked onto the front passenger seat. The grey seat material was stained with blood that had dripped onto the grey rubber floor mat.

"Oh, Chelsea," she cried out. Removing her jean jacket, Madie covered the seat to hide the stain. She sat behind the wheel for a few minutes, trying to ground herself.

The drive home down Black Sage Road was uneventful and less than half the time compared to travelling up with Chelsea. The vineyards and farmlands she passed, normally a pleasant view she enjoyed, disappeared without a glance. She might as well have been driving in a tunnel.

The sun was about to drop behind the hills, and the air had cooled. Madie shivered and turned on the heat. She tried to push the day's events away, wanting—needing—her mind as numb as her body felt. Her hand continuously wiped her eyes, which wouldn't stop tearing, making her vision blurry.

She pulled the car over to the side of the road and watched the sun go down in the west as dark shadows spread across the flats, creating eerie shapes and ominous darkness to the fading light. Robotically, she pulled onto the road and drove on.

CODY HEARD the sound of Madie's car pulling into the driveway. He headed to the door and opened it as she stepped onto the porch. She looked exhausted and he took in her dishevelled appearance and the blank expression on her face. "Hi, I'm glad you're home."

Madie hesitated a moment when she saw him, walked past him into the cabin, and dropped in the armchair.

Cody shut the door. "I called you on Chelsea's phone. Syd told me you were heading home, so I came straight here when I finished at the Centre."

She stared straight ahead, saying nothing.

"Madie?"

He knew she was in shock and wasn't sure what to say to snap her out of it. What he did know was she shouldn't be alone. He decided not to push her to talk until she was ready. "I'll make you some tea. Are you hungry?"

"No, thanks," she whispered.

Cody was rummaging through the cupboard for the teabags when a knock came at the door. "I'll get it." He opened the door to find Sergeant Davis on the other side.

"Good evening, Cody. Is Madie in?"

"Uh—yeah, come in. She just got in from the hospital in Oliver."

The officer looked surprised. "Oh?" He glanced at Madie still in the armchair. "Nothing serious, I hope."

"Chelsea Grey's water broke two weeks before her scheduled Caesarean. Madie had to get her to Oliver along Black Sage Road."

"I see. That must have been a difficult trip, what with the accident closing the highway. I hear it was a zoo out there. How's Chelsea doing?"

"Umm, please come in … they did a Caesarean and she has a daughter. The baby is in MICU, but Chelsea is in an induced coma. She lost a lot of blood but, apparently, she's stable."

"Glad she's stable." So far, Madie hadn't acknowledged his arrival. He looked at Cody quizzically, who shrugged and gave him an I-don't-know look. He sat down on the couch in front of her and leaned forward. "Hi, Madie. We found your cell in the rocks by the compound." He placed it on the coffee table. "I stopped by because I promised to let you know if we found anything on site."

That got her attention, and she lifted her head and stared into his eyes in silence.

Cody sat on the arm of her chair.

Sergeant Davis focused on Madie, speaking in a soft voice. "Madie, I want you to know we found something out there."

Her eyes grew big and her body stiffened. "What?"

"The remains of a female."

"Tara?"

"We haven't identified her as yet."

Madie swallowed hard. "Was she wrapped in a blue tarp?"

Davis glanced at Cody and back to Madie. "I can't give you any details at this point, but I promised to let you know before the media, and they're already asking questions. As soon as I know more, so will you."

Madie started to gag. Her hands flew to her mouth and she ran to the bathroom. She left the door open and the two men saw her kneel on the floor and vomit into the toilet.

Cody turned to Sergeant Davis. "She arrived just before you did. I haven't had a chance to talk to her. You can see the state she's in."

"She's in shock. It was a difficult morning for her on-site and then having to handle the situation with Chelsea." Davis paused, running a hand through his hair. "And my arrival just added to it."

Cody heard the toilet flush and looked back at Madie. She stood, reached into the shower stall, and turned on the water. After testing it with one hand, she stepped in, clothes and all, leaving the shower door open.

The two men exchanged glances and rushed to the bathroom. By the time they got to the door, Madie had slid down the wall of the stall. They found her curled into a fetal position, the water pounding down on her, her body convulsing as she broke into loud sobs.

Cody turned the water off, stepped into the stall and sat down beside her. He cradled and rocked her in his arms. "It's okay, sweetheart. Let it out. Everything's going to be okay."

Madie clung to Cody, trying to talk through her blubbering. "It's all so fucked up, Cody …"

"Ss-ssh." He held her tighter.

"It's her, Cody. I know it's Tara." Madie took some deep breaths. "Life, death." She gulped loudly. "Tara died, I was born, Chelsea might die, her baby born, people on the highway dead—all those poor sheep—so much pain. What's the point of it all?"

"Chelsea's strong, she'll make it." Cody held her until her sobs subsided. "Come on, babe. You're exhausted. Let's get you out of these wet clothes." He pulled her to her feet.

Sergeant Davis, who'd stood by as a quiet observer, asked, "When did you eat last, Madie?"

"I—umm—this morning on the hill with Corporal Jennings."

"Well, I think some fluids, a bite to eat, and a good night's sleep is in order. You did well today. Considering all that you've had to handle, you've been brave and strong. I believe a lot of people will be indebted to you."

Madie managed a wry smile. "You might be back to arrest me in the morning. I broke a lot of laws today, getting Chelsea to the hospital."

He cocked one eyebrow. "Really? Maybe we should leave this conversation right here. I'll forget you even mentioned it and take my leave."

"Thanks, Sergeant Davis, and thank you for stopping by." Madie turned to Cody. "I think I'll take a real shower while you make my tea."

"Okay." Cody kissed her on the tip of her nose and the two men backed out of the bathroom.

Before she could close the door, Sergeant Davis gave her a mischievous look. "By the way, I heard some chatter on the scanner earlier about this crazy lady who crossed the highway through solid double lines in front of oncoming traffic, bounced over the meridian to Hospital Road, and raced like a bat out of hell down the road, exhibiting rude gestures and spouting profanity. Know anything about that?"

Madie's face reddened, but she shrugged, "Not a thing."

"Umm ... thought not."

Madie shut the door and Sergeant Davis turned to Cody.

"Would ya like some tea?" Cody asked.

"Thanks, but no. It's been a long day for us all; I'm off home."

Cody walked the man to the door. "Thanks for your help. I'd no idea how to deal with all that."

"I wouldn't say that. It seemed to me, you handled it very well. I think Madie will be okay now. Good night, Cody."

🐝 38 🐝

Constable Friesen entered his superior's office and sat in a chair facing Sergeant Davis. "I locked the exhibits I gathered in Penticton in the evidence room with the rest. Here's a copy of the exhibit paperwork." He placed a folder on the desk.

"Good job. The helicopter from Kelowna Detachment will be here in an hour to fly them to the forensics lab outside of Vancouver. They'll stop to pick up the remains in Penticton first. I just got off the phone with head office, begging for clearance and fast-track service. The lab has committed to four weeks for exhibits and any evidence found on the remains or tarp."

"Which is standard, hardly fast-tracking," Friesen scowled.

"*But* they did promise to provide the confirming DNA results on the skeleton in two weeks." Sergeant Davis tapped his fingers on some papers in front of him. "I just finished reading the Coroner's initial report. Since he's already identified the remains through dental records, with her DNA and familial DNA on file in the database, it will be a simpler process for the lab to classify and officially confirm the skeletal remains as that of Tara Crawford's."

"That's something."

"It'll be everything to her family. I'd like you to accompany me to Cherryville to give the news to her parents. We'll stop to see Douglas Crawford on our way out of town."

"When do you want to leave?"

"Once the chopper leaves for the Coast. Meanwhile, you can set up Conference Room #2 for the MCU Investigator. You'll be working for him on this case priority one. Triple-copy all exhibits, photos, reports, etc. He'll be joining us tomorrow."

"I'll get on it."

As Friesen left, Constable Timmons came in. "I've been fielding calls from the media. They know something's up."

"Okay, set up a news conference, noon tomorrow outside the main door. I'll tell them what I can."

Ninety minutes later, Davis and Friesen left the detachment and drove to the Crawford home. His second wife led them to the living room and went out to the workshop to get him.

The two men stood beside a black leather couch. Sergeant Davis took in the stark room, freshly painted white walls, one abstract painting on the wall in white and muted tones of grey, a glass coffee table with magazines stacked in a neat pile in the centre. Even the red cushions on the couch and matching leather armchair were placed upright and perfectly symmetrical to each other. *Nothing cosy about this room; everything in its place. Controlled.*

Crawford appeared puzzled at their unannounced visit. "Officers? What can I do for you?" he asked as he entered the room.

"Mr Crawford, I'm Sergeant Davis and this is Constable Friesen. May we sit?"

"Of course." Crawford gestured the couch. He sat opposite in an armchair.

"Sir, we wanted to inform you that, yesterday, we found human remains out on the flats."

Crawford's eyebrows shot up. His facial expression was passive, but his body stiffened. "Oh dear, how sad. I heard the helicopter flying overhead a couple of times and wondered what was up. What does that have to do with me?"

"Today, the Coroner matched dental records to the skeletal remains. We believe the remains are those of your missing wife, Tara."

Crawford was visibly shaken. His wife let out a cry and left the room.

"Tara? Are you sure?"

"Judging by the Coroner's description of the remains, jewellery found in the gravesite, and the dental records, we are. But the forensics lab will confirm it through DNA. We should know officially in about two weeks. Meanwhile, we wanted to share what we do know before the media reports it tomorrow."

"Do you know how she died?"

"The Coroner confirmed death by strangulation."

Crawford blanched.

"Your wife's case is now a murder investigation, sir. We have an Investigator, Serge Patrova, coming from Kelowna. He's with the Major Crime Unit and he'll be handling the case. Constable Friesen will be working with him. At some point, Detective Patrova will be in touch with you."

"Where in the desert was she found?"

"In a rock enclosure by the foothills."

"I see. How on earth did you find her?"

Sergeant Davis noted he looked almost angry. *Was that anger because we found her, or anger that someone buried her not far from home.* "It was a tip, Mr Crawford."

Crawford's jaw dropped. "A tip? From whom?"

"I can't give you all the details at this point, sir. It's an ongoing investigation."

Crawford stared at the two men. He stood and nodded to them. "Thank you for letting me know."

Davis and Friesen stood also. "We're sorry for your loss, sir. We'll be in touch when you can claim the remains," Sergeant Davis advised.

"It was a long time ago, Sergeant. I have a new wife, with a baby on the way. Perhaps her family would like to claim the remains."

Sergeant Davis bit his lip. "Thank you for your time, sir."

Back in their car, Davis drove them back to the highway shaking his head. "Isn't he a piece of wasted skin? He couldn't have cared less. And then, he just dismissed us, like we were bothering him."

"And dismissed her remains. I know people react differently to these things, but he didn't react at all, except to ask who the tipster was," Friesen said gravely.

"In an indignant tone, I might add. His file mentioned that he had an arrogant attitude back when his wife went missing; twenty-two years later, he hasn't changed a bit."

Three hours later, they were in Cherryville, pulling into the driveway of Francis and Tom Wood. The house was one of those old-fashioned two-story wooden houses with an attic. The egg-white paint was faded and the steps and railings up to the verandah were peeling. But the gardens were well kept with flowering bushes and shrubs lining the front of the house. They got out of the car, climbed the stairs, and rang the doorbell.

"I guarantee this call won't go like the last one," Sergeant Davis whispered to his officer.

The door was opened by a man in his sixties with silver hair and inquisitive blue eyes. "Good evening, officers."

"Good evening, sir. Is this the home of Francis and Tom Wood?"

"It is. How can we help you?"

"May we come in for a few minutes? We'd like to talk with you and your wife," Sergeant Davis said.

"Of course, follow me."

As they followed him into the living room, Mr Wood called out to his wife. "Franny? Franny! We have company, dear."

A small woman with blond hair and warm brown eyes joined them. When she saw them, she stopped in her tracks, looked from one to the other and said, "You're here about our dear Scarlett, aren't you?"

Sergeant Davis wasn't surprised at her question. He'd learned over the years that a lot of mothers were intuitively tuned in and knew when news of a missing child was about to be provided. "Yes, Mrs Wood, we're here about Tara —Scarlett."

"Please, sit," she said.

The couple sat beside each other on the couch with the officers both sitting in armchairs.

"Yesterday, a gravesite was discovered. The remains of a young, pregnant female were found. Today, the Penticton Coroner identified her from dental records as your daughter." He paused, waiting for his words to sink in.

Mrs Wood began to shake and her husband placed an arm around her shoulders. "We hoped and prayed she'd be found one day. A day like today is what's kept us going," he said solemnly, "but it couldn't prepare us for … for … hearing the words." Tears filled his eyes and he placed his head against his wife's.

The two officers sat in silence while the couple clung to each other and cried. Constable Friesen picked up a Kleenex box on a side table, reached over, and handed it to Mrs Wood. After a few minutes, when he could see they were in control, the Sergeant said, "The remains have been sent to our forensic lab for DNA testing. We'll have confirmation in about two weeks."

Mrs Wood straightened and sat up. "But your sure it's her?"

"Yes, there was identifiable evidence, jewellery, and dental records. The DNA results will make it official."

"How did she die? Do you know?" Mr Wood asked quietly.

Sergeant Davis took a deep breath, knowing he was about to cause them pain once again. "The Coroner has determined that your daughter died of asphyxiation."

There was a long silence in the room. Franny stared at the floor. Tom Wood spat out the words, "You mean that bastard, Crawford, strangled her."

This time it was Franny who reached out and squeezed her husband's hand. She turned to the Sergeant. "How did you find her?"

"It was a tip. I can't go into details, as your daughter's case has been re-opened as a murder investigation."

Tom grunted. "About time. I hope you nail that murdering bastard and put him away for life."

"The case is in the hands of our Major Crime Unit. Constable Friesen will be working with the Investigator. The media will be given a briefing tomorrow. We wanted you to be prepared when you see it on the news, and you can expect them to phone or knock on your door. You might want to screen your calls first and not open the door to strangers for a while."

"Thank you, Sergeant," Franny said softly.

"One more thing, Mr Crawford suggested you might like to claim your daughter's remains …"

Tom lost his temper yet again. With eyes full of fire, he said, "Of course *he* wouldn't, the asshole. After murdering her, why would he do the right thing and pay for her funeral?"

Franny pleaded with him. "Please, Tom, stop. You're not helping."

Tom calmed down. "Sorry, Franny." He looked at

Sergeant Davis. "I apologize. Of course, we'll claim the remains. We want her to come home and be near us anyway, not him."

"No apology needed. We'll notify you when you can claim your daughter's remains."

The two officers stood.

Tom and Franny led them to the door. Before leaving, Sergeant Davis turned to them both. "We're so sorry for your loss. We hope that finding her helps with your pain."

Franny gave him a partial smile. "You've given us some closure. It means a lot."

Tom shook hands with the officers. "Put Crawford away; that'll give me closure."

❧ 39 ❧

Madie stood in the barn at Sydney's, watching Cody check the sheep rescued from the accident. Some of them had been released the night before into the second meadow with their flock. It was her first day back to work, as Wenner insisted she take a day off. Sydney and Jax had returned last night from Emerald Lake and they were in the house, having breakfast.

Cody stood. "These last three should be able to join the rest in the paddock in a couple of days. The owners are picking them up Saturday. Wenner has one left at the Centre that can be moved in with these sheep tonight."

"Not much of a flock is it? They've lost so many."

"Good morning, Madie. I hope you got lots of rest yesterday."

Madie spun around to see Sydney entering the barn. "Hi. I slept half the day away and stayed in my pyjamas for the rest. All good. So, how's Chelsea and Maisie?"

"Having gone through the same thing with my girls, I know what to expect with Maisie, and she's doing great. As for my mom, they've finished the transfusions. Her vitals are stronger, and the doctors say if that continues, they'll wake her up tomorrow or the next day."

Madie let out a long breath. "That's great news."

"I'm on my way there now but knew you'd want an update. Nan's keeping the girls until she's awake; Chaz and I've been spelling each other off. Today, I'm going to read one of her favourite books to her. We want Mom to know we're there and waiting for her to come back to us and Maisie."

"Tell her we're all waiting at the Centre to see her too," Madie said.

"Second that," Cody added.

"I will. Gord's watching the girls for a bit, so Mom can pop in for a while. Well, I'm off. Have a good one, you two."

"Talk to you later," Madie said.

"See ya!" Cody echoed, leaving the last stall. He turned to Madie. "I'm all done here. I'll check on them again at lunch."

"I'll walk back with you. Time for me to clock in."

They walked arm-in-arm past the magnolia grove and over the hill to the Centre. It was early and they hadn't opened the gates. As Cody unlocked the compound, Madie noted a car pull into the parking lot.

Sergeant Davis got out and walked towards her. "Good morning," he said with a quick smile.

"Morning, Sergeant," Madie said.

Cody swung open the gate and they walked through and stood by the steps to the Administration building.

"I wanted to catch you early before my day begins," he said. "You're looking better today, Madie ... well-rested."

"I'm feeling fine. What's up?" she asked.

"We've identified Tara's remains with dental records. DNA from the lab will make it official in a few weeks. I wanted to let you know we're having a news conference today at one. It'll be on the evening news."

Madie nodded. "Thank you. I appreciate it. I always knew it was her, but having you confirm it—well, it's still a bit unnerving." She sucked in her lips, shaking her head. "I guess that means you've notified her family."

"Yes, last night."

"I'm sure it was a shock after all these years, but I'm glad they have some closure," she said.

"And Douglas Crawford?" Cody pressed.

"Notified, as well," the officer said with a stoic expression.

"So, what happens now?" Madie asked with a furrowed brow.

"It's an ongoing investigation with our Major Crime Unit, thanks to you. You can expect them to contact you at some point. Now, I must get to the office. Have a good day."

They watched him leave the compound.

Madie started up the stairs, "This has been so much a part of my life; I can't believe it's over."

Cody followed her. "It's not over until they nail Crawford."

The entrance door was unlocked and he held it open for her. "Wenner's been in; let's see if he made some java."

MADIE STOOD in the new suite of her mom's house with Cody. "It's beautiful, Mom. Jax did a great job, didn't he?"

"I'm very pleased with it. It was his suggestion to replace the small window at this end of the room with a larger one … makes the room look bigger and brighter."

"So, when's the new tenant moving in?" Cody asked.

"She'll start bringing things in mid-month, but officially she's in November 1st. I was lucky to find her. A recent graduate from the nursing program at Kelowna Hospital, she started here at the Oliver Hospital last month. She's been commuting and looking for the right place to rent."

"That's awesome, Mom. I love the natural colour scheme and the new wood floors. Very today."

Her mother sighed. "Umm, it makes my place upstairs look so tired and old fashioned." She giggled. "I may have to get Jax to upgrade my place too."

"Why not? You deserve it," Madie nodded. "And with the money coming in from the rental, you can well afford it."

Val looked at her watch. "Oh, news in five minutes. We don't want to miss the broadcast. Let's go up."

They settled in the living room and Val found the news channel. "I can't believe you found that poor girl's gravesite. Thank you both for coming and sharing this with me."

Madie slipped an arm around her mother's shoulders. "I can't think of anyone else I'd rather share it with. After all, you're the one who had to deal with my night terrors as an infant, with no answers as to why they were happening."

They turned their attention to the television as the newscaster began her broadcast. "Good evening, I'm Kara Bromley. Tonight, we begin with the story of the startling discovery on Tuesday of a gravesite in the Strawberry Creek area in Osoyoos. The RCMP identified the skeletal remains to be those of Scarlett Crawford, who went by Tara Crawford, a young woman who has been missing since 1998. Our own Marcia Turnbull reports from Osoyoos. Marcia?"

They listened as the reporter played excerpts from the news conference held by Sergeant Davis and the MCU Investigator. None of what they said was new to Madie. She did note the questions asked by reporters covering the scene, and how deceptively the officers avoided answering them.

"I wonder if they'll have enough evidence to convict her husband," Val asked.

"I don't know, but I sure hope so. He's an evil man," Madie said flatly.

Her mother patted her knee. "I'm glad they didn't reveal where the tip came from, leading them to the discovery. I'd be so worried about your safety, otherwise."

"No worries, Mom. Sergeant Davis assured me that as long as the investigation is open, I'd be kept anonymous."

Her mom nodded. "Good. Perhaps now, you can put this whole business behind you, and not suffer from any more nightmares or visions."

"I would think so."

Val stood. "Now, I have coffee made, a freshly-made peach cobbler cooling on the counter, and vanilla ice cream in the freezer. What say we move to the kitchen and spoil ourselves?

Cody jumped to his feet. "I'm up for it. Peach cobbler's my fav. Yum!"

❧ 40 ❧

Sergeant Davis stood by the one-way mirror, observing the interview of Douglas Crawford. Present in the interrogation room with Crawford were the detective in charge and Constable Friesen. This was a preliminary interview and Mr Crawford had agreed to come into the office to talk with them. He turned up the intercom and listened to the conversation on the other side of the glass.

"We appreciate your coming in, Mr Crawford. Would you like anything? Coffee, water?" Detective Patrova asked.

"No thank you. I hope I won't be here that long; got a busy day ahead," Crawford said indifferently.

"Shouldn't take long. As you know, your wife's case has moved from a missing person to a murder investigation. For that reason, we'd like to go over your statement about your wife's disappearance." Petrova told him.

"Ex-wife. I'm re-married. Do you think I can still remember exactly what happened twenty-two years ago? Whatever I said in my statement, those were the facts and they still stand."

Petrova smiled. "Mr Crawford, it's possible to forget some

details after all this time but, then again, you may have remembered something since that you forgot to tell us back then. Let's begin the last day you saw her. You stated you left for work that morning at your usual time at 7:30 am. You arrived home at your regular time of five o'clock that evening. Is that correct?"

"If that's what my statement says."

"You told the officer that you left after dinner to go to the office for some papers you'd left behind."

"I think that was the reason."

"And why did you need the papers that night? Couldn't they wait until you went to work the next morning?"

Crawford sat back in his chair and stretched out his legs. "I have no idea. What did I say in my statement?"

Petrova read the paper in front of him. "You had a meeting the next morning—a commercial property deal—and wanted to be well-prepped and on your game."

Crawford flipped a hand in the air and said, "There you go. I guess that was why."

Sergeant Davis muttered under his breath on the other side of the mirror, "Arrogant prick!"

"Do you remember what time you left home that evening?"

Crawford shrugged. "Sixish."

"And what happened after you left?"

"I went home again because I forgot my wallet."

The detective's radar went off. He glanced down at his notes and then studied his person of interest while Crawford appeared to squirm in his chair. "When you got home, what was your wife doing?"

"I don't remember."

"Did she know you forgot your wallet?"

"Yes. She said she knew I'd be back for it and we shared a laugh over it."

Petrova's stomach churned. "So, you retrieved your wallet and what did you do then?"

"I went to the bathroom, and I felt ill. Something I ate, I think. I decided not to go to the office for my notes. We turned in early and watched a movie in bed."

"Do you remember the name of the movie?"

Crawford smirked. "Of course not. Would you?"

"You said in your statement your wife was leaving early the next morning to visit her family in Cherryville for a week. Do you remember the events of that morning?"

"All I remember is we got up per usual time. Her bags had been packed the previous day and put in the back of her pick-up under the canopy the night before. She wanted an early start and left while I was eating the breakfast she'd cooked me."

"Your statement says you never heard from her for two days, then left a message, but didn't connect with her parents until the third day. Is that right?" Petrova asked.

"If I said that, then that's right."

"Why did you wait that long to call her parents? I mean, wouldn't you expect her to call the same day to tell you she'd arrived safely?"

"I did, but when she didn't call, I assumed she was excited to be home and forgot to ring me. I was busy at work, so left her to enjoy herself. But after two days, I began to get concerned."

"I see. And you never heard from or saw your wife again?"

Crawford appeared to bristle. "Ex-wife and, no, never."

Detective Patrova opened a file in front of him. "I want to show you some pictures, Mr Crawford." He pulled out a few. "Do you recognize this pendant, sir?"

His interviewee blanched at the photo. "It was Tara's."

"And this one?" The detective pushed it across the table.

Crawford hesitated. "It looks similar to one I had."

"Had?"

"I lost it a long time ago. Where'd you find it?"

Petrova ignored his question. "They're very unique arrowheads. Did you buy them together?"

"Yes, on our honeymoon. We attended the Osoyoos Medieval Faire and bought them at one of the sale tables."

Petrova showed him another photo. "Do you recognize these?"

Crawford picked up the photo and stared hard at it. He threw it down on the table. "Tara's wedding rings."

The detective noted Crawford was sweating and appeared a little less arrogant. "We're almost finished here. But I need a coffee. How about you? Whatcha take in it?" He closed his files and stood, picking up the folders.

"A little cream."

Both men left Douglas Crawford alone and joined Sergeant Davis in the other room. They watched their person of interest through the glass. He sat perfectly still, blankly staring at the table.

"Whatcha think?" Sergeant Davis asked the detective.

"I expected him to forget some details after all this time, but he's changed some details and added other things to his story he never put in his original statement."

"Such as?"

"For one, he said in his statement he returned home because he fell ill. Today, he says he went back home because he forgot his wallet and then felt ill. The wallet was never mentioned in his original statement. Now, he says Tara knew about it and figured he'd come back for it—and they laughed about it."

The hairs went up on the back of Sergeant Davis' neck. "Madie Hayes said in one of her visions, Crawford returned home that night because he forgot his wallet, surprising Tara, who was about to leave him."

"Well, he confirmed her vision about the forgotten wallet at least," Constable Friesen added.

Davis looked to the detective. "And all that means?"

"It's normal to forget some things, but not to add new details and embellish them. He either lied back then or he's lying now. I think it's a little of both. We'd best go back in. Don't forget to make the call when I say the keywords."

Sergeant Davis nodded.

The two men left Davis and rejoined Crawford with their coffees.

"Just a few more things, Mr Crawford and you'll be on your way." The detective fussed with his files, pretending to search for a particular one to buy time while Crawford drank some of his coffee. Taking a few sips of his own coffee, he began. "Last Sunday morning, can you tell me where you were?"

Crawford eyebrows shot up, revealing he hadn't expected this line of questioning. "I was at home, with my wife."

"Did you stay home that morning, or go out?"

His body tightened. "As I said, I was home."

"Inside, the whole morning?"

Crawford straightened and his eyes travelled between the two men. 'What *is* this? What's my Sunday morning got to do with Tara's disappearance?"

"You mean Tara's *murder*. Mr Crawford, were you on the desert flats last Sunday morning on a dirt bike?"

Crawford became cagey. "I don't remember. Why?"

"We have a witness who saw a dirt bike on the flats, and they've identified you as the rider."

"A witness? I … I never s-saw anyone." Crawford fumbled over his words. "I mean, I usually go out on weekends on my bike … but I don't remember if it was Saturday or Sunday, and I never saw anyone else out there."

"We also have these." Petrova spread a series of photos in front of the man. "Saturday night there was a major thunderstorm with record rains; the desert surface was very soft and moist Sunday morning. The tire imprints in the photos lead from your backyard to the foothills near Strawberry Creek— and back again to your home."

Anger flared in Crawford's eyes; his arrogant tone returned. "So? As I said, weekends I usually go out on the flats with my bike. What of it?"

The detective spread more photos in front of him. "The rider left his bike close to the rock facing and these boot prints lead to an enclosure. Not one that's visible to the average person. You'd have to know it was there to find it."

Crawford stiffened. "Where are going with this?"

"What do you think the odds are, Mr Crawford, you'd be out on a frivolous ride in the desert and end up in the exact spot where your wife, Tara Crawford's hidden gravesite was found two days later?"

Crawford blanched and, for the first time, he didn't correct the detective to the fact that Tara was his ex-wife.

On the other side of the one-way mirror, Sergeant Davis pulled out his cell phone, punched in a contact number and waited for the recipient to answer. When he did, the officer said, "It's Davis, you can go in now."

Meanwhile, Crawford's eyes hardened. "I have nothing more to say."

"Neither do I, sir. We're done here—for now." Petrova rose. "Thank you for coming in today, Mr Crawford."

The other man stood and walked toward the door, with the detective following behind. Petrova stood in the doorway, watching his person of interest walk down the hallway. He heard the cell phone ring in Crawford's pocket, observed the man answer it and then rush down the hallway and disappear.

The detective smiled and turned to Constable Friesen who was gathering up files on the desk. "Right on cue. Must be the current Mrs Crawford letting him know that my men just presented her with a subpoena to search the premises. I guarantee they'll have confiscated his bike and riding boots before he arrives home."

Crawford retrieved a small forensics kit from a box under the table. With tweezers, he picked up Crawford's coffee cup and placed it in a plastic bag. "Off to forensics for finger-printing and DNA."

❧ 41 ❧

Chelsea opened her eyes to bright lights. Everything appeared blurry and she blinked a few times to clear her vision. It was like looking through a long tunnel and at the end was a room, and a man in a white coat with a woman in blue scrubs staring at her.

"Hi, Chelsea, I'm Dr Phillips."

As he came up to the side of the bed, she tried shifting her position and felt pain shoot through her abdomen. In those few seconds, her focus returned and, realizing she was in a hospital room, her hands flew to her stomach. She stared at her flattened belly and was hit with instant panic. "My baby!" Her widened eyes flew to the doctor, who smiled and nodded.

"Congratulations, Chelsea, you have a healthy baby girl. She's in our MICU unit and doing very well."

No sooner had she breathed a sigh of relief, she was overcome with confusion. "I can't remember anything beyond driving in the car, wha-what happened?"

The doctor sat on the edge of the bed. "On the way, you haemorrhaged and lost consciousness. We kept you in an induced coma after the Caesarean because you were very weak. You've received blood transfusions; over time your blood levels increased, your vitals stabilized, and we decided it was safe to wake you up this morning. A few more days in here, and you should be able to go home."

"How long was I under?"

"Ten days. You came in Tuesday afternoon of last week and this is Friday morning."

Chelsea's eyebrows shot up. "Omigod—*ten days*? And my baby's okay? When can I see her?"

"Your daughter's fine. We're going to start you on some soft foods and fluids. I'd like you to rest this morning, and we'll see about wheeling you down to meet your little girl this afternoon. How's that sound?"

"Okay." Her eyes fluttered, and Chelsea realized how exhausted she felt, but that couldn't take away her sense of relief or the happy sensation of peacefully floating in space.

"There are a few family members who'd like to see you for a few minutes if you're up to it?"

"Yes, please."

Chaz entered and leaned over her, brushing his lips against hers. "Hi, sleepyhead, about time you woke up." He sat on the bed, holding her hand. "You gave us all quite the scare, especially poor Madie. She was a real trouper though and broke a few traffic laws to make sure you got here."

"I'll be forever grateful she showed up when she did." Madie shuddered, thinking about what could have happened.

"All's well that ends well. Let's not go there now."

"Tell me about our daughter. What does she look like?"

"She's small, but not as tiny as the triplets were, and a little beauty. She has those beautiful blue eyes of the Grey women, your nose, and my hair—thinning brown, with tinges of grey on the sides."

Chelsea began laughing, "Ouch," she cried out, her hand touching her abdomen. "Don't make me laugh; it hurts."

His facial expression turned serious. "How are you feeling, apart from the pain?"

"A little weak and spacey from some pretty good drugs."

He let go of her hand and fumbled in his pocket and pulled out his cell phone. "Got a video to show you. One sec —aw, here it is." He turned the phone towards her. "Say hello to our little Maisie."

Chelsea's mouth dropped, her eyes became misty, then a big smile spread across her face. "Oh, she's precious. Play it again." She watched it two more times. "So beautiful, isn't she?"

Chaz lifted her hand and kissed her fingers. "Just like her mama. I'm so happy to have you back with me and our new daughter. I love you, Chelsea Grey."

There was a knock on the door and it opened, and Sydney and Elizabeth joined them. Chelsea gave them a big smile. "Hey, family, so good to see you."

Hugs and kisses were shared all around, along with congratulations and questions to Chelsea about how she was feeling. Chaz stood to one side, chuckling at the amount of noise the three women created together in their enthusiasm. Once they'd settled down, he pulled two chairs to either side of the bed for Chelsea's mother and daughter to sit.

"I'm going to leave you three. I need to check in at the office but I'll be back this afternoon to wheel my beautiful wife down to see our dear, sweet Maisie." He blew Chelsea a kiss and turned to leave.

"Wait—what happened with the gravesite Madie found?" Chelsea asked.

The others stared at one another in silence.

Chaz walked back to the bed and took Chelsea's hand in his. "They found the remains of Tara Crawford right where Madie said she would be. She was identified the next day through dental records, and yesterday DNA results confirmed it."

Chelsea was stunned but she didn't have the physical or mental vigour to deal with it. "Oh ... and how's Madie?"

"It knocked the stuffing out of her for a few days, but she's strong. The case is now an open murder investigation. But you don't need to hear this right now. You concentrate on getting strong yourself." Chas leaned over and kissed her. "See you later."

Chelsea looked at the others. "I guess it's good news for Tara's parents ... gives them some closure."

"Yes, I imagine it would," Sydney said. "Now, let's talk about this new baby sister I have. I can't believe it. Wait 'til you see her."

A smile spread across Elizabeth's face. "And I have another granddaughter."

Chelsea stared from one face to the other in silence, soaking up their excitement. Her eyes grew wet with tears as a lump formed in her throat.

Elizabeth stared at her daughter and, noting the change in her manner, asked, "What is it, hon? What's wrong?"

Chelsea put a hand out to both of them and Elizabeth reached across the bed and took Sydney's free hand in hers. Chelsea smiled through her blurred eyes. "It's just over three years since you both found me and freed me from Arne. Remember my first night at the farmhouse, when we sat in the bedroom on the bed? Sydney got her mother back and just learned that Jax wasn't her brother. Mom, you got your daughter back, and I got both of you. We held hands like this, forming a circle."

Chelsea gazed fondly at her mother. "You said we would put the past behind us, celebrate life, and look to the future. That circle sealed our bond—a bond formed from pain, compassion, and love. Look how far we've come."

TWO WEEKS LATER - STONEY CREEK REHABILITATION CENTRE

The two owners and three employees sat around the conference table, having finished an impromptu meeting called by Wenner. He and Chelsea were seated at each end of the table, facing each other. Kelly sat alone on one side, with Madie and Cody opposite her on the other. As the initiator of the gathering, Wenner chaired the meeting.

They'd covered their season, accomplishments, improvements needed to house the animals, and the breakdown of job assignments, with Chelsea about to become a full-time mother. Maisie was due to be released soon and her initial focus would primarily be her daughter.

"We're finished with our business agenda," Wenner announced. "We have one more item to cover: a presentation from Jordy. Chelsea and I are fine at either end of the table, but if Cody and Madie could join Kelly, facing the two rows of chairs set up on our left, I'll call Jordy in with his guests."

Wenner left the room, returning with Jordy, Chaz, Jax, Chelsea's mom and stepfather, Elizabeth and Gord, Madie's mom, Val, and Cody's grandmother, Kat. They all sat in the rows. Wenner rejoined the others at the conference table. "It's all yours, Jordy."

Jordy stood beside Wenner so he could address the table and those in the chairs. "Hi, everyone. Thank you all for making time to come here this morning. For the few of you who don't know me, my name is Jordy Lewis. I'm a freelance writer, mainly in magazines. I spent the summer hanging around here, writing a story on the rehab Centre for a wildlife magazine, which will be published in its May, June, and July issues.

"A publisher friend of mine signed me to a contract last month for a series of photography books and I'll be moving here to Stoney Creek. I've recently returned from a trip back home to Toronto to visit family and met up with my publisher. I told him all about the Centre and the wonderful people I've met. He'd like to put the current contract on hold and, instead, have me write a full-length book about the rehab Centre."

Jordy turned to the table. "Apart from covering the wonderful work you do here, equally important would be the story of you, the people who work here." He paused and surveyed the family members. "And that would include all of you, as family members. Past and current events could make this a very unique book. And that's why I wanted all of you here today. To get your feedback on being part of this book. If you chose not to be included, that's okay too, but I hope you'll all see the wonderful thing that's happening here. There's a synergy and spirituality I believe bears sharing with the public. You aren't only a business, but a family. Now, I'm open to any questions you may have."

Chelsea spoke first. "By past and current events, do you want to include my abduction by Arne?"

"I would, but only if you're comfortable with it. There are ways to include some backstories without all the details."

Chelsea nodded. "I'm fine with it—all of it. Just wanted to know what to expect in the way of questions."

Madie spoke next. "And does current events include my journey to Tara Crawford?"

Jordy nodded. "It's certainly an important part."

"I'm a little uneasy, putting my name out there as the one who led police to her remains. But if the telling of it would help bring justice to Tara's life, I'm okay with it. But if Douglas Crawford isn't charged with Tara's murder before the book is published, how can we publish my visions about him killing her or my belief he's guilty? We could all be sued."

"I have a lot of work to do ahead of time, so we could leave your interview for the story until last. That gives us time to see if there's final closure to the case. Believe me, the publisher's lawyers will know what should and shouldn't be included in the book. How's that?" Jordy asked with a warm smile.

She looked at her mom. "What's your take, Mom?"

Val sucked in her lips, looking from Jordy to Madie and back. She let out a deep sigh. "I'm on the fence. I have no problem talking about Madie's night terrors and our struggles back then, but I'm concerned about her being exposed. Not only to Tara's killer, but to the public in general. They can be very cruel and—no offence to you, Jordy—but the media can be relentless and focused only on the story, not always taking into consideration the human factors and consequences."

"No offence taken, Val. I promise you all, I'll write this story truthfully and give each of you the respect you deserve."

"Okay, I'll agree to be interviewed last, but only if I have control over the content," Madie advised.

Jordy spoke to the room. "Each of you will be allowed to approve the final words and negotiate any changes you feel more comfortable with."

"I have a question," Sydney put forth.

All eyes turned to her.

"Go ahead," Jordy nodded.

"Jax and I are under contract with *Snuggle Butts* until June, with one more commercial to finish out. We're not allowed to sign contracts with any other kinds of media until theirs expires. What's your timeline on this?"

"My publisher anticipated a problem when I told him about the girls' commercials. He's already spoken to *Snuggle Butts*. As long as the book is published after your contract expires, they don't have a problem—and, I might add, they're quite happy with the publicity to be garnered for them, if I write about the girls and their commercials for *Snuggle Butts*."

They all laughed.

Jax snorted. "Of course they are."

Wenner spoke next. "Jordy and I spoke about this last

night. I'm all for it. When he covers how Chelsea and I met at Emerald Lake, which started us on the road to this Centre, he'll include Brian's murder and that outcome, as well."

Kelly interjected. "I don't know why you'd put me in the book. You've all had terrible tragedies in your lives but, also, experienced such interesting and adventurous events. I'm only nineteen, born and raised here. Nothing much to tell about me."

Amidst the other comments supporting her role, Jordy said, "Not true at all, Kelly. You're an integral part of the work-family here, and equally important to its story. Having lived in Stoney Creek your whole life, your understanding of local history is integral. And I bet, once we start talking, you'll have some very interesting tales to tell about your childhood."

Kelly turned pink and grinned, appearing pleased to be validated by Jordy.

"You certainly have a lot of photos you can put in the book," Wenner added.

"Some, but I used the best ones for the magazine article, and they have the rights to those. But I'm sure spring and summer at the Centre will offer more photo opportunities. Talking about the magazine, they're okay with me writing the book as long as its publishing date is three months after the magazine's release. My deadline would be mid-August and the publishing date is slotted for October 1st. So, no worries there."

Wenner turned to the table. "Let's take a vote. If you agree with Jordy doing this book, raise your hand."

Five hands reached into the air simultaneously.

"Done," he said.

Jordy turned to the family members in the rows. "If you don't have any more questions, can we do the same? Who's in favour of being part of this book?"

All hands were raised, and Jordy beamed. "Thank you.

You'll all receive a document to sign, permitting me to write your story and my publisher the right to put it into print."

Wenner looked up at Jordy with a big smile. "Congratulations. Are we done here?"

"One more thing," Jordy said. "I left this until the last, so you wouldn't accuse anyone of bribery. I'd like to announce that fifty per cent of my royalties for this book will be donated to the Centre and that includes half of my advance. I'd like to present the Centre with a cheque for $2500."

The noise level in the room rose as exclamations and whistles sounded while they clapped.

"I'm not done. I have one more cheque from the wildlife magazine printing the articles on the Centre; they'd like to donate $5000 to the Centre. And when my book is released, my publisher friend plans on donating one hundred copies to the Centre to sell to the public for fundraising." He handed the cheques and a letter of commitment from his friend to Wenner, who stood and embraced him.

Everyone stood and clapped.

When things quieted down, Wenner turned to the table. "Wow! How lucky are we for the day Jordy Lewis walked into our lives? What a great start to future fundraisers." He nodded to Jordy. "Thank you so much. And with that, I'd like to adjourn this meeting, and invite you all to the table in the corner for coffee and goodies."

Madie rolled over, cuddled into Cody's back, soaking up his warmth while she pulled the covers tighter to her neck. It was early November and the nights had turned chilly. She'd almost fallen asleep again when a knock came at the door.

She lifted her head and listened as another harder knock sounded. "Huh?" *What time is it?* She looked over Cody's shoulder at the side table. *What? 11 a.m.?*

She pushed herself up and out of bed, grabbed her house-coat, and padded to the door. She flung it open and looked through the locked screen. Her mother stood on the stoop with a worried look on her face.

When Val saw her daughter, relief flooded her face and her shoulders relaxed. Madie glanced over at the bed. Cody was up and in his jeans, pulling a shirt over his head.

Unlocking the screen door, Madie let her mother in. "Mom? What's wrong? You look so scared."

"Oh, Madie. Thank God you're okay. I tried calling you since last night, but you weren't answering the phone, or my texts, and messages."

She gave her mother a hug, who clung to her tightly.

"Umm … I guess I didn't turn my phone back on. Cody and I were at a concert in Kelowna and, afterwards, we went out to dinner. It was a late night for us, and we slept in." She led her mother to the couch. "Have a seat and tell me why you're so spooked—and why wouldn't I be okay?"

Val pulled a newspaper out of her pocket. "This was in last night's paper." She handed her a copy of a Kelowna newspaper. The heading on the front page jumped out at Madie, and she sat with a thump on the coffee table. "What the hell?"

Cody was making coffee when Madie reacted to the title. "What is it?"

She steeled herself and read the heading out loud. *"Remains of missing Okanagan woman found by psychic."* She read through the story. "For crying out loud, I'm not a psychic. It's all here, everything I told the cops, finding the gravesite, and—omigod, my name … and that I live in Stoney Creek is in here too." Stricken, she threw the paper down on the table.

Cody picked it up and read the story. "For fuck's sake," he blurted. Glancing up at Val, he said, "Sorry for the language."

"Don't be. I've used that word a few times since last night," Val told him, her expression solemn.

Madie looked at her mom. "No wonder you were worried when you couldn't reach me. Sergeant Davis promised to keep my name out of this. Who *did* this?"

"I think you need to talk to him. Give him a call," Cody advised.

"You can't stay here alone after this. I'm worried for your safety," Val declared, apprehensive. "And you're going to have the media after you."

"Damn, maybe I should have called them back. I had a couple of calls from the paper and I was busy and ignored them." She picked up her phone and checked her messages. "Oh, fuck! The reporter who wrote the story left me a message on Friday telling me about yesterday's paper. They wanted to ask me some questions. I should have returned his call."

An angry Cody snatched the paper and flipped to the end of the story so hard, the page ripped. "Wouldn't have mattered. They would've run the story no matter what you said. The reporter says here you couldn't be reached for comment."

Val looked distressed. "What are you going to do?"

Madie realized she needed to snap out of her initial shock and deal with her mother. She reached out and squeezed her hand. "It's okay, Mom. I'll be fine. I have no intention of talking to them. Eventually, they'll leave me alone and move on to the next story."

Her mother didn't look convinced. "But what about Douglas Crawford? He knows who you are now."

"At least the story didn't mention you envisioning him killing his wife. That would be harsh," Cody added, his expression dark.

"I suppose, legally, they could get in trouble if they did since he hasn't been charged with anything. But if he ever is indicted for Tara's murder, it won't be me who puts him away. I wasn't even born yet. It'll be because they find tangible evidence to convict him. So, for him to come looking for me would just make him look guilty. I'm really not a threat to him."

A stern look crossed Val's face and her body stiffened. "Maybe not, but don't be naive, Madie. He could come after you just because he's crazy. After all, he got away with it for twenty-two years, and you're threatening his new life with a pregnant second wife. He's got to be beyond angry with this and, according to your visions, it was his anger that caused Tara's death."

"You're right about that, Val," Cody said. "Look, until this is all sorted, Madie's staying with me at my cottage. We'll travel together to work and back. I won't leave her alone for a minute."

Val visibly relaxed. "Thank you, Cody. I appreciate that."

Madie stared at Cody with her arms crossed over her chest. "Hey, don't I have a say in any of this?"

Cody stared back, incredulous. "You're kidding, right? This is no time to pull the independent woman shit. You shouldn't be alone, and it makes sense that you stay with me—unless you'd rather stay with someone else."

Their eyes locked in silence until a slow smile spread across Madie's face. "Couldn't think of anyone better than you, lion tamer. A girl never knows when she might need someone to catch a lion."

Cody reached out and squeezed her hand.

Val smiled for the first time since she'd arrived in a nervous state. "You two are so cute together."

Madie raised an eyebrow at Cody, giving him "the look", as he called it. "Maybe," she teased.

"You know it," Cody winked.

"I need to call Sergeant Davis." Madie called the Osoyoos Detachment and reached Constable Friesen.

"Hi, Madie. Sergeant Davis is off today. Can I help you at all?"

She told him about the newspaper story. "Sergeant Davis told me my name would be kept out of this. I need to know what happened and who leaked this information to the press."

"I haven't seen it myself, but I'll check into it, and I'll let him know. I'm so sorry, Madie."

"When's he back at work?"

"Tomorrow morning, but I'll see if I can reach him today. Where are you, right now?"

"I'm home, but I'm going to pack up and stay with Cody for now."

"Good plan. We have his address and cell on file. I'll get back to you."

"Thank you." Madie rang off. "He's calling me back after he talks to Sergeant Davis. I don't know about you two, but I need coffee and some food. Let's eat, then I'll pack, and we can head over to your place, Cody."

"I'll make breakfast while you get dressed and pack," Val said and headed to the kitchen.

Cody stood. "And I'm going next door to let your landlady know you'll be away for a bit and if she sees anyone unfamiliar hanging around, best to call the police."

An hour later, Cody drove into the driveway to his cottage on the river. Madie decided to drive herself and park her vehicle at Cody's house. Her mother pulled in behind her. Once Madie's things were carted into the house, the three of them settled in the enclosed sundeck facing the river. Cody turned on the ceiling heater over the table, creating enough warmth to make them comfortable.

"Still able to enjoy it back here. Another few weeks, it'll be too cold," Cody said.

Val took in the open view through the floor to ceiling windows and watched a common loon float with the gentle current downriver. "You have a lovely spot here, Cody."

"Don't I know it. I was lucky to find this place. Anyone want a beer?"

Madie nodded. "Yes, please."

"Do you have a light beer?" Val asked.

"Sure do."

"Just one for me, since I'll be driving home later," Val said. When Cody disappeared into the house, she turned to Madie. "I'm glad you have him to help get you through this. I'm feeling a little better about this whole thing. How about you? You okay?"

Madie gave her mother a faint smile. "I will be. No worries about Jordy's book now, since the world knows all about me."

Cody returned with the beer and they settled around the

table. A short time later, a figure appeared from around the corner of the house, wearing blue jeans, a black bomber jacket, and a Blue Jays baseball cap. He climbed the deck stairs and waved at them through the glass door.

Cody stood and walked over to the door. "It's Sergeant Davis," he threw over his shoulder, as he opened it. "Come in, I didn't recognize you at first in your civvies." He pulled another chair over to the table. "Have a seat. Want a beer?"

The officer joined them. "No thanks. I figured you were back here when no one answered my knock." He joined them at the table.

Cody introduced him to Val. "This is Valerie Hayes, Madie's mom. Val, this is Sergeant Davis from the Osoyoos Detachment."

The two acknowledged each other and the sergeant turned his attention to Madie. She'd been silent since his arrival, filled with mixed emotions. She was angry with the man because of what had happened but, then again, she felt surprised that he'd showed up on his day off. She decided to hold back and let him make the first move, afraid of what she might say.

"Madie, I'm truly sorry. This story should never have reached the newspaper. I've—"

Her anger got the better of her. "You promised me! Now my face and name are out there for everyone to see. I want to know how it happened and I deserve some answers!" *So much for holding back, too late!*

"Yes, you do. I've made some calls and I can assure you it didn't leak from our detachment or the Integrated Crime Unit. This case has a lot of people involved from various offices and localities; we'll continue to investigate and, if we find the culprit, there'll be consequences."

The words "*if* we find the culprit" stuck in her mind, but she let it go for now. "Can I ask what's happening with the case, if anything?"

"We're still waiting for the final forensics report from the lab. The detectives are following some leads that have come in and done follow-up interviews, but these things take time."

Madie fell silent again. She wanted to ask him if they'd interviewed Douglas Crawford, but she knew Davis would never tell her anything, so she refrained.

"I don't anticipate that you're in any danger because of this, but your safety is foremost. Yours and Cody's addresses have been flagged in the system. Officers on street patrol will do scheduled drive-bys during the day and night shifts to watch for anyone or anything suspicious in the vicinity."

Madie nodded. "Thank you."

Val let out a sigh of relief. "That makes me feel so much better."

"It's good that you're staying with Cody for the time being, if only to let him ward off any reporters from bothering you. I'd suggest you don't talk to them, on the phone or in person."

"Don't worry, I won't."

"Work may be a problem. You can be sure the media will show up at the Centre, and since you work alone most of the time in the Admin building, maybe keep the entrance door locked."

Madie's anger rose yet again. "Dammit … anyway, I don't want any of this to infringe on the Centre. They don't deserve this either."

"Don't worry, it won't last long. Once the media sees there's no more story, they'll move on." The sergeant stood to leave. "Enjoy your afternoon. The next few days will be hectic, but it will pass."

❧ 43 ❧

C ody pulled into the compound and hit the brake pedal. "Holy shit! Look at them all."

The parking lot was full of reporters, a few with cameras.

He inched his way up to the gate. "Stay in the car. I'm going to drive right into the compound and up to the Admin building."

While he got out to swing open the gate, the car was surrounded by reporters. Some knocked on the windows. They called her name and shouted questions at her. Madie stared back at them in anger and defiance but said nothing. Cody pushed his way back and honked the horn as he inched forward and into the compound. He closed the gate before continuing to the offices.

As they got out of the car, Wenner raced towards them from the direction of the animal shelters. "I didn't even know they were here. I just got a call from Chelsea, who can see them from her deck. Let's get inside. Wenner locked the door behind them and they went to the coffee room in the back of the building.

"This is ridiculous," Wenner said, annoyed. "There's more

here today than yesterday. I don't want to lock the gates, but we can't have them wandering around the compound either."

"I'm so sorry, Wenner. Maybe I should work from home for a few days," Madie mused aloud.

Wenner handed her a cup of coffee. "It's not your fault. I'd rather have you here with us. Besides, they'd hang around anyway, waiting for you to reappear."

Cody threw in, "And Wenner needs me at work, and we don't want you at home alone. At least we're fenced in here. At home, they can sneak around the property, undetected. Like Sergeant Davis said, they'll go away after a while. We just have to out-wait them."

"I guess you're both right."

"But I don't want you alone in the office either. Cody and I have surgery to do and it's Kelly's day off. Jordy's coming over shortly. He's bringing his laptop and files. He can use Kelly's office to do his work."

As if on cue, a knock sounded on the reception room door. Wenner poked his head out of the room and stared down the hallway to the windowed door. "Here he is now."

He disappeared and Madie heard the door open, close and voices talking.

A minute later, Wenner and Jordy joined them.

"I really appreciate this, Jordy. I hope I'm not interfering with your work," Madie said. She sighed in exasperation. "I'm upsetting everyone's routine."

Jordy sat down beside her. "No, you aren't. I can work from anywhere. Have internet, will travel. I'm one of the family at the Centre now and family looks after one another. Believe me; no one is getting past me."

"Now, stop whining and drink your coffee," Wenner said with a wink.

Madie balled up her napkin and threw it at him.

Later that day, as she sat in her office trying to focus on a government grant application, the phone rang. The number wasn't identifiable or recognizable to her, so she let it pass to voicemail. A few minutes later she picked up the receiver to the beep of an interrupted dial tone, telling her she had a message. She punched in her code and waited. An agitated male voice began talking, and her heart skipped a beat.

"This is Douglas Crawford. I don't know what you're playing at, girlie, but I know you're the one who came to my house weeks back. You and your boyfriend lied to me about why you were there. Then, you go to the cops, and now you're talking to the papers. It's all crap, you hear me? If you know what's good for you, you'll stop interfering in my life, because next time, you'll be seeing me in person. And you don't want to be near me when I'm angry—trust me. Stay away from me and my family, and if you ever come on my property again, I'll have you charged with trespassing."

Madie heard the slam of the phone, ending the message. "Whoa!"

She hung up the receiver and sat staring at it. *Was that a threat? Sort of an indirect one, but not enough of one for Sergeant Davis to do anything about.* She turned back to her computer to work on the application. Five minutes later, she gave up. *Can't focus!*

She stared at the phone again. Her anger began to build. *How dare he try to intimidate me. Well, at least I saved it. I should turn it over to the police.* She picked up her cell phone and searched contacts for Sergeant Davis. Her finger stopped midway to punching his number. *All he can do is tell Douglas to keep away from me. Fuck this—I'm not going to be bullied.* She glanced at the clock and noted it was mid-afternoon.

Madie knew what she had to do. She slipped her cell into her jacket pocket, left her office and stopped at Kelly's. Deeply engrossed in what he was reading on the computer, Jordy didn't notice her.

"I'll be back in a couple of minutes. Just running something over to Wenner."

He glanced up. "Oh, okay. See you in a few," he said, his eyes sliding back to the screen.

MADIE HAD no concerns about the compound. Wenner had posted a sign this morning on the gate: Authorized Personnel Only Beyond this Point, All Others will be Prosecuted for Trespassing.

She slipped behind the surgery building and through a side gate that took her onto Sydney's property to the magnolia grove. She stayed on the low side of the hill and made her way to the back deck of the home. She knocked on the door, glancing towards Chelsea's property, in case any strangers were hiding there and about to jump out.

"Madie, hi, come in," Sydney said, opening the door.

Once inside, she spoke quickly before Sydney could engage her in any conversation. "Hey, I have a big favour to ask. I'm in a hurry to get to town and I was wondering if I could borrow your car for a couple of hours. I want to slip away before the media in the parking lot see me."

"Of course, but I thought you were travelling with Cody? Can't he take you where you need to go?"

Madie hated to lie to Sydney but if she didn't, she couldn't follow through with her plan. "Wenner needs him; besides, the reporters would just follow us, and I'd never get my work done. I really appreciate this."

"Not a problem, let me get my keys. I'm parked on the far left side of the driveway, so if you turn around and use that exit, no one next door will see you leave."

She took Sydney's keys. "I'm sorry for running in and out so quick. You're a godsend."

"Maybe when you come back, we can have some tea and a chat?"

"You bet," she said, slipping out the front door.

She slid into the car and drove onto the road that would

take her into town and south towards the Canada/US border. A look in the rear-view mirror confirmed no one had spotted her; the road behind her was devoid of traffic. A smug smile crossed her face as she glanced at the dash clock. *Just enough time to get there and initiate my plan.*

●

Sergeant Davis entered the conference room and joined Detective Petrova and Constables Friesen and Dennings. The room was packed with boxes, files scattered on the table or pinned to the wall with photos of the crime scene and people in Tara Crawford's life. Petrova motioned for him to sit to the left of Friesen. Pointing to folders in front of the three officers, the detective said, "We got the final forensics file from the lab."

"About bloody time. They promised us four weeks; it's been almost six," Davis said with a scowl.

"I'll give you a few minutes to read it through." Petrova went to a side table and poured himself a coffee before turning to the window, where he stared out across the flats, leaving the others to read the report.

Sergeant Davis skipped through the first few pages introducing the case, information he already knew. When he got to the determination of Tara's death, he slowed down. It confirmed the Coroner's report that her left cheek had been shattered by blunt force trauma and death had come from asphyxiation due to strangulation. Sample bone fragments confirmed her pregnancy.

Reading the findings of the loss of the baby wrenched at his heart. But it was the determination of evidence he'd been waiting for, and that part of the report sent his blood racing. Each sample of the evidential exhibits provided to the lab connected the dots. By the time the Forensic Scientist signed off at the bottom of the final page, Davis let out a whistle, followed by a deep sigh. He closed the report and sat back.

The detective joined them at the table. He turned to Davis. "Whatcha think?"

The Sergeant sucked in his lips, pushed them out, and a slow smile spread across his face. With a glint in his eye, he said, "I'm thinking we've found our victim's murderer—and this report proves it without a doubt."

Petrova nodded in agreement. "Twenty-two years and because of the dry, arid location, all that evidence was preserved inside that blue tarp for us to find. If he hadn't buried her in the tarp, we may not have gathered enough evidential exhibits to convict. His fingerprints on the tarp, his hairs in the tarp and on her body. His pendant wrapped in her hand. Tire tracks, and boot prints of his visiting the gravesite. The poor bugger's offered himself up to us on a silver platter."

"That he has. We'll have to thank him," Davis smirked.

The detective chuckled as another man came through the door. "Aw, here he is. Davis, you remember Detective Art Wasserman?"

Sergeant Davis nodded to Wasserman. "Yup, we've worked together before. Hi, old man, been a while."

"Wasserman's been to the courthouse to visit the Judge. Did you get it?"

"I did," the detective said, handing Petrova an envelope. "One signed arrest warrant in the name of Douglas Crawford."

Petrova stood and grabbed his jacket. "Okay then, what say we five go find ourselves a killer?"

❧ 44 ❧

Madie stood with her coffee and a fat muffin in her hands, searching for a spot to sit in the crowded coffee shop. A couple left a booth by the window and she hustled over and claimed it for herself.

Pulling her cell phone from her pocket, she noted it was 3 p.m. She glanced around the room. *Not here yet!* He should be here for his afternoon coffee any minute. *Perfect timing!* Her phone also showed she had messages. *Probably, Cody. They'd have figured out by now, that I'm not there at the Centre. He's going to be so angry with me for sneaking off.*

She thought of her grandmother's warning during her reading with Cody's grandmother, Kat, telling her to be careful, because she could be in danger. She shook off the feeling of dread that spread through her body. *Stop it; you have to do this.*

Madie put her cell phone on the table and tackled her muffin. The plastic knife slid through the still warm, freshly baked goodie and the sweet fragrances of raspberries and melted white chocolate wafted up. *Mmm ... my favourite.* She placed a piece into her mouth and savoured the taste, along with the butter melted into the surface. Her coffee cup was halfway to her mouth when a man slipped into the booth opposite her. Her hand froze for a moment and she put her cup back down. Her body became taut. Fear bubbled up inside as Madie fought the urge to flee. *Stay strong, girl!*

In contrast, Douglas Crawford sat back and gave her a wide smile. "Relax. I just want to chat. Nothing can happen to you—here."

Madie's eyes narrowed. "Are you threatening me?" She took her cell phone off the table and placed it on the bench seat beside her.

"And why would I do that? Are you a danger to me, Madie?"

She squirmed in her seat but forced herself to stay put. "What can I do for you, Mr Crawford?"

He spoke in a soft but arrogant tone. "Douglas, please. I think the question is, what can *I* do for *you?* What are you doing here, Madie Hayes?"

Madie thrust out her chin. "I got your phone message, and I knew you'd be here, as you are every day at three. I want you to know I won't allow you to bully me."

"Ballsy little thing, aren't you? Since you're here, let's chat. I understand from the papers you're the one who told the police where to find my long-lost wife's body. Her family are certainly grateful to finally have some closure as to her disappearance."

"I'm sure they are. It's a terrible thing to have a family member disappear without a trace." Madie weighed her next words carefully. "And how about you, Mr Crawford? Are you grateful your wife was found?"

His eyebrows rose in surprise. "It's Douglas. Tara was everything to me. It saddens me, of course, but after all these years, it confirmed what I suspected. She met with foul play at the hands of a sadistic murderer. But I don't want to discuss that; I want to know how you knew where she was buried."

Her heart was racing, but she stayed calm. "What did the police tell you?"

"When they first found her, they told me it was a tip and an ongoing investigation." He pulled the newspaper article out of his pocket and dropped it on the table. "Then, this story comes out. By the way, you're prettier in person than in this photo." He gave her a sinister smile. "They still won't tell me anything. So, I'm asking you. How'd you know?"

Madie knew she was at the tipping point and hesitated. Either she should get up and walk away, refusing to talk to him ... or ... the moment had come to jump in with both feet. She chose the latter. She sucked in a deep breath to calm her jagged nerves. "No one told me, Mr Crawford. I knew."

"Impossible. How old are you, Madie? Twenty-something?"

"Twenty-three."

He flipped his hand up with a smirk. "Then you weren't even born when my wife disappeared. The person responsible for my wife's death must have told you."

"You aren't listening, Mr Crawford. I said no one told me anything. I know what happened."

A sardonic laugh escaped his mouth. He leaned forward and placed his elbows on the table. "So, you're one of those so-called psychic people. How interesting. So, tell me,"—he wiggled his fingers in front of her—"what do your voodoo psychic thoughts think happened?"

Now she was all in, Madie decided to enjoy what she was about to tell him. *I'm going to wipe that cocky, smirking look off your face.* "Psychic? No. Incarnate."

He frowned. "And *what* is incarnate?"

"Incarnate is the reincarnation of someone from a past life. In my case, I was Tara in my last life."

His face contorted with mixed emotions: surprise, fear, disbelief, and then returned to that arrogant, wide-mouthed toothy smile. "Wow." His hand rubbed his cheeks and mouth. "I wasn't expecting that. It's a good one." He pointed a manicured finger at her and tilted his head sideways. "You caught me off-guard for a moment there. Reincarnation, eh?"

Madie took a sip of her coffee, holding the cup with both hands to keep her shaky hands from spilling the liquid. She said nothing, waiting for his next move.

"Okay, Madie, why don't you tell me about your life as my wife, Tara."

"I was a timid, naive schoolgirl who was in love with love. You were older than me and talked me into marrying you the moment I graduated from high school. By the time, I realized my mistake, it was too late. You were a physically and mentally abusive asshole who controlled my every move and thought. You cut me off from family and friends. You expected dinner on the table when you walked in the door after work and a spotless house. You thought you owned me body and soul. You drank way too much— although, you didn't need to drink to be abusive, except it made it worse when you did."

Crawford's eyes narrowed. "Tara had a beautiful house, all she wanted in clothes and jewellery. Other women envied her as my wife. I worshipped her."

"Until you didn't." Madie fell silent, waiting again for his lead. This time she acted nonchalant and ate her muffin.

"Nothing you said proves you're a reincarnation of Tara. You could have found a lot of that info online or from her family. It's all bullshit."

Madie leaned across the table. She stared directly into Douglas's eyes. "Then, how did I know where you buried her?"

His face clouded over.

Madie continued. "You said it already. I wasn't born yet. There were no witnesses. The only one who could have told me was you—or my former self, Tara."

He looked amused again. "Since you're accusing me of killing you Tara/Madie, tell me how I did it." Douglas slouched back in the booth and folded his arms across his chest. "This should be an entertaining story."

Madie hesitated a moment. The whole situation was becoming too real and she was more than a little frightened. *But I can't stop now. Ignore his blatant arrogance and don't show your fear.* "I wanted to visit my parents. You said it wasn't the time and we fought about it for a few days. It was almost like you sensed that if I left, I wouldn't come back. You were right, you know. I *was* planning on leaving you. That night, after you left, the moment you were gone, I pulled out the suitcases and packed them. I went to the kitchen to get my car keys. Unfortunately for me, you forgot your wallet and came back to find my bags in the hallway. Five more minutes and I'd have been gone."

He stared at her unblinking, his face blank, but she noticed his lips twitched.

"You surprised me as I returned to the hall for my bags. You beat me, broke my left cheekbones. A while later, as I dressed my wounds in the bathroom, you pulled me out and threw me against the wall. Remember? You told me I was feeling sorry for myself and you needed the bathroom." Madie paused waiting for a reaction.

His expression was still unreadable. "And? Don't stop now."

Madie saw his body tense and he sat up straighter. "You found me staring out the sliding doors at a rainstorm that was fast becoming a fierce lightning squall. I knew from the look in your eyes that you weren't done punishing me. I couldn't take anymore, so I slipped through the doors onto the back patio and disappeared into the dark."

Crawford's forehead creased but he remained still and quiet.

"You chased me into the desert. The ever-increasing lightning strikes lit the desert floor and I ran for my life towards the foothills where I thought I could hide."

Madie noted a slight hint of a smile at the corner of his lips. They both knew what he was thinking about her last comment. *Hidden for twenty-two years. Bastard.*

Once again, his face became stoic. "Continue," he said.

"I crouched down as a lightning strike hit the plateau right in front of me. When I stood, you caught me from behind by my ponytail and pulled me down to the ground."

His body stiffened and he leaned forward. She knew she had his attention.

"I remember seeing your legs straddle me. You were wearing your new black and white sneakers ... Nike Air Max."

His eyes narrowed and he pursed his lips. He glanced around the room and when his eyes returned to her they were full of anger. "And?"

"You strangled me. And buried me amongst the rocks at the bottom of the craggy hills I'd been trying to reach for safety. Oh, did I mention you wrapped me in a blue tarp?"

A pregnant silence hung heavy in the room and the pair stared at each other in silence. Madie didn't know what to expect next. His face revealed he was processing her words as his eyes darted around the room and back to hers. Her body tingled from tension, but she swallowed her fear and once again waited for him to speak first.

Crawford appeared to regain his composure. "I'm assuming the police have your ridiculous story on record. Right?"

She nodded. "They do."

"They obviously didn't believe you because I'm still walking around free."

"They believed my ridiculous story, as you call it, enough to let me take them to the spot where you buried my body. And they believed me enough to bring cadaver dogs along to confirm something was there."

The arrogant smile returned to his face. "No prosecutor

would ever charge me with Tara's murder and take this case to court without evidence to substantiate it. They have no proof and, after twenty-two years, all they have are a pile of bones."

Madie's heart began to pound. She couldn't believe his callousness. "I thought you said, Tara was your life—and now she's just a pile of bones?"

Crawford shrugged. "It was a long time ago; I have a new life now. Let's get back to you. All they have is a crazy star witness, the *only* so-called witness, who believes she's the incarnation of my murdered wife. No jury would ever convict me on the testimony of a reincarnated soul. I doubt any prosecutor's ever used testimony from a past life in court."

"You're probably right." She needed him to say more. Afraid to move or even breathe, she deliberately spoke softly to sound confident. "You know, I was born the morning you buried Tara's body? She sat on top of the hill and watched you dig her grave." She paused as Crawford's face turned white. "That's when she decided to reincarnate with the hope that her new soul carrier would remember the past and help bring you to justice. Even as a baby I had nightmares every time it stormed about a sad young woman running in fear from her abuser husband … only bits and pieces that never really made sense … until I became an adult. The dreams became more detailed and intense, and then the visions started."

Crawford sneered. "Try convincing a jury of that."

"You know why Tara finally found the strength to leave you? She was pregnant. She never told you because she knew she had to protect her child from you. It was her motivation to leave. It must have been a shock to you when the police told you they'd talked to her doctor. Not only did you kill your wife, you killed your baby."

Crawford turned white and looked like he was going to throw up.

Madie knew she needed to push on. She willed herself to

stay calm and shrugged. "I guess you're the killer who got away with murder—two murders."

Douglas began to shake. He leaned across the table and grabbed her wrist, eyes filled with anger. "That's right, Madie. I killed Tara. But it's your word against mine. And it all stops here. If you so much as look at a reporter or talk to the police again, the next stormy night you experience will be in real-time with a visit from me."

Madie recoiled. "Now you *are* threatening me. And you're hurting my wrist." She struggled to pull her hand free.

Crawford relaxed, let go of her wrist, and smiled sweetly. "Oh, yes I am, sweetheart. If you think dreaming about my killing Tara was frightening, wait until you feel my hands squeezing *your* throat. Definitely a nightmare you don't want to experience firsthand."

Madie couldn't hide her fear after that threat. *But he said it. He murdered Tara.* Her eyes searched the room. The noise level in the room was too loud for anyone to hear them. No one had witnessed the exchange between them. They were either on their cell phones or talking to someone else. It was time for her to get away from this man. The door to the cafe opened and she saw Sergeant Davis come in with Detective Petrova and another man she didn't recognize.

Two officers stood outside guarding the door. Her eyes locked with Sergeant Davis' and she saw the look of surprise on his face when he saw her with Crawford.

Madie knew it was over and she was safe. She stared across the table at the man who'd threatened her. "Mr Crawford, you've been the cause of my nightmares all my life. But guess what? I've just become *your* nightmare."

She slipped out of the booth and backed away while Detective Petrova slipped into her empty seat. Sergeant Davis and the other man blocked Crawford's way out.

"Douglas Crawford, you're under arrest for the murder of

your wife, Scarlet Louise Crawford, and the murder of your unborn child."

Petrova read him his rights while the other detective pulled him from the booth and cuffed his hands behind his back.

"You've got nothing on me. Just her word against mine." Crawford spat out the words and glared at Madie.

"No sir, we've got a lot more than that," Petrova told him grimly.

Madie stepped forward and held out her cell phone. "And you've got this. His recorded confession."

❧ 45 ❧

The two officers escorted Douglas Crawford to their car to escort him back to the detachment. Sergeant Davis turned to Madie and gave her a stern look. "You alright?"

She felt contrite, knowing she had some explaining to do. "Fine," was all she said.

Davis turned to the detectives. "I'll travel with Madie back to the station. We'll see you there." To Madie, he said, "Come on, take me to your car."

Madie led him to it and when she pulled the keys out of her jacket pocket, he put his hand out. "I'll drive. You're white as a ghost. Get in and relax." As he pulled away, he said, "This isn't your vehicle. Whose is it?"

"Sydney's. I snuck over to her house and borrowed it, so the media wouldn't follow me." Madie had a ton of questions but doubted Davis would give her the answers, so she said nothing.

"I got a call from Cody. You've got a lot of people out there worried about you. What part of my telling you to stay away from Crawford, did you not get? You put yourself in real danger here."

"I know."

"You're lucky we came when we did," Davis said sternly.

"I know that, too."

Sergeant Davis pulled into the parking lot and stopped the car. Madie got out and followed him into the building. They stopped at reception.

"Can you call Cody Diaz and let him know Madie is safe here with us? Ask him if he could come with a friend to pick her up and drive Sydney's car back. And call her mother and tell her the same. I expect the media will be on to something soon, and I don't want her being caught off guard if she hears something and can't reach Madie."

As he led her to the interrogation room, Madie sighed. "Cody'll be so mad. He's gonna kill me."

Sergeant Davis stopped and stared. "Is this something else I should be concerned about?"

Madie's face turned red, realizing what she'd just said in a police station. "Figuratively."

He sat down opposite her. "What were you doing, meeting with Crawford?"

"I've been scared to death for the past three days, ever since that article came out in the paper. All the phone calls and reporters shouting at me. Then, Crawford called today at the Centre and threatened me. I didn't take the call; he left a voicemail. I started to call you, but realized it was a veiled threat, nothing you could charge him with.

"Something snapped, and I got angry. I decided I wasn't going to live in fear or be bullied and hatched a plan to be at the cafe he goes to every day at three. I knew if he saw me, he'd come over; and I decided if I could record him threatening me, you'd have something on him. It was the threat I was after." Madie's eyes grew big. "Who knew he'd confess to murdering Tara?"

Sergeant Davis shook his head. "Do you realize how dangerous that was? It could have backfired."

Madie twisted her mouth and shrugged. "I do ... but it worked."

Detective Petrova came into the room. "We left Crawford cooling his heels in Room 1. He won't say a word without his lawyer present—so we wait." He pulled Madie's cell out of his pocket and placed it on the table. "How're you doing, Miss Hayes? You have a little bit of colour back in your face."

"I'm still a bit shaky, but glad it's over."

"I thought we'd give your recording a listen, so Sergeant Davis can hear what you gave us. I listened on the way back in the car and I must say I'm impressed."

Madie sighed. "Right about now, you're probably the only one who is."

He hit the recording and the three of them listened to the end. Madie couldn't believe how calm she sounded through most of it. But hearing Crawford's words again, on safe ground where she could concentrate on them, made her skin crawl. *Sgt. Davis was right, I put myself in extreme danger.*

Patrova shut it off and looked at Davis. The two men stared at each other and nodded their heads. "What say you, Davis? Did she do good or what?"

He stared at Madie. "As much as we don't encourage civilians to get involved in investigations or play detective, what you just gave us is a solid case. The forensics report came in this morning with enough evidence to charge Douglas Crawford with murder, but we may never have gotten him to admit to it. This recording gives us a stronger case for conviction. I suppose it's time we thank you."

Petrova slapped the table with his hand. "If you ever consider going into law enforcement, let me know. You have good instincts, a calm, deliberate approach, and perfect timing. You're a natural."

Madie smiled, pleased to get past the point of being chastised. "Thanks, but no thanks. I'd rather face the four-legged wildlife at the Centre than the two-legged likes of Douglas Crawford."

A knock came to the door and the receptionist poked her head in. "Cody is here."

"We'll be right out," Sergeant Davis said.

The three of them stood and the Detective held up her phone. "Have to keep this for awhile, I'm afraid. Evidence." He left ahead of them.

When Madie entered the reception area with Sergeant Davis, Cody and Jordy were waiting for her. She gave them both a weak smile and a wave. "Hi, guys."

Jordy gave her a look of concern. "Are you okay?"

Madie nodded and said, "All good. Thanks for coming."

Cody's expression, on the other hand, was stoic. He may have appeared unreadable, but Madie knew full well he was holding back his anger in front of the others.

Sergeant Davis looked at Cody. "Don't be too hard on her. In the end, what she did today helped seal a foolproof case against our suspect. Madie was very brave, and we're very appreciative." He handed him the keys to Sydney's car and turned to Madie. "Now, go home Madie Hayes, it's time for you to enjoy some peace. You're a remarkable young woman —but do I have to say it again?"

Madie grinned. "No, sir. I'm done."

Sergeant Davis shook hands with the three of them and they left the building.

Madie got into the passenger side and waited for Cody to say something. *Nothing.* "I'm sorry, Cody. I ..."

His voice rang out loud and sharp. "Not now."

Madie studied his profile, noting his tension. "But—"

"Don't. I'm too angry and I don't want to fight while we're driving."

Okay, you knew he'd be angry. "We don't have to fight; we can talk like two adults."

Cody spoke through clenched teeth. "Sneaking away from

us wasn't very adult, Madie. I don't want to talk to you right now. Let's just get back to the compound, okay?"

Madie stared out the window and said nothing. *I guess I deserve that.* With Cody locked in his anger as he drove, and Madie wanting to make it right, they both suffered in silence for the rest of the painful trip home.

Cody pulled into Sydney's driveway and parked by the side of the house, away from prying eyes. He stared straight ahead out the windshield and shouted, "Why did you do it? Where'd you go?" He punched the steering wheel with his fist. "You scared the hell out of us all."

"Stop shouting at me and I'll tell you."

Cody leaned back and rested his head on the headrest. In a softer tone, he said, "Go ahead."

"I got a threatening voicemail from Douglas Crawford. He tried to intimidate me, but it wasn't enough that the authorities could do anything about. I was upset and I got angry. I went to the coffee shop at three, knowing he'd be there."

Cody turned to face her. "You did what? Why would you do such a stupid thing?"

"Shut up and listen, or I'm not going to tell you anything."

They stared each other down.

Madie began again. "I thought if I could record him threatening me on my cell, Sergeant Davis could charge him with something. I don't know, Cody. I've been living with this since last June, the nightmares, the visions, Tara's remains and living in fear for three days—I went a little nuts, okay?"

Cody was back to his stoic expression. "So, what happened?"

"In a nutshell, he threatened me, and then he … he confessed." Madie said the words like she didn't believe it had happened.

"To murdering his wife?"

"Yes, then he threatened to do the same to me and—"

"To kill you?"

"Yeah, then the police arrived and arrested him."

Cody was staring at her in horror. His voice got louder and louder. "You could've been murdered, Madie! You could've disappeared just like Tara. Fuck, sometimes you're so naive. You have to stop doing these things! I can't keep worrying about you and what you're going to do next."

Madie's face contorted with anger. "There you go, yelling again. I'm so sorry, I've been such a burden to you." She swung open the door and jumped out, and started around the corner of the house.

Cody followed. "Madie, come back."

She kept moving at a faster pace, headed to the side gate to the compound. "You didn't have to experience the nightmares and visions of Tara's life, Cody. I did. So, I haven't always acted rationally; you try living my hell."

A male voice from the deck broke into their argument. "Uh-oh. Hey guys, everything alright?"

Madie looked over to see Sydney and Jax standing on the deck. She didn't have the energy to face another person she'd lied to today and pushed on into the magnolia grove. *Sorry, Sidney.*

She glanced back over her shoulder to see Cody had stopped to talk to them and hand over Sydney's car keys. *Good!* By the time, she reached the Admin building, tears were streaming down her cheeks. She found Wenner in Kelly's office with Jordy, packing up his laptop.

Wenner took one look at her face and opened his arms to her. "Come here, sweetheart."

"I'm okay, really." She lay her head on his shoulder and let him hold her for a moment. Stepping back, she said, "I owe you all an apology, and Jordy, I'm so sorry I lied to you earlier. I know everyone is mad at me."

Jordy nodded and gave her a smile and a thumbs up.

Wenner handed her a Kleenex and said, "The important thing is you're back and you're safe. Where's Cody?"

She wiped her eyes. "At Sydney's, returning her keys. We aren't really talking right now."

"Yeah, well. We were *all* worried, but Cody—he was beyond panic mode. He'll get over it. I think you should go home, have a hot shower, a glass of wine, and a good night's sleep. Things will seem better tomorrow."

Madie turned to Jordy. "Am I asking too much for a ride to Cody's to pick up my car?"

"Not a problem. I'm parked in the parking lot. The media got wind of Crawford's arrest; they've all gone to Osoyoos."

"At least that's a positive."

"Let's go."

On the way, Jordy lent her his cell phone so she could call her mother and assure her she was okay, and Crawford was in jail. When they reached the cottage, Jordy asked, "Are you alright to drive?"

"All good. My place is five minutes down the road. Thank you, Jordy."

"Hey, get a good night's sleep. Things will get better now that this whole Crawford thing is over."

"Maybe, but not everyone is as forgiving as you, Jordy." Madie pulled out her keys, got in her car and drove to her cabin. Whatever she'd left at Cody's could stay there.

Twenty minutes later, she'd had a shower, donned her pyjamas, and crawled into bed. The moment her eyes closed, an exhausted Madie fell into a deep sleep.

❧ 46 ❧

Madie opened her eyes to the sound of distant thunder. As her senses came into focus, reality set in. It was still dark and the alarm clock read five a.m. She'd slept eleven hours straight. On a trip to the bathroom to relieve herself, she peered out the window to see lightning flashing across the sky. A shiver passed through her and she added more wood to the fire, stoking up the still-hot embers.

Madie remade her bed, snuggling under the covers pulled around her neck. In a matter of minutes, she felt warm and cozy, and rolled onto her back to stare at the ceiling. The pounding of rain on the tin roof of the cabin pulled her back into comfortable drowsiness.

Then, it hit her. *No nightmares, no visions, for the first time in six months.* A memory tickled the edges of her mind of Cody telling her once how he loved nothing more than laying in bed and listening to the sound of rain hitting a tin roof. A smile spread across her face and a giggle escaped her lips. *My fear of storms is gone.* She closed her eyes and concentrated on the rain.

A deep, pounding boom-boom-boom followed by a tinny ping-ping-ping formed the rhythmic verse of the water song, while gentle splashes of droplets dripping from the tree branches formed the chorus, building to a crescendo as over-flowing eaves released a cascading waterfall to the ground, ending with a light show and roaring clap of thunder—back to the beginning, the song started again.

I love it!

A knock at the door broke through her imagery. *What? So early?*

Madie threw back the covers, reluctantly leaving the warmth of the bed. She peaked through the curtains to see who it was. *Oh!* She padded to the door in her bare feet, pulled it open, and stared through the screen door. Cody stood on the other side, with two cups of coffee and a bag of something. The two locked eyes and stared at each other in stoic silence.

Cody spoke first. "Any lion tamers allowed to enter?"

Madie reached out, unlocked the screen door, and walked away, leaving him to balance his offerings and struggle to open the door on his own. She stood by the table while he put his goodies down. Once again, they faced one another in silence, gauging each other until Madie couldn't stop a tiny, quirky smile from forming at the corner of her mouth.

Once Cody saw it, he grinned and they both began laughing; within seconds, they fell into each other's arms and held each other tight in silence.

They sat at the table and Madie opened the bag. "So, whatcha got in here? Oo-ooh, raspberry with white chocolate—and it's hot. I didn't get to finish mine yesterday at the cafe. This is going to be *so-ooo* good."

Cody handed her a knife and some butter for the muffin. "Fresh out of the oven."

"Thanks, I'm starving." She glanced at Cody. "You're up early."

"When the storm started, I thought, oh great, just what Madie needs: another storm. I had to check on you."

What Madie saw in his eyes at that moment wasn't just

concern, she saw love. She reached out and squeezed his hand. "You know what I was doing when you knocked at my door? Laying in bed, listening to the rain hit the tin roof. It's all in the past, Cody. Gone! It's just another rainstorm."

"Really? That's great." Cody hesitated, then said, "Sorry I yelled at you yesterday. I'm an idiot. I'm ready to listen to what happened if you want to talk about it. For sure, the media will be back, and I want to hear about it from you, not them."

"You were scared, and I shouldn't have snuck off." Between bites, Madie filled him in on what he didn't already know and, when she finished, asked, "Any questions?"

Cody put down his coffee. "Just one."

"Me first. You want that last muffin? I haven't eaten since yesterday's breakfast."

"All yours," he said, pushing the muffin towards her.

Buttering it, she said, "Okay, shoot."

"Should I gather your things at my place and bring them back tonight? Or should I leave them there and stop at the market for some empty boxes to pack up the rest of your stuff here?"

Madie's hand stopped halfway to her mouth as his words sunk in. A slow smile spread across her face as she looked around the cabin. "How many boxes do you think it would take to pack up the rest of the cabin?"

THREE WEEKS LATER

Excitement filled the Centre as they gathered in the lunchroom. Wenner and Cody only had two patients under their care and all the volunteers and interns were finished until spring. Their days were filled with repairs and expansions to the surgery and compounds. Madie kept busy with grant applications, spring fundraisers, and planning presentations at schools. Kelly had settled in with part-time financials while continuing her online studies. They were quiet times to be enjoyed before the next hectic season began in the spring with orphaned and injured newborns.

Today, Chelsea was visiting for lunch with *her* newborn, her first visit since Maisie had come home. Or so she thought. In truth, it was a surprise baby shower. Bea, who had been hired to cater the special occasion, bustled around the room, setting up veggie, fruit and cheese, and deli meat trays. The centrepiece of the table featured a two-tiered cake decorated in butter yellow. The exposed edge of the bottom tier was lined with baby animals, and on the top tier, a bassinet sat holding a baby girl.

Val, Madie's mom, arrived at the same time as Lizzie and Gord, who had the triplets in tow. Next came Jax and Chaz. Jordy was moving in and around everyone, snapping pictures. The last to arrive, as pre-planned, was Sydney and Chelsea with Maisie.

When they entered the room, everyone shouted in unison. "Surprise!"

And it was. The shocked look on Chelsea's face was price-less and caught on camera by Jordy.

Chelsea moved around the room to give them all a good look at the newest addition to their family. When she finally settled in a chair decorated especially for her, Chelsea placed Maisie in a bassinet beside her. The perfect guest, the baby promptly fell asleep, leaving them all to passing Chelsea presents to open, and finally, great food to eat.

Chaz moved over and sat beside Madie. "I haven't had much of a chance to talk to you these past weeks. How're you doing?"

"I'm good. Thanks for asking."

"I hear you and Cody have moved in together. He's a good guy."

Madie's eyes searched out Cody and saw he was talking to her mother. She smiled at Chaz. "He is. He keeps me out of trouble."

Chaz laughed. "I remember my grandfather telling me to find a good woman to keep me out of trouble, 'cause that was their job."

"Your grandfather would be shocked how times have changed, but the emancipation of women comes with challenges if we women can't handle the consequences of our choices."

Madie watched Chaz seek out Chelsea in the room; his eyes found her and instantly softened. "Yes, strong, independent women have new issues to contend with. But women like you and Chelsea will come through."

"Thank you. You know, everyone thinks I call Cody lion tamer because he worked on a reserve in Africa, but the truth is he's my rock ... but don't tell him I said that."

Chaz smiled. "Your secret is safe with me. I wish you and Cody all the best."

Madie's eyes settled on Maisie, who was awake and being cuddled by Elizabeth. "You have a beautiful daughter. She's a combination of you and Chelsea, all eyes and that dark hair; she's like a little cherub."

He beamed. "Yeah, isn't she? I couldn't be happier." He turned back to Madie. "So, I read that Crawford took a plea deal. It's good he won't be getting out."

Madie clouded over. "I guess, but it means he could get out in ten years. Sergeant Davis told me Crawford wanted to plead not guilty, but his lawyer convinced him there was too much evidence and he'd never get off. Second-degree murder has a minimum sentence of life in prison with no parole for a minimum of 10 years, but the judge could give him life without parole for 25 years if he thinks the case warrants it. His lawyer asked to reduce the charge to manslaughter if he pleaded guilty because it was a crime of passion, and he's no threat to anyone else."

"No way," Chaz said, stunned.

"That's what the prosecutor said. His second wife was willing to testify he was abusive to her and she feared the same fate as his first wife ... and then, there were his threats to me. And the unborn fetus is considered murder as well. In the end, they offered him life in prison, ten years minimum before he could apply for parole. He accepted."

Chaz shook his head. "It doesn't seem enough, does it? Considering how much damage he's done to people's lives. Still, ten years is a long time. And the parole board may not grant him parole either."

"His wife has gone home to Alberta to her family. She's filing for divorce. She's been given the chance for a normal life that Tara didn't get," Madie said solemnly.

"She's a lucky woman. Speaking about Sergeant Davis, he just came in the room."

Madie looked towards the doorway and sure enough, Davis was talking with Wenner. They both turned and looked at Madie. The hairs stood up on the back of her neck. Instinctively, she knew there was more news to be heard on the subject of Douglas Crawford.

Cody came over and stood by her, placing a hand on her shoulder as Wenner clapped his hands. "Hey, everyone, can I have your attention, please? If you could all have a seat, Sergeant Davis would like to speak to us all."

He remained just inside the door. "First, I'd like to congratulate Chelsea and Chaz on the birth of their beautiful daughter. I wish you both many happy moments like this one, and nights filled with hours of blissful sleep—you're going to need them." They all laughed and when the noise settled, he continued. "I must apologize for interrupting your party with police business. But, as I've found myself saying too many times lately, I want you to hear this from me and not from the media," he paused and looked directly at Madie. Her body stiffened and she braced herself for what he was going to say next.

"Today, we received notification from the prison where Douglas Campbell was being housed temporarily, awaiting transportation to a federal institution. Early this morning, he was involved in an altercation with another inmate and I'm here to inform you that Douglas Crawford succumbed to his injury and died."

The silence in the room was deafening; the shock of his words left them all speechless. Madie digested the information, accepted it, but felt there was more to hear.

She stood and all eyes moved to her. "Sergeant—how did he die?"

The officer paused a moment. "The altercation was between him and the inmate he shared a cell with. Crawford died from asphyxiation—he was strangled."

Gasps and cries echoed around the room.

Madie's knees gave out and she sat hard on her chair. She spoke so low, her words couldn't be heard.

Cody leaned over, taking one of Madie's hands in his.

"What was that, Madie?" Sergeant Davis asked.

Madie looked up and spoke in a strong, clear voice. "Karma finally found Douglas Crawford's address."

✣ 47 ✤

The drive from Stoney Creek to Cherryville had been a challenge due to the first heavy snowstorm of the year, but it was imperative to Madie she be there. She'd been invited to join a Celebration of Life for Tara Crawford that early-December Saturday. They'd made good time on the highway to Vernon, having pulled in behind a snowplough, following its tracks along the freshly ploughed roadway.

Heading west on the secondary road through Lavington to Lumby, they stopped for some take-out coffee. This was a slower trek as the snowplough hadn't cleared the road as yet and Cody's driving skills were put to good use. Lumby was a small community sitting at the edge of the Monashee Mountains, mainly a logging and agriculture village with its many trails along the creek beds, known as the Salmon Trail. They welcomed the short stop to stretch their legs, but soon continued on the final leg of their journey into the Monashee foothills.

Large flakes hit the window, making it harder to see. Madie glanced at Cody. "This storm isn't easing up any."

"I have a feeling, we'll be spending the night here," Cody said with a dry smile. "The forecast is calling for more snow throughout the evening and overnight. Far from what they originally predicted. The ploughs will be out in full force all night, so the trip home should be safer tomorrow."

Madie took in the snow-covered meadows and the rolling hills. "It's beautiful to look at, isn't it?

He glanced out the window. "Not far now. We've joined the Shuswap River on the left."

Madie picked up her cell and checked hotels in the area. "The only thing out this way is about six minutes past Cherryville, probably more in this storm. Should I call and book a cabin?"

"Yeah, let's do it. Otherwise, we'll have to drive thirty minutes back to Lumby."

A few minutes later, Cody passed the general store and Madie clicked off her phone. "Done, the last one available. We got lucky."

"Our turn off to the hall should be coming up on the left any minute. Here it is," Cody said, carefully turning off the highway.

The hall came into view and Cody made his way into the parking lot. "I think I'll back in and make it easier to pull out later." He found a spot amongst numerous other vehicles and they came to a stop.

"Wow," Madie said, surprised. "This weather sure didn't stop people from coming out."

She and Cody walked into the Cherryville Community Hall to a group of about sixty people. The only person she recognized was Sergeant Davis, who stood talking with another couple, and a woman by his side she assumed was his wife.

Fran and Tom Wood joined them at the door. "You must be Madie," Fran said. "I recognize you from the paper." Fran put out her arms and embraced her. "Welcome. We wondered if you would even make it here in this horrid storm."

Tom introduced himself to Cody and they shook hands.

He turned to Madie. "Would it be too weird for me to give you a hug as well?"

Madie smiled. "Not at all, Mr Wood."

The two embraced and when they broke apart, he said, "Call me Tom and this is Franny." He turned to Cody. "So, how was the drive?"

"Not too bad, just had to take it slow. We've booked a cabin down the road for the night. Not gonna take a chance driving back today."

"Smart man," Tom said.

"We're so glad you could come and share this day with us, Madie. We wouldn't be here celebrating Tara if it weren't for you," Franny declared, her expression one of gratitude.

"I wouldn't have missed it."

She slipped her arm through Madie's. "Come along with me, I want to introduce you to some people."

Tom took charge of Cody and led him over to another group.

The apprehension Madie had been feeling about the day soon left her. Everyone she met was so happy to meet her and treated her like family. They told her stories about Tara that were near and dear to them personally. That was part of her discomfort before arriving because she worried they'd think of her as Tara, not an incarnate of her, and the whole reincarnation thing might upset some. The only uncomfortable moment she experienced was from a couple in their forties: the husband was a cousin of Tara's. After a chitchat with Franny, the man, Jonathan, turned to her.

"The family is certainly grateful for your help in finding our Scarlett. But you must know, Carol and I don't believe in reincarnation." He and his wife stared at her like she was the devil incarnate. "In fact, our beliefs don't allow it. Still, we thank you." The pair hurried away.

"Never you mind them," Franny said.

"They looked at me like I was something evil."

"That's only because they fear anything they don't understand. Now, listen up. Tom and I never believed or disbelieved in reincarnation. It was something we never thought about. So, when the article appeared in the paper, we were a little shook up with people saying you were our Tara in a previous life.

"At the time, we chose to believe Tara reached out to you from beyond, for whatever reason, for your help to bring her home to us, and to lead Douglas to justice. Having had time to adjust to this whole thing, our minds are open to anything. Obviously, you aren't our Tara, but we feel a connection to you, and will forever accept you for giving us closure. There's a magic to life that's sometimes beyond our understanding; we don't always know the answers."

Madie smiled at the woman. "Thank you for that. Tell me something? They called her Scarlett, but you all call her Tara. When I first started to search for her, I only knew her as Tara and couldn't find her until I came across the name Scarlett Crawford."

Franny laughed. "Oh that. Her legal name is Scarlett, which as a teen she came to hate. It seemed so old-fashioned to her—not at all in with her school friends. She knew she'd been named after Scarlett O'Hara from the movie *Gone with the Wind,* and one night, when she was sixteen, we watched it together. She loved the story but still hated her name. She declared she was going to use the name Tara, the name of the plantation in the movie. We all went along with it because it seemed so important to her, except her cousin, who said her given name was Scarlett and in God's eyes that's who she was. To this day, he's refused to call her Tara."

"That explains it. I'd love to look at the table with Tara's photos. Maybe you could show them to me and tell me a little about her life."

"Of course. Come along."

Later on in the gathering, Tom's brother, who was hosting,

went to the stage and spoke into a microphone. Behind him on a screen videos played from Tara's childhood. One by one, family members and friends went to the microphone and spoke of Tara and shared a special memory they'd carried with them over the years.

Madie and Cody stood with Sergeant Davis and his wife, Sandra. Franny and Tom were the last to speak, and when they finished, Tom spoke to the group. He asked them to welcome a new friend to their circle, inviting Madie to come up and say a few words.

She froze as all eyes turned to her and applauded. She looked up at Cody in fear. "I wasn't expecting this."

"Go on, hon. Just be you and you'll be fine," Cody said reassuringly.

Sergeant Davis leaned over. "Where's that strong-willed girl who wouldn't be stopped? Get on up there."

Madie made her way to the microphone, her eyes focused on the video of a smiling teenaged Tara on the screen behind the podium. She stopped to stare for a moment into the face of a young woman during happier times of her life; turning to the microphone, she faced the gathering.

"When Franny and Tom invited me here today to join your celebration of Tara's life, I felt honoured to be a part of your special gathering. I also felt a little apprehensive. My concern lay in the strange happenings that led me to find Tara. Fearing some of you wouldn't be comfortable with the stories flying around the media, I worried my appearance would be an intrusion of your privacy and would take away from what today is really about. Because it's not about me, or what happened to Tara, or how it happened."

Madie paused and took a deep breath, to steady her nerves. "Today is about remembering Tara. Today is about finding closure for all of you who knew and loved her. Today is about healing. You've all shared some wonderful, happy stories about her childhood, school days, and young adulthood. Up until today, my memories of Tara came from a dark place where a fearful young woman wanted to come home to her family.

"You've told me how grateful you are for my help in bringing Tara home. Let me just say, I'm grateful to all of you because of what you've given me: memories of the happy times in Tara's life instead of just the sad. Thank you so much … because you've given *me* closure. Today, along with your healing, mine too can begin."

The End

Dear reader,

We hope you enjoyed reading *Storm Dreamer*. Please take a moment to leave a review, even if it's a short one. Your opinion is important to us.

Discover more books by June V. Bourgo at https://www.nextchapter.pub/authors/june-v-bourgo

Want to know when one of our books is free or discounted? Join the newsletter at http://eepurl.com/bqqB3H

Best regards,
June V. Bourgo and the Next Chapter Team

AUTHOR BIOGRAPHY

Born and educated in Montreal, Quebec, June V. Bourgo lives with her artist husband on Vancouver Island, off the west coast of British Columbia. The author finds inspiration for her writing in the raw beauty of nature and the Salish Sea that surrounds her home.

The author writes suspense/thriller series that encompasses a touch of magical realism, with empowered female protagonists. Her debut novel, *Winter's Captive, Book 1, The Georgia Series* is inspired loosely by the author's survival from a previous abusive relationship. *Chasing Georgia, Book 2* continues Georgia's search for self and *Missing Thread, Book 3*, a psychological testament, rounds out *The Georgia Series*.

Magnolia Tree, Book 1 of The Crossing Trilogy was released in 2018 and Chameleon Games, Book 2 was released in July 2019. Storm Dreamer, Book 3 was released In August 2021. Book 1 encompasses the disappearance of a mother and the search by her daughter to solve the mystery and continues throughout the trilogy with the aftermath of her search and how it affects the lives of the Grey family and their circle of friends. Again, the author's writing style follows a suspense/thriller adventure with a touch of the Supernatural.

The author is currently working on a stand-alone book, *Beyond Impact*.

Storm Dreamer
ISBN: 978-4-82410-195-2

Published by
Next Chapter
1-60-20 Minami-Otsuka
170-0005 Toshima-Ku, Tokyo
+818035793528

23rd September 2021

Lightning Source UK Ltd.
Milton Keynes UK
UKHW040833070622
404062UK00002B/231